The Agony of It All

The Agony of It All

THE DRIVE FOR
DRAMA AND EXCITEMENT
IN WOMEN'S LIVES

Joy Davidson, Ph. D.

JEREMY P. TARCHER, INC.
Los Angeles
Distributed by St. Martin's Press
New York

Excerpts from the following are reprinted with permission:
Sleeping with Soldiers, by Rosemary Daniell (Holt, Rinehart & Winston, © 1986)
Watching Dallas, by Ien Ang (Methuen, Inc., © 1986)

Library of Congress Cataloging in Publication Data

Davidson, Joy.
  The agony of it all : the drive for drama and excitement in
women's lives / by Joy Davidson.
    p. cm.
    Bibliography.
    ISBN 0-87477-445-4
    1. Women—Psychology. 2. Senses and sensation. 3. Interpersonal
conflict. I. Title.
HQ1206.D34 1988   88-4263
155.6'33—dc19   CIP

Jeremy P. Tarcher, Inc.
9110 Sunset Blvd.
Los Angeles, CA 90069

Design by Deborah Daly

Manufactured in the United States of America
10 9 8 7 6 5 4 3 2 1

First Edition

To a boundless future for the children,
Jessica, David, and Riahna Davidson Hanson, and SBJ.

Contents

CHAPTER SIX

The Rebel, Part I: Sex and the Sensation-Seeker

CHAPTER SEVEN

The Rebel, Part II: Crimes, Compulsions, and
Addictions

Part Two: The Excitement

CHAPTER EIGHT

Toward an End to the Agony

CHAPTER NINE

Change-Making: The Thrill of It All

APPENDIX I: THERAPY, THERAPISTS, AND YOUNG
SENSATION-SEEKERS

APPENDIX II: RECOMMENDED READING LIST

Acknowledgments

Fully expressing appreciation to the people involved in the "birthing" of *The Agony of It All* could produce acknowledgments equal in length to a chapter of the book. I hope each of them will accept instead my brief and heartfelt thanks:

Jeremy Tarcher, for recognizing the import and potential of this project in its earliest stages, for his ongoing participation and incisive input, and above all for his absolute faith in, support of, and commitment to this book.

Sherry Robb, for her remarkable insight, and for her perseverance as my agent and dear friend, for always knowing when to step in and when to let me be, and for lending me "Comfort."

Ted Mason, for sensitively guiding me through and sharing "the agony" of the first four drafts, and for his forthright and on-target editorial suggestions.

Lynette Padwa, for her priceless feedback during the final stages of writing, and for taking time beyond the call of duty to add to the quality of this work.

Liz Williams, for her excitement about this project, and for her creative efforts and commitment on behalf of the book.

Mary Nadler, for so sensitively and skillfully copy editing the final manuscript.

Deborah Daly, for her striking cover design.

George Hodgkins, with special thanks.

Connie Zweig, Shari Lewis, Mimi Brien, Marta Tarbell, and Lee Wood, for their timely and helpful editorial input.

Lisa Chadwick, Nathaniel Sherrill, and Steven Winslow, for their kindness and assistance.

Douglas Amiel, Susan Paglia, and Diane Pezzullo at U.C.L.A. for their invaluable research assistance.

Cindy Lemak, for keeping my finances in shape; and trainer Susan Shane, for keeping my body in shape during months of sitting at the word processor.

Bart Andrews, for sharing with me his knowledge of TV history.

Dennis Roach, for his contract expertise.

Stacy Prince, for her enthusiasm, suggestions, and backing when this book was still in its embryonic stages.

Harold Schechter and Sarah Nissim Kalevitch, for their assistance with the initial proposal.

Rosemary Daniell, Kay Dryden, Linda Fiero, Sandi Gosten, Ann Hayman, Mary Jensen, Shari Lewis, Gloria Monty, Tina Shelton, Barbara Tropp, and the women whose names I agreed not to use, for their candid interviews.

I could not have had a stronger, more loving and understanding support system than I did during the past year and a half of daily writing and social "hibernation." For these dear friends and associates I am truly grateful:

Bonnie Pinto, for ceaselessly prodding me to begin writing back in the days when I wasn't sure I could or should, and for being an additional "backbone" during these many months of concentrated work.

Beverly Engel, for twice reading drafts of the manuscript, and for speaking the truth.

Jeannine Gregory, for typing her weary fingers "to the bone!" and for providing vicarious thrills.

Jeannie Himmelstein, for being a true friend as well as a thoughtful "editor."

Jordan Buck, for maintaining unflagging belief in me and in this project.

Joan Magner, for her far-reaching vision and wise words of counsel.

Bill Magner, for being my energetic "ski patrol."

Tara Madden, for having "been there" first, and for providing timely advice.

Edith and Jack Davidson, Debra Davidson-Backalenick, and Shari Hanson, for sending love across the miles.

Susan Andrews, Suzanne Aran, Karin Bryant, Barbara Cowen, Linda Culbertson, Helen Engleton, Andrew Erlich, Obron Farber, Adele Feinstein, Ann Hayman, Margaret Hogan, Michael Klinger, Jay Pinto, Lucy Pinto, Ray Polisano, Leon Williams, and Lucille Versailles, for providing encouragement, support, or ideas during my work on this project and throughout the years.

And, especially, all my wonderful clients . . . for their courage, for sharing their lives with me, and for being the heartbeat of this book.

Part One
The
MELODRAMA

Before We Begin ...

*L*ife is either a daring adventure or nothing."
—Helen Keller

This is a book about drama. Not the drama you see in the theater or on TV, but the drama you create in your own life, upon the stage of your own personal experience. It is about you, me, and the other women whose lives sometimes manifest the chaos and instability of a soap opera. But it is also about our search for excitement, a hidden motive that leads us to do so many of the wonderful, fulfilling, agonizing, awful, and utterly thrilling things we do. It is about how many women with a healthy drive for novelty, passion, and a sense of aliveness—a drive known to psychologists as *sensation-seeking*—have been misinformed about that drive, and as a result have misunderstood and misused it, turning an ability to create rewarding excitement into self-defeating melodrama.

As a therapist, I have often seen how living with drama can sabotage one's happiness, livelihood and self-respect—and I've learned it firsthand from hard experience. Our personal dramas may involve unproductive fights with lovers, family, and friends; exhausting daily crises and emergencies; doomed affairs and love triangles; futile attempts to please moody, difficult people; abuse of drugs and alcohol; shopping, eating, and dieting binges; dangerous theft; destructive gambling; and sexual thrill-seeking. This book is about the women

3

whose lives consist of episode after episode of drama that, to various degrees, revolves around one or another of these themes.

As you read about the many facets of drama-making, it will probably occur to you that some men behave in similar ways, and do some of the same destructive things. Why isn't this a book about them, too?

Although it's true that men can act melodramatic, they rarely do so for the same reasons that women do—nor does drama become such a pervasive, consuming part of their lives. For women, drama-seeking extends from restrictive, sex-biased conditioning imposed by both society and family. As we will see, women often learn to create drama as the *primary* means of satisfying their sensation-seeking needs. For men, unencumbered by the same conditioning, drama-making is only one of many available sensation-seeking options (and, for men, a socially unapproved, "feminine" one at that).

No matter how dramatic any of our lives might be, it is important to understand from the outset that we don't create drama because we are sick, hysterical, or have a disease. We do so because we were prepared by society and by our childhood experiences to perpetuate a drama-making lifestyle: our culture has penalized women's *direct* expression of natural aggression, daring, and personal power, and as a result these attributes are often channeled into negative drama-making.

Our tendency to seek drama is societally based, and we are certainly not to blame for it. But I sincerely believe that each of us has tremendous power to consciously redirect and redesign our life for the better once we face our own role in shaping its quality.

Just as any of us can learn self-defeating patterns of behaving, we can also develop new patterns of living that increase our self-esteem, enhance our sense of adventure, reinforce our personal power, and enrich our relationships. This book, above all, is about how we can rediscover and acknowledge the many strengths and positive traits that have been directed toward drama-making, so that we can apply them to success in our personal and professional lives.

In focusing on sensation-seeking in women's lives, I don't mean to discount the wealth of other, sometimes contradictory, needs that also drive us forward, such as the needs for security and freedom, variety and stability, activity and peace, intimacy and detachment. All of these have been explored by psychologists and philosophers for many decades. In this book, however, I cast light on a need that has not yet come out of the shadows, in the hope that all of our yearnings will be considered together and our knowledge of ourselves enhanced.

This book does not deal with men, sex, love, or relationships in the tradition of most self-help books. Although relationships are integral to the drama-seeking styles of many women, this book is not about finding a relationship, analyzing a relationship, putting up with a relationship, changing a relationship, or leaving a relationship. Here, no matter how deeply involved we become in examining relationships, the focus will always remain on *ourselves:* what we do to diminish our potential, what drives us to do it, and what we can do to renew ourselves.

The issues raised here are relevant to all women, of all ethnic and socioeconomic backgrounds, races and religions, and sexual orientations. Specifically, the drama-making patterns relating to sex and love may be applicable whether a woman is heterosexual, bisexual, or lesbian. In the book, however, I've characterized sexual relationships as woman/man and friendships as woman/woman. On the surface, dramatic encounters between friends and relatives can often resemble the scenes that occur between lovers (and vice versa), yet the deeper dynamics of romantic and platonic relationships are generally quite different. In view of that, I've made these distinctions so the reader may easily distinguish between sexual/romantic and platonic bonds. It is by no means my intent to dismiss the drama or significance of love relationships between women or of friendships between men and women.

As you read, you may sense the genuine affection I feel for the women whose stories I share with you. In part, this is because they embody such tremendous potential for accomplishment, so many worthwhile attributes and abilities. It's also because I can empathize so completely with their pain and confusion. Many therapists are said to find psychotherapy a process of "healing from one's own wounds," using one's personal suffering to assist others through similar travails. That is certainly true in my case. My dedication to helping women understand the role of drama in their lives comes from facing my own drama-seeking patterns and striving to overcome them.

In addition to recognizing the fondness I feel for the women in this book, you may think I am being unduly hard on them at times—and by proxy hard on you. If that is so, it is partly because I have known these women to be capable of so much more than they had been receiving or producing in their lives, and I feel zealous about illuminating the possibilities for reward and achievement they (and you) have the capacity to create. And if I am hard on anyone, it is also because I know that changing is not easy. To the contrary, it is a process few of us are motivated to begin unless we first subject ourselves to frank, sometimes unflattering scrutiny, and thus begin to see that the costs of staying as we are are simply too great to further endure. It is out of my compassion for all drama-seeking women, and my respect for their strength and potential, that I have taken such a straightforward approach in describing to you the circumstances of the women in this book.

As you become acquainted with the real[1] women on these pages, some of their lessons will speak loudly to you, others will barely whisper. Because the spectrum of drama-making possibilities is so broad, you may find yourself identifying with certain aspects of many women's stories instead of relating completely to any one woman's experience. You need not feel deeply bonded to any of the individual women on these pages. It is only important that you open yourself to taking a fresh look at your own actions, exemplified by theirs, and begin to face the drama-seeking patterns that have been causing you pain.

Part one of *The Agony of It All* is a forthright examination of the ways women create self-defeating melodrama in their lives, the roots of drama-seeking, and the underlying emotional themes that influence one's personal style of drama-making. Part two describes how you can change drama-making patterns and explores the prospect of creating drama of the most productive and exhilerating kind. Since I don't believe that drama-making is a sickness, this section is not about recovery in the mode of many self-help books. Instead, it is about becoming reaquainted with all the vitality and power you have channeled into negative drama-making, and about redirecting your energies toward creating genuine excitement—without sabotaging your happiness or forfeiting your self-respect.

---

[1]All actual names and identifying details have been changed.

1 &

Setting the Stage for Personal Drama

I can still see Kelly as clearly as if she were sitting in front of me now, with her eyes darting about the room and her slender fingers nervously twirling a long strand of hair into a tight coil.

I vividly remember Kelly's third therapy session with me ten years ago, shortly after I began my private practice. As always, she and I sat facing each other, close enough that even when she grew quiet I could hear her inner tension. Yet on that day I recall perceiving still another, hidden facet of Kelly, an energy I could suddenly sense, like an extra pulse beating in the room.

"I was late for work again yesterday," she announced defiantly. "I've been put on warning, and—and I don't care. Let them fire me."

Kelly was late for work with amazing regularity. "What happened this time, Kelly?" I asked.

"Oh, you know," she said brightly, laughing. "That stupid car of mine wouldn't start. But first my friend Judy called and woke me out of a dead sleep—that was okay, though, because I forgot to set my alarm—and I had to talk to her because she was crying. She and her boyfriend had had another fight. And then I spent fifteen minutes looking *everywhere* for my big silver hoop earings, the ones I wore here last week—but finally I remembered I'd left them at Ron's house!"

Kelly's life was littered with "little traumas" like this. If she wasn't having a problem with her car, she was arguing with her landlord or was unable to find her keys—again. A minor crisis seemed to erupt at every turn.

"I'm twenty-eight years old, and I'm beginning to wonder if I'm the only one in the world who hasn't gotten it together yet," she remarked. "I'm always worn out before I even *get* to work! But then I think of Judy . . . she's not doing much better. Anyway, it doesn't really matter. I hate that job."

"Like you hated the last one," I reminded her.

"Yes! I hate my job, I hate where I live—*I hate my life!* And you know what?" she hurtled on, ignoring the gravity of her last statement. "Ron called from Dallas on Monday . . . said he'd be back on Tuesday. That was *two days ago,* and I haven't heard a word from him. Can you believe it? I should be worried, but I know he'll turn up. . . . He does this a lot, actually . . . telling me one thing, doing another. I can't count on him for anything but trouble!"

With that, Kelly smiled, her eyes glimmered, and her face took on a mischievous expression—but just for a moment. Then her features became like those of a very sad child about to burst into tears. Swiftly, she tried to compose herself.

How incongruous. In less than five minutes Kelly had alluded to at least a half dozen problems that must have been truly agonizing. Yet, in describing her frenetic, unsatisfying lifestyle and her rocky relationship with her lover, Ron, she had at first looked almost delighted in spite of the obvious discomfort she was in. I was both intrigued and concerned.

"Kelly," I ventured, "you tell me that you can't seem to 'get it together.' You say you hate your life and that Ron is nothing but trouble, but you looked pleased when you said those things, and then you turned very, very sad. Would you tell me about both of those feelings?"

For the first time Kelly stopped fidgeting and simply stared at me. The room was so quiet I could have counted each of her breaths. In the seconds before she spoke, the unidentified current of energy I had noticed earlier coursed through her with such force that the air around her seemed charged.

"I really don't know how to answer you," she said finally, her voice barely above a whisper. "I'm sort of confused." She paused, as though trying to determine how safe she was, how much of herself she should expose.

"My life has always been kind of crazy, unsettled." She shook her head, and her expression was once again tinged with sorrow.

I nodded, inviting her to continue.

"Before Ron there was Tim, but I guess he was as unreliable as Ron. And before Tim there was Arnie, and . . . I was *obsessed* with

Arnie. I didn't *love* him—I don't think that's what it was about, at all."

"What was it about?"

"I don't know—maybe it was about never knowing what would happen next. That's the story of my life, I guess. Arnie and I would have awful fights, then make love. We were always trying to make each other jealous. It hurt, and it was terribly exhausting, but it was exciting . . . until it ended one night at a party. I was dancing with someone else, and Arnie went crazy . . . smashed an antique mirror, then came after me with one of the pieces. I ran into the bathroom and locked the door. The police were called. It was awful, but still. . . ."

"Still?"

Again, that mischievous look crept across her face.

"Still," she said simply, *"it was never, ever dull."*

Never, Ever Dull

Kelly's words stayed with me. Why did some women go to such extreme lengths to lead a life that was never, ever dull?

As the years passed I began to see over and over again in the lives of the women I treated a sometimes subtle, sometimes distinct straining toward the acting out of intense scenarios that were highly distressing and equally stimulating. As I looked more closely, I saw the same pattern to differing degrees in some of my friends and family members, and in myself. I realized that many women habitually extract excitement from their turbulent relationships with lovers, family, friends, and coworkers—compelled *not* out of a hidden wish to suffer or a belief that they deserved pain, but out of a *restrained or severely misdirected, but essentially healthy, drive for the heightened stimulation* that could be wrung from these entanglements. Their suffering, however, was real—the most pronounced consequence of repeated, poorly focused, and ultimately unsuccessful attempts to find pleasurable stimulation in living lives that were "never, ever dull."

Sensation-Seeking Through Melodrama

While Kelly's search for excitement was desperate and unproductive, the motivation behind it was in no way abnormal. "Sensation-seeking"—the drive to seek varied, novel, and complex sensations and experiences, coupled with the willingness to take risks in order

to find them—is a potentially healthy personality trait. While some
people naturally crave greater stimulation than others, the basic drive
for sensation, for excitement, is part of our physiological heritage.
For an array of cultural reasons, however, many women learn to
pursue a particularly unrewarding kind of thrill—a circular, self-defeating cycle of daily *melodrama* that upsets both their personal and
professional lives.

Most women have not been provided access to the same healthy
outlets for excitement-seeking as men, nor have they been invited, as
men have, to digest all the stimulation they need and at whatever
potency they need it. Instead, women have traditionally been raised
to meet their sensation-seeking needs through their relationships or
inner emotional lives. They have been given preparation to play only
supporting roles in the world, with men remaining the major stars.
Drama-seeking is a learned way of satisfying a basic need for stimulation by building high sensation into everyday situations. When we
create our own dramas, *we* are the stars, while other people (men
included) become supporting players or audience members.

Women who thrive on melodrama as a means of meeting their
excitement-seeking needs are everywhere. While their private
dramas are highly individualized, the scripts are often predictable. In
many drama-seekers I sense a bristling tension that rarely eases, and
I feel the presence of an undefinable energy (much like Kelly's).
There is an engaging intensity about these women, often manifested
as a highly expressive, occasionally explosive nature. Always, there
is a raging fire inside, and one can feel its heat even without understanding its source.

I believe the source is the burning, generally unacknowledged or
misunderstood drive for excitement and sensation. When unhar-
nessed and unproductively channeled, the drive for excitement can
stir a woman up, then let her down. It can take her to incredible
emotional heights, then plunge her into the depths of despair. The
dramas she creates can exhaust and deplete her—until it is too difficult to deny the pain that so much melodrama brings.

What Is Melodrama?

Many life experiences are unavoidably dramatic and correspondingly
painful or tragic. Divorces, deaths, illnesses, accidents, and major
disappointments can severely upset even the most balanced, satisfying life. Other life experiences are dramatic, but in a healthy, invigorating way. All of the most rewarding, confidence-building, hap-

pily remembered moments of life—a wedding, a major professional promotion, the birth of a child—contain elements of *drama,* of heightened realism and pleasing emotionalism.

Unlike these naturally occurring dramatic aspects of life, the kind of drama this book is concerned with is, strictly speaking, *melodrama.* In theatrical terms, melodrama demands excessive, violent, extravagant emotional displays, bordering on the manipulative or unauthentic. Sensational incidents, crises, and exaggerated reactions are ever-present. Soap opera is the quintessential melodrama.

When we create our own exciting melodramas, whether deliberately or unconsciously, we set up or build upon potentially dramatic or explosive situations so that they are exaggerated, sensationalized, and pushed to the limits. As these scenarios become more volatile, they also become more thrilling.

Personal melodrama can take a variety of shapes other than those seen in Kelly's life. Some are extreme and self-destructive. Women whose self-esteem is fragile or low are more easily lured into the most damaging dramatic scenarios, for drama feeds on negative self-concepts like a parasite off a weakened host. Other melodramatic formats are so subtle that it's easy to discount their importance, but their self-defeating effects are cumulative and serious.

Some women occasionally just *sound* melodramatic. At one time or another anyone can say, "I have to return a *million* phone calls" or "I've just had the *worst* day of my life!" Many women become dramatically enthusiastic about people or projects, or dramatically expressive about ideas or events. Dramatic declarations by themselves do not a melodrama make. But when frustrating and unproductive scenes occur *regularly* in a woman's life, with dramatic declarations coming from pain, not from pleasure or humor, the drama becomes a genuine cause for concern.

Throughout this book, I will use the terms *drama* and *melodrama* interchangeably in referring to any of these personal, melodramatic formats. To distinguish self-perpetuated drama/melodrama from naturally occurring or positive dramatic moments, genuine drama will be called "real" or "true" drama.

Are You a Drama-Seeker?

One of the tragedies of living amidst drama is that we are frequently unconscious of our part in making it happen. Our failures and troubles seem to be out of our control, our mishaps unavoidable. Our perception of helplessness adds sting to our emotional wounds.

If you suspect that drama may have become a detrimental element in your life, you'll want to address the following questions.

- Does it drive you "crazy" when your routine is the same for too long?
- Are you sometimes accused, in a manner that feels insulting or judgmental, of being "dramatic" or "high-strung"?
- Are you prone to sudden, sometimes unexplainable eruptions of anger or tearfulness?
- Just when things are going smoothly, do you find yourself in a fight with someone close to you or faced with a new crisis?
- Do you wonder if you'll ever be satisfied by anyone or anything?
- Would you go to any lengths to help out a friend, even to your own detriment?
- Do you become strongly attracted to men who are already involved with other women or who don't appear interested in you?
- Do people accuse you of "making a big deal out of nothing"?
- Do the people closest to you seem to be in frequent upheaval or turmoil?
- Do you long for career success, but find that it continues to elude you?
- Have you tried, more than once, to "conquer" or "change" an emotionally distant, troublesome, or cruel partner?
- Have you ever been a binge eater or used alcohol or drugs to excess, especially when bored or frightened?
- Do you complain to friends of being mistreated by others, or by "life"?
- Do you take secret pleasure in breaking social rules or minor laws and getting away with it?
- Does your life seem more like a jumble of unrelated chapters than a whole book?
- Is passion usually mingled with conflict and turbulence in your relationships?

If you honestly don't see yourself mirrored in any of these questions, you have probably found healthy, productive ways of generating all the excitement your system demands. The relationships and activities you engage in offer a kind of stimulation that doesn't boomerang on you later, leaving you to contend with severe consequences after the thrills are gone. As a result, your relationships prosper, your confidence soars, and you feel complete, content, and proud.

But if, like so many women, you saw your actions reflected in some or many of the preceding questions, you are probably generating excitement through personal drama in a way that forces you to pay for quick-fix emotional thrills with ongoing frustration and unhappiness and dwindling self-esteem. You are entitled to much, much more. By becoming aware of your learned, self-defeating behaviors and using the techniques for overcoming them found in this book, you can have it!

The Three Styles of Drama-Seeking

There are three distinctive styles of personal drama:

The Drama of Conflict and Crisis

The Drama of Challenge

The Drama of Rebellion

For most women, just one of these dramatic orientations is an ongoing, primary mode for seeking stimulation and has a lasting appeal. We are often introduced in early childhood to the style of drama-seeking we will eventually favor. Although we may "jump" drama-seeking boundaries and experiment with a noncustomary style when it suits our purposes, in most cases we return to the melodramatic format that is most familiar.

Once we have found a predictable, even partially successful means of generating excitement, we will continually repeat the actions, extract the pleasure, and put up with the anguish relating to our personal drama—usually without recognizing its patterns or understanding why they recur. It isn't that we enjoy the agony of it all, but that we find satisfaction in drama's stimulation and may unconsciously believe that a trade-off is necessary—a pound of excitement for an equal ration of hurt and confusion. However, by understanding how these erroneous beliefs come into being and by uncovering the scenarios that rule our lives, we can move forward to create true excitement that does not carry with it the backlash of pain we've learned to tolerate.

Courting Disaster: The Drama of Conflict and Crisis

What could be more highly charged, more scathingly dramatic, than conflict—the emotional upheaval of a good, hard fight? What gets our adrenaline pumping faster than a serious crisis or calamity? Very little. For we are human animals, built to react immediately in the face of danger, physiologically designed to "get high" on trauma.

When we are angry or fearful, the brain sends signals to various hormone-producing glands, instructing them to release chemicals that ready us for fight or flight. One of the by-products of this stress response is an "adrenaline rush"—a biochemically induced feeling of power and pleasure, a necessary motivator in battle and a source of extraordinary strength in a life-threatening crisis. This response is often accompanied by waves of a sinking sensation in the pit of the stomach, extreme alertness, and sharp reflexes that jar us into action.

In today's world, this biological alarm system is seldom set off for the purpose of meeting survival needs. Since it is rare that we must face actual life-threatening situations, we often have to garner our stress-related "stimulation pleasures" from more prosaic events, such as personal conflict or crisis. Conflicts and crises do give our systems exciting jolts, take us to heights of arousal, and invite floods of emotion. But they can also exhaust us, deplete us, and make us emotionally and physically ill.

Conflict, as we'll be using the word here, means interpersonal dis- sension—verbal or physical confrontations in which two or more people behave toward one another in ways that are oppositional. A heated argument with a lover, boss, or friend is conflict. Even a testy confrontation with a waiter in a restaurant is conflict.

Crisis, as the word will be used here, refers to any situation, event, or chain of events that is perceived as critical, urgent, perilous, or disastrous. "Perception" is the key ingredient, for what seems critical to one person may seem ordinary to another. A divorce generally precipitates a personal crisis—but, for some women, so does a flat tire.

While conflict and crisis are treated together as a single style of drama-seeking, women may generate more of one than the other.

However, these elements are highly interrelated. We cannot live in the throes of crisis without upsetting the people close to us to the point at which conflict finally erupts, nor can we engage others in conflict indefinitely without damaging our relationships and provoking crises.

For women, interpersonal relationships commonly provide the stage upon which dramatic conflict and crisis is played out. This "play" can assume a multitude of forms—explosive confrontations with lovers (the thrill of breaking up and making up), drawn-out feuds with family members (the thrill of indignation, rage, and revenge), procrastination on critical work deadlines or personal promises (the thrill of coping with an emergency), overinvolvement in other people's crises (the thrill of being needed) . . . and so many more.

I call women who create drama through conflict and/or crisis "Fighters," since either approach leads to a preoccupation with fighting—against something, someone, or both.

Rebecca is a Fighter. The daughter of an alcoholic mother and a chronically ill father, she was witness as a child to continuous family chaos and crisis. Accustomed to the strife of early family life, as an adult she was stimulation-dependent upon crisis and confrontation. Barely out of her twenties, she had already divorced, remarried, and separated. In therapy, Rebecca admitted that she found nonconfrontational relationships dull, lacking in passion. "If a man won't fight, he's probably kind of wimpy," she said. "I'd be bored."

Until Rebecca sought therapy, she was not consciously aware of her drama-seeking pattern or of why, whenever things were going smoothly in her marriages, fights would suddenly erupt. She couldn't see that it was she who had provoked arguments by criticizing her husbands until her complaints over small annoyances turned into serious altercations. "I don't understand why I blew up," she said. "I felt stupid and hateful the next day. But I felt a sense of relief, too, as if now that the fight was over everything between us would be all right—though it never was."

Rebecca's conflict orientation overshadowed her occasional attempts to solve the legitimate problems that existed in her relationships. Her penchant for crisis led her to overreact to the irritations of daily life, regarding them as calamities. Her friends could always count on her to rush to the telephone in a frenzy, eager to share the details of her latest disasters. "The toilet overflowed and practically *drowned* the cat, the rug is soaked—everything's *destroyed!*" she would exclaim dramatically. But when asked if she had called a plumber, the answer was invariably something like this: "A plumber?!! What good is a plumber going to do me *now*? I need an *ark*, not a *plumber!!"*

Putting herself and others through so much distress by creating drama out of incidents that were, really, just part of life took its toll on her both emotionally and physically. She was hyperstimulated but never content. She wondered why she was so fatigued, so vulnerable to colds. Despite its attendant discomfort, immersion in conflict and crisis was Rebecca's way of creating excitement. It was the only way she had ever known of feeling really alive.

Not all women replicate their childhood dramas in the same fashion. Some people brought up in severely unhealthy circumstances even manage to break away from the mold by vowing never to repeat their parents' behavior themselves and, miraculously, succeeding. However, most of us are so affected by our upbringings that, even though we may swear we'll "never be like that," we carry our family's emotional lessons with us into adulthood. These lessons are often in a form that is vaguely disguised and therefore insidiously incapacitating.

Living on the edge of interpersonal conflict and crisis, we may generate fleeting feelings of aliveness and excitement. But because this kind of drama demands that we remain on guard against the next catastrophe, we also trap ourselves in a world where peace of mind does not exist. Our emotional energy is constantly depleted through drama, so there is little energy (or time) left to channel productively. What's more, we imprison ourselves in a place where love cannot be perceived unless it is accompanied by turmoil. On an emotional level, we often fail to associate gentleness with loving; instead, we equate volatility with passion, and we embrace passion as love. We might deny these perspectives intellectually, but we live them nonetheless.

We do not cultivate misconceptions about love on our own. Most women have been conditioned, through exposure to the unhealthy relationships around them as well as through the barrage of melodramatic stories in books, films, and television shows, to perceive of love as a synthesis of physical attraction, heightened excitement, inflammatory episodes, and emotional dependence. This is an explosive combination, at best. We are not taught the difference between high drama and healthy excitement; we don't know what genuine passion is. As a result, most women grow up expecting dramatic conflict to be a requisite component of love.

Fighters rarely experience true, shared love. Though they begin their relationships feeling impassioned and excited, they wind up feeling uncared for and unfulfilled because their fights and struggles become a barrier to intimacy. How can partners stop and listen to each other's innermost feelings, trust each other, or give and receive emotional support when they are preparing for the next battle or when one of them is coping with the most recent crisis?

In conflict/crisis-ridden scenarios, there is plenty of action, and in some cases plenty of passion. But no matter how stirred up a woman gets, she is usually left with a sense that something is missing. She remains emotionally undernourished, yet she can't quite grasp the basis of her amorphous sense of dissatisfaction. Dramatic conflict and crisis can fill our time and even turn us on, but it can never appease all our emotional hungers or bring meaning, closeness, or love into our lives.

High on the Contest: The Drama of Relationship Challenges

For many women, excitement stems from the drama of competing to "win" a succession of difficult, seemingly unattainable partners. While some of these contests are played out without sexual overtones in the business environment, where attracting a powerful mentor can feel like a great conquest, most are inspired by romance and eroticism.

Women attracted to dramatic relationship challenges live in the netherworld between wanting and having, between striving and achieving. They are like the hunters who prefer the chase to the kill. Aroused by change, risk, and trial, their greatest high comes from defying the odds they see working against them. It is a sad irony that this urge to test oneself against obstacles—a quality that can help to make someone a dynamic frontrunner in the world—is primarily expressed in romantic relationships, where it often does the most damage.

While many women have found romantic challenge exciting at some point in their lives, not all women transform these feelings into consistent, highly charged dramatic styles. I refer to women who become hooked on relationship challenges as "Challengers." For these women, the more remote the desired partner, the more appealing he is. For instance, a married man is more desirable than a single man; a dispassionate partner offers a greater test of seductive skill and worthiness than a willing, romantically inclined partner; and an uncommitted or nonmonogamous partner is more engaging than a stable partner. There is tremendous potential drama in the effort to attract, get, change, and *keep* a difficult, unattainable lover—but there is also tremendous danger.

Paula was attracted to this type of romantic drama. When I first met her she was the manager of a café at the beach, an "almost" kind of place—almost comfortable, almost trendy, with food that was almost great. Walking in, one got the feeling that there could be something very special there if the restaurant only took itself more seriously. One got the same feeling about Paula.

Her first flirtation with romantic challenge had occurred years earlier, when she was working as hostess in a San Francisco bistro. Her handsome boss, a married man with a new baby on the way, intrigued her. She wanted to dazzle him, and she did, enticing him into an affair.

At first Paula thought she had the relationship under control, but she soon found that just having a "sometime" affair wasn't enough for her. She wanted to see more of her lover, illogically thinking of his wife as a rival who had no right to his time. Looking back on this period, she realizes she was less in love than she was enraged. How dare he favor another woman—even if it *was* his wife! Paula applied pressure, and the relationship turned into a test of wills. She called her lover at home, hanging up if his wife answered the phone. He became angry. Then she spent tearful hours alone, writing sentimental or plaintive letters and poems that she slipped into his pockets at work. Each of their encounters became an exciting episode in an ongoing saga of pursuit and resistence. Though Paula might have continued the chase indefinitely, her lover eventually tired of the drama and withdrew.

Paula became despondent. The feeling of failure and the comedown from the high of the challenge, which had been keeping her going, were unbearable. She moved to Los Angeles, determined to make a success of herself in the L.A. business community and hoping to one day launch her own restaurant. But she continued to be sidetracked by the drama of romantic challenge, and she exhausted herself in captivating and attempting to capture the most elusive of partners. Her relationships lasted about six months, at most a year.

In romantic challenge Paula was able to seize the quickening moments of aliveness that all drama evokes and to magnify those sensations by telling herself that this time she was really in love. Just as importantly, she was able to regard herself as special and valued each time she convinced herself that another woman's man preferred *her* or proved to herself that an "impossible" man really wanted

her (if only temporarily). It was never enough to be loved or desired by someone sincere, for whom she didn't have to fight. It
was more important to charge up on excitement while proving her
self-worth, again and again, through the challenge of acquiring a
hard-to-get man.

Paula didn't take more meaningful challenges seriously. Despite
her dreams, she merely dabbled in the restaurant business, working
for others and never quite getting her own enterprise off the ground.
Because her energies were always focused on bewitching a man,
Paula remained an "almost," just like the restaurant she managed.
The drama that sustained her did not allow room for any other
challenges to be met, and her "almost" relationships never quite
compensated for the deep loneliness she reluctantly admitted to
feeling.

The drama of romantic challenge condemns such women to live in
a desolate limbo of high-intensity struggle and meager reward. They
keep themselves stoked on striving, eternally reaching out but never
able to grasp anything they can hold onto. In contrast, some people
extract *true* drama, and far greater reward, from the same state of
limbo. No matter what they covet—a job, a promotion, a creative
accomplishment—there is unparalleled excitement in striving to get
it, in working, maneuvering, and competing for the prize.

Any good challenge begins with a *want,* a powerful, intrusive, undeniable sensation of profound yearning. You might insist, "I want
that job. Even though there are twelve other qualified applicants, *I
want it."* Out of such unshakable desire flows a series of passionate
efforts extended toward *getting.*

"The getting" is a period of exquisite tension, of consuming, almost obsessive thought and focused action breeding an excitement
so sharp it borders on pain. At its most intense point there is a feeling
of nerve-wracking uncertainty, of breathless suspense as you await
the outcome and wonder whether you've met your goal. The sensation is emotionally blistering and almost—but not quite—intolerable.
It is this precarious balance between tolerance and agony that imbues
even a healthy challenge with its final, quivering thrill.

The Challenger exists in such a state, but her passion is directed
toward a person rather than an achievement. Unlike those who find
satisfaction in the chasm between desire and attainment, the woman
immersed in romantic challenge usually becomes a prisoner of that
realm. She may try to convince herself she is chasing a happy ending,
but she neglects to see that her failure to attain it is related to the
doomed nature of the type of contest she has chosen to enter. In-

stead, she sets up another destined-to-fail relationship challenge, hoping that *this* time she can meet it. While romantic challenges produce flashes of powerful, delectable sensation, they offer only the illusion of achievement. What most women are really hoping to acquire—self-worth, love, success, happiness—simply cannot be attained in this way.

Playing with Fire: The Drama of Rebellion

Sometimes, life is never as good as when we're bad. Many women thrill to violating established rules of conduct, thumbing their noses at convention and testing limits to see just how far they can go. There is something delicious about "getting away with it," whether "it" is stealing from department stores without getting caught or padding expense accounts without getting fired.

Some of the women who enjoy "playing with fire" are easy to spot. They're the hard-core excitement junkies who never feel completely alive unless they are behaving in dramatically antisocial ways. Danger is their drug, and taking chances their way of life.

Many others rebel more covertly. Such women possess some desire for security and middle-class comfort but at the same time have a constitutionally low tolerance for tranquility. As a result, they contrive clever ways of roiling the placid waters of their otherwise normal lives without ever permanently disrupting the status quo. These women, whom I call "Rebels," crave the excitement of rebelling against the "good-girl" rules but are often drawn back to doing what is expected of them, torn by the conflict between their innate drive for novel sensation and the cultural conditioning that impels them to "behave." Their rebellion is often self-destructive and is rarely in the service of meaningful personal growth, social change, or noble causes.

Clarissa, a bright, vivacious woman, feels trapped playing the part of the good wife in a rather bland marriage. Her favorite drama is overeating until she is almost sick, then hopping on the remorse-filled, emotional roller-coaster ride that inevitably follows. Her preoccupation with food serves an array of psychological purposes, but the one that is most important to her is the sensation that comes from doing what is supposedly forbidden. Whether the mini-dramas that surround her eating behavior offer her a chance to "stick it" to her husband (who insists she be thinner and repeatedly sends her to weight-loss clinics) or to share her unhappiness with a friend and a carton of ice cream, they are the only sensational aspects of her otherwise controlled life.

Laurie's story is different. A member of a weekly therapy group I conducted a few years ago, Laurie always arrived at least ten minutes early, often bringing freshly baked pastries to share during the break. She looked as innocent as a fashionably updated "Harriet Nelson," and it was hard to picture her as the former radical protester who more than once during the sixties had been teargassed by campus police. It was just as difficult to envision her seducing the nineteen-year-old son of her husband's business partner, and then throwing a barbecue for both families—a story she told with great relish.

"I asked him [her young lover] to come into the house and help me make the potato salad while everyone else was still in the yard having drinks. Needless to say, we got our hands full of more than mayonnaise . . ."

"That's crazy," one of the group members interrupted. "What if someone had walked in on you? Maybe one of your own kids . . . *then* what?"

"We were careful," Laurie insisted. "We kept our eyes open."

Others in the group were highly amused, but Laurie's questioner wriggled uncomfortably in her chair. Then, leaning forward, she said with absolute finality, "I think you *wanted* to get caught."

"Not true," Laurie retorted. "I have too much to lose." There was a moment of silence. Then she said, with a half-smile, "Well . . . maybe it wouldn't have been half as much fun if the *possibility* of discovery hadn't been there."

In one concise sentence Laurie had voiced what I consider to be a Rebel's manifesto. It wasn't that she wanted to be punished for her actions; it was only that there could be no excitement if that prospect didn't exist. The sex and the boy were, at best, secondary. Without the gamble (the real source of stimulation), she would never have toyed with him.

When we speak of playing with fire, we are talking not only about sexual risk-taking but also about a variety of compulsive or addictive behaviors, ranging from binge eating or shopping to the abuse of alcohol or drugs. We're also talking about crime—shoplifting, bouncing checks, dope dealing, fraud. In all of these activities, the excitement is born in the mysterious realm between action and consequence. Similar to the Challenger, whose thrills are found in the breach between desire and attainment, the Rebel's sensation peaks in another state of limbo, where the dramatic episode and the potential for consequence are wrapped together in one exhilarating package.

This kind of drama demands that you momentarily suspend the belief that consequences might ever have to be faced. It is rather like walking a high wire, knowing you could tumble to the ground at any moment and feeling excited because that prospect exists, yet convinced of your balance and invincibility. You must, in essence, hold two paradoxical realities in your mind at the same time: "I cannot fall" and "I could fall." It is the potential for success tinged with the fear of failure that makes the action exciting. However, the difference between the Rebel's typical drama-seeking behaviors and the wirewalker's act is that an experienced tightrope walker calculates the risks and depends upon skill, concentration, and deliberation as her backups. An impulsive shoplifter, on the other hand, relies for her feeling of safety on an illogical sense of invulnerability, but this belief is coupled with a realistic awareness that many shoplifters get caught. The contradiction between "I might get caught" and "I won't get caught" spurs her on. If she knew for certain that she *would* be caught, she would be unlikely to steal. But if she knew for certain that she *wouldn't* be caught, she would not find stealing exciting. In the titillation of rebelling, we are buttressed by the irrational belief that we are special, that *we* can get away with it. At the same time, the tempting question "What would happen if . . . ?" teases us. For the Rebel, the thrill of uncertainty always holds more power than any outcome.

Despite the excitement this kind of drama generates, many women who repeatedly engage in it suffer from a nagging sense of worthlessness. It is not uncommon to find incidents of severe abuse or neglect in their backgrounds, traumas that confer to them the belief that they are inherently worthless and unlovable. Their quest for excitement is often extreme, as they attempt to momentarily obliterate their profound inner pain. Unfortunately, when the thrill of the moment wanes, they are left feeling as anguished as ever.

In many instances, the Rebel's drama-seeking style is the saddest and most self-destructive of the three orientations. It is especially tragic to witness the Rebel squandering so many latently outstanding qualities. If channeled productively, her hearty appetite for sensation, willingness to risk failure or danger, natural curiosity, and inability to accept many of society's limitations at face value could be remarkable assets, a potentially uplifting source of power within her. When indulged destructively and without substance, purpose, or sincere conviction, these qualities become emotional liabilities that further undermine the Rebel's self-respect.

The Nature of Drama:
Living Episodically

Whether we are Fighters, Challengers, Rebels, or a mix of more than one style, the nature of our dramas is episodic. The excitement is wrung from the intensity of the given moment, often without regard for its significance—or its consequences—within the context of our lives.

To capture the flavor of these episodes, consider the things you have done on impulse, only to ask yourself later, "What made me do something so stupid?!" Perhaps you bought something you couldn't afford, only to berate yourself afterward because of the financial bind in which it put you. Maybe you abruptly quit a job, suddenly ended (or jumped into) a relationship, or said things to a friend in the heat of the moment that you later regretted. At one time or another we all indulge in episodes like these. We make mistakes. We pay the price. We learn.

When drama-seeking is our primary source of stimulation, we make mistakes and we pay the price, but we never really learn. We can't afford to. To recognize the dramatic episode for the damaging, agonizing affair it is, to admit how it perverts our lives, would be to take its heat and its payoffs away. Instead, we not only savor episodes of heightened intensity, but we allow the presence of those episodes to determine the contours of our lives.

The excitement of drama overshadows the cumulative meaning of events and relationships. Our lives become a series of disjointed vignettes, strung together only by the residue of pain, sadness, and failure left by dramatic episodes. We often feel like characters in a soap opera who exist only for short scenes and quick cuts, trapped within an endless story line and forced to endure constant commotion and periods of hope, but never allowed to experience a happy ending.

Thriving on episodic drama, we are unable to experience any resolution to our problems, for they must be kept alive if the drama is to remain at fever pitch. Life begins to feel incongruously empty, oddly purposeless—a surprising, paradoxical feeling, given the maelstrom we are in. Episodic drama leaves us without a strong, comforting thread of meaning to connect the events that punctuate our existence, and deprives us of the personal growth gained through understanding and resolving each of our life issues.

The betrayal, the false promise of satisfaction in the episodic style of living is this: although we are excited by the drama, it can never fulfill us. Subsisting episodically, "out of context," becomes a taxing, depleting, frustrating, and ultimately deeply disappointing way of life.

Drama-Seeking: Rewards and Consequences

Many women include some aspects of more than one primary dramatic style in their excitement-seeking patterns. They may even incorporate consistent features of two or more drama-seeking styles into a kind of hybrid style. But all drama-seekers find similar emotional rewards in creating drama, and they incur many of the same, exacting costs.

The Rewards of Drama

Feeling Alive through Excitement.   Drama can transform lives of boredom, of quiet desperation, into lives that seem *never, ever dull.* Drama makes us feel alive, excited, and turned on to the moment; this is its most seductive facet, the most compelling reason we seek it.

Getting through life from day to day is not always "naturally" exciting. In fact, many people experience life as predominantly tedious and mundane, filled with demands and survival requirements that brush only slight color over the muted backdrop of existence. They don't find their jobs stimulating or their spouses fascinating, and they're bored with the daily drudgery and frustrations of parenting. Waking up each morning signifies an end to the blissful oblivion of sleep, not the beginning of an adventure.

Other people find that each day presents endless opportunities for creativity, novelty, challenge, and adventure. Though their survival needs are the same as those of the bored folk, they go beyond mere survival in their concentrated efforts to extract the unusual from the mundane. It isn't that they live in a different world; it is, instead, that they approach the same world quite differently. They find excitement because they seek and create it. They *insist* on bringing excitement into their lives, and they will go to extraordinary lengths in search of adventure.

While there are many consequences to seeking excitement in personal melodrama, the relief it provides from dullness and tedium, the very thrill of it, is a true reward for the person who demands a stimulating, sensory life. The sensations of excitement to be found in drama can engulf and dissolve boredom and briefly strip away unwelcome memories.

To be excited is to be raw, susceptible to an extreme inflammation of the senses. Feelings are remarkably altered: pain recedes, while pleasure is exaggerated.

Excitement can shoot through you in waves. It can make you shudder with cold, or flush crimson and hot. It can clutch at your gut or go to your head, leaving you weak and dizzy. Excitement can make your breathing come shorter, your skin tingle, and your hands tremble; it can make your palms sticky, your underarms wet, and your lips dry. It can be like a rampant infection, sparing no part of you.

Excitement can swallow your thoughts or inspire them. It can make you giddy or furious; it can diffuse your attention or narrow your focus to near-microscopic acuteness. It can magnify fear or diminish it. To be excited is to be passionate, zealous, demanding, invigorated, forceful. It is to be tense, frightened, amorous, sexual. It is to be totally alive. To be excited is to experience any human desire, any thirst, and to feel utterly compelled to quench it.

Drama can provoke all the sensations of excitement. During a conflict you might feel unbearably enraged, hurt, fearful, or hateful. No matter which sensation you experience, you are in a primitive state, you are bursting with emotion and thoroughly aroused, both mentally and physiologically.

Whether we generate crises, become obsessed with romantic challenges, sexual conquests, or acts of outrageous defiance, during the rush of immersion in the drama our feelings rise to the surface as if a switch had been pulled to engage a dormant electrical circuit. Through drama we know what it means to feel fully charged. In fact, the excitement of drama has a druglike effect upon our systems; though we may crash later, during the brief dramatic episode we can get high on our own experiences, drunk for an instant on the elixir of our own lives.

Dangling on the Edge: Uncertainty and Suspense.   Not only does drama offer a generalized sense of excitement, but the fact that many of our dramatic episodes are cliff-hangers also gives them a specific, penetrating edge. Whether we reenact "the perils of Pauline" as new crises constantly beset us; pursue challenging, unattainable relationships; or take sexual or physical risks, in our created dramas we live on the edge of suspense. Few experiences in life are able to stir greater tension than that of stealthily approaching the edge of failure, disaster, or danger, all the while wondering if we're going too far.

The Fighter, never knowing which catastrophe will strike next, lives on the verge of uncertainty and suspense.

The Challenger, never knowing how her contests will end—Will the object of her passion succumb to her or reject her?—lives on the edge.

The Rebel, in the uncertainty of never knowing whether she has pushed "being bad" one step too far until *after* she has committed a given act, lives on the edge.

Stress and excitement, suspense and fear mingle to magnify our dramas. For many, the tension of dangling on the edge of these emotions is a heady, pleasurable sensation.

Establishing Specialness.   Most people have an enduring wish to feel special, to be a unique, important "somebody." I call this the need for specialness. Through drama, it is possible to create the illusion of specialness.

Specialness is a belief about oneself that each person defines by her or his own terms. For instance, you may feel that you're special because you are more attractive, kinder, smarter, or braver than others. You may feel you're special because you have overcome greater obstacles, suffered more, achieved more, or risked more. You may think you're special because you work for a Fortune 500 company or because your daughter is president of her class.

It is a normal, human trait to seek a sense of specialness. After all, most successes occur because an individual strives to rise in status, either financially or in terms of peer respect. Even our religions confer specialness, saying that some of us are God's chosen, and some of us are doomed.

Some women who wish to be special only *suspect* that they are, or could be. They aren't sure at all—in fact, their greatest fear may be that they are really quite ordinary. Burdened with this insecurity, they will usually set up arbitrary, personally relevant tests, the outcome of which either affirm or refute specialness. Many dramatic scripts are written (often unconsciously) with the necessary "specialness trials" in mind.

The Fighter may seek specialness in situations that permit her to be righteous, tough, or martyred. The Challenger finds validation of her specialness in relationship challenges, and the Rebel in getting away with "playing with fire."

Unfortunately, these specialness "fixes" are short-lived. When a woman's self-esteem is fragile, a single "win" is rarely satisfying enough to warrant an end to the trials. In order for the feeling of specialness to be preserved, proof of it must be established again . . . and again.

Holding Center Stage. In the midst of a dramatic episode, a woman can experience a momentary sense of stardom by engaging other people in her personal dramas while she commands center stage.

Recall Rebecca, the Fighter, whose conflict/crisis orientation kept her in an exhausted frenzy. Each time a crisis occurred, her vocal, dramatic reactions made *her*—not the problem, not its possible solutions—the center of attention. Her friends and her husbands were accustomed to either standing by as sympathetic audiences or entering into the drama as angry, impatient actors. In either case, their presence lent Rebecca an aura of importance, of visibility, that she didn't know how to gain in other, more productive ways.

It is common for women to feel invisible in the world. In social groups of men and women, *both* sexes often direct the majority of their attention to men. A woman is less likely to be seen, to be regarded as important—either by men or by other women—unless she is outstandingly attractive or renowned. Even the most successful businesswomen often complain of being discounted by associates. It is this kind of discrediting that often leads women to concoct their own dramatic styles of gaining visibility.

By creating drama a woman can hold center stage only briefly, and in a manner that eventually brings her as much dissatisfaction as pleasure, but the experience of stardom is exhilarating while she can hang onto it. Suddenly, she is not on the periphery of life, she is at the heart of it—and at the time, that seems worth all the costs.

The Consequences of Drama

Exhausting Our Energy. Many women have strong, focused goals and dreams that they hope to actualize one day. Others are anxious to discover where their professional and personal potentials lie. These ambitions are part of the structures that add meaning and purpose to all of our lives. Drama, however, is an exacting "mistress." After spending too much time submerged in drama, we come up for air devitalized—and suddenly lost. We look around, shocked to realize that *this* is not where we intended to be at this point in our lives. We wonder how so many of our plans and dreams got away from us. There is a jarring emptiness inside, a sense of panic. I often hear such questions as "What *happened* to my life?" and "How did things turn out this way?"

The story of Paula, the Challenger you met earlier, exemplifies what can happen when a relentless search for excitement in drama saps energy that could have been devoted to personal accomplishment. In Paula's case, immersion in romantic challenges turned her desire to own a restaurant into an impossible dream while sabotaging her chance to have a real relationship. The anguish of this finally shocked her into taking stock of her life. As Paula told me:

> I woke up one morning to discover that I had been sobbing in my sleep. The pillow was all wet . . . my eyes were filled with tears, and I didn't know why. I realized that here I was, thirty-five years old, and what did I have to show for it? No real relationship, no family . . . a good job, yes, but no business . . . nothing I thought I wanted. I felt like a worthless nobody. How could this have happened to me . . . ?

The answer is the drama. It seduces women like Paula, possesses them, and eventually drains away much of their potential.

Losing Personal Power and Self-Esteem. As noted earlier, the intense gratification of drama is limited and fleeting. Our heightened sensations dissipate, our feelings of specialness wane, and the curtain comes down on center stage. We are left needing another shot of drama to bring the excitement back.

Usually, this entire transition occurs outside our consciousness. Because we often don't recognize the degree to which we are making choices or the extent of our responsibility for directing dramatic scenarios, it is a simple matter for us to blame God, our parents, our husband, our boss, our lover, the police, the economy, the traffic, the state of the union—anything or anybody outside ourselves—for "making" us feel this way or "doing it" to us.

The truth is, while others may in fact have hurt us badly, and luck may at times have not been on our side, the ways in which we *perceive* and *react to* occurrences are completely within our control. For example, a fender-bender accident can be seen as either a major catastrophe with endless possibilities for drama or as an unfortunate occurrence, to be handled efficiently and then forgotten. When we are immersed in drama-seeking, our tendency is to become so overwhelmed by emotions, so stimulated by the drama, that we lose sight of our options. Swept up in the drama, we imagine that *it* is controlling *us* and that we are without personal power.

There is no pleasure, no electric charge in this aspect of drama. It's *awful* to feel powerless. Yet, it is a sensation that begins to shape our experience of ourselves and the world, for when we feel powerless we act as if we *are* powerless. In doing so we become, operationally, as powerless as we believe we are. A downward spiral begins: First, the illusion of powerlessness becomes our reality. Then, the sense of powerlessness demoralizes us. Finally, our self-esteem declines, driving us to seek greater drama, much of it designed to help us feel more alive, more special—more powerful. Thus, while drama drains us of a sense of personal power, it offers us the illusion of temporary power. We are caught up in a truly agonizing cycle!

Losing Touch with Our Deepest Feelings.   When energy and emotion are expended on drama, we can become distracted or detached from our deepest feelings, those "other," buried feelings that aren't revved up during dramatic episodes. While the constellation of masked feelings may be different for each of us, it often includes grief, anger, fear, betrayal, mistrust, envy, hate, guilt, and shame.

All the women described in this chapter hide their feelings and insecurities from themselves. Their dramas serve the dual purpose of satisfying their needs for sensation and distracting them from, or setting limits on, the pain they experience. Clarissa, the Rebel whom you met earlier, overeats compulsively, and in generating her drama manages to not only be bad but also to stuff down the anger toward her husband that frequently wells to the surface—an anger she fears could threaten her social and financial security. Brought up to believe that the right husband could provide her with "acceptability," Clarissa never really felt important on her own. Rather than dealing with the pain that lies at the root of her poor self-image or facing the unhappiness and potential collapse of her marriage, she creates drama. And *drama inevitably conceals insight.*

If denial of unpleasant feelings could really make them go away, there would be no reason to encourage people to deal with them. But masking feelings only forces them to rise to the surface in a disguised form—a form that *always* does far more damage and creates a worse, although different, kind of pain than the one being hidden.

There is, finally, no escape from ourselves, nor should there be. Our deepest feelings, both good and bad, are essential to our characters, our personalities, our essences. They are an important part of what makes each of us *genuinely* special.

Losing Out on Intimacy and Emotional Security.   Women who seek excitement through drama rarely experience lasting intimacy in their love relationships. Although sharing tales of drama can enhance the intimacy of friendships between women, in romantic relationships drama often substitutes for the intimacy that is missing.

Intimacy, in which two people are able to share with each other the deepest truths about themselves, is difficult for lovers to achieve under any circumstances. It requires space, time, and nurturing to blossom. To create an intimate relationship, we must be willing to repeatedly risk self-revelation. We must provide for our partners—and they for us—an inviting, loving atmosphere in which to take those risks.

When drama-seeking plays a role in our relationships, dramatic conflicts and challenges chip away at the foundation of trust and safety that must be present if intimacy is to flourish. When drama pervades other areas of our lives, the sweeping turmoil around us leaves insufficient space for intimacy to expand or grow. Though we may long for a relationship combining intimacy and passion, drama usually precludes our having a relationship that encompasses both qualities.

In dramatic, nonintimate relationships, we often feel unsure of where we stand with our partner (or vice versa) and of the relationship's future. While this uncertainty contributes to the thrill of living on the edge, it also leads to a profound sense of emotional insecurity. We often beget excitement, strong sensation, and heightened feelings at the expense of our yearnings for closeness and commitment.

The Agony of It All!!

A life of drama-seeking is painful and self-defeating. It brings us excitement, but it also brings us great agony. The title of this book reflects not only the anguish we experience as an outgrowth of the melodrama, it also reflects the melodrama itself.

It is my hope that in this phrase you will find an honest mirror of your feelings and a humorous way to look at your own behavior. If in the midst of the excitement, intensity, and excessive nature of a dramatic episode, you can hear yourself silently cry, "Oh, the *agony* of it all"—if you can just tickle your mind with that thought—you will have stepped outside your melodrama and will no longer be submerged in it. By even momentarily removing yourself from your attachment to the drama, you open yourself up to rethinking it and understanding it. In doing so, you are actually taking the first steps toward finding a happier, more fulfilling, and more genuinely thrilling way of living.

The Thrill of It All: Pure, Healthy Excitement

If, right now, you could magically rid your life of unproductive drama and move beyond the agony of it all, you would still be left with a normal need for excitement, for stimulation, novelty, and sensation. Would you know how to fill it?

In contrast to melodramatic highs, pure excitement is the kind of stimulation that leaves us with a feeling of confidence, a sense of glad-to-be-aliveness, rather than a backlash of pain, disappointment, and despair. Healthy excitement takes many forms, but it contrasts with drama in two essential ways. First, healthy excitement is neither self-defeating nor self-destructive; rather, it is self-actualizing. Second, healthy excitement offers substantial pleasure and/or concrete reward.

Let's look at some examples of healthy excitement my former clients have shared with me:

- When I surpassed my company's sales quotas for the year by nearly 200 percent, I was really proud and excited. Then, at the annual banquet, I received an "outstanding salesperson" award. It was incredible to feel such a sense of accomplishment and to be recognized and applauded.
- The first time I skied a black diamond run [the most advanced and dangerous] was one of the all-time exciting moments of my life. I was scared, but never more thrilled.
- After I had my twins, I decided not to go back to work for a while. I discovered that being a new mother was challenging and exciting. And for the first time in years I've had a chance to paint—I'm doing portraits of the twins now. It's wonderful.
- Every time I face a jury, I'm excited. As a lawyer I'm constantly challenged, always putting myself on the line with my client. There is tremendous responsi-

bility in what I do, and sometimes tedious work, but
the rewards are there at the end of the line.

● One of the most exciting things in my life right now
is my relationship with Allan [the man with whom
she lives]. I'm an executive secretary, and I work
very long hours. But when we do spend time together, it is exciting just to *be* together, no matter
what we're doing. Just talking can be as intense as
making love.

Each of these experiences is personally rewarding or immensely
pleasurable. All are self-actualizing, meaning that the experience
either maintains or strengthens self-esteem, furthers goals and ambitions, or enhances growth as an individual on the mental, emotional,
spiritual, or physical plane. A self-actualizing experience is not damaging to oneself or to others.

Whether it is experienced alone or with another, whether it is an
outgrowth of genuine intimacy or an extension of individual goals,
healthy excitement is always distinguishable from drama because it
doesn't take more than it gives in return. Following are some of the
costs of drama versus the corresponding rewards of healthy excitement:

Drama	Excitement
gives an illusion of specialness	builds real confidence
depletes your energy	energizes you
lowers your self-esteem	builds your self-esteem
leaves you stuck in old patterns	offers choices and brings growth
obscures your real feelings	illuminates your feelings
creates barriers to intimacy	furthers intimacy
distracts you from goals	furthers your goals

The possibilities for including healthy, self-actualizing excitement
in your life are limited only by your personal preferences and imagination. Starting a business, advancing your education, taking up
bodybuilding, giving a well-planned party, running for organiza-
tional office, and taking part in a marathon race are all potentially
healthy, self-actualizing experiences. Which activities will appeal to

you, individually, will depend upon the level of pleasure and reward you can derive from them.

In healthy excitement, the pleasures and rewards of an experience always outweigh the struggles. The pleasure may be its own reward, as in the sensory adventure of trying a new exotic restaurant. It may be an outgrowth of the achievement level of an experience, as in the excitement of successfully negotiating an important contract. In many of our most exciting endeavors, pleasure and reward mingle, as they do when we play in a tennis tournament or when we make love.

Any goal that is challenging and exciting has difficult, anxiety-producing, tedious, disappointing, and frustrating moments. It is in getting through and beyond the difficulties that we grow as individuals and aspire to greater levels of accomplishment and excitement.

Paula, the Challenger, finally knows how rewarding true excitement can be. The night she woke up to find she had been sobbing in her sleep was a turning point that brought her a painful, but necessary, awareness of her drama-making patterns. As she grew to understand them, she chose to work toward changing them. Paula is now putting together the financing for her own restaurant and has become involved with a man who "wants me as much as I want him." Of course, the road ahead is still uncertain. There are no guaranteed outcomes in her business or her new romance, but for Paula that only enhances the challenge and intensifies the suspense.

The final section of this book is devoted entirely to the process of healthy excitement-seeking, to the process of learning to step outside our dramas and to let them go. We discover that despite the costs of drama, there are actually many *positive* aspects of all three drama-seeking styles that can become very useful in seeking healthy sensation. Many drama-making strategies reflect valuable personality traits that need only to be redirected, not changed. In order to find healthy excitement we don't have to douse our internal fires or restrain our energies. In fact, the guidelines offered are specifically oriented to helping any woman become more in tune with her innate strengths rather than rejecting them. Where drama causes heartache today, pure excitement and self-love can bring fulfillment tomorrow.

2 ❧

The Roots of Drama-Seeking

Drama generates a feeling of aliveness that is important because it satisfies a basic human urge: the drive to seek sensation.

Biochemically, a domestic crisis, a love challenge, and a 10,000-foot parachute drop from an airplane can be equally stimulating. From an emotional point of view, however, the love challenge is potentially far more disastrous than the jump. In chapters 2 and 3, we will explore the reasons why women tend to go after love challenges (or other forms of interpersonal drama) when equal stimulation can be attained by exploring the risks and challenges available in more productive thrills.

In this chapter we'll look at the biological side of the sensation-seeking trait in men and women, as well as at the cultural norms that have traditionally dictated how this urge is satisfied or restricted. Despite the drama you may be creating in your life, the message of this chapter is that you are not a "sick" or "diseased" woman, but rather one who has learned to adapt to society's traditionally imposed limitations upon your sensation-seeking options.

In chapter 3 we'll explore the compounding influences of early-childhood experiences and family relationships upon women's drama-seeking patterns.

With these two chapters taken together, we'll see how our sensation-seeking drives have been perverted by cultural indoctrinations and unhealthy family dramas that enveloped us in a tight web of emotional conditioning. Our task is to scrutinize and tear away that confining web.

The New Science of Excitement
The Meaning of Excitement

"Sensation-seeking" refers to the human need to seek novel sensations and experiences and to the willingness to take risks for the sake of those experiences. Before we delve into the science of sensation-seeking, we ought to clarify the meaning of the terms *sensation* and *excitement.*

For our purposes, *sensation* is a general term referring to the feelings that arise when any of our senses is stimulated—sight, sound, touch, smell, taste, and even the sixth sense, intuition or extrasensory perception (ESP).

Sensation can also be created out of a mental state or emotion, since these have physiological counterparts. While the physical changes may be subtle (perhaps just a slight increase in perspiration or a tendency to fidget) or great (a wildly thumping heart, or a sick feeling in the pit of the stomach), we usually recognize, or "sense," that a shift in our perception or mood has occurred. We often identify that new state by describing it as anxiety, fear, love, anger, hate, sadness, depression—or excitement.

The word *excitement* can be confusing, for it has two distinct meanings. First, it can refer to a specific, recognizable state associated with certain familiar sensations. Some people apply the term primarily to happy or positive feelings of anticipation and tension. Others acknowledge that for them excitement is associated with danger or risk. In addition to describing these specific feelings or sensations, excitement can also be used to denote a more general, physiological precursor to *any* category of sensation.

By arousing or stimulating a sensory or emotional capacity, we can physiologically "excite" that capacity. That is the second meaning of excitement. Any specifically identified sensation—hunger, heat, cold, anger, happiness, pain, fear—is achieved through stimulation, or excitation, of certain combinations of senses. For example, the sensation of fear is experienced when biological excitement is achieved as a result of an outside event or its mental anticipation. However, most of us are unlikely to describe the sensation of feeling fearful as excitement. It is more natural to refer to a specific form of excitation by using its most distinctive name—in this case, *fear*. While most people use the word *excitement* to describe only the precise, familiar group of sensations they consider pleasurably thrilling, the meaning of the word is broader in relation to the sensation-seeking drive.

Since sensation results from arousal and stimulation—in other words, from excitement—of the mind and senses, the general meanings of *excitement* and *sensation* are so closely aligned as to be almost interchangeable. Certainly, they are inseparable. This means that negative excitement, which produces the sensations of fear, anger, hate, pain, anxiety, and so on, is no less stimulating and, therefore, no less satisfying of our sensation-seeking needs than is positive excitement.

The Basis of Our Drive for Excitement

In order to respect the depth and importance of our sensation-seeking needs, we must understand the biochemistry that motivates us.

Long before sensation-seeking was isolated as a distinct personality trait, Carl Jung pointed to the existence of five instinctual human tendencies. These included hunger, reflection, creativity, sex—and the "drive to activity," which encompassed the urge to travel, the love of change, and a tendency toward what Jung called "restlessness." His conception of the activity drive is sufficiently similar to the current operational definition of sensation-seeking to be identifiable as the same trait.

Today, one of the most eminent researchers in the field of sensation-seeking is psychologist Marvin Zuckerman of the University of Delaware. Zuckerman's initial exploration of the subject nearly thirty years ago grew out of his desire to predict the ways in which different people would respond to experiments in sensory deprivation. He was also curious about why some students repeatedly volunteered for experiments, and he speculated that novelty and excitement were greater enticements than the small fee the students received.

In 1961, Zuckerman began testing the first version of his Sensation Seeking (SS) Scale, a questionnaire built on the premise that human beings attempt to increase or decrease external stimulation as necessary to maintain an internal "optimal level of arousal." The optimal level of arousal was considered to be a state of nervous-system stimulation (or excitement) that produced a sense of functional well-being. It was regarded as a subjectively positive state that could be reached by either painful or pleasurable means.

According to this early theory, some of us have "strong nervous systems" that are insensitive to low levels of stimulation but that react to excitation at high levels of intensity. Such people demand intense, thrilling experiences to charge up their systems to the optimal level. Other people have "weak nervous systems" that respond to relatively light stimulation and that cannot tolerate intense stimuli. These people are already revved up inside; they don't need acute levels of experience to reach the optimal level of arousal.

Zuckerman's SS Scale scores people on their relatively high or low need to seek adventure and avoid boredom. It consists of four sections: a Thrill and Adventure Seeking subscale, which poses questions about risky sports such as mountain climbing and parachute jumping; an Experience Seeking subscale, which concerns the attraction to seeking sensation through the mind, the senses, or a nonconforming lifestyle; a Disinhibition subscale, which focuses on drinking, partying, and sexuality; and a Boredom Susceptibility subscale, which assesses tolerance for monotonous, routine, repetitous experiences. Through the use of these subscales we not only know what high-sensation seekers do and how they think, but we also know more about what makes them biologically different from more subdued people.

The strong versus weak nervous-system theory of arousal has given way to more advanced, neurochemically based hypotheses. Currently, scientists are exploring *which* brain chemicals control the sensation-seeking trait, and exactly *how* they go about doing it. Although everyone is driven to seek some sensation in some way, there is general agreement that certain people are neurochemically driven to demand greater sensation than others.

In his current theory explaining the biological basis of sensation-seeking, Zuckerman has pointed to the catecholamines, a family of neurotransmitters (or chemical messengers) that carry signals between the neurons of the brain. He uses the term *catecholamine systems activity* (CSA) to summarize the effects of all the chemical action within this specialized arousal-control system of the brain—including the influence of the neuroenzyme monoamine oxidase, which is found in lowest quantities in the blood plasma of high-sensation seekers. Zuckerman believes that there is a general level of CSA that is optimal for desirable mood, activity, and social interaction.

When our CSA level is substantially different from its optimal level, we have to do something to bring it up, or down, as the case may be. People who score lower on the SS Scale may have levels of CSA that are greater than those of high-sensation seekers, who apparently have constitutionally lower levels of CSA. Both must adjust their systems through the external environment by reducing or increasing stimulation. Meditation, for example, has a calming affect, theoretically lowering levels of CSA and bringing an uncomfortably hyped-up system back to normal. Giving a speech before a large audience could stimulate one's system, bringing CSA levels up and "balancing" a system that had wound down to an unpleasant level.

The attempt to activate or reduce CSA could explain why some people are disposed toward quick-fix excitement—that is, stimulation that has the fastest, most efficient effect on CSA. Zuckerman suggests that risky, even fear-provoking, activities will immediately raise the level of CSA to a point where certain individuals feel "normal." The line between excitement and fear is perpetually blurred for such people. Dangers that would inhibit some of us are perceived differently by those whose systems quite literally thrive on threat. CSA can also be raised by situations laden with almost any highly charged emotion. All the emotions attached to melodrama, such as rage, jealousy, and fear, can be equally satisfying on a neurochemical level. So can the sensations associated with extraordinary happiness. *The issue is not whether the source of stimulation is objectively positive or negative, healthy or unhealthy, but whether the stimulation is intense enough to alter the CSA.*

When our CSA is stimulated to a degree that is well above our optimal level, we are likely to experience anxiety, depression, and, ultimately, panic. *Anyone* can be thrust over the neurochemical edge by more stimulation than his or her system can tolerate. By the same token, when our CSA level is less than optimal, we may feel depressed or anxious, as well as apathetic, bored, or withdrawn. If we don't mobilize to increase our level of stimulation and thereby alter our mood, we will probably sink deeper into ennui. You may have had the experience of becoming suddenly edgy because you were bored. You might have impulsively sought stimulation—maybe by drinking or eating too much, picking a fight, going dancing, or going to see an action/adventure movie—in an attempt to raise an insufficiently activated level of CSA. Within a certain range of CSA activity, such activity appears to constitute a normal, even desirable adjustment, denoting a personality trait rather than a clinical disorder. Only at the extreme low end of the CSA spectrum is it more difficult to achieve a healthy adjustment.

Some individuals experience major clinical depression because, in Zuckerman's terms, their characteristic levels of CSA remain seriously below the optimal. Without treatment, they may surrender to their depression. Some become enervated, lethargic, and apathetic. Others become driven and desperate in their search for stimulation and inject huge measures of drama into their lives, often in self-destructive or self-defeating ways that can leave behind even deeper depression.

While sensation-seeking and depression can be biochemically related, only the smallest proportion of women I've known have actually engaged in drama-seeking to compensate for biochemically based depression. It is true, however, that continued drama-seeking can foster depressed feelings in people who are not otherwise predisposed.

In terms of Zuckerman's theory, mood-elevating drugs or antidepressants work because they intervene chemically to bring the CSA up to a closer-to-optimal level. Research has shown that high-sensation seekers are frequently multidrug users. Not only do they get high on such CSA heighteners as cocaine and amphetamines, but they will also gladly stimulate another chemical system of the brain—the endorphins, or "pleasure centers"—by smoking marijuana or taking opiate-type drugs. Zuckerman theorizes that high-sensation seekers may be aroused by any form of change. This makes complete sense if we consider that, by definition, sensation-seeking involves a craving for experience that is not merely intense, but *novel*. And no experience remains novel for long.

One of the differences between sensation-seekers who occasionally get high on drugs and those who become addicts involves the comparative search for novelty. As Harvey Milkman and Stanley Sunderwirth wrote in their book *Craving for Ecstasy,* "The human body eventually adapts to most novel stimulation by reducing the potency of its effects. The user or performer soon needs more of the mood-altering activity in order to experience similar alterations in feelings." When the original experience is repeated more frequently, and at higher and higher levels of intensity, an addiction can develop.

According to Milkman and Sunderwirth, it is theoretically possible to become neurochemically addicted even to certain forms of risk-taking activities. For "risk junkies," activities that bring excitement and pleasure at first eventually become muted in their effects. Like heroin addicts who have to shoot up just to function but who can no longer get high, risk junkies eventually lose the intense sense of thrill that attracted them to an activity in the first place.

In the nonaddicted individual, sensation is maintained through novelty, which demands that one intermittently institute a change from the status quo. In terms of sensation-seeking pleasures, change carries no value judgments. A change from sober to stoned, happy to sad, or joyful to mad is satisfying simply because it is change.

Zuckerman's SS Scale has been utilized by numerous researchers throughout the world to reap substantial information about the personality characteristics of the high-sensation seeker. Statistically speaking, high-sensation seekers prefer the color red over blue, would rather have spicy, sour, and crunchy foods than bland foods, and enjoy all kinds of rock 'n' roll. They also tend to have a greater variety of sexual experiences and partners, to use more alcohol and drugs, to smoke more, and even to switch television channels and consumer products more frequently. High-sensation seekers are also more likely to enjoy violent, fear-provoking, or erotic films. Runners tend to score somewhat lower on the SS Scale than athletes involved in body-contact sports, and much lower than those who pursue more daring ventures such as surfing, skiing, or scuba diving. Married women who tested high on the sensation-seeking scale were found to be more sexually responsive, more inclined to masturbate, and more apt to have multiple orgasms. High-sensation seekers are more likely to take an interest in gambling and are more sensitive to the probabilities of winning or losing. They also tend to drive above the speed limit more often.

High-sensation seekers are leaders in groups, but they do not cope well with sensory isolation. Overall, they are also less anxious than low-sensation seekers, as well as more extroverted. They are more creative, and they are more inclined to favor variety and complexity in sensory stimulation.

Most studies of sensation-seeking show that it declines with age; especially among men, sensation-seeking extremes tend to lose their appeal after about age thirty. Some evidence suggests that this shift is biologically based. It may also be that as we grow older and our priorities change, we put the riskiest activities aside because we got them "out of our system" earlier. Interestingly, some studies show that women's tendency to seek sensation actually *increases* over the years, peaking from ages thirty to thirty-nine and beginning to decline in the forties and fifties.

Psychologist Frank Farley calls high-sensation seekers "Type T Personalities," with the "T" standing for "thrill-seeker." He says that "these high-profile people are risk-takers and adventurers who seek excitement and stimulation wherever they can find or create it. For some, the thrills are mainly in the physical domain; for others, they're mainly mental; and for still others, they're a mix of both." Farley believes that "thrill-seeking can lead some Type T's to outstanding creativity . . . but it can lead others to extremely destructive, even criminal, behavior."

He implies that it is primarily social circumstances that determine whether people become "creators or destroyers." For example, an occasional shoplifter may not be a high-sensation seeker, while a cat burglar probably is—but both channel their need for stimulation in a destructive fashion. A portrait photographer might be an average-sensation seeker, while an entrepreneur may be a very high-sensation seeker, yet both would seem to have found creative, self-actualizing means of expressing their drives. The high need for stimulation does not in itself pose problems for individuals. Rather, it is the productive or destructive choices made to satisfy this need that are our ultimate concern.

Is Drama-Seeking an "Addiction"?

As we've seen, it is possible for potentially addictive activities, such as drug use, to fill sensation-seeking needs. It is also theoretically possible to become biochemically addicted to risky, excitement-producing activities. The question we turn to now is this: Can drama-seeking be an addiction used to create excitement?

Some experts believe that *any* activity can become an addiction if it induces changes in the action of the brain's neurotransmitters, with behavioral problems resulting. However, even within this framework an addiction does not develop unless a person becomes unable to control when he or she starts and stops the activity.

Since the drive to seek excitement appears to be modulated by the levels of neurotransmission in the catecholamine system, it is conceivable that one could become biochemically dependent upon, and unable to control, the thrilling activities that trigger alterations in the system. However, to the extent that we are capable of managing those activities, we are nonaddicted.

Of course, capability for control is different from manifesting control. For example, some people may be fully capable of yelling or not yelling at their children. Yet, for these people yelling may be so ingrained a pattern and may produce such consistent results that they do not exercise, or even consider, their capacity to stop it. Similarly, though a woman is able to stop creating drama once her awareness has been raised, until then that capacity may lie dormant. Yet during the period of dormancy it would be inaccurate to suggest that the woman was addicted to the drama.

The issues of addiction and nonaddiction are often confused as they pertain to excitement and drama-seeking. Some self-help groups for

adult children from alcoholic or dysfunctional families consider an
addiction to excitement to be one of the predictable consequences of
growing up in such a family. While these adult children often do seek
higher levels of sensation than others, in most cases this is an indication of a personality trait, *not* of an addiction to excitement or to the
drama from which the excitement is often derived.

When the inherently healthy drive to seek excitement is channeled
unsafely—even into abuses that later become addictive—the drive
itself is often misunderstood and labeled an addiction. This obscures
some of the real treatment issues. It is rather like trying to cure
unhealthy eating habits by calling hunger a pathological compulsion,
and seeking to repress the need instead of addressing the destructive
eating habits that corrupt it.

The tendency to seek drama does not indicate an addiction to
either excitement or drama. Drama-seeking is a learned behavior
pattern that is to some extent *adaptive* rather than pathological, and
which over time becomes self-defeating. In my clinical experience, as
women come to understand the nature of their sensation-seeking
drive and the purpose of their drama-making, they begin almost
immediately to stop much of the drama and to make new choices for
bringing healthy, self-fulfilling excitement into their lives. Like a
natural appetite well fed, their hunger for sensation begins to be
satisfied in the most nourishing ways possible. Only when their problems are compounded by the abuse of drugs, alcohol, and so on is
it crucial that addiction be addressed.

Growing Up as High-Sensation Seekers

Since our predisposition to high, low, or moderate sensation-seeking
is thought to be determined by our neurochemical systems, we may
wonder if the operation of those systems is genetically determined,
and, if so, whether it is possible for our environment to intervene and
actually alter our neurochemistry.

Animal studies have shown that the brain is a remarkably "plastic"
organ, capable of drastically changing its shape in response to various stimuli. In a series of famous experiments performed by psychologist Harry Harlow at the University of Illinois during the 1950s and
early 1960s, monkeys reared in sensory isolation became withdrawn
and violent, spending most of their time rocking back and forth or
cringing in corners like sad autistic children. The pleasure centers of
their brains were unable to develop because of the deprivation to
which they were exposed. The opposite occurred when rats were
raised in "enriched" environments, with lots of mazes, wheels, and

toys. These animals grew thicker cerebral cortexes and became much "smarter" than rats provided with low sensory input.

The bulk of scientific evidence indicates that the brain is a dynamic open system that reacts biochemically to the environment, changing in response to an individual's experiences and then reacting to the further experiences one has as a result of those chemical transformations. It follows that the brains of children raised in a highly stimulating environment will adapt cortically and neurochemically to their situations. If we accept the validity of Zuckerman's theory, we would expect many such children to grow up to be higher-sensation seekers, with correspondingly lower levels of CSA, than those raised in a relative absence of stimulation. This becomes clearest if we remember that the term *stimulation* doesn't carry good or bad connotations; a slap can be just as "stimulating" to the system as a hug. It becomes an especially important concept to remember when exploring how our childhood experiences affect our sensation-seeking patterns as adults.

A New View of Female Sensation-Seekers

Based on the SS Scale, high-sensation seekers are slightly less likely to be female than male. If they're female, they possess stereotypically "masculine" personality traits: autonomy, dominance, adventurousness, curiosity, aggressiveness, exhibitionism, and radicalism. Because biochemical evidence for gender differences in sensation-seeking is vague and conflicting, a good case can be made for the role of social and cultural conditioning in creating male/female differences in test scores.

No matter what a woman's fundamental drive for sensation may be, few of us are raised with access to the same healthy outlets for excitement-seeking as men. For instance, women aren't generally encouraged to take up "daredevil" sports. Growing up, we received the message that these activities are macho for men but inappropriate for women, and this double standard holds true even today. Yet there are numerous items on the SS Scale concerning risky sports. Because women generally don't respond enthusiastically to questions that relate to these principally male avenues of exploration, their test scores when compared with men's may, indeed, be lower. Instead of pursuing daredevil or risky activities, many women seek excitement in daring or risky relationships. Since the questions on the SS Scale don't reflect this tendency, women's drive for sensation may be significantly higher than scores on the scale indicate.

Most experts in the field agree that high-sensation seekers are quite zealous in their quest for sensation. According to Polish researcher Zbigniew Zaleski, "high-sensation seekers would involve themselves in events that either strongly excite them, make them happy or irritate them, satisfy or disgust them, make them angry, or help to give them 'highs'." It is logical, he states, that "they will try to create such situations if the natural and cultural environment does not offer them." For Zaleski, sensation-seeking "involves not only seeking after existing strong stimuli, but also creating such incentives" if they are not readily available.

Drama-seeking—creating intense sensation in day-to-day situations—is the way women have learned to fulfill their innate need for stimulation in the face of restrictive injunctions about their role and their "place."

Women and men in the Western world are traditionally socialized quite differently. Most people would concur that adult women today, especially those ages thirty and over, are the offspring of a distinctly unliberated era, a time when prevailing attitudes about women's status and potential were stultifying. Women were subjected to diminution of their natural powers and capacities in every realm of life except that of "catching" a man, keeping the home, and nurturing the children. For many women, drama-seeking became a way of creating necessary sensation within acceptably "feminine" domains: their relationships and emotional life.

The women's movement has helped open previously locked doors to other forms of sensation and excitement, but women still reel from the impact of their psychological and cultural legacies. Most "today" women—liberated, career-oriented, sophisticated—have not yet left all the lessons of their upbringing behind nor dropped the patterns of drama-seeking that they learned, while growing up, could provide consistent emotional payoffs.

How We Learned to Behave as Women

Many powerful lessons about womanhood are acquired through exposure to models of femininity that reach us from all sides—magazines, television shows, movies, novels, schoolbooks, advertisements, jokes. It is through these seemingly "lightweight" sources that we come to grasp some exceptionally heavyweight messages about what it means to be a woman and, most importantly, about *how* to be a woman. These messages—which are perhaps the most potent messages about our culture's perceptions of femaleness—become primers that teach girls and young women what to do and what not to do, seriously hampering their desire or capacity to develop outside the confines they see.

The far-reaching capabilities of radio and television have enabled the fastest, broadest transmission ever of these cultural messages. Long before radio or television, however, there was print. Through the pages of glossy ladies' magazines, women have been instructed in domestic arts, social graces, and skills for pleasing their husbands. Whether the magazines were read in the 1900s, 1930s, or 1950s, the predominant cultural mood was reflected in essentially the same message: "Your proper place is in the home, serving your husband and children. And your special 'female' qualities—tact, patience, diplomacy, and charm—should be used for nurturing children and transforming your hardworking, tired husband into a new man when he comes home." A "true" woman was expected not to demand greater fulfillment than this.

The magazines' helpful hints relayed a parallel, but hidden message: a "real" woman should not seek excitement outside her clearly delineated boundaries. Of course, sensation-seeking surely was as innate (though unrecognized) a drive in women in the past as it is now. For many women of the early and mid-twentieth century, creating drama undoubtedly became a means of satisfying the need for heightened stimulation without risking the consequences of pursuing it out of bounds.

Although it seems clear from the vantage point of the present that during the first half of the twentieth century drama-seeking was an adaptive mechanism for women with few other sensation-seeking outlets, the medical establishment of those years presumably regarded dramatic behavior as an illness (as it often still does). One might speculate that many women back then—especially the high-sensation seekers, who probably suffered the most from their cultural confinement—became diagnosed as the "hysterics" who were treated for mental disorders by the new breed of Freudian psychoanalysts.

Unfortunately, changes in the social structures that predispose women to drama-seeking have occurred slowly and incompletely over the years. Even as late as the mid-1960s, when Vietnam war protests and sexual revolutions were fomenting across college campuses nationwide, the role of women had expanded only nominally. While we may have begun to seek sensation through sexual exploration and political agitation, it was usually the men who were the movement's leaders and the women who kept the coffee cups filled during protest-planning meetings and intellectual bull sessions. According to social-science investigator Carol Erlich, the sociology textbooks being utilized on those campuses were primarily collections of folklore and sexual stereotypes, confirming the fact that the establishment still regarded women as entirely different from, and inferior to, men. In 1971, Erlich wrote:

> In sociology, woman as an object of study is largely ignored. Only in the field of marriage and the family is she seen to exist. Her place in sociology is, in other words, the traditional one assigned to her by the larger society: woman's place is in the home.

Throughout the seventies (and even into the eighties), many cultural instruments played this same old off-key tune. Yet, as long as women accepted—even partially—society's view that they were meant for a domestic role, as long as they believed that tending to relationships should be their life's priority, they would be inclined to satisfy their needs for intensity and excitement by creating drama within the confines of their restricted personal universe. For most women, even becoming "liberated" and having careers could not substantially change these deep-seated, unconsciously motivated, and misunderstood drama-making patterns.

Many of us were growing up or coming of age in the period between 1950 and 1970. There was no need to rely entirely on textbooks or on magazines like *Cosmopolitan* for definitions of ourselves; all we had to do was turn on the television set to receive a long-lasting lesson about excitement-seeking and womanhood. While female roles in nearly every show were stereotyped, I believe that two immensely popular programs, "The Donna Reed Show" and "I Love Lucy," had an especially formative impact upon millions of young women, conveying some of the most damaging messages to hordes of viewers.

Television's Impossible Role Models

"The Donna Reed Show":
Domestic Contentment and Homebound Excitement

Donna Stone, the picture of selfless, contented perfection, was the sweetest, most loving mother a child might wish for and the prettiest, most efficient wife a man might win.

In the opening of almost every scene, Donna could be found attending to one household task or another or tending faithfully to her temperamental, penny-pinching but handsome and adoring husband, Alex. In this impeccably organized TV family, traditional female/male roles were clearly delineated; unlike many real-life homemakers, Donna was exquisitely comfortable in her part.

Donna didn't work outside the home. All of her needs—including her need for excitement—appeared to be met easily through Alex and her children. In her case, life produced relatively low-intensity excitement and only minimal drama. But then, Donna was the perfect, perfectly *unreal* female stereotype, so she seemed to be fulfilled without requiring more.

Donna did have her little secrets from Alex, and every so often she got a charge out of being devilish—buying an extravagantly expensive hat, for instance. But she really thrived on her role as caretaker, manipulator, and, at times, outright meddler in her family's affairs. She became deeply involved in whatever her husband or children got into, always offering honey-drenched advice, yet endeavoring to control circumstances whenever she could. If conflict erupted between Alex and the children, she intervened, especially when Alex became too ornery and unreasonable—which happened weekly. It was in this role that her hunger for sensation was best appeased.

Donna was utterly fulfilled. Because she was so perfect, viewers tended to believe that such perfection could exist and was something to strive toward, and that undeniable happiness could be reaped from such a life. This was dangerous, since the character was completely fabricated. Impressionable girls or young women were likely to get caught up in this fantasy, accepting whatever viewpoints the show offered. Consequently, "The Donna Reed Show" instilled in them a desire to be something they could never be—and even if they *could* have become like Donna Stone, they could never, in real life, have achieved the bliss that she did.

Watching the show also provoked certain questions, then inexpressible, but irksome. If a woman's stimulation was supposed to be found in family life, in her relationships, how could many young women account for the boredom and frustration they observed in the women around them, in their own mothers—so unlike Donna? How did they explain the yearnings for a more *exciting* life that they felt stirring within? Many simply ignored the contradictions, suppressed their questions, and stumbled forward. Others looked to different role models for guidance.

Some looked to "Lucy Ricardo," who provided a rebellious, madcap counterpoint to Donna Stone's domestic conformity.

"I Love Lucy": The Excitement in Rebellion

When we think of 1950s-era television, most of us think first of "I Love Lucy," a situation comedy that was described in the October 15, 1951 issue of *TV Guide* as a show "revolving around problems arising in a household where the wife is stage-struck and the orchestra leader husband thinks she should stay home."

Part of the show's overwhelming popularity surely hinged on the way it gave the well-behaved women of America a chance to experience, if only vicariously, the thrills of being truly naughty. It was a kick to watch that zany culprit, Lucy, slither her way in and out of mischief, and it was a scream to hear husband Ricky bellow "LUU-UCEEEEE!" when he got wind of her antics. The effects of this kind of humor are serious, however. While I loved Lucy as much as anyone, I also feel that the show incorporated some disturbing themes that helped shape our real lives.

Lucy's life was exciting, but her excitement was always an extension of her naughtiness. She was a bad girl, a rebel, who made a career out of doing anything and everything that Ricky had forbidden her to do. *Forbidden.* The very fact that a husband assumed he had the right to forbid a wife to do *anything* was a sign of the times. The fact that Lucy thrived on disobeying was another. She had an amazing drive for excitement, and she was bent on getting all she needed, in spite of the potential costs.

Lucy spent most of her time trying to carry off imaginative, often semicriminal plans without having Ricky find out what she was up to (all of which is detailed in Bart Andrews' *The "I Love Lucy" Book*). She disguised herself and sneaked onstage to perform in Ricky's nightclub act after he had insisted she not come near the club. She was put on an efficiency schedule and allowed "ten minutes for this and fifteen minutes for that" while Ricky told everyone that he had her jumping around like a trained seal. Lucy thwarted him, as always, by serving dinner to his boss and wife, each course rushed to the table and then "efficiently" whisked away before the diners even tasted it. No matter what Lucy tried to get away with, Ricky got wise, and got *mad.* His job was to clip his wife's flighty, thrill-seeking wings and attempt to keep her at home, and in line.

When Lucy didn't get her way with Ricky she begged, pleaded, and pouted. Her famous facial expression—the wide eyes, the lower lip thrust out—was a little-girl pose, played to Ricky's symbolic "parent." In fact, most of Lucy's adventures were reminiscent of those of a not-too-smart adolescent. Ricky's reactions were like those of a frustrated but grudgingly tolerant, and occasionally amused, father. When he got tough, Lucy tried to cajole him, and, failing that, to manipulate him—and if that failed, she simply disobeyed him.

While Lucy must be given credit for refusing to knuckle under, her rebellion did not take a constructive form, and none of her adventures led to a change in the basic power structure of her relationship with Ricky. In that respect her escapades brought high sensation, but low reward. She did not get, or demand, either respect or equality; rather, she subsisted on the excitement of playing with fire, living day-to-day in the realm between actions and consequences.

Just as melodrama is exaggerated drama, farce is exaggerated comedy, and "I Love Lucy" was certainly that. Through farce, Lucy exhibited the same yearning to be center stage that many women display when they create personal melodrama. For Lucy, this need was spotlighted in her attempts to force her way into Ricky's nightclub act and share center stage, for real. Ricky's resistance, rather than being considered a comment on his wife's questionable talent, might be seen as a broader reflection of male reluctance to welcome women "front and center" in the world.

The episodic quality of dramatic scenarios in women's real lives is reflected in the obvious episodic quality of Lucy's farcical life—dictated, in this case, by the realistic demands of the sitcom format itself. No matter how "bad" Lucy was, Ricky always forgave her. In fact, most of her previous escapades might never have occurred, because each episode of the show had to stand on its own merits. Viewers watching Lucy were easily lulled into suspending awareness that this was "just" fantasy. Many became willing recipients of another, covert message about drama-seeking for women: there are no real consequences or dangers in lying, manipulating, or making trouble to get your way—it's fun and exciting to be bad. But when they extended this axiom to their own lives, the result was painful family drama with lasting emotional consequences—*not* episodes of uproarious comedy.

The Message for Female Excitement-Seekers

Through role models like Donna Stone and Lucy Ricardo, women were influenced to fulfill their sensation-seeking needs by caring for a husband and children and becoming dramatically involved in every detail of their lives, or by misbehaving, acting out against the authority of the men they loved.

Since the stimulation of action or power in the world at large was explicitly out of bounds, finding excitement by sneaking behind hubby's back, being a bad girl, was one of the most thrilling outlets legitimately open to women. On such shows as "I Love Lucy," "The Honeymooners," and "Burns and Allen," women were at their comedic best when they were digging up excitement at their defiant, childlike worst.

Television throughout the 1950s and 1960s was a formidable influence on developing minds, as it still is today. Rules about what girls or boys, men or women could do were re-created from life and enacted on the television screen, with the power of the medium leaving us with indelible impressions of suitable male or female roles. Little boys had a multitude of choices—heroes like the Lone Ranger or Elliot Ness, renegade survivors like the Fugitive, brooding saviors like Dr. Ben Casey, or benevolent dictators like Jim Anderson. Excitement, involvement, and power could take unlimited forms in boys' imaginations, and later in their lives. For girls of that generation, however, television, like much of real life, offered no Christine Cagneys or Mary Beth Laceys, nor even any Alexis Carringtons. In comedy there were women like Donna and Lucy. In drama the women were mostly virtuous victims or ladies gone wrong, absorbed in the challenges of wooing, rescuing, or—in the hard-action shows—killing off difficult men. They were, in all cases, excitement-dependent upon their men. Women and girls watching at home received a deceptive, subliminal instruction about seeking excitement: *get it with a man, through a man, or by rebelling repeatedly against the man you depend on.* With few exceptions, the television shows we grew up with both reflected and designed a world in which a woman's opportunities for excitement were delimited, where her drive for sensation could best be vented through the bits of drama she cooked up at home.

Today's Dramatic Dilemma

One of the most serious consequences of our culture's long-standing antifemale bias is that women have learned to resort to personal drama as a primary means of satisfying a complex, natural human drive. We might imagine that by now our drama-seeking problems would be over, since we can work outside the home and, we are told—often by the same women's magazines that once relegated us to the kitchen—we can do and be almost anything we choose. Yet our drama-seeking patterns, along with many of the same old role injunctions, remain.

It is still some of the women's magazines, as well as today's movies, commercials, and TV shows, that offer a mixed bag of messages. On one hand they dangle the "power carrot" before budding "super-women," and on the other they depict us as playing out our tired, gender-appropriate roles—while they sensationalize (and manage to make enticing) the day-to-day melodramas born of those roles.

Whether we're liberated or not, career-oriented or not, the lessons we learned as girls and young women still live inside of us and unconsciously shape our perceptions of ourselves in relation to the world. No matter what we've gone on to do as businesswomen, sportswomen, or creative individuals, the force of our early conditioning—our emotional heredity—continues to affect our feelings about ourselves and to dictate much of our behavior and our choice of thrills. For a majority of us, life still remains tightly organized around our relationships and our inner emotional life, and we automatically seek our excitement through drama within these familiar borders.

Drama-seeking is most damaging when it is done without awareness of one's motivation. It is especially debilitating to women who are striving to achieve recognition and success in the world but who are unwittingly sabotaging themselves. Their tendency to become sidetracked or distracted by hazardous but intense relationships or to let important goals become overshadowed by repeated dramatic crises is part of a drama they have been programmed to find appealing. Further undermining their ambitions, many women also gravitate to dramatic episodes on the job.

No matter how impressive our positions or how much of our own money we have in the bank, the deep patterns that have been etched within us can live on. Only by learning to recognize and honestly evaluate these patterns, their usefulness or their detriment, can we let go of the ones whose costs are greater than their rewards.

As if biological demands and social forces weren't enough for us to contend with, a third, equally powerful faction has had enormous impact upon our sensation-seeking styles: our families. Their influence truly confounds the issues relative to sensation-seeking, because no matter what biology and society dictate about how much excitement each of us needs or how we ought to go about getting it, our families often have the last word.

3

The Family Melodrama

Not long ago I wandered into a little gift shop to buy a birthday card for my sister. While cruising the card racks, I noticed a cluster of casually dressed women checking out the novelty coffee mugs displayed on a nearby shelf. I could tell that one item had really caught their attention, because their voices suddenly tripled in volume.

"Isn't *that* the truth!" exclaimed one.

"Somebody sure knew what they were doing when they wrote *this* line," laughed another.

"One for me, one for my daughter!" the first woman announced. She held a matched set aloft, one in each hand, like trophies—two bright red cups with glossy white lettering that read MY LIFE IS A SOAP.

It's not surprising that these women related so strongly to the idea that their lives were like soap operas. The lives of many drama-seeking women resemble soaps. In fact, the essential components of the soap opera are identical to three features of dramatic sensation-seeking: *relationship orientation, emotional conflict,* and *episodic living.* Just as the situation comedies of the 1950s and 1960s both dictated and reflected cultural norms about the status of women and their relationships, the soap opera both imitates and creates a world in which emotional turbulence occupies a central place.

The types of sensation women crave as adults are usually rooted in the family melodramas of their childhoods. It was also in childhood that most drama-seeking women developed an affinity for the emotional ups and downs that characterize TV's serial melodramas. Though a soap is not a perfect reconstruction of anyone's actual family, in its dramatic exaggeration of family life the truth about our own experiences can be most plainly seen. Even women who aren't avid soap-watchers—or who never watch them at all—are usually still aware of, and in some sense affected by, this popular entertainment medium and cultural phenomenon.

Before we delve into how family dynamics influence the drama-seeking patterns of women's adult lives, it's important to consider the soap opera as a *structural paradigm* for understanding the nature of real-life family drama, in our childhoods and in our present.

Viewing and Living the Soap-Opera Life

I know very few women who haven't been smitten with soap-opera fever at some point. I once discovered that my most esteemed psychology professor could be found at midday—every day—in front of the tube, lost in "The Young and the Restless" and "As the World Turns." I realized that if such a studious woman could become hooked on soaps, they must offer something quite special.

Dutch social scientist Ien Ang explored what that elusive "something" might be in her book on nighttime-soap "addicts," *Watching "Dallas".* She points out that we watch "Dallas" (or any soap) because we enjoy seeing ourselves in the emotional life of the show. Ang says that viewers seem attracted to an "emotional realism" that has nothing to do with the specific events of the plot. Our lives may not resemble J. R.'s or Sue Ellen's in wealth, but the situations and complications that beset these characters reflect our own experiences—family arguments, intrigues, tragedies, and miseries—and we empathize with what the characters *feel.* In watching soaps, we seek pleasure and identification in a world where only emotional highs and lows count.

Taking this theme one step further, Ang states that the program arouses a *tragic structure of feeling:*

> . . . tragic because of the idea that happiness can never last forever but, quite the contrary, is precarious. In the tragic structure of feeling, *emotional ups and downs occupy a central place.* . . . [my emphasis]

From "Dallas" to "Dynasty" to "Days of Our Lives," the tragic structure of feeling in a soap is created through the use of three script constructions: a focus on relationships, the depiction of constant emotional conflict, and the serial, episodic nature of the soap format itself. Within the dramas of women's lives, the tragic structure of feeling is created through similar constructions.

Just as personal relationships are usually central to women's lives, they are at the heart of the soap. Conflicts with family and friends, divorces, deaths, marriages, and affairs bring the scripts to life. Although events in the world at large—politics, business, and so on—are also depicted, they are included only in order to affect the *relationships* among the characters. In this way, soaps display sensation-seeking at its interpersonal best, built to heights of improbable proportions. The improbable, extreme nature of the occurrences within a soap opera make it *melodrama.*

Melodrama demands *continual, exaggerated displays of intense emotion.* In most soap operas, as in real life, the tensions and conflicts that induce emotional outbursts occur between people connected by love or blood—people bound by family or quasi-family ties. As Ang put it, in a soap "the imaginary ideal of the family as safe haven in a heartless world is constantly shattered." The soap's ongoing emotionalism is wrested from the broken pieces of this fantasy. Those of us who were reared in settings we perceived as anything but harmonious and safe will instinctively respond to this struggle.

It isn't only the emphasis on discordant relationships and heightened emotional displays that accounts for a tragic structure of feeling in soaps (or in life). Fused with them, and emblematic of both, is an *episodic nature of living.*

Characters in a soap opera live from scene to scene, episode to episode, with no definitive ending and no prospect of lasting resolution in sight. As one crisis ends, another appears; as one problem is solved, new ones are created. Each dramatic moment exists as if it were the *only* moment, as if time stopped there. Yet the feelings, relationships, and circumstances are neither permanent nor secure. In "Dallas," Sue Ellen may despise J. R. one minute, then make love to him the next. Pam's a widow; Pam's not a widow. Although nothing is certain, each scene is played as if it might be, and viewers must stay on guard against expecting consistency in their characters' lives. In the kingdom of soaps, anarchy and disorder always reign.

All of this is fun to watch on TV, but it is torturous and unproductive to live it off-screen. Although we don't live with the constant trauma or dramatically condensed time frame of soap characters, we often structure our lives as unending private melodramas, squeezing maximum intensity from each emotional involvement. We may ascribe undue significance to actions and events that, objectively, are not distressingly important. We may create scenes that arouse us temporarily, take on relationship challenges of epic proportions, or tolerate irresponsible, inconsistent behavior in our partners. Of course, unlike characters in a soap, we can't healthfully tolerate emotional turbulence "season after season." As we move from one exhausting emotional episode to another we feel increasingly forlorn. What we lack in our lives is continuity, a sense of proportion and purpose.

To differing degrees, it was in our childhood homes that most of us became acquainted with the episodic, emotional ups and downs that produce the tragic structure of feeling. We find this quality again in our adult relationships. In the soap opera, with the pleasure and comfort afforded by distance, we recognize and relive it again.

Sensation-Seeking and the Family

Not only can our style of seeking excitement—Fighter, Challenger, or Rebel—be determined by the emotional dynamics that dominated our childhood years, but the quality and intensity of our search can also be influenced by early experiences.

Sensation-seeking may be a biologically determined tendency, but, as noted in the previous chapter, the early environment can exert a tremendous impact on nature. By viewing the sensation-seeking trait as a continuum of experience, with very high sensation-seeking at one end and very low at the other, we can see a great range of possibilities between the two poles. In my clinical experience, women reared in relatively stimulating environments—whether painful or pleasurable—appear "trained" to demand levels of stimulation in their adult lives that place them above the mid-range of the continuum. In a sense, they are conditioned to seek stimulation that comes close to the heightened level with which they grew up. We can surmise that if these women had come from calmer environments, they would now require less stimulation in order to achieve an optimal level of arousal.

A person's sensation-seeking drive is raised an "octave" when the family environment is sensation-rich. This does *not* mean that all children who grow up in such environments become extremely high-sensation seekers. They are, however, unlikely to become low-sensation seekers.

Of course, a need for high sensation does not automatically imply a need for high drama. Sensation can be found in healthy excitement, too. But if a woman is a drama-seeker, she will create as much or as little drama as she needs to balance her neurochemical system.

Families reflect the traditions, roles, and values of society at large, vis-à-vis women. In every individual case, the ways in which a woman seeks excitement or drama are sternly influenced by the quality of her early family relationships.

Recognition of the Family Drama

We learn our dramas at our parents' knees, at the family table, standing in front of closed bedroom doors, listening to "private" phone conversations, and huddled in the backseat of the family car. We learn our dramas from scoldings, lectures, and praise; from silences heavy with fear; from shouts of frustration; and from tokens of love. We learn our dramas from watching, listening, feeling, and refusing to feel. Our family home is our theater, and the relationships among those who live there produce the first comedies and tragedies we are ever to know—a template for all the dramas that follow.

As a therapist I have been privy to the family histories of hundreds of women. Although each story is different, the formative family dynamics and later behavior patterns common to these women often bridge distinctions in age, lifestyle, race, religion, sexual preference, intelligence, and occupation. One common thread among these women is the wish to have had a better family. And one way that wish is revealed is through denial of the pain inflicted by the families they *did* have.

Clients usually enter therapy eager to talk about their current difficulties but hesitant to share details about their childhoods. They bring into therapy a set of immediate, pressing problems, but are completely unaware of the wealth of hidden, deep, profoundly important issues lying behind those they introduce. In one way or another, these buried troubles hark back to childhood. Unless we acknowledge the past, respect it, and resolve its pains, as adults we are no more than little children rattling around in big bodies.

It's difficult for many of us to accept that our past has the power to determine our present and future, or to believe that our troubles today are brilliantly disguised repeat performances of past events. Accepting these truths is especially hard when unhappy memories have been blocked or diminished in importance and replaced with more comforting images. That's why, in the first session or two, clients often make such statements as these:

"I had a normal, happy childhood."

"My childhood was okay—no better or worse than most."

"Oh, it wasn't great—but it wasn't that bad. Anyway, that's not a problem I came here to talk about."

After a few weeks or months these clients often reveal that the "okay" childhood was actually experienced as miserable, that the "normal" family was headed by a critical and withholding parent who always put the children down, or that the "not that bad" childhood was actually traumatic because of sexual or physical abuse.

Even in the absence of abuse, the real miseries of childhood are the subjective miseries of experience, sometimes invisible to both the spectator and the participating parent.

A child, too young to discern emotional or intellectual subtleties, experiences events only *from her point of view,* no matter what happens within her household or what is done to her. For example, if she's scolded for knocking over a display in a supermarket, her mother may forget the incident within minutes, but the child may experience the event as a painful public humiliation or as a sign that her mother "hates" her. She will remember only her own reality: embarrassment and hurt, plus any interpretation of the incident that makes sense, from "Mommy hates me" to "I hate the supermarket and I'll never go there again" to "I can never do anything right." Eventually, her personal dramas will incorporate the "lesson" of that early experience.

By the same token, a parent who is overly affectionate, hugging and patting her child incessantly, may do so out of great love. From the child's emotional point of view, however, the touching may seem smothering and disgusting. In reaction, she might make a permanent, unconscious decision about *all* forms of touching. The decision may haunt her, becoming a factor in all of her adult dramas.

It doesn't matter whether the acts the child found painful were well intentioned or stupid and irresponsible. To better understand ourselves, what matters now is what mattered then: the world from our childhood points of view.

Women who grew up loving their parents in spite of misunderstandings, mistreatment, or even abuse fear that facing feelings about growing up in their households would be like issuing indictments against their parents. Some believe that being sad or angry about the way they were raised is equivalent to hating or rejecting their parents, and they are afraid that as a consequence of those "bad" feelings their parents will reject or abandon them. Instead of risking such outcomes, they safeguard their fantasies about their families. After a lifetime of protecting their family relationships with beliefs they can live with, it is frightening for them to contemplate ripping away the curtain of those beliefs to reveal a different tableau. Most people harbor fantasies for so long that the truth gets lost in the make-believe.

Denying the troubles in our families serves another purpose besides sparing us pain. When we confuse our *selves* with our dramas, when we believe that "my drama is *me*," we become reluctant to accept any information that might prove that belief false and thus threaten our basic perceptions of ourselves. Facing the truth about the impact of our families' on our developing personalities is likely to provide that proof, for the truth often reveals that we learned our dramas through our parents' teachings—that the drama is *not* "me."

After ending the melodrama in their lives, many women say that it was initially difficult to admit that their struggles, which looked and felt so genuine, were episodes in a cleverly constructed, carefully *learned* dramatic scenario. Said one client:

> I remember calling one of my friends to tell her about the latest episode in the continuing saga of "Why Is Life So Cruel to Me?" She actually accused me of being dramatic, of making a big production out of tiny problems I could have handled more efficiently. I was wounded. "You're trying to take my feelings away. You don't understand," I told her. Now I know that she was right . . . and I recall my mother making big productions, too. I didn't see it before.

When we identify ourselves with the drama we create, it is natural to resist suggestions that the depths or expressions of our feelings are extreme or inappropriate. Any questioning of the influences or motives behind our actions may seem like an attack on, or an invalidation of, our individuality, our "self." We can't help but take offense at the idea that we could be different. To be is to exist. When someone criticizes our way of being, we feel they are negating our very existence.

There will be places in this section where you may feel comfortable in discounting any connection between what you are reading and your own life. In reading about various family situations, you may be able to truthfully say, "Oh, well, *that's* not me" or "My family wasn't like *that,*" because the minor details are dissimilar to your own experiences. However, the minor details don't really count—and the major ones often don't count much, either. What does count is your willingness to see the larger picture, to recognize the *patterns* that have meaning for you. I encourage you to open your mind and heart to these pages and to pay attention to the dynamics that seem familiar and relevant. Recognizing the truth about the way your childhood was experienced is the first step toward gaining a deeper awareness of yourself.

Patterns of Family Drama

Each of us grew up in a private world in which special laws of nature, language, and justice applied only to the inhabitants. We call these private worlds "families." The following is a basic, but emotionally accurate, description of growing up in a family.

The Family Universe: A Story of Childhood

In the world of the family, the rulers are generally known as parents, and the subjects are called children. As children, it was our role to adapt to the customs and rules dictated by our parents. Some of us adapted by obeying, some by rebelling, and some by withdrawing. But we all had to adapt.

The emotional temperatures in our families varied. For some of us, it was always cold; for others it was sometimes so hot it burned. For a fortunate few it was enjoyably warm, for others it changed, day to day, from freezing to stifling. Whatever the emotional climate of our family, we adapted. No matter how intense or unpredictable the temperature, it became part of a familiar constellation of sensations we called home. We adjusted—sometimes uncomfortably, but we did adjust.

When we leave our families and move out into the world at large, we instinctively look for places to live that reproduce the emotional climate, laws, and customs of our family environment. In most cases, we try to re-create the sensation called home, the feeling of familiarity, no matter where we go or with whom. Although our new home might look different and we might believe we are far away from our families, we always find similarities in the sensations, in the feelings that arise. Our adult drama-seeking patterns, especially, reflect our need to again and again reexperience the *inner sensations* of home.

The story of childhood, in the simplest terms possible, depicts the cumulative effects of upbringing on the adult lives of most people. The key formative elements are *adaptation*—the way we react to and find a way of fitting into our family environment, based upon our unique perception of events—and the resulting, unconscious, *longing for the familiar.* As you read on, keeping those two concepts in mind will aid you in understanding the influence your family had on the ways you seek excitement in drama.

Being a child is not easy, even in the best of circumstances. You are small and powerless, controlled by and subject to the whims of the grown-ups around you. But if you are a child in a family that cannot provide a consistent, nurturing, and emotionally honest climate, your confusion and anxiety are tremendous.

As a child, you made sense of—that is, adapted to—the unpredictability of your environment and your lack of control over it in many different ways, and you used whatever means seemed natural at the time (active, such as throwing tantrums, or passive, such as getting sick). You did what you had to do in order to cope. Yet the way you adapted then probably fostered a reassuring pattern of thought and behavior; you did the same things over and over, in one form or another, because you did them well. It is those adaptation mechanisms that have become running themes in your adult dramas.

Although no two families are exactly alike, certain situations and patterns of relating are common to many households. People who were raised in families that shared similar characteristics and emotional climates may reflect those commonalities in similar patterns of thinking, feeling, and behaving. *The coping strategies developed as a child will become lifestyle and drama-seeking patterns for the adult.* Many women share the same basic pattern of drama-seeking because they were raised in comparable cultural and family environments and adapted to those environments in similar ways.

Certain especially common family scenarios seem to have the most profound effects upon the drama-seeking patterns of adult women. These scenarios include the physically, sexually, and emotionally abusive family; the alcoholic family; the maritally distressed family;

the ideal family; the insecure family; and the tragic family. All of these families instill in their children an episodic approach to living.

Some of the above family types appear quite "normal" to the outsider. Others are clearly abnormal and seriously emotionally disturbed—that is, dysfunctional. A child brought up in a dysfunctional family does not usually know there is anything atypical about her family. She accepts and adapts to the circumstances in which she finds herself. Problems arise much later, when the very survival skills that protected the vulnerable child and helped her adjust to the family climate become maladaptive and destructive to the grown woman.

The Abusive Family

It's important to begin with the most extreme family circumstances, even though many of you will be unable to identify personally with them. By developing a familiarity with the most dysfunctional family environment, you'll be able to see the less obvious but painfully experienced violations that occur within even the seemingly normal home.

While children are abused in myriad ways, three categories tend to encompass all such damaging behaviors: physical, sexual, and emotional abuse. All abuses leave deep scars on the victim, leading to patterns of thinking and feeling that are typical of many adults who were abused as children. In terms of the effects on sensation-seeking, however, subtle differences can exist, depending on the type of abuse to which a child was subjected and the way she adapted to it.

In most cases of abuse, more than one type was inflicted. For example, neither physical nor sexual abuse occurs in the absence of emotional abuse. Emotional abuse, however, can exist unaccompanied by either physical or sexual cruelty.

It is impossible to do justice to a topic as complex as that of child abuse in less than a full volume. In the back of this book you will find a reading list that cites other references on the subject.

The Physically Abusive Family

Physical abuse is any bodily contact that leaves marks or injuries upon the body. It can include "cruel and unusual punishment"—for example, locking a child in a closet or making her stand with arms outstretched for hours.

Most physically abused children are unaware that they are being subjected to abnormal treatment. Furthermore, they are likely to minimize or rationalize the severity of the punishments. Saying something like "It wasn't that bad" or "I deserved it" is a common way of *adapting* to an out-of-control situation and making sense of an irrational world.

In addition to punishment, some abused children must contend with the remorse and effusive apologies of the abuser. The child feels sorry for the parent who seems to be in pain because he or she was "forced" to hurt the child. In this way children learn that love comes mingled with pain, and that in order to receive love they must suffer. Elaine described an all-too-usual scenario:

> After she punished me my mother would come into my room, take me in her arms, and tell me she loved me and that she was sorry she'd hurt me, but that I had upset her too much. She'd cry, and she'd hug me so tight I could hardly breathe. The next day she'd hurt me again, and apologize again. I thought the same thing happened in everybody's family.

Elaine's confusion was normal, for child abusers are not easy-to-hate "monsters." They are disturbed people unable to control their impulses or handle the pressures of child rearing, and they are people who generally were abused as children themselves. The very humanity of the abusive parent is the "hook" that often keeps a child deeply attached to the person who hurts her most. She is emotionally seduced by the parent's sporadic attention or affection, and she must then adapt to the contradictions inherent in the abuse. One moment Mommy or Daddy is kind, and the next, vicious. In these cases the child usually adapts to the confusion by blaming herself. She must be very bad, very wrong, if she can drive her "loving" parent to such violence. This sense of badness becomes a deep belief about herself that is later manifested in her adult dramas: if "I am innately bad," then I will seek excitement that reflects and reinforces my badness.

In most families, physically abusive punishments are unpredictably and inconsistently meted out. Consequently, accidentally slamming a door might lead to a severe beating on one occasion, while skipping school might be practically ignored. One woman told me about the time her father stood lecturing her about one misdeed or another, then suddenly slapped her across the face for "unfocusing her eyes"—a punishment that could never have been predicted. The physically abused child lives in a constant state of neurochemical arousal, subjectively experienced as fear and anxiety, never knowing what will bring a parent's wrath down upon her next.

The adult who was physically abused as a child learns to seek high sensation in intense and unpredictable situations that mirror the emotional climate of her or his childhood. Males often turn to crime or become child abusers themselves. Some studies indicate that nearly 100 percent of incarcerated male criminals were physically and/or sexually abused as children. Some women take this route, too, but more often they unconsciously seek difficult, even abusive relationships that have a potential for cliff-hanging drama. Their systems are attuned to scenarios tense with the suspense of what will happen next. They seek strong sensations in relationships that seem *familiar* and that are therefore less anxiety provoking than the unfamiliar.

If a child adapted to abuse by trying harder to win her parent's love, in adulthood she will generate a drama that is excitement-dependent upon striving to get what she cannot have—possibly a Challenger drama. If she actively fought with her parents and struggled against the abuse, her dramas may be conflict-oriented. If she repeatedly ran away or attempted to rebel against her environment by being as "bad" as she believed she was, her adult dramas probably will involve playing with fire. If she attempted to protect or rescue other abused siblings or a battered parent, as an adult she may seek victims to help or rescue, generating a series of crisis-dramas—but if she is repeatedly unsuccessful (as most rescuers are), she will ultimately become resentful of those she has sought to help.

As a result of any form of childhood abuse, a woman may turn to drama-seeking behaviors that reflect her early experience of, and adaptation to, the trauma of her youth.

The Sexually Abusive Family

According to various studies, an estimated 25 to 38 percent of all women in America were sexually victimized as children. While boys are also victims of sexual abuse, the numbers are comparatively smaller (though no less appalling), with abuse of male children estimated to be 30 percent of all sexual-abuse cases.

Most sexual abuse happens to girls between nine and twelve years old. It is almost always perpetrated by a man known to the child. Usually the abuser is a relative, and according to some statistics, approximately 75 percent of the time it is the father or stepfather. All sexual-abuse statistics are estimates, since abuse is often unreported.

In addition to overtly sexual acts, sexual abuse includes inappropriately touching a child, talking sexually to a child, showing pornographic pictures to a child, demonstrating sexual acts before a child, and even excessively and vigorously washing a child's genitals.

It is common for a sexually abused girl to blame herself for what is happening. She may be told by the perpetrator that she is at fault, or she may feel she is actually responsible for the abuse because she is afraid to resist the adult. She may also be torn between her attachment to the abuser and her sense that the sexual acts are wrong. And, like the physically abused child, she is likely to live in an agony of uncertainty, never knowing when the perpetrator will abuse her next. This sense of uncertainty is a precursor to the cliff-hanging drama of her later life.

When the abuse occurs at home and is perpetrated by a father or stepfather, much of the girl's pain will stem from her feelings toward her mother, from whom she must keep the secret of her abuse. Again, she is in conflict—this time between her desire to reveal the abuse and her fear of the consequences of doing so. She may also be split between her wish to be rescued and protected from the abuser and her desire to protect her mother from knowledge of the abuse. She may be concerned with protecting the abuser from going to jail or from being told to leave the house.

Magnifying her trauma, her intuition sometimes tells her that her mother *knows* of the abuse yet is doing nothing to stop it. This is a puzzling and painful awareness. The child feels angry and betrayed, yet guilty for having such feelings. It seems that there is nowhere to turn, no one to trust, nothing to do but tolerate further abuse.

Under these circumstances, the abused child learns to cope at a very primitive emotional level. Her initial reactions to the abuse—fear, confusion, hurt, anger—are often turned into guilt and hate: guilt about her participation in the abuse and about her anger, and hate of herself for "allowing" or "deserving" it, and, eventually, rejection of her own body. In adult life such rejection may be evidenced by obesity, illness, an inability to experience sexual pleasure, or a willingness to allow anyone to use her body, either for pleasure or for inflicting pain.

Sensation-seeking, most often at very high levels of intensity, later becomes a mode of acting out the guilt and self-hatred the woman-child continues to carry. Because the abuse occurred in the context of a relationship, and because women are conditioned to be relationship-oriented, relationships often become the stage upon which the abuse drama is reenacted. Since the sexually abused child learns not to trust others and learns, too, that her needs for love, kindness, and safety will not be met, as an adult she may seek highly chaotic relationships in which the drama substitutes for the intimacy and caring she does not know how to find or offer.

Like the victims of physical abuse, the sexual-abuse victim incorporates into her drama the adaptive responses she used to cope with impossible circumstances. If, for example, as a child she came to believe that putting up with the abuse "kept Daddy home" and therefore kept the family together, she may later seek relationships in which her personal dramas surround her unsuccessful attempts to save troubled and abusive people. If, on the other hand, she coped by going into a sort of "trance," blocking out the physical and emotional feelings generated by the abuse, she will later seek sensations designed to block off her emotions and numb her body. Compulsive and addictive behaviors—for example, abuse of drugs, alcohol, shopping, or sex—may be her way of creating internal excitement while limiting her capacity to feel pain. Such behaviors are among those in a category I refer to as auto-arousal.

Auto-arousal is a form of stimulation that can either positively or negatively augment the relationships we have with ourselves. Certain forms of fantasy or self-hypnosis might be considered positive means of creating auto-arousal. On the negative side, auto-arousal is a self-induced, internally generated form of sensation-seeking that excites us and, at the same time, selects and limits the types of feelings we are able to experience. For example, a sexually abused child may later turn to the addictive use of cocaine or alcohol, which numbs her immediate suffering, quells her pain and sadness, and reinforces the sense of "badness" that has become a part of her identity. At the same time, it helps her to produce an experience of auto-arousal: it "turns her on" or gets her "high"—that is, it stimulates her on an internal level, irrespective of anyone else's participation. She may not be able to trust others, but she thinks she can trust her drugs. Auto-arousal produces intense, episodic, inner drama, while the extreme behaviors that induce auto-arousal generally provoke further interpersonal drama. Amidst all this commotion, the victim of abuse is distracted from the memories and suffering imposed by her trauma.

The Emotionally Abusive Family

For our purposes, emotional abuse consists of many different behaviors, ranging from emotional neglect—which can be as damaging as active abuse—to emotional overconcentration.

Neglectful abuse may occur when parents refuse to touch or hug their child. They may ignore her or neglect to talk to or speak affectionately to her. They may unfairly restrict her activities, or they may be emotionally unavailable—often an invisible abuse in families that seem perfectly normal, even "ideal." Emotionally overconcentrated parents may perpetrate abuse if they constantly criticize, belittle, humiliate, or threaten their child. They may call her names or deliberately embarrass her in front of others. They may demand to know everything about what she does and who she's with, and they may be unsparingly harsh in their judgment.

Families that perpetrate any form of abuse are dysfunctional. According to family therapist, theologian, and world-renowned addiction expert John Bradshaw, 96 percent of all American families are dysfunctional *to some extent.* His conception of dysfunction is based upon the recognition that children in those families are *emotionally abandoned* by parents who neglect their basic dependency needs. Dependency needs involve far more than the needs for food and shelter. They also include the needs for love, kindness, safety, physical and emotional care, *consistent parenting,* and *emotional honesty.* Yet, it is unlikely that 96 percent of the population would consider their families dysfunctional. Emotional abandonment of children is so much the norm in our culture that we disregard it.

In many dysfunctional, emotionally abusive families, the climate is hot, intense, chaotic, and unpredictable. Rules about which behaviors and feelings are acceptable change daily, and sometimes minute to minute. Changes can occur even on the simplest level of interchange. For example, on Sunday evening Susie's mother may be warmly receptive to hearing about the party Susie went to on Friday—but on Monday morning, when Susie tries to tell her mother that she has an earache, her mother tells her to shut up and go to school. The next time Susie tries to engage her mother's attention she brings up the party again, thinking she's on safe ground. "Who wants to hear more about your stupid party?" her mother replies. Susie is deeply hurt, ashamed, and confused. Next time, she thinks, she'll have to try a different tactic.

A child raised in such a family grows up reacting to and being conditioned by sudden detonations of emotion and onslaughts of pain. She learns to live on guard, in a state of suspense. I believe that the majority of these children, reared in such intensely stimulating, sensation-rich environments, are prone to demand equivalent levels of stimulation in their adult lives. Because the sensations of rejection, shame, fear, and sadness are so familiar to them, their adult dramas often incorporate the same agonizing sensations.

Two specific types of emotionally abusive families are most likely
to contribute to a child's potential for being an adult drama-seeker,
and they also influence the type of drama to which she may become
attracted. These are the alcoholic family and the maritally distressed
family. Both characteristics can be present within a single family, in
which case the turmoil increases and the drama heightens.

The Alcoholic Family

The issue of alcoholism and the family has garnered a great deal of
attention in the past five years, as awareness of the huge numbers of
afflicted families has come to light. Among the literature on the
subject is Robin Norwood's book *Women Who Love Too Much,* an
account of the way in which women from alcoholic and other dysfunctional families develop predictable patterns of relating to partners
who are emotionally unavailable.

According to Norwood, girls reared in alcoholic families often
adopt the role of helper, or care-giver, in relation to the alcoholic
parent—a role they cling to throughout adulthood. Growing up in a
home where one or both parents is alcoholic means growing up in
an unmanageable, unpredictable world. For the drinker, all family
needs are subverted to the need for alcohol; for the nonalcoholic
spouse, all other needs are subverted to the desire to control the
behavior of the drinker. The needs of the children are lost in the
chaos, and the family lives in a state of perpetual crisis.

Many female children in such families can achieve a sense of importance or competence only by becoming a "little woman" and helping
out in these crises (or trying to control them). As a result, a daughter
from an alcoholic household may grow up to seek drama, stimulation, and self-esteem in crisis, and to seek crises in order to feel a
familiar sense of aliveness. It is also through crisis that she is able to
distance herself from the unrealized pain of her childhood. As Norwood puts it, "Without uproar, stress, or a desperate situation to
manage, the buried childhood feelings of being emotionally overwhelmed would surface and become too threatening."

In adulthood, daughters of alcoholics often become dependent on
the auto-arousal potential of their relationships. Auto-arousal can be
achieved in many different ways. On an emotional level, it can be
achieved by drumming up dramatic, exaggerated feelings. The "the-
atrics" that often characterize the relationships of these women are
usually products of the misdirected need for heightened sensation.

This is not to say that daughters of alcoholics seek drama only in conflict/crisis-ridden relationships. If a child adapted to the family climate in a manner not representative of the helper or rescuer, her adult dramas will reflect the way she actually *did* adapt. Perhaps her gut-level response to the turmoil and lack of emotional care in her family was anger. She might become a teenage rebel (and later, an adult Rebel), seeking stimulation and drama in taking careless risks, acting out her anger toward her parents by doing what she knew they would find unacceptable. In this way she could punish them for being bad parents while satisfying her need for stimulation in ways that provided salve for her deep-seated emotional pain.

The Maritally Distressed Family

Not all families in which marital problems exist are dysfunctional, nor do all parents with marital troubles become emotionally abusive. But when marital discord is continuous and extreme enough to prevent the spouses from providing their children with adequate, consistent parenting, a troubled marriage blossoms into a fully dysfunctional, emotionally abusive family.

In many instances, marital discord, alcoholism, and child abuse occur in the same family. In such families there is no relief for the children from the traumas that beset them. Even in the absence of other abuses, however, children suffer in families where the parents are so consumed with their marital problems that the children's needs are abandoned.

Providing little security, maritally distressed families are especially frightening places for children. Mom or Dad is always threatening to leave, if not actually leaving and returning. "I'm taking you with me—we're going to live with Grandma in Florida!" Mother might say—only to change her mind the next day. By this time the child is in a state of panic, imagining having to say good-bye—maybe forever—to Dad, friends, and maybe siblings. Then, the crisis is over. For the parents, perhaps, the calm is a relished period of normalcy, but for the children it is merely a break in the horrible, constant action. They know the fighting will begin again, and they wonder if next time the explosion will be unbearable.

Children brought up amidst this unrelenting chaos become conditioned to the stimulation of their parents' drama, and they become strangers to the notion of love that is unaccompanied by turmoil, fear, and, in some cases, physical violence. Like all children of abuse, the way they react to their environment dictates the type of sensation they later seek.

Boys frequently react by withdrawing from the home and becoming involved in outside activities—sometimes healthy, sometimes not. Girls tend to become far more emotionally involved in the excitement of their parents' dramas. They may try to comfort the parent they believe has been most severely wronged or intervene in an argument to make their parents stop fighting. Clients have told me of banging on locked bedroom doors, screaming "STOP IT!" over the raised voices of their parents, to no avail, or of being drawn into the parents' relationship, forced to listen to each describe "how awful" the other can be. In these situations, drafted as helpers and quasi-therapists, they begin to feel responsible for the parents and for their relationship. Since the children, in fact, have no control over the adults, they are left feeling ineffective and powerless. As adults, they often direct their drama toward overcoming the sense of powerlessness by taking on relationship challenges that are almost impossible to meet. Thus, their powerlessness is reaffirmed.

Because the household is such a noisy, emotional minefield in many maritally distressed families, daughters may attempt to tune out the din by becoming lost in fantasy. Novels, movies, and television become passive means of redirecting their attention. While there is nothing overtly unhealthy about this, these materials can reinforce the explosive, melodramatic nature of the home life. A tragic structure of feeling is experienced, first in life and then in fantasy. The two worlds become entangled and interconnected. Growing up with melodrama in both their outer and inner worlds, the girls expect and seek similar drama as adults.

In all abusive family climates, the tragic structure of feeling is palpable and ever-present. However, this sense of emotional unstability and unpredictability can also exist in homes that, at least on the surface, appear to be "normal." That even the average, or "ideal," family can qualify as dysfunctional on the basis of the parents' emotional unavailability is a frequent unacknowledged reality. The following circumstances usually engender a tragic structure of feeling in the emotional life of an ordinary family.

The "Ideal" Family

The ideal family climate can be clearly seen through the eyes of Margaret, who entered therapy because she was depressed—"enveloped by a big grey cloud." No specific misfortune in her life accounted for those feelings.

When I asked Margaret about her childhood in the first session, she picked at her already chipped nail polish and then gazed at me through a tangle of streaked blond bangs. "I had a perfectly normal childhood. We were just your average, all-American family," she said expressionlessly. Then she changed the subject.

After a few weeks Margaret admitted that "ideal" and "normal" were superficial descriptions of her family. Beneath the placid surface lay many strong feelings that were denied or unexpressed. "I wish I had a movie of my family at dinner. It was unbelievable," she told me. She painted a sparkling picture of a family who, in appearance, could have rivaled TV's Nelson family as family of the year. At six every evening, Mother, Father, Margaret, and Brother gathered around the table for dinner. Mother and Margaret served, while Father inquired politely of Mother, "And how was your day?" and of Margaret, "And how was school?" Mother: "Lovely, dear. Broccoli was on sale today." Margaret: "I got an A on a math test today." Father: "Good, good."

"We never *talked* about anything important," Margaret told me.

> Every time I tried to tell them how I *really* felt about school, friends—anything—they had the same response: "Don't get excited, dear, nothing is important enough to get upset about—why don't you go wash your hands for dinner?"
>
> If I had a problem, forget it. No one wanted to hear about problems. And even if I was mad at someone, I had to hold it back. No one ever got mad. I felt so dammed up with feelings, but I knew I couldn't talk about them. "We don't yell or raise our voices, dear," my mother would say.

In such households, children are exposed to two worlds. There is the dishonest surface world, where rules demand that you refrain not only from expressing strong feelings but also from experiencing them. Then there is the inner world of sensation, of feelings. Despite the rules, children experience unacceptable feelings. Even more confusing, they intuit that their parents have inexpressible feelings, too. Sadness, anger, sexuality, grief—all the intense "imperfect" feelings are negated.

When a parent becomes withdrawn because she is angry but refuses to admit that she is mad, the child who clearly perceives that something very real is wrong is forced to doubt her perceptions. Eventually she sees that *her* feelings, *her* perceptions mean nothing. They are not validated by her parents—the people with the greatest power to shape her developing sense of self—so they must be useless.

That means *she* is useless, stupid, wrong. Since she cannot trust herself to perceive the nature of the world around her correctly, it becomes natural for her to look to others to make decisions for her.

In some "ideal" homes, although feelings *are* expressed, those the family members acknowledge and those they experience are not the same. The family emotional life is built on a foundation of lies—fear is expressed as anger, love as indifference, concern as criticism, and so on. Mothers, for example, often fear the consequences of their adolescent daughters' emerging sexuality. Instead of expressing their concerns, parents in emotionally dishonest families restrict opportunities for dating and become furious if a daughter is fifteen minutes late coming home. The daughter realizes, on some deep level, that more than the issue of time is involved, but she doesn't know what it is or how to deal with it. A mother's lack of honesty about her fears, and her consequent rigidity, may actually set the stage for the daughter to seek drama through sexual rebellion.

In any home where massive contradictions exist between what is spoken and what is unsaid, the child senses the subtle descrepancies but rarely trusts the accuracy of her perceptions—nor would she know how to voice them if she did. Children growing up in such environments have trouble reconciling the inner world of perception with the outer world of avoidance and denial. Consequently, their inner emotional worlds become confused and chaotic. The tragic structure of feeling for children from "ideal" families is created by this inner turmoil.

It is the constant influx of discrepant messages that makes this kind of household what is often called a "crazy-making" situation for children, who are torn between what they feel is true and what they are told is true. Depending on the severity of the family circumstances and a child's innate temperament, this conflict may be intense (so that the children grow to adulthood having higher sensation demands) or moderate (leading to relatively lower sensation demands). As a result of the conflict, nearly all of these children will learn to mistrust and deny their own feelings, intuitions, and observations. As adults, they are apt to look outside themselves toward anything or anyone who will define what is real.

Male and female children adapt in similar ways. However, because it is culturally acceptable for men to avoid their feelings, when boys reach adulthood there are many male-oriented institutions willing to welcome those looking for an essentially emotionless structure—for example, the military, corporate, and academic worlds. Men who enter these systems may never have to deal with the emotional vacu-

ousness of their lives because their deficit represents a socially per-
missible, common masculine trait.

On the other hand, a woman is more inclined to re-create her past
by becoming attracted to relationships in which her role is well defined; she chooses male partners who dominate her and who maintain narrow standards of behavior to which she must continuously
aspire. Men become reality barometers. *His* assessment of her, of life,
of the world, and of what is good and bad becomes gospel. Predictably, the drama in her life often revolves around the crises that beset
her difficult, repressive relationships.

At the opposite extreme, some women react to an emotionally
unavailable or dishonest "ideal" family background by rebelling
against structure of any kind, and their adult dramas incorporate the
Rebel's style of playing with fire. Whether women become compliant
or rebellious, in shutting off their feelings in order to adapt and make
sense of their complex worlds, they may also suffer from serious
depressions—for depression is frequently the sense of vacancy,
meaninglessness, and despair imposed by longstanding rejection of
one's real feelings and true self. Depression often leads to dangerous
forms of drama and sensation-seeking (including auto-arousal
through self-medication with street drugs) in an attempt to temporarily quell the sensations of depression.

The Insecure Family

The tragic structure of feeling—the sense that happiness can never
last, that emotional ups and downs are the only "constant" in one's
episodic life—is also cultivated in many emotionally available and
nonabusive families. Here, it is based upon the presence of inconsis-
tencies and unpredictabilities that may seem reasonable to adults but
that cause severe stress and insecurity in children. In families that are
beset by frequently shifting financial conditions or that are repeatedly uprooted, it is especially likely that events adults consider to be
temporary hindrances will be perceived by children as wrenchingly
painful.

The Financially Insecure Family

When parents are sporadically employed or have fluctuating income
levels, children's lives become subject to the emotional ups and
downs that even the most well-adjusted couple can experience under
such circumstances.

I am speaking of people whose financial lives undergo *drastic* and *repeated* reconfigurations—for instance, actors, writers, artists, and others whose incomes and work lives are unpredictable; workers who are subject to sporadic layoffs and strikes; and entrepreneurs who continuously start up new ventures, none of which provide stable income over the long term. The children may attend private school one month, and public school the next; they may move from apartment to house to apartment and from one neighborhood to another. And they may switch friendships as often as their parents switch credit cards.

Children realize they are powerless to control these ups and downs and comings and goings, and they are afraid to relax or to settle into a new situation because they know it could change again. They must adapt to living in a state of chronic, low-grade emotional suspense as they warily observe the family drama unfold.

As a result of these experiences, in adulthood these children may seek rigid financial security, living in fear of losing a job or of taking a financial risk. They continue to live with the anxiety and suspense that was characteristic of their childhoods. Their dramas are often composed of panic and crisis reactions to every potential change in their financial status. For example, a small item on the news about a possible "someday" recession can fuel dramatic agitation that lasts for days.

Others believe that financial security is an impossible dream, so there is no point in striving for it. Such women seem to have developed a sixth sense that draws them to men who have "potential," but who nevertheless remain "losers." The dramas in these women's lives incorporate the same elements as those in their parents'—money crises, often leading to relationship crises.

The Geographically Insecure Family

Children who are periodically uprooted from their homes and then planted in others are subjected to stresses similar to those experienced by children in financially insecure homes. Parents in the military, the diplomatic corps, entertainment, and international business are among those whose travels can painfully disrupt the lives of their children again and again.

We must remember that as children it is our perception of events and our mode of adaptation to them—not always the events themselves or the intentions of our parents—that cause us difficulties later. Some children adapt beautifully to traveling and thrive on opportunities for novelty and adventure. They may even learn healthy patterns of sensation-seeking from these early encounters. But being uprooted can also prevent some children from forming lasting relationships with friends and teachers. It may decrease their motivation to take relationships seriously or approach them fairly. Knowing they will have to leave eventually, some children may not be willing to invest themselves in caring too much for anyone or in developing skills for relating to others.

Some of these children, especially those whose parents express their own reluctance to move again, experience so much emotional hardship that a fear of change is instilled. Others become so stimulation-dependent upon change that as adults it is impossible for them to slow down long enough to achieve goals or actualize ambitions. When girls also absorb traditional messages about appropriate female behavior, they may become reluctant to pursue real adventure. As exciting substitutes for the ever-changing relationships and environments they learned to thrive on as children, they build drama into relationships with friends, families, and eventually lovers.

In some families, the potential effects of this mobile lifestyle are complicated by other relationship dynamics. For example, if a child harbors competitive feelings toward a highly successful parent or perceives herself as being abandoned to the interests of the parent's career, the problems are magnified. If the successful parent is the mother, the child's dramas in adulthood are likely to incorporate both her mode of adaptation to being uprooted and an enormous, almost desperate drive to be special.

The Tragic Family

The emotional turmoil in the financially or geographically insecure family is but a fraction of the turbulence found in the genuinely tragic family. No matter how essentially "normal" a family environment may be, when its members are forced to cope with tragic events, stresses of abnormal dimension are imposed upon everyone.

Tragic families are those besieged by multiple disasters—death or serious illness, destruction of the home by fire or natural disasters, rape or other violence—in relatively swift succession. In this unfortunate group is Katy, who spent months in the hospital with rheumatic fever, lost her father and, a few years later, her mother, and was adopted into the unwelcoming home of a near relative—all before she was ten years old. Katy learned very early that nothing good in life lasts—and that if she expected the worst she wouldn't be surprised or disappointed later on.

Some people attempt to control the onset of disaster by creating their own calamities. Women who as children were conditioned by crisis or punishment often become involved in relationships that are virtual setups for tragedy. Katy generated her own brand of stimulating, catastrophic drama by twice marrying alcoholics. Through her work in therapy she discovered that she had been trying to control their behavior in the unconscious hope that doing so would give her control over life's unpredictable miseries. The pain she knew, and could count on, seemed to her far less debilitating than the unfamiliar agonies life might inflict. Her sensation-seeking patterns reflected her style of emotional adaptation to the events of her childhood.

When Feeling Good Has Its Price

In some families, events that adults would never consider disastrous *seem* disastrous, even punishing, from the children's point of view. For example, the child from the geographically insecure family who had finally made friends in one town could experience the next move as a punishment directed at *her*. When a child feels that punishment—whether real or interpreted—repeatedly follows happiness or excitement, she may develop the belief that pain inevitably follows pleasure.

Coming home from having fun in the schoolyard only to hear Mommy and Daddy yelling at each other may seem like punishment. Coming home excitedly with a B+ on a math test only to have Mommy, drunk and mean, tear up the paper because it wasn't an A would certainly feel like punishment. When good things are continually followed by bad, when excitement appears to bring on pain, children grow to expect that feeling good will always have its price. Through repeated experiences like these they learn to create their own problems, disasters, and punishments. The pain they can prepare for or control may seem most bearable.

Children can learn through an endless variety of means that bad things follow good things. This is why, as grown-ups, so many people become anxious after they've enjoyed a short roll of good fortune. "Too good to last," they say. They *know* something awful will happen, because it did when they were kids, didn't it? So they create conflicts and crises that are *theirs*. Though they may be unaware of the degree to which they manipulate events, they do it to gain control over their lives.

The Episodic Lifestyle

We've seen how parent-child relationships, marital relationships, and inconsistency and unpredictability within the home can generate a tragic structure of feeling. The way a child reacts and adapts usually determines her adult lifestyle and drama-seeking patterns.

For many women, adult drama-seeking may fulfill two distinct, seemingly paradoxical, human needs: the need for intense sensation, and the need for familiar experience. The style of drama-seeking we are drawn to allows us to satisfy our biological craving for exciting sensation *and* reexperience the familiar sensations of "home."

A paradox exists because sensation-seeking, by definition, is the drive toward intense and *novel* experience. Since drama so success-fully conjures up familiar emotional experiences, we might wonder how it can reflect full-fledged sensation-seeking.

In fact, drama-seeking is an adulterated, incomplete, misdirected, and poorly implemented substitute for pure, healthy sensation-seek-ing. Drama's payoffs—especially the qualities of excitement and sus-pense—arise from its sensation-seeking component, but the costs are directly linked to its subtle avoidance of true novelty and to its utiliza-tion of emotionally familiar, self-defeating scenarios. In all of these scenarios, and in all of our dramas, one of the most devastating ingredients is the episodic quality.

Children raised in family climates that evoke a tragic structure of feeling are conditioned to the episodic life. Children of abusive, maritally distressed, alcoholic, insecure, tragic, and even "ideal" families survive, in part, by learning to function episodically. We initially seized this approach only because in our early experience *there was no other.* But as adults we can make lifestyle choices, and we can learn to trust ourselves enough to let the old ways go.

The following story illustrates how an affinity for episodic drama developed in the life of one client, Angela. If you, too, grew up amidst emotional unpredictability and inconsistency, you will probably be able to relate to Angela's experience. Though the details of her childhood are likely to be quite different from yours, the basic emo-tional dynamics may have been found in your household as well.

The Birth of the Episodic Lifestyle: Angela's Story

Angela was the first-born daughter of a tempestuous union between a dockworker's saxophone-playing son and a wealthy importer's daughter. Angela's father used to tell her how much she looked like her mother, who had deep auburn hair and huge violet eyes. "Your mother's eyes talked of passion," he often said. But in her passion, Angela's mother never let anyone forget she had married "beneath her station." And Angela's father never let his wife forget that she would always play second to his first love, music.

Angela told me that for as long as she could remember her parents had fought, usually hurling records, dishes, and vicious words in a rising crescendo of sensation. She recalled with mingled fear and excitement the night her mother was out of ready ammunition, but, spying her husband's saxophone beside the sofa, grabbed it and tossed it out the second-story window. Seven-year-old Angela watched, terrified, as her father stood trembling with rage. She was sure he was about to hit her mother. Instead, he walked out the door and didn't return for two days.

While her father was away, Angela's mother was inconsolable. She would pull little Angela to her one minute, tearfully whispering that everything would be fine, then seconds later turn on the girl, finding irrational fault with whatever leaped into her sight. When her husband returned, peace was restored briefly, but within a few days their marital *pas de deux* resumed.

For Angela, growing up was a continuous adjustment between loving sequences and noisy, painful ones. Even the simple act of returning home from school was filled with unpredictability. Sometimes her father was sound asleep after having worked all night at a jazz club, and Angela had to tiptoe for hours in order not to wake him. If she forgot, he might rise, yelling like a wounded giant, to reprimand her. On other days, she arrived home to find him waiting for her like an excited, childlike pal who couldn't restrain his exuberance over a new record or game he wanted to share—immediately.

Angela's home was a huge, hyperventilating monster of human emotion. Both parents were capable of expressing great tenderness toward each other and toward their child, yet they were equally prone to making wanton, unreasonable demands and accusations. Angela could trust only that nothing in her world would remain the same for long. She had to be prepared to handle anything in an environment dense with strong sensations, ranging from the emotionally agonizing to the delightful. She had to learn to cope from moment to moment, without continuity, as if each day were a fresh dramatic episode and each event just another twist of the plot. Episodic living became the crux of her reality. In later years, though she imagined she was living differently, she would incite this familiar kind of high-sensation drama herself.

As a teenager, Angela began to dabble in minor trouble, sneaking out of the house to see boys she wasn't allowed to date because they were too "wild," smoking pot at parties, cutting classes at school. Yet she was basically a "good girl" who never strayed too far.

At nineteen she enrolled in college, but she quit after three years to take a job in an art gallery. A few years later she married an advertising executive whom she had met at an art show. She left her job, thinking, "Now, here's a man who can provide the stability my father couldn't offer. I'm not going to have a marriage like my mother did." And for a while it seemed that her life was, indeed, "together." Less than a year into the marriage, however, the relationship began to deteriorate. Angela found it surprising that her husband, whom she had thought was so unlike her own father, now seemed to place the relationship second to his career—much as her father had done. Like her mother, Angela tried to put life back into her relationship by provoking arguments—but her husband refused to fight back.

In the midst of these problems, Angela decided to go back to work at the gallery. The moment she returned, she realized how bored and hungry for stimulation she had become staying home, and she plunged voraciously into the art world by enjoying a brief fling with a photography instructor, then a lengthier affair with a married sculptor. Her relationship with her husband began to seem very remote, yet she continued trying to spark his interest by inciting his anger.

Angela had begun to live life as a series of disconnected episodes. The hours she spent with her lovers were like capsules of time that were severed from her "other life." She couldn't see the meaning of her actions in relation to one another or to her life as a whole, because she had been conditioned during childhood to deal with only one emotional episode at a time. She was honestly unaware of the significance of hopping feverishly into bed with one man, then going home and trying to fight with her husband. Each episode was separate and all-important at the moment. Predictably, she gave little thought to birth control.

Shortly before she entered therapy, Angela was horrified to discover she was pregnant. "I've made a real mess of my life," she said to me during our first session. "I don't want to have a baby—and I don't want to have an abortion, but what else can I do? How could this have happened?"

"I haven't had sex with my husband in months, so I haven't had to use anything," she admitted. "Maybe I imagined that what went on in one corner of my life had no bearing on the rest of it, so that carrying over a pregnancy was . . . impossible."

Angela's statement personalized the common dilemma faced by women who grew up in an environment of unpredictability and emotional turbulence. No matter what type of family we grew up in, we learned that each emotion-packed episode exists, and must be coped with, unto intself. What we may not realize is that the long-range effects of such episodes upon our maturing psyches were cumulative.

Those of us who come from backgrounds similar to Angela's have difficulty seeing our lives in an overall context, for we just aren't accustomed to thinking in such terms. We rarely ask ourselves what our behavior *means,* or what our life's *purpose* is and how our actions will affect it, since those are not considerations that ever helped us to get through the day. Having grown up in households where just getting through the day *was* our purpose, we often carry the same, episodic approach to living into our adult lives—and dramas.

The consequences of living episodically are not experienced in isolation. In time, they will affect our own children. To the same extent that we learned how to seek sensation from our parents, our children will learn how to do it from us—from what we do and how we act, rather than what we say *they* should do. In becoming more aware of our drama-seeking patterns and beginning to change them, we will not only benefit ourselves, but by our example we will also touch a new generation of women.

The Real "Dallas"

When we say, "My life is like a soap opera," we do it with humor. But living the soap-opera life is not funny at all. The turbulence that characterizes the relationships in "Dallas" or any other soap may be engaging to watch, but it is painful to live.

As we've seen, our style of drama-seeking and the intensity of our need for excitement are influenced by many factors: biochemistry, cultural indoctrination, family dynamics and emotional climate, and our manner of adaptation. Yet, it has been my observation that there are trends in the interactions of these elements:

- If you were raised in an unpredictable or emotionally turbulent family climate, you will most likely
  need high levels of stimulation in your adult life,

and your dramas will reflect your early adaptation to your family's dynamics.

- If you were abused physically, sexually, or emotionally, your adult dramas will tend to reflect the ways you survived the pain and adapted to your situation. Through your dramas, you'll act out the beliefs about the world and your place in it that were instilled in childhood.

- If your family climate was seemingly placid but emotionally disordered or dishonest behind the facade, you reacted and adapted to the disorder, not to the sham of composure. Depending on your biochemistry and the severity of your family's emotional dishonesty, you may at present be a high- or average-sensation seeker. In either case, your adult dramas will either evoke or help numb the surges of pain and frustration that you first experienced in childhood.

- If you grew up in any of the above circumstances, you will have most likely adopted an episodic style of living.

As you read on, you'll begin to see even more clearly how your early experiences and your present style of sensation-seeking have fused. In the next four chapters we'll explore in detail the intriguing manifestations, ready excitements, and pitfalls of all three dramatic styles—the Drama of Conflict and Crisis, the Drama of Relationship Challenges, and the Drama of Rebellion.

4 ❧

The Fighter:
Lost without a Crisis,
Bored without a Conflict

Cheryl had been my client for about eight months, ever since her divorce had been finalized. Upset about the ending of her marriage, she had sought therapy. She had proved to be a hard worker, committed to making positive changes in her life. During our most recent session, Cheryl had talked excitedly about how well she'd handled the latest of her ex-husband's regular phone calls, as he once again tried to wriggle out of his child-support obligations. It was a trick she would have fallen for just a few months before, precipitating a crisis, a torrent of drama that could have kept her on edge for weeks. As Cheryl once explained,

> After listening to him and fighting it out for a while, I always cave in. I even feel a little sorry for him sometimes. So I say, "Okay, pay me when you get your next check"—but there never seems to *be* one. I know he lies to me. And I hate myself for putting up with it, just like when we were married. Only now I have to struggle to pay the bills on my salary alone. I'm always broke!

This time Cheryl proudly told me, "I did something I couldn't have done before. I told him I was on my way out, and that if there was a problem with his payment I didn't want to hear about it. 'Have your attorney discuss it with mine,' I said. 'Otherwise, I'll expect a check as agreed.' I got the check in the mail two days later."

A week later Cheryl came in still smiling, but when she sat down she just looked blankly around the room. "I don't have much to tell you," she began hesitantly. "Everything's been going smoothly and I still feel really good, but . . ." She paused, obviously disturbed about something. "I know this will sound strange," she finally blurted out, "but . . . I almost miss those fights with him! I guess I feel a little *lost* without a crisis."

Cheryl's feelings were understandable, and her ability to recognize and articulate this unavoidable transition was testament to how far she had come.

If you, too, have lived your life in the throes of dramatic conflict, leading to one emotional crisis after another, you are bound to feel "a little lost" when all the commotion stops. After all, if you are attuned to noise and commotion, tranquility is confusing and frightening. When the havoc stops, it is painfully necessary to face yourself.

Are You a Fighter?

Everyone becomes embroiled in legitimate conflicts at one time or another. All of us face life crises. But some of us, like Cheryl and other women whom I call Fighters, have learned to provoke arguments and crises or to seek situations that offer them—to use conflict and crisis as a favored *style* of sensation-seeking.

Below is a series of questions I'd like you to ask yourself. The answers will help you to determine the role that conflict and crisis have been playing in your life and the degree to which they may provide drama and stimulation.

1. Do you feel that you have to get angry in order to get your partner to listen to you?

2. When you are feeling particularly good, do you expect something awful to happen soon?

3. Could fights with your spouse or lover be described as frequent, vicious, or theatrically intense?

4. Do you become intensely involved in the personal problems of the people close to you?

5. After a serious fight or confrontation with your partner, do you feel a sense of relief, of satiation?

6. In the most heated stage of some arguments, are you vaguely aware that you're no longer fighting about the issue that started the altercation?

7. Do you often seem to be on the edge of missing a deadline at work?

8. Were fighting and yelling a familiar part of your childhood?

9. Do people ever tell you that you make too much of "little" things?

10. Do your friendships sometimes end after explosive confrontations?

11. Do you get angry and yell at other drivers in traffic?

12. When you have a problem or crisis, do you talk about it at length to many of your friends?

Give yourself one point for each "yes" answer. If your score is 4 or greater, you probably have a strong, and potentially damaging, tendency to garner stimulation from dramatic conflict and crisis.

Women who seek drama by being Fighters have found a method that guarantees a very high level of stimulation indeed. Fighting— whether against a person, as in conflict, or against a real or perceived disaster, as in crisis—always produces biologically supercharged waves of sensation.

Melodramatic conflict and crisis "fool" our systems into a state of heightened arousal because our bodies can't distinguish among threats that are serious, imagined, or exaggerated for dramatic effect. At the physiological level we only have to define a situation as critical for it to *be* critical. To better understand the body's response pattern, let's look at a typical, nonmelodramatic situation.

If you are driving your car and someone runs into the street in front of you, you perceive a critical situation. Your body's stress-response system—that is, your internal alarm—switches to "red alert." Stress hormones rush into action to enable you to quickly size up the situation, and you then brake or swerve to avoid hitting the pedestrian.

But what if there were no pedestrian there? What if, in the dark, you mistook a broken tree branch blowing in the wind for a person, and though no real crisis existed, you *perceived* one? Your physiological warning system would still kick into gear, and you would react just as you would have in the first scenario. Whether a threat is legitimate or imagined, the same physiological stress-response system is activated to help you move out of the way, defend yourself, or attack.

As long as you perceive a crisis—whether this means facing a mugger or a flat tire—it *is* a crisis. Likewise, as long as you engage in conflict—whether it's over a broken contract or your place in line at the movies—your system revs up for the confrontation. The same adrenaline rush is experienced in the midst of any kind of fight, whether the source of conflict or crisis is genuine, misperceived, or melodramatically contrived.

In spite of the rush Fighters get from their dramas, as a mode of sensation-seeking fighting is fraught with very real personal dangers. Because constant fighting induces so much stress, the costs may include illness—for example, ulcers, headaches, high blood pressure, rashes, and heart disease—as well as the agonies of emotional emptiness, depression, directionlessness, and powerlessness that result from living the dramatic, episodic life.

An additional consequence of creating Fighter-style drama is loneliness. Fighters are often perceived by others as boring or annoying. Friends, family members, and coworkers may grow tired of listening to a Fighter's complaints or of being dragged into her dramatic scenarios.

This chapter consists of brief vignettes illuminating a variety of these sometimes hard-to-swallow Fighter-style behaviors. The directness (and perhaps even harshness) of the vignettes is deliberately unmitigated by background details or glimpses of the many genuinely admirable qualities underlying the Fighter's more observable, off-putting traits. If you are a Fighter, it's terribly important that you see the dramatic elements in your life as others may see them, and that you recognize how they detract from the best that is in you. And if you are close to someone who is a Fighter, it will be helpful for you to see the behavior you may have previously found boring or irritating for what it is—learned, sensation-seeking *behavior*—and to recognize that behavior alone by no means constitutes the whole or the core of any woman.

Since the pain that emanates from the Fighter's drama-seeking can be so great, it is also important for us to explore the forces that motivate a woman to generate dramatic conflicts or crises, as well as to explore why, despite the terrible costs, she often feels satisfaction—however fleeting—from the presence of such conflicts in her life.

The Elements of Drama-Making

Standing back and viewing our own dramatic crises and conflicts gives an opportunity to learn more about the feelings and needs that are stored inside of us, unacknowledged. Examining the composition of our dramas gives us a chance to break them down to their basic elements and to see what they, and we, are truly all about.

Whether we are fundamentally Fighters, Challengers, or Rebels, nearly all of us find some stimulation in conflict, crisis, challenge, and rebellion. In drama-making of any kind the same five basic components are often involved, frequently within the same dramatic episode:

Exaggeration and Magnification

Playing for an Audience

Seeing Others as Adversaries

Making the Mundane Exciting

Intense, Unresolved Episodes

These components are especially pronounced in Fighter-style drama. Through the vignettes that follow, we can examine each of these features to find ways of identifying and judging our own patterns of dramatic living.

Exaggeration and Magnification
Dottie: The Invisible Woman

When Dottie found a single flea on her dog she became frantic. It had FLEAS. Her pet was infested, her house was infested, her yard was infested, she was infested. It was UNBELIEVABLE. "I'll kill that guy at the dog wash!"

When the dry cleaner couldn't get a tiny ink spot out of the sash to Dottie's dress, she flew into a rage. "My dress is ruined, just ruined!" she railed. "It cost a FORTUNE, and now it's ruined."

When Dottie's bus was late she told the driver that "the damn thing might as well have *never* come because my WHOLE day is wasted now, anyway." He told her she could turn right around and get off the bus if that was how she felt. Angrily, she did. Then Dottie phoned her boyfriend and told him, crying, that something "HORRIBLE" had just happened—"You've GOT to come pick me up!"

Dottie's days are strewn with normal problems or disagreements inflated to the size of national crises. Each episode contains all the elements of melodrama on its own. Dottie is perpetually distraught and exhausted; her motor is revved up, but her wheels just spin in place. She complains a lot about life's being unfair, but what she really means is that it is especially unfair to *her.*

Dottie is dramatic and self-absorbed. Not only does she exaggerate the importance of most problems, she also magnifies her own. It is easy to criticize her, but it is more important to try to understand her. If Dottie didn't make more of small incidents than they warranted, she wouldn't feel noticed or important at all. For women like Dottie, making melodrama is a way of creating necessary sensation and, at the same time, fighting their way out of the "invisible woman" trap.

When a woman's self-esteem is low, it is not uncommon for her to feel invisible—unseen and unheard, discounted and discredited by others. Nor is it unusual for her to become involved in situations where she *is* unseen, where she must battle her way toward visibility. Dottie, for example, is a secretary. She works for two executives, both of whom refer to her as their "right arm." At first Dottie was flattered, believing they thought her indispensable. She soon learned, however, that being a right arm meant just that—she was simply an appendage, expected to respond automatically but never viewed as a person in her own right with independent thoughts, feelings, and valuable ideas. Only when one of Dottie's constant personal crises is carried over to her work life do her employers seem to respond to her as an individual.

Dottie complains that her boyfriend takes her for granted, too, so she frequently calls upon him to come to her aid in the midst of "disaster," knowing that her tears and tantrums will get his attention. Dottie feels momentarily special when she can get her boyfriend to rescue her. Says Dottie, "He wouldn't go to all that trouble for just *anybody!*"

Like many women, Dottie learned early in life that men respond to tears, and that she could get their attention by making their efforts on her behalf seem terribly crucial to her happiness. "If you won't take me to the new disco I'll just *die,*" Dottie once beseeched her boyfriend, insisting in her inimitable fashion that the disk jockey at the club played absolutely the most PHENOMENAL music he would ever hear in his LIFE!! Dottie couldn't imagine anyone, especially a man, respecting the fact that she wanted to go dancing at a nice club just to have a good time. She felt she had to fight to get her way—with "the *best* club," where they could have "the *best* time *ever,*" as ammunition—or her needs would be ignored altogether.

Some women feel as invisible as Dottie does, even though they appear to be quite independent and hold down fairly high-powered jobs. How these women are perceived by others is secondary to how they perceive themselves. The lenses through which they look out upon the world are distorted by their poor self-images.

If these women are managers, they often have a tough time developing good working relationships with their subordinates because their self-images have not caught up with their job titles. They compete ferociously with other staff members for center stage and find it difficult to delegate work. They maneuver to receive *all* the recognition for every project they touch, even if this means withholding needed information from coworkers. Fighters who feel invisible often quit their jobs with great fanfare, making angry accusations against others and blaming them for their own mistakes. They walk away still fighting, believing that unless they magnify the importance of their leave-taking it won't matter to anyone at all.

Pat: Creating "Incidents"

Pat hangs wallpaper for a living. It is physically demanding but mentally numbing work, and Pat regards most interactions with people on the job as momentous encounters.

"Sometimes I hate getting up in the morning," Pat told me. "I know there's going to be another hassle with somebody, and when I'm really tired I'm just not up for it."

"And when you're not so tired?"

"Oh, then I'm ready to take on anybody," she laughs.

Almost every one of Pat's workdays is turned into an event by an "incident." When an electrician didn't complete his wiring on time and Pat had to postpone starting her job, she fumed and fussed as though the Second Coming had been delayed. And when a male client showed polite interest in her background, she complained to other workers that she was terribly uncomfortable working in the home of someone who was "in love" with her.

Pat lent great importance to each dramatized scene and recounted them all to her friends at length. But she once admitted to me: "What I do is really pretty simple. The problems are all in a day's work. I don't know why I make such a big deal out of these things."

Pat, like Dottie, lacked genuine confidence and a feeling of personal power and importance. By adopting a Fighting style of sensation-seeking, by making a "big deal" out of everything, she compounded her problems, creating distance from people while she stewed in exaggerated conflicts and magnified ordinary events until they became crises.

Pat's working circumstances, like Dottie's often reinforced her inner sense of invisibility. As a tradesperson, she frequently encountered what she called "middle-class snobbism" among clients who considered her to be just a part of the wallpaper she hung, not worthy of serious conversation or personal attention. On occasions when someone did become friendly, Pat exaggerated the significance of the encounter. What might have been an uncomplicated, enjoyable conversation, a light break from the job, was magnified—and usually turned into a fiasco.

Women who grow up with the message that their presence, ideas, or feelings don't count may find it necessary to go to far greater lengths to become "visible" than do people who feel intrinsically valuable. Being melodramatic is one way for these women to ensure that they are noticed, that they are seen and heard. But the apparent magnification of their significance through drama is just a smokescreen. "Invisible" women are so frightened of being "nothing" that they are ready to do whatever is necessary to become "something." Dottie, Pat, and other such women often have a strong built-in need for excitement, along with precariously low self-esteem. Dramatic behavior is one way of becoming visible, of feeling special, while simultaneously generating vigorous—and necessary—sensation.

Playing for an Audience
Penny: Performing for Family and Friends

"I'm forty pounds overweight, my boyfriend and I fight all the time, and my mother won't get off my case," Penny declared by way of introduction during the first minute of her first therapy session with me. In one sentence she had revealed far more than the "facts" of her problem. She had shown the face she presented to the world; her problems and her persona were one and the same.

Penny grew up feeling invisible in the shadow of her older sister, the favored child. She becomes visible through her physical size and through her role in an ongoing personal drama that demands the presence of an appreciative audience.

Penny is a compulsive overeater, and she also abuses diet pills. The conflicts with family members that her behavior provokes and the peaks of emotional crisis it leads to allow her to act out inner conflicts in front of a select audience of viewer/participants. There's the boyfriend, who wishes Penny would lose weight but who hates the moods that set in when she takes appetite suppressants; the mother (also a Fighter), who alternately prepares feasts for Penny and "suggests" that she take off a few pounds; the older sister, who feels guilty that the mother's favoritism toward her causes Penny to overeat; and the best friend, who comforts Penny and offers "helpful" solutions to her problems. Without these emotionally vested coconspirators, Penny's dramas would play to an empty house.

Penny's personal universe is composed of interchangeable players who can rapidly switch from being costars to audience members. For Penny, a fight with her boyfriend about her diet would be excitement-deficient if she couldn't describe it to her sister. In turn, her sister's efforts to prepare a gourmet diet dinner would be unremarkable if Penny couldn't tell her best friend about the half-gallon of ice cream she secretly wolfed down afterwards. All told, the melodrama that surrounds her food and drug dependency would lose its sparkle if there were no audience there to reflect it.

Dawn: Backstage Woman

Dawn is Penny's best friend. "I really pride myself on being a good friend," she told me. "Penny is a good person who just has a lot of problems with her weight, those pills, and her family. I do what I can to help her. I want her to feel she can call me anytime, no matter *what* she's done. I told her I'd be angry if she *didn't*. That's what friends are for, don't you think?"

Dawn seeks excitement in a slightly different way. She is a passive, rather than active, Fighter, who loves to hold her more aggressive Fighter friends' coats while they indulge in mental fisticuffs. She lives her life through other people, making their struggles, crises, and immediate needs her own. As the ever-available "ear," she creates drama in her own life through her involvement in other people's conflicts. This pattern began in childhood, when she became a surrogate parent for her two younger brothers and a caretaker for her depressed mother, who was a single parent and often worked double shifts in her job as a waitress. Though Dawn never received much mothering herself, she learned how to give what she couldn't get. She discovered that if she could help and give advice, she could have a place—she could be "seen." As she put it, "There's an exhilaration to stepping in when someone you care about is in trouble. I feel good when I can make a difference, but it depresses me when I can't."

Backstage women like Dawn perform by lending support in a crisis. They believe their role in each new drama is a critical one.

Dawn sees herself as generous, unselfish, and pure. What she doesn't realize is the degree to which her "unselfish" acts have ulterior motives. Women like Dawn can be *selfish* in a self-defeating way. Because their competence in the midst of other people's distress is the only real measure of their worth, the responses of those others becomes the primary barometer of their achievement. If the loved ones are not appreciative enough, or if they actually begin to help themselves and work out their troubles, women like Dawn can become deeply hurt, and often angry. Their identity, their purpose for being is threatened, and the pain they experience is very real. Such women are not conscious of the symbiotic quality of their relationships, of how desperately they depend upon the very people they imagine are needier than themselves. Instead of dealing with their own feelings, they clutter their lives with other people's, while priding themselves on being "together."

In short, though Dawn is Penny's audience, Penny is no less Dawn's. The crises and conflicts that Penny provokes sustain them both.

Ruth: The Agony Queen

Ruth sits at the kitchen table, sipping coffee and puffing on a cigarette, the telephone receiver seemingly welded into her hand. She dials her daughter's work number. "I'm sorry, I can't talk now, Mom. I'm just about to go into a meeting," her daughter says.

"What do you mean? This is your *mother!* What do you have to do that's so important you can't talk to your mother for a few minutes? I don't feel good—my headaches are killing me again. I need you to take me to the doctor . . ."

"I guess you'll have to call a cab. I've got to go now. I'll talk to you tonight. 'Bye," says the daughter, hanging up.

Ruth fumes for a moment, then dials her son at work. She is put on hold. When her son picks up the line, she begins: "That damn secretary of yours keeps me on hold every time I call. I hope you can talk to your poor old mother. Your sister can't be bothered, as usual.

Too busy, Miss Big-Shot Executive. . . . I want you to take me to the doctor today. . . . What? No, it can't wait until tomorrow. No, it's not my arthritis, it's my headaches. I *know* the doctor told me to stop drinking coffee . . . sure, I quit . . ." (as she takes another gulp of black coffee) . . . and on . . . and on.

Ruth is sixty-nine years old. She is of a generation of women who had few life choices but to get married, have children, keep house, and cook—and maybe, for excitement, play a little gin.

Ruth was a child of the Great Depression; her affluent parents lost their wealth in the stock-market crash. Ruth grew up expecting that good things don't last, that troubles are always around the corner, and that happiness should not be too loudly expressed, lest "the fates" see her glee and bring tragedy in its place. Ruth finds stimulation, manages the unpredictability of life, and maintains her visibility by creating crisis-oriented dramas in which she plays the role of victim and/or martyr. Her children and friends either provide an audience for her complaints and sorrows or unsuccessfully attempt to change her—as Ruth's daughter did by bringing her to a mother/daughter workshop I conducted some years ago.

Women like Ruth—whom I refer to as "Agony Queens"—remain passive reactors to life rather than active participants in it. Their Fighter drama stems from the crises that arise when "bad" people take advantage of them and bad things happen to them (usually because they failed to take reasonable action to prevent it) or from the conflicts that result from their covert manipulation. Ruth, for example, has severe headaches because she drinks too much coffee, but she refuses to give up her habit. Instead, she lies about it and uses her resulting discomfort to manipulate her children.

Agony Queens, by and large, refuse to take charge of their lives or to take responsibility for the state of their relationships, and they view themselves as somehow "meant to suffer." Such women often feel victimized by life, and their specialness seems to evolve from their "poor me" position. They are special, in essence, because they suffer. It is through this setup for suffering that they are also able to control the people closest to them, as well as to control the drama that protects them from the feared, impending catastrophes they've come to believe are punishments for happy excitement. The unconscious, irrational, but deeply ingrained theory they hold, is this: "If I provoke many "little" disasters, if my life is fraught with minor troubles, then 'the fates' [or God, or whomever] won't single me out for the more horrible tragedies that befall people who dare to be happy."

Melissa: The Deadliest Crisis

Melissa attempted suicide three times. Once, she cut her wrist with a razor while three people banged on the locked bathroom door. Another time she swallowed half a bottle of aspirin five minutes before her ex-husband was due to pick up their daughter for the weekend. The third time she overdosed on sleeping pills, but she made sure to call her lover on the phone to tell him. He hung up on her, and she called the paramedics herself.

Of the four women discussed thus far, Melissa has certainly taken the term *dramatic crisis* to its farthest reaches, but there can be no minimizing her pain. Only someone who feels invisible to the core would need to try "materializing" herself in so dangerous a fashion. For Melissa, playing to an audience has been an integral—and almost lethal—part of her drama.

Melissa grew up in a household where communication centered around conflict and crisis; anyone who wanted to be noticed had to participate. The child with the the loudest argument or the worst cold always drew the most attention. Melissa learned how to play the game better than anyone.

> I knew how to get my mother to spend time with me instead
> of my brothers. Because I was a girl she was more protective
> of me, so if I got in trouble at school, she'd come running. If
> I got hurt playing, or if I said one of the boys was picking on
> me, she was there.

Melissa has minor "accidents" regularly and is often ill. While the unhappiness and stress of her life whittle away at her immune system, her body seems to cooperate to bring on the illnesses she knows her audience will respond to best. For example, she doesn't get colds—she gets *pneumonia.*

When she isn't actually fighting an illness, she finds reasons to rush to the dermatologist, the plastic surgeon, the internist. Melissa has had her eyes done, her thighs liposuctioned, and her teeth straightened. She doesn't quietly go about improving herself, as some women do. Instead, every new procedure—and each of its stages—becomes the focal point for tremendous drama over possible complications, medical bills, doctors' egos, and so on. No matter how hard Melissa fights to change her body, she is unhappy with herself. "Sometimes I feel like starting all over again and building a new me," she tells me sadly.

Regardless of the content of her dramas, Melissa stages them with the audience in mind, and she fills that audience with intimates. Not only are melodramatic incidents stimulating in themselves, but the telling and retelling of them after the fact add to the potency of the drama. Though her friends have often given advice, Melissa—just like Penny—really wants the opportunity to share her fights and remain the center of attention.

Although Penny, Dawn, Ruth, and Melissa procure stimulation, visibility, and attention from their style of drama-seeking, these pay-offs obviously are not sufficient for building a satisfactory life. All four women are deeply troubled and desperately unhappy. None feel as though they have accomplished anything worthwhile. All feel painfully empty inside. Their repeated failures to fill themselves on bits of self-defeating sensation only lead to an escalation of the drama.

Seeing Others as Adversaries

Linda: Family Feuds

Linda has not spoken to her mother-in-law, Arlene, for three weeks. "The woman's impossible. No matter what I do it isn't right," she says. "When I had her over for dinner and I served chicken, she spent twenty minutes describing the wonderful *fish* her daughter had cooked the night before. She's a bitch, and she's just trying to upset me. Well, I have nothing to say to her until she apologizes."

Linda's husband and his sister have tried to intervene, with no success. Linda and Arlene are both aware that the holidays are approaching and that the family is hoping they will patch up their differences in time to avoid spoiling the festivities. The family remembers only too well how the similar feud last year between Linda and her own sister brought tensions to the table at Thanksgiving that were sharp enough to carve the turkey. Though Linda resolved her differences with her sister shortly thereafter, it seems that she is continually on the outs with someone in her family.

Beth: The Troublemaker

Shelly and Donald had just been married, and the ceremony had been tender and touching. When the gala reception was about to begin, Donald's cousin Beth approached Shelly and hugged her tightly. "Congratulations," she said, smiling. "You know, some things are a blessing in disguise. If Candy had said yes to Don, this might not be happening, and I think you're so-o-o much better for him than she was." Shelly was speechless. She knew that Candy and Don had been involved once, but marriage had never entered into the equation. Or had it?

Ronda: The Litigant

"You have to be on your guard," says Ronda. "There's always someone out there ready to screw you over, and they will if you don't watch out for yourself."

Some people would consider Ronda a professional litigant. Though she is an aerobics instructor, not a lawyer, she has a legal mind honed through personal experience. She has been to small-claims court nine times, has settled three personal-injury suits, one worker's compensation claim, and a divorce, and she is about to file a new suit against a local department store. This is more legal action than most people see in a lifetime, yet Ronda is only twenty-nine.

When Ronda is involved in a case, the details overshadow all other aspects of her life. "I sink my teeth in and I don't let go," she told me proudly. "When I'm into a case, I'm into it all the way, for better or worse—nobody gets the best of me without a fight!"

Linda, Beth, and Ronda are Fighters who create drama by starting trouble. Beth likes to stir the soup of other people's emotions, then walk away from the drama and let them simmer.

Linda and Ronda, on the other hand, are always in the thick of the conflicts they initiate. For them, the controversy is the thing. The excitement flows from the conflict and attaches itself to every mini-crisis that arises in the course of battle. Because Ronda is less concerned with finding a resolution than with keeping the action going, her fights often drag on for years. Throughout the duration of each case, episode upon episode add up to create an ongoing saga. In the end, Ronda has lost as many legal battles as she's won and has sometimes settled for far less in damages than her time and energy were worth.

Linda, Beth, and Ronda seek out other people (or organizations) to cast as the opposition, as intentional bad guys. In their private melodramas, "the fight" is a pervasive theme, one that twists all their relationships and turns trust and generosity of spirit into a weakness. Linda and Ronda engage quite directly in their fights, which are often over issues that allow them to feel self-righteous. Beth is both manipulative and often deliberately vicious.

Beth was an emotionally deprived, unloved child. Her deep core of insecurity and sorrow is disguised by her ferocious rage over the desolation of her childhood. She is resentful of people who received the love and care she never experienced, and she has developed a pattern of creating internal excitement by fantasizing about the upheaval she can cause in their lives. After walking innocently away from the scene at Shelly and Donald's wedding, Beth entertained herself with images of the discord she most likely stirred up between them on what should have been a joyous occasion for them. Not only do fantasies of this kind excite her, but her vicious acts also make her feel heady with power over the lives of her victims.

Some women are, like Beth, troublemakers, but they lack her consciousness and deliberation. Such women often make catty or cruel remarks, but when asked why they would say such things, they reply, "Oh, I was just kidding." While they don't perceive themselves as unkind, they are actually sitting on powderkegs of anger, jealousy, and insecurity, which eke out from time to time in the form of personal barbs. All troublemakers seem to have an intuitive knowledge about the location of other people's raw spots, and whether they do so intentionally or unconsciously, they use that knowledge to wreak emotional damage.

If conflict is excitement for us, we need to see others as adversaries, for without a nemesis to fight there is no source of stimulation. But when it becomes more thrilling to do battle than to simply resolve our legitimate problems and get on with life, our losses will always outweigh our potential gains.

Our fighting style may be direct, like Ronda's and Linda's, or covert, like Beth's. In any case, the thirst for blood usually distorts our perception of events, and our other important priorities—ethics, friendships, careers—collapse. Wrapped in animosity, we are also removed from intimacy. As others distance themselves from us they prove to us that, as we suspected, they can't be trusted. A vicious, closed circle is formed, and the force and number of our adversaries can only grow.

Making the Mundane Exciting

Casey: Picking a Fight

Casey tells me that she reads romance novels avidly. "I usually daydream about a man who sweeps me off my feet and carries me to the bedroom," she admits, giggling with embarrassment. "Sometimes I wish my husband could be as dashing and as passionate as the heroes in my books."

When her husband, an accountant, arrives home with talk of balance sheets and client demands, Casey is jarred back to reality by the obvious difference between her exciting fantasies and her ordinary life. Suddenly she begins criticizing her husband, picking a fight so senseless that she can barely remember the reason for it the next day, in an unconscious attempt to imbue her everyday world with the drama and the special intensity of emotion that it lacks.

Casey, like many women, has been brought up to extract excitement primarily from her love relationships; when those relationships become dull, she finds that a good fight relieves the tedium for a while.

Casey might be typical of those homemakers who are bored with grocery shopping and cleaning; frustrated with their kids, sick of PTA meetings and car pools; and tired of hearing about their husbands' jobs and annoyed with having to nag them to help around the house. Not only are such women legitimately bored and frustrated, but they are also unconvinced that what they are doing at home matters. Yet they are reluctant—even afraid—to change their lifestyles, to change themselves.

Bored housewives can temporarily alleviate their dissatisfaction by immersing themselves in such accessible melodramas as romance novels and soap operas, experiencing thrills vicariously. They long for the inaccessible "real thing," yet they are unwilling to risk creating it. Eventually, they discover the next-best option: they can make even their mundane marriages appear briefly exciting again if enough drama, enough emotion is injected into them. Even petty conflict has the power to stimulate a mundane relationship to the point at which it *almost* resembles passion.

Casey, out of touch with her feelings and unwilling to admit she is bored or to do anything constructive about it, maintains that her marital arguments are rooted in justifiable anger. She has a right to be mad, she says, because her husband is not holding up his end of the wedding bargain. It's his duty, she feels, to excite her, to keep their honeymoon passion kindled, even after twelve years. Unaware of her own contribution to the ardorless quality of the marriage, she is angry that her husband has failed in what she believes is his responsibility. Instead of talking openly with him about her feelings, she needles and picks at him. For Casey, fighting becomes a poor means of filling two legitimate needs—the needs for excitement and for self-expression—at once. For her husband, however, the arguments are merely puzzling. Unaware of Casey's hidden agendas, he can't respond to her needs, and he can't satisfy her. He can only disappoint her over and over again, as the fighting goes on.

Bored women find that conflict can be a strong stimulant that, like a drug, shifts their systems into overdrive. The downside of this sort of kick is that—again like a drug—it undermines the relationships they value, stunts any real growth between them and their loved ones, and strengthens their belief in the melodramatic, adversarial nature of love.

Eileen: In Conflict with Time

Eileen races through my office door and practically throws herself into a chair. She's five minutes late for her therapy appointment and is out of breath. "I can't *believe* this day," she gasps. "I can't *believe* how much there is to do. I've got to slow down or I'll have a heart attack."

Eileen seems always to be in conflict with time, and it is this conflict that produces one critical episode after another. Her husband says that if anyone would be likely to have a baby in a taxi, it would be Eileen.

In college, Eileen crash-studied the night before each exam. Today, she crashes through project deadlines at work; she is unprepared because she has added so many extraneous activities to her schedule that there isn't enough room for the priority item. To make matters worse, Eileen's secretary has problems following through on the work delegated to her, so Eileen must complete her secretary's work as well as her own. Yet, Eileen can't bring herself to fire the woman.

All told, Eileen creates her own pressures, then panics in the midnight hour and wastes most of her energy trying to regain control of a situation that never needed to become so urgent. "Why can't anything ever run smoothly?" she asks ingenuously. "I need to be three people to get everything done!"

Despite an ulcer, Eileen thrives on these challenging, stressful, self-induced crises. Her system demands constant, heightened stimulation, but she has developed self-defeating methods of procuring the excitement she needs. And she operates in a stressful, crisis mode because only in this way does her otherwise unintriguing job feel exciting and meaningful.

Eileen's life has become a workplace soap opera that produces high sensation but only a modicum of reward. Her immediate crises always burn themselves out, but the minute one race against time has been won she dashes off on another. She even staffs her office inadequately, relying on a secretary who is as much of a drama-maker as she. Functioning amidst crisis, Eileen can hyperstimulate herself, then take pride in how well she has overcome the emergency.

Eileen's husband, who jokes from time to time about her frenetic style of living, has been growing more unhappy with the marriage. "I can never pin her down for a relaxed evening, or even a full-blown conversation," he complains. "I know how much her work means, and I realize she's under pressure, but I don't feel as though anything else—including our relationship—matters much at all."

Eileen's situation is the reverse of Casey's, but it is no less debilitating. Women who try to create conflict- or crisis-based excitement in a work or a home situation that has grown dull usually avoid asking the kinds of questions that could help them to reevaluate their circumstances: What happened to change my relationship or my initial enthusiasm for my job? What part did *I* play? What, if anything, can I do about it?

By making drama instead of addressing similar questions, these women add stress to their lives and risk damaging the very relationships they hold most dear.

Intense, Unresolved Episodes

Kim: High Drama in Mad, Passionate Scenes

"We were in the middle of the street, and the car was still moving slowly when I opened the door. Chuck yelled, 'What the hell do you think you're doing?' and I screamed back, 'I'm sick of you and I'm leaving—right here and right now!' and with that I opened the car door and jumped out. But I fell onto the pavement, and that's why my arm is all scratched up. Chuck saw me fall, but the minute I started to pick myself up he reached over and slammed the passenger door shut and drove off. Nice guy, huh?"

By the time Kim told me about this latest scene, she and Chuck had already gotten back together.

Highly charged scenes such as the one above are scattered throughout Kim's relationship. She has come to crave the intense sensation that is as tightly linked to episodes of major conflict as it is to times of impassioned sexuality. Without the fiery drama she feels incomplete.

Unlike Casey's situation, in which a dull marriage is brought to life by fighting, there is nothing dull or ordinary about any aspect of Kim's relationship or of Kim herself. She is the type of woman who personifies the word *dramatic,* from the tips of her red spiked heels to the top of her pitch-black spiked haircut. Kim has never read a romance novel in her life, and she is far more likely to rent videos of *Rambo* and *Aliens* than to tune in to "The Guiding Light." She is a high-sensation seeker, incapable of sitting still long enough to become bored with anything. She fulfills her abundant need for stimulation primarily through her extremely volatile relationships with equally high-strung men. With Kim, we observe a new level of heightened dramatic conflict that borders on, but never quite reaches, physical violence.

Kim and Chuck put the fire back into their tempestuous union every time they end it. They break up and get back together with remarkable regularity. And, although the rare happy "highs" they experience appear to hold them together, Kim and Chuck live most often amidst churning conflict. Their arguments are cruel, their words aimed at each other's most vulnerable spots. If a few days pass without incident, one of them—usually Kim—will take a verbal swing at the off-guard partner. Kim, particularly, likes to go for the sexual jugular. "You think you're so hot," she'll say snidely. "I could tell you about hot—but you wouldn't want to hear it." This kind of ploy can be counted on to make Chuck strike back.

"I don't know why I started it," Kim says of each fight. "Everything was so calm; it was nice for a change. But he ticked me off again, and I just lost it!"

In a relationship like Kim and Chuck's, real closeness is lacking, but the conflict creates an illusion of involvement and excitement. It is a way of getting a partner to respond and "take notice" while keeping him or her at a distance that, for many people, feels safer than intimacy. Conflict stands between their longing for intimacy and their even greater fear of getting too close, of being swallowed up or lost in another person. Intense conflict is a "connector," a form of communication that acts as both a stimulant and a buffer, and it can imbue an otherwise insubstantial relationship with life.

In circumstances where dramatic episodes actually replace the emotions aroused by genuine caring and depth of affection, the episodic quality of the conflict is spotlighted. By relating only to the feelings aroused by the immediate, heated episode, it is possible for people to avoid examining or drawing upon the more uncomfortable feelings and needs buried deep inside. In these cases, conflicts are not the forerunners of resolutions to meaningful problems. They are sensational ends in themselves. Each episode provides its own dramatic form of gratification, but nothing worthwhile is achieved.

In many Fighters' conflict-ridden relationships, the partners may come close to the resolution of a problem, only to turn and run from it. Whenever Kim or Chuck actually concedes to the other in the midst of a scene, the partner refuses to be appeased and instead escalates the conflict. For most serious conflict-drama seekers, there is an emotional point of no return. This is a juncture at which, no matter *what* the partner says—even "Okay, I see that you're right about that"—the other finds it unacceptable. "Oh, *now* I'm right," Kim might scream. "But I was 'stupid' five minutes ago. How dare you call me stupid?! . . ." and on and on.

At an emotional point of no return, a combatant may feel so out of control that she actually believes she is incapable of stopping the fight or justified in her continued outrage. The truth is that even in a verbal brawl, she is in complete control. Any woman who has ceased creating this kind of drama will tell you that she discovered she could stop immediately, if she chose to do so. As one client, Marilyn, told me, "There was always a part of me observing and almost commenting on the goings-on. I knew when I was purposefully saying things to keep the fight raging, and I knew I just didn't *want* to stop—even though I could have." Any woman who becomes invested in the drama of the episode will prefer to think she can't help herself or that her behavior is warranted. Genuinely aiming to resolve the conflict and deal with the real problems buried in the altercation would end the drama—and quell the excitement.

In many relationships, even the healthiest ones, a verbal "knock-down-drag-out" fight can occur a few times over the life of the relationship. Some couples may have heated battles two or three times each year. Others, like Kim and Chuck, may create volatile, explosive scenes three, four, or five times in a single month—or even in one week. Such people's lives become warped by the *prevalence* of their battles. There is no question that conflict itself, no matter what a couple is fighting about, is damaging to a relationship in which it seems to be more the norm than the exception. Although a count of "fight days" versus "peace days" may actually reveal a greater number of peace days, if a relationship *feels* characterized primarily by conflict, it is sure to be a debilitating, nonnurturing partnership.

Although there is no real intimacy between the partners in a conflict-laden relationship, intimacy frequently *appears* to exist during the time between conflicts. During this short period of calm, the couple can have fun together and relate quite normally. While this is an enjoyable time, the "intimacy" is really just a mirage—an experience of the contrast between conflict and its absence. Compared to the anger and hostility present in the fighting, it is a warm relief—but it is not intimacy.

Intimacy demands that two people be capable of sharing their most subtle and personal feelings and needs with each other without judgment or censure. It also implies that if those needs conflict, both people will lovingly and respectfully endeavor to find a resolution. When high drama and mad passionate scenes permeate the relationship, trust is usually absent, and real intimacy is too great a risk. The partners may think, "What if he [or she] *really, deeply* hurts me by using what I said in confidence against me during a fight?" For most people, that is a prospect too awful to contemplate for long, so confidences are withheld and conflict becomes the more powerful connector.

For couples who thrive on conflict, living on the brink of dramatic episodes means that deep feelings are rarely revealed, and the real problems that lie beneath the boiling surface of the relationship are barely considered. A sure sign of the fact that one is living an episodic lifestyle is the unresolved quality of these deeper issues. For Kim and Chuck, resolution of emotional conflicts is elusive in the furor that erupts between them, so their fights eventually just peter out, ending without victory and without defeat. In the end, the partners wind up using their rocky relationship to provide the highs and lows that masquerade as love.

In her case Kim has found a willing partner, a man just as attached to drama as she is. Although sensation-seeking through personal drama is usually a woman's issue, our radar sometimes helps us to home in on that rare man who becomes just as deeply involved in drama as we do. I say "rare" man, because while most men will engage to a point, they have not been raised to be as dependent upon drama as women have, nor to have as much need for it on a consistent basis. In fact, their very *reluctance* to become equal participants in the melodrama of our lives is often so infuriating that it provokes us to generate more and more drama of our own.

Sue: High Drama in Episodes of Internal Crisis

When Sue broke up with Jonathan, she thought that she had seen the last of the man who had "made her life miserable" for nearly a year. But Jonathan was not one to let a woman walk out on *him*. He continued to call her, leaving lengthy, plaintive messages on her answering machine. Finally, Sue agreed to see him again. When she did, it was a humiliating experience: Jonathan first made love to her, and then he viciously attacked her verbally. In describing the incident to me, she wailed, "I'm so dumb—how could I have done something so ignorant? I never should have gone to see him. What's wrong with me? I'm so *ashamed.* It was the worst night of my life! I guess I wouldn't do something like that unless I was *addicted* to him!"

Sue is a relationship Fighter, but her dramas are slightly different from Kim's. Although conflicts similar to Kim and Chuck's often rage between Sue and Jonathan, Sue can create an added level of crisis drama through her attachment to auto-arousal, even in the absence of contact with Jonathan. The emotional crises that stem from the auto-arousal component of the Fighter's dramas are often misperceived as products of "addiction" to a man.

Recently, there has been much attention given to the subject of "relationship addiction." Women diagnosed as relationship addicts are said to be suffering from a disease. They are highly dependent upon their partners (frequently, troubled men whom they imagine they can help or change), and they often feel they "can't live" without those partners.

In her book *Women Who Love Too Much,* Robin Norwood characterizes relationship addicts as women who find that "being in love means being in pain," and who are "strung out on pain, fear, and yearning." She calls such women "man junkies." The addiction, Norwood states, "is not to a substance but to a person."

The pattern of relating known as relationship addiction is certainly unhealthy, counterproductive, and progressively debilitating. However, it has been my experience that such women are not "addicted" to a person at all. The need they seek to fill is *primarily* the need for the intensity of sensation generated by these relationships, and only *secondarily* the need for the person who appears to give their lives focus and meaning. The sensation to which most "man junkies" become particularly attached is that of auto-arousal.

Auto-arousal is, in a sense, a "mind trip." For example, the feelings associated with the high of stealing or taking drugs are auto-arousal. And the drummed-up, self-generated emotions achieved by some women in the buildup to, or the aftermath of, an episode of relationship drama are also auto-arousal.

It's crucial for us to realize that women like Sue rarely get hooked on the particular object of their frenzy, no matter how severe their dependency on a certain man may *appear* to be. Relationships provide a setup for drama-making for these women, and they can become dependent upon the auto-arousal component of the dramatic scenarios. For example, when Sue insisted she was addicted to Jonathan, she was mistaken. She was really hung up on the internal process— the emotional crises—that a "Jonathan's" presence in her life justified. Jonathan could have been Ted, or Mike, or Bob. The need Sue feels is, in part, for *someone* to focus on, someone to fill the emptiness in her life, someone to "love." But just as significantly—and, in relation to her pattern of emotional dependency, even more importantly—her yearning was for intense sensation, and she achieved it through the self-generated crises that she alone created. The men that Sue tended to become involved with simply manifested the particular chemistry that helped to ignite this process.

For many reasons, both biological and historical, Fighters like Sue are often high-sensation seekers whose systems require megadoses of stimulation. Episodes of auto-arousal can provide that stimulation just as efficiently as episodes of interpersonal drama. Best of all, they are accessible, since auto-arousal can be achieved anytime, anywhere. Neither audience nor participants are necessary. The supply of crisis is self-generated and endless.

According to Norwood, women who become "relationship addicts" always come from dysfunctional homes, most commonly from alcoholic ones. Norwood states that as a result of their upbringing such women thrive on crisis and become caretakers of troubled people; they have addictive relationships because they grew up with addicts. Like Norwood, I—and most other therapists—have found that adult children of alcoholics, who grew up with little confidence or self-esteem, have developed many profoundly damaging, often confict/crisis-oriented patterns of relating to others. But I have also observed that these people learn to rely for emotional gratification upon their own self-induced sensations, their own internal excitement and drama. In childhood, this was a drama they could count on, while they had no real control over the painful family drama produced in their homes. Consequently, as adults such women often become attracted to the kinds of relationships that are fertile ground for creating both interpersonal conflict and crisis *and* the self-induced sensations and internal crises of auto-arousal.

The Fighter's internal drama can be played out around any aspect of her relationship. It can begin early and continue on through the "changing" or "rescuing" period, during which the woman attempts (and inevitably fails) to change her partner. For many women, the most intense episodes of auto-arousal occur when they try to break up with a lover.

Sue entered therapy immediately after her second attempt to break away from Jonathan. Jonathan, a psychologically manipulative and emotionally abusive man, as well as a therapist, had been the object of Sue's agonizing obsession for over a year. During the time before she capitulated and agreed to see him again, Sue experienced great internal drama—enormous, self-generated Sturm und Drang. She spent days in a heightened, tumultuous state of crisis, preoccupied with analyzing nearly every word of Jonathan's phone messages and looking for hidden meanings. She reread all his old letters—both love letters and hate notes—and reran their love scenes and fight scenes over in her mind. She spent hours fantasizing how it would be if she saw him—the best outcome, the worst-case scenario. Should she call him, or shouldn't she? She worried about what would happen if she didn't—would she miss out on her last chance to make it work?

She called her friends, pleading, "Tell me what to do—I have to know *now.*" If she was told not to call him, she countered with rationales for doing it anyway. If a friend said she should go ahead and call him, she came up with all the reasons not to. She went back and forth until she was exhausted. Finally, in a state of excited tension, she dialed Jonathan's number and agreed to see him. Her worst-case scenarios paled beside the reality of their meeting.

After Sue's devastating night with Jonathan—a dramatic episode in itself—she began a new inner drama that provoked a new emotional crisis. She became obsessed with having been "stupid enough, sick enough to let him suck me in again." She continuously visualized scenes from that evening. She flipped through the pages of one self-help book after another, because it was *urgent* that she find out what was "wrong" with her. She begged for answers from her friends. By the time she arrived in my office (after telling me she was having a "terrible crisis" and needed to see me "right away!!!"), she was already on automatic pilot—steering herself down the exciting auto-arousal course she already knew quite well but did not understand.

Because Sue was accustomed to creating emotional crises, it was difficult for her to view the incident of her meeting with Jonathan proportionally. If her perspective had been clearer, the encounter would have yielded a strong message, giving her a much healthier recognition of the dangerous nature of the union as well as deeper insight into her own feelings and motives for being with him. But Sue was still attracted by the possibilities for inner drama that Jonathan represented. Before and after the encounter, she allowed herself to become literally high on the trauma. She began by fighting against her own confusion—should she or shouldn't she, what if this, what if that? Later, self-recriminations and feelings of shame were magnified and exaggerated. Each despairing but theatrical repetition of "I'm so ashamed, I'm so ashamed" revealed how aroused Sue was by the emotional intensity of her inner turmoil.

Like most women who think of themselves as being addicted to a person, she was unconscious of the degree to which she was controlling and manipulating her own feelings and manufacturing her own melodrama. Preoccupied with internal dialogues, Sue lost sight of the self-understanding her experience might have provided. Like Kim's conflicts, each episode of Sue's drama produced ultimate sensation and a measure of emotional gratification, but led nowhere.

Women who self-induce internal emotional crises actually stimulate themselves and become auto-aroused. Each time the experience of auto-arousal generates an internal monologue that they allow to preoccupy or obsess them, they relinquish the potential benefits and lessons of the life experience that precipitated it. Yet, contrary to the belief of some therapists that women in such circumstances are powerless over their "addiction," it has been my observation that in the act of making drama, these women are exerting tremendous power, control, strength, and creativity. They are, however, misusing these attributes. In effect, they are using their strengths—their survival tactics—in the ways they learned as children, in the ways they unconsciously believe these attributes *should* be used. Unfortunately, those strategies no longer work for them. To change those patterns is a matter not of recovery from a disease but of reeducation and reacquaintance with one's deepest self.

Misusing and misdirecting our abilities are not signs of illness or disease. Recognizing that we have misused our abilities means recognizing that we are capable of making conscious choices to develop new patterns of relating to others and of satisfying our own needs. It is important that all women begin to "own" their strengths instead of reducing them to weaknesses. It is crucial that we acknowledge our attributes rather than naming them as deficiencies, for we have been denied—and have denied ourselves—the recognition and use of our genuine power for far too long.

In order to develop healthy patterns of having relationships and of living as free, psychologically independent women, we must come to terms with our motives and methods for seeking any form of drama, whether it is interpersonal or internal. Once we have stepped back from our dramas long enough to observe the ways in which we create them, we will find that there are few limits to the forward strides we can make in all aspects of our lives.

Similarities Among Fighter Styles

As we have seen, the Fighter's style of drama-seeking encompasses a large variety of behaviors and situations, as well as all kinds of relationships. Naturally, each woman who adopts this style of drama-seeking will tailor it to fit her own personal circumstances. She will also include all five elements of drama-making in many of her scenarios: Magnification and Exaggeration, Playing for an Audience, Seeing Others as Adversaries, Making the Mundane Exciting, and Intense, Unresolved Episodes.

There are more important similarities than differences among women's drama-seeking scenarios. Any time we adopt aspects of the Fighter's style of drama-seeking we achieve the following:

- We generate tremendous stimulation and drive ourselves to peaks of passion—but we experience sadness, emptiness, and hollowness between episodes of drama.
- We maintain control of our lives by directing dramas that have predictable consequences—but we forfeit the genuine pleasures and surprises of healthy excitement.
- We gain visibility by exaggerating and magnifying ordinary situations—but our true selves remain unseen and unappreciated.
- We hold the attention of an audience—but all of their applause doesn't soothe our pain.
- We vanquish our adversaries and win our battles—but we distort events and relationships through our hostility.
- We transform the mundane into the extraordinary—but we damage the relationships and sabotage the achievements we most value.
- We experience intense episodes of passion and excitement—but we never resolve the feelings or find solutions to the problems that prevent us from experiencing love and intimacy.
- We wallow in our perceived weaknesses—but we never uncover, and use, the strength and power that are hidden inside us.

If the Fighter's style of creating drama sabotages love and prohibits intimacy, it is no more self-defeating than the Challenger's. In the next chapter we will see how the relationship-challenger's style of sensation-seeking, while appearing to be in the service of love and romance, is actually a setup for failure and pain.

5 &

The Challenger:
The Thrill of Relationship
Contests and Competitions

If he didn't already have a girlfriend, I probably wouldn't want him!"

"Everyone thinks he's such a bastard . . . but he's so different when he's with me."

"He's been getting away to see me on weeknights. Now, if I can only get him to spend a weekend with me . . ."

"I know I'm really important to him, so why won't he admit it? I guess I just have to be patient, or try harder."

Most us have heard women make comments like these. Many of us have made them ourselves. If so, we probably find relationships with hard-to-get or hard-to-please partners a tremendous source of excitement, challenge—and drama.

This chapter is about the women who are repeatedly drawn to challenging relationships, whether in love or at work; women who are tantalized by the most seemingly unapproachable, unavailable, or unattainable partners; women for whom serious obstacles are not stop signs, but green lights.

This chapter, however, is *not* about the drama in certain other difficult relationships. It does not concern the drama in violent or sexually risky relationships, which is usually fueled by danger, not challenge, and which will be dealt with in a later chapter. Nor is it about painful and unpredictable relationships with emotionally troubled partners or with those who abuse drugs, alcohol, or the like. The drama that is characteristic of those relationships generally centers around the kind of conflict and crisis we explored in chapter 4. In such relationships, women often operate in the Fighting mode— fighting with, fighting to change, and fighting to handle the crises of the partners they already have. In this chapter we'll be dealing with women who create drama in a *striving* mode, in which they work to *attract and manipulate* the partner who is out of reach.

Over the past few years, Fighter-style love relationships have been explored in depth by authors writing about women involved with men who are sick or troubled, who can't love women, who hate women, who love and leave women, and so on. Such books tend to focus on issues related to why a woman becomes involved with such men, the conflictual dynamics of the relationships, and what the woman can do to change the man or change herself to better deal with him. The psychology of the men is usually examined to help women understand why men behave as they do.

This chapter is not about men, their psychology, their motivation, or their concerns. It is about the women—the Challengers—whose personal dramas revolve around striving to elicit the adoration or passion of others. To understand the Challenger, it is not important to understand the emotional dynamics of the men or to focus on their motives. To do so would be to detract from the importance of understanding the nature of the Challenger woman, and why she seeks the kind of relationship she does.

The Challenger: Who Is She?

Challengers don't pursue just *any* others. They experience the thrill of striving only if the object of their desire appears to be out of reach. For them the relationship is a contest, and for the contest to be exciting it must be difficult, taxing, even impossible to win.

Challengers are quite different from Fighters. Although conflict may play a role in the relationships of Challengers, it is the *contest* upon which the excitement is based.

In the Challenger style of drama-seeking, the challenge component of a relationship is generally more attractive than the potential for intimacy or satisfaction. The excitement of relationship challenges is unlike the excitement of a healthy, loving relationship—or of healthy excitement, per se—because it is neither self-actualizing nor genuinely rewarding. In a loving, mutual relationship, both partners strive to overcome obstacles to intimacy, both are committed, both seek similar levels of involvement. In the Challenger's relationships, she alone strives to overcome obstacles, and she alone is committed—but even here, her commitment is more to the contest than to the man.

Women do not belong in the Challenger category simply because they may develop an attraction to a man who is unavailable. It is natural to be attracted to people who have qualities you admire and whom you find appealing, but it is the choices you regularly make with respect to those attractions that help you to create—or avoid—more drama in your life.

A woman is also not definitively a Challenger simply because she once fell in love with an unavailable man. Certainly, there are situations in which the attraction and deep feelings between two people compensate for the problems that ensue when one of them is not free. However, in relationships where challenge is not a strong component, both partners are equally committed to each other and are clearly involved in creating a future together. The real drama in such relationships is an outgrowth of the intense, sincere feelings between two people, not part of an exaggerated pursuit-and-resistance scenario.

Challengers are women whose relationships evidence a specific *pattern* over time. A Challenger repeatedly becomes involved in difficult, competitive love triangles, and/or consistently seeks relationships with men who are impossible to please, uncommitted, and often involved with other women.

For a woman hooked on the thrill of the struggle, the realm between desire and attainment is her home, her "thrill zone." In the heat of a love challenge, she may fantasize about happy-ever-after outcomes, about how wonderful it would be if "he and I could be together" or "if he would only realize how important to him I am," but the reality of those moments (if they come at all) are rarely as thrilling as the fantasy. Although the prospect of actually winning the contest *appears* to be the Challenger's goal, the actuality of conquest usually pales beside the fervid quality of striving. Simply put, for the Challenger the excitement is in the quest, not the conquest.

The Rival

Women who grew up believing that their identities, fulfillment, and excitement would come from demonstrating their sexual allure and/or capturing and pleasing a man also learned to invest the bulk of their energies in those pursuits. For many of these women, the most difficult men can come to represent the most dramatic source of personal validation. Attempting to conquer them becomes an utterly thrilling challenge.

Challengers often view other women as competitors for a seemingly unattainable—and therefore highly desirable—male. Having a rival not only heightens the excitement and magnifies the importance of the potential conquest, it also allows the drama to be extended beyond the relationship to include the "other woman" in a passionate, conflict-tinged triangle.

The presence of a rival provides possibilities for high drama that are *not* inherent in relationships where there is no rival, for one cannot "win" or "lose" a contest if there are no other contestants. Where rivalry exists, however, great drama can be invested in "psyching out," playing with, and scoring oneself against the competition.

Among women, it is traditional to view other women as adversaries. From the time we learn to "hate" the little girl next door with the lovely golden ringlets or the prettier party dress, we are culturally conditioned to regard one another with jealousy and suspicion. We grow up believing it is natural to compete among ourselves for everything from beauty, to clothes, to men, to jobs. The introduction of a rival in an intense love challenge merely adds magnitude to a conventional, long-standing contest of woman versus woman.

Patterns in Dramatic Love-Challenges

When we are really interested in love and happiness, we invest our time in nurturing relationships that present minimal obstacles and maximum potential for becoming a partnership of equals. In dramatic love-challenges, the potential for true romance and intimacy is limited.

In confronting the material in this chapter, you may say, "Yes, but *my* situation is different. This is *real love,* and it can work." It's important to realize that there are certain attributes of challenging relationships and patterns of Challenger behavior that distinguish these relationships from others. While specific details can vary considerably, the existence of these patterns points to a drama-seeking, challenging quality in the relationship.

The following guidelines may help you to clarify whether your current and/or past relationships evidence the patterns characteristic of love-challenges. While few situations reflect all of these criteria, all love-challenges include many of them:

- It's not the first time you have entered, or stayed in, a relationship after learning that your lover was living with, married to, or still in love with someone else.
- To make your lover do what you want him to do (for example, see you on weekends, stay the night at your house, call you from home, or tell you he loves you), you deliberately manipulate, argue, cajole, and demand—and you push him as far as you can.
- Each time you achieve a victory (that is, get him to do or say something you want), you feel tremendously powerful, and your determination to conquer him is renewed.
- You genuinely believe that you know what he needs and that your attempts to manipulate him are for his benefit.
- You live in a state of almost chronic jealousy, which is relieved only briefly each time you win a battle against the other woman.
- You tell yourself and your friends that even though the relationship is difficult, you can make it work.
- Your reunions after fights or separations are exquisitely passionate.
- You often fantasize about deliberately upsetting the status quo in his other relationship, but you fear the consequences too much to do it.
- You have fantasies about him, her, or them that involve violence or revenge.
- When you accuse him of lying to you or deceiving you and he provides reasonable explanations, you're torn between your desperate desire to believe him and your fear that he is covering up.
- You believe that the special moments of tenderness and passion between you make up for the occasional miseries.

- You often test the strength of your lover's bond to you. You "can't help" calling him when and where you shouldn't or dropping in at his office unannounced. If his response is favorable, you're aglow, but if he's displeased you feel as though you've lost a round in the contest.
- One moment you're excited, the next depressed—and your mood swings depend entirely upon what is happening between you and your lover.
- When you're feeling down and without hope, you wonder how you can face your friends if you fail to win your lover. You worry about your pride and the "I told you so's" you'll likely hear.

In the story that follows, you'll recognize most of the above elements. Barbara's relationship exemplifies the kind of painful Challenger drama that stems from a preoccupation with a lover, and with his wife: the rival. In other women's scenarios the rival may take the form of a girlfriend, or even of a "ghost" love from the past whom your lover can't forget.

Because Barbara's story illuminates the major themes that shape the emotional lives of Challenger women—no matter what the specifics of their individual relationships—I have chosen to deal with her affair at some length, and in detail. Although I will offer my interpretation of the events in her story as we move along, I will also tell it to you much as she told it to me when her affair ended and she sought therapy.

In many ways, Barbara's story is a common one. Tune in to any soap opera and you'll find a similar scenario; love triangles are predictable plot staples. But there is nothing trite about the anguish Barbara felt when her difficult love-challenge ended, nor about the depletion of energy, self-esteem, and professional respect she experienced as a result of her year of obsessive competition.

The Challenger Drama
The Contest Begins

Barbara, thirty-two, described her first meeting with Steven as "straight out of paperback heaven." She had been convinced by her friend Monica to take a few hours out of her hectic schedule and enjoy an *al fresco* lunch in Malibu. Barbara, an architect, was just beginning to make a name for herself in the firm she'd joined a year earlier. It was rare for her to leave the office during the week except to visit building sites or see clients, but on the day she met Steven she had surrendered to a break from her routine.

Barbara and Monica sat in the sunshine, contentedly sipping wine and eavesdropping on the conversations of people at neighboring tables—especially the intriguing couple beside them. The man was quite distinguished looking and appeared to be in his late forties. The woman was a designer-clothed beauty of about the same age. They were having a civilized fight. You had to listen carefully, which Barbara did, to catch words such as "thoughtless" and "liar" being tossed back and forth. The man seemed able to maintain his composure well, but the woman was on the edge of crumbling. Barbara saw that they both wore wedding rings.

"Hmmm, marriage on the rocks," she whispered to Monica.

"That's assuming they're married to *each other,*" Monica whispered back.

A few minutes later the woman left the table, but the man remained seated—and was suddenly gazing with clear interest at Barbara. He *was* awfully attractive, she mused, but probably meant real trouble. Prefering for the moment to avoid the situation, Barbara stood up to make her way to the ladies' room. When her hip accidentally brushed his shoulder as she squeezed by, she excused herself. He smiled warmly. She tingled, barely noticing his wife returning to her seat.

When Barbara exited the ladies' room he was waiting for her, and his wife was nowhere in sight. Their eyes met.

If this were a soap opera we would go to a commercial here, leaving the viewer hooked by unanswered questions: Who is he? What will happen next? What about the wife?

For Barbara, reality was rife with the same questions, and her excitement emmanated from them—as it would continue to do throughout their emotionally dangerous, yearlong affair.

His name was Steven, and he was a lawyer. He and Barbara spoke to each other briefly and exchanged business cards. Barbara returned to her table, too excited to continue eating but able to give a breathless description of the encounter to Monica. As she talked, however, a disturbing warning chime pealed in her mind, and she said to herself, *"No, Barbara, not another married man. You've been there once already. It's not worth it."* For a few moments the thought nagged at her—then it was gone, and she joined Monica in weaving a complete fairy tale out of the thin strands of information they had. They imagined a successful career, a marriage gone stale, children torn between their battling parents. Then there were the lies—surely hers; the sadness, the loneliness—surely his.

Finally, Barbara turned to the topic of The Wife, Herself: Who was she? Why couldn't she make him happy? Barbara was actually as entranced by this woman as by Steven, faced as she was by the task of turning someone she knew practically nothing about into an antagonist. This was necessary, however, since the only facts she really had at her command—a distressed woman married to a cheating, or certainly a willing-to-cheat, husband—said more about Steven's contribution to his marital problems than his wife's. If Barbara had been more realistic in her assessment of the situation, she might have avoided an involvement. Instead, barely moments after meeting Steven, Barbara was comparing herself to his wife and envisioning the possibilities for play-offs with her.

What excited Barbara so early in this affair—really, even before it became one—was the lure of challenge, contest, and conquest sheathed in a wild, romantic garment. It was the perfect mingling of sexual, mental, and emotional arousal that someone with an especially high demand for sensation—someone like Barbara—could find irresistible.

The fact was, Steven himself didn't really count. He could have been almost *any* attractive married man, for his unique appeal hinged on his involvement with another woman. Though Barbara was not consciously aware if it, for her love without rivalry was water, not wine.

Barbara waited three days for Steven to call. Then, finally, he did. They had lunch, and it was magic. As Barbara told me much later, when the affair was over, "The chemistry between us was breathtaking. When we finally made love it was beautiful, but I couldn't help wondering how it was with Elizabeth, his wife—so I asked. Big mistake. He was angry, but that only made me more curious."

Barbara had already begun a pattern of provoking Steven with queries about her rival. Challengers often keep their drama fueled by taking on the role of provacateur, trying to elicit the information that will reveal where they stand in relation to the competition.

As time passed, it became apparant that Barbara was in a sense having an affair with two people, not one. Barbara's involvement with Steven hinged on Elizabeth's imagined presence, for in relating to Steven she would not have known what to do or how to act unless it was as a *reaction* to, and in competition with, Elizabeth.

Barbara became almost obsessed with Elizabeth. "I wanted to know everything they talked about, where they went, and who they saw. I wanted to know what she wore, so that I could outshine her, and what her body was like, so I could be sure mine was better. I even asked him how she kissed."

Barbara continually drove herself in an effort to best her rival. She even went to the antique shop Elizabeth owned, not to confront her but just to observe her. What did Steven's wife *have* that still intrigued him?

"I just watched her," Barbara said. "I felt so paranoid, as though she would *know* about us just by looking at me. Of course, she didn't have a clue. But I still couldn't figure out what she had going for her that made him stay with her!"

She told Steven what she had done, and he exploded. It *must* not happen again—she had to promise. Barbara promised, but she never intended to keep her word. For most Challengers, there comes a point when the fantasy of the rival is not enough to keep the intensity of the drama going. They yearn to stalk and observe the woman in the flesh, to make their rivals *real*.

For Barbara, the contest with Elizabeth became her first priority. During hours when in the past she would have been working, she imagined what life would be like if she and Steven were together and plotted ways of outdoing his wife. Completely disregarding the fact that in a sense she was a trespasser, having jumped deliberately into the midst of an existing marriage, Barbara viewed Elizabeth as the obstacle that prevented her from having a full-time relationship with Steven. She drove herself into a white-hot fury each time she thought of the woman that stood between her and her lover. "I wanted to kill her," she said later. "I thought of horrible ways to wipe her off the face of the earth. Then I'd come back to reality and would instead dream up ways to show Steven that I was better for him than she could ever be."

An essential component of drama for Challengers is the special "performances" they arrange for their lovers. Barbara told me how she orchestrated romantic dinners for two that culminated in hours of lovemaking. Often, with delightful anticipation of the evening ahead, she left her office early and shopped for champagne and pâté before going home to slip into silky little nothings. On those days she could barely concentrate on anything but the exciting prospect of seeing Steven. Until the moment he rang her doorbell, she was filled with electrifying suspense, wondering what he might say or do tonight that would indicate she was edging out her competition and burrowing her way into his heart.

As the relationship wore on, these sultry evenings frequently turned ugly when Barbara, a little drunk and reckless, again maneuvered the conversation around to Elizabeth. Prove to me, she seemed to be saying, that your love for me is greater than for her. Leave her—for me.

Eventually, there were fights—Barbara yelling, pleading; Steven coldly angry, storming out, slamming the door. Usually Barbara was left alone in a fit of anguished sobbing, only to pick up the phone and call Monica—the friend who most consistently served as the audience for Barbara's dramas—to spill the whole story.

"This is destroying you," Monica would comment sensibly. "Look what's happening—you're falling apart. You're lucky you still have a job, you're so out to lunch most of the time."

Barbara would become extremely defensive, "Yes, I know, but you just don't understand. He's going to leave her—I can feel it. He loves me."

"You're dreaming. This is just like the last time with Andrew. He has no intention of leaving her. He's having it all, with two beautiful women—and you're going to wind up with nothing."

"This *is* really different, I just know it—we're meant to be together. He says so, too. You'll see. I can make him leave her."

It was this last response that most graphically revealed the challenge Barbara had set out to meet, the no-win predicament in which she had placed herself.

"I Can Make Him"

When a woman is more committed to the stimulation of challenge and drama than to the prospect of finding a loving, caring, *real* partner, she usually responds to anyone who confronts her with reality by saying, in effect, "Yes, I know that what you're saying is true, *but* I can rationalize it differently. I can deny my pain and convince myself that this relationship was *destined* in order to justify striving to meet the challenge I've created."

And that challenge is clearly stated in the phrase, in the very words, "I can make him . . ."

The "I can" attitude imbedded in these challenges is not an extension of healthy, self-actualizing, positive thinking. The purpose is not to enhance one's personal performance or achieve something worthwhile by and for oneself. Because it involves an attempt to control another person, and because the weighty consequences of the challenge are only rarely or fractionally considered, the "I can" reflects a self-defeating pattern of thinking.

Despite the costs, in most challenging affairs a chain of "I can make him's" varying in intensity is manifested in stages throughout the relationship. The special excitement emanates from the episodes of dramatic suspense and stimulation that revolve around striving to "make him do" whatever we want him to.

Below is a typical list of the progressively more difficult and "advanced" goals that Challengers struggle to achieve throughout the life of their romances:

I can make him notice me.

I can make him desire me sexually.

I can make him ask to see me.

I can make him see me again.

I can make him compare me to her.

I can make him prefer me.

I can make him want to make love to me constantly.

I can make him think of me all the time.

I can make him love me.

I can make him want to be with me all the time.

I can make him want to leave her.

I can make him leave her.

I can make him move in with me.

I can make him marry me.

It is at this point, however, that the Challenger's goals usually run out. Since challenging relationships survive on the excitement of striving to make the lover do one's bidding and of competing with the other woman, the Challenger doesn't seriously consider what will happen if she actually gets what she has said all along that she wants. However, confronting success only rarely becomes a problem. Because so many challenging relationships are doomed to break up painfully, most women never have to face the reality of reaching the end of their "I can make him" list. Instead, they must face the pain of losing their contest, their lover, their confidence, and their pride.

Jealousy

In trying to get a man to do what they want, most Challenger women experience a myriad of intense emotions, ranging from exhilaration to anguish. All such feelings appease their sensation-seeking needs to some extent, but the one most provocative of further drama is jealousy.

Every time Steven appeared to consider Elizabeth's needs or feelings, Barbara experienced powerful surges of jealousy. Often, after a wonderful afternoon with Barbara, Steven would call Elizabeth on Barbara's phone to inform her that he was "just ending a meeting" and would be home shortly. Barbara would leave him alone in the bedroom to make the call, but she would listen intently outside the door. A sudden burst of laughter would infuriate her—how dare he seem to *enjoy* talking to that woman? She wanted to grab the receiver and "scream at the bitch until her damn eardrums burst," but, terrified of the consequences of such an extreme act, she did nothing. It was only after Steven hung up that she partially vented her feelings. "Well, *that* sounded cozy," she might remark snidely. Sometimes an argument would follow, and sometimes Steven would soothe and reassure her, insisting that it was *she* he loved above all—and Barbara would calm down temporarily. But no matter what Steven did to comfort Barbara it wouldn't be enough for long.

She was just as tied to her jealousy as she was to her man. A few years later, when love-challenges were no longer part of her life, Barbara admitted to me that the highs and lows, the jealous frenzies had made the affair even more exciting.

> The jealousy was what made it so dramatic, so much like a novel or a movie. Looking back, I see that it was almost *fun* to be in the middle of something so intense. It hurt a lot at the time, but I can hardly remember that now. I just remember how strongly I felt, how stimulating it was.

In challenging relationships the jealousy is, in a sense, "fun" because it is part of the romantic game of conquest. It is superficial jealousy. It is melodramatic, exaggerated, self-serving, and flamboyant. It is not the kind of heart-rending jealousy that, for example, a wife would feel on learning that her husband was involved with another woman during the tenth year of a basically happy marriage. The jealousy in such a situation would be mingled with shock, a sense of betrayal, the feeling of suddenly living inside a nightmare, and the experience of deep grief. Barbara's jealousy, however, could not have been mixed with shock or betrayal because her relationship never included trust. And she was hardly trapped in a nightmare out of her control; she was, instead, playing a self-scripted role in a drama she had been directing from the begining.

Like most women in this situation, Barbara had entirely lost sight of the emotional benefits she was (or wasn't) getting from the relationship. Assuming Steven would ever leave Elizabeth, Barbara never considered whether her relationship with him could survive without all the drama.

Tunnel Vision

When a woman becomes obsessed with dramatic episodes in any relationship, she develops "tunnel vision" with respect to other aspects of her life and becomes blind to her other emotional needs. Her sight is fixated solely upon the titillation provided by the immediate experience. And if she does take the time to consider the dubious quality of her future, no matter how loud the warning bells clang in her mind she often finds a way to ignore them and to convince herself that everything will work out in the end.

While Barbara was focused on the challenge of her relationship, another, eminently more worthwhile challenge was being neglected. Her career, formerly an important and meaningful part of her life, was suddenly an intrusion, an unwanted distraction from her obsession with Steven and Elizabeth. She was making mistakes at work, and she had begun to take half-days off to wait at home for Steven, who often said he "might" come by in the afternoon—but rarely did. She had even walked out of a meeting with a client to take a phone call from him, and had then become so upset by the conversation (in which he canceled their plans for that night) that she left the office, fighting back tears. Her colleagues, who by this time were thoroughly annoyed with her, concluded the business meeting.

Barbara was vaguely aware that she was systematically alienating everyone in her business life, but it seemed to her as though that life had receded in importance. It even seemed unreal, compared to the heightened emotionalism of her challenging affair with Steven. Later, it would take many months for her to repair the professional damage done during that year of impassioned challenge.

The Challenger's Family Drama

Adult Challenger dramas are rooted in many different kinds of childhoods, but as we saw in previous chapter 3, most women who develop this drama-seeking style do so as a result of their particular modes of adaptation to—or emotional survival in—their family homes. Family circumstances can range from the dysfunctional to the "normal," because children must adapt to the content as well as the severity of the family drama.

Barbara's propensity for Challenger drama can be easily understood in retrospect. The youngest of four children, Barbara was the little princess, the focus of her family's affections for the first years of her life. But when she was seven, her mother died of a stroke.

After the mother's death, Barbara's family was too busy to give her the attention she had become accustomed to. While Barbara missed her mother deeply, she missed the attention even more. Only her father occasionally made her feel special again, though she often felt she practically had to do cartwheels to catch his eye. For him she did whatever was necessary, perfecting a charming performance that was aimed to please. It was essential that Barbara prove herself "special"—as special as she had been before her mother's death transformed everything.

When Barbara was twelve, her father remarried. Now she had serious competition for his attention, and she tried even harder to attract him. Later, she even went so far as to choose the profession—architecture—that her father, a structural engineer, had encouraged her to enter, so that she could create a professional bond with him that her stepmother couldn't equal.

In her childhood Barbara had learned that in order to be loved she had to be special, and in order to be special she had to expend great effort, she had to perform—and she had to compete. This background set the stage for all her adult relationships. Only men who provided a challenge became appealing; only in a series of turbulent triangles could she feel any of the intense sensations she called love.

The Dramatic Climax

Consumed by her relationship challenge, Barbara continued to escalate the drama. It reached a crest one Friday when she visited Elizabeth's antique shop again. Barbara stood at the back of the shop, pretending to admire the merchandise but secretly watching Elizabeth. Suddenly she saw Elizabeth answer the phone, and she was horrified to hear her speaking lovingly to Steven. It was in this way that Barbara discovered they were about to leave together for a weekend in Palm Springs—the same weekend that Steven had told Barbara he would be spending in San Diego with a client.

Barbara went straight home, put a Billie Holiday album on the stereo, and slowly downed half a bottle of scotch. Always a controlled social drinker, Barbara was now at the edge of losing control. Too despondent to go back to work, she called the office and said she was sick.

She was dozing when the phone rang. It was Steven. The "meeting" had been called off, so he thought he might stop by for the evening. Since he wasn't expected home, if she had no other plans he could spend the night.

"Other plans! Of course I had no other plans," Barbara said later, reflecting back on that moment. "I felt like someone who'd just been reprieved from death row! I didn't know what could have happened between him and Elizabeth to change things so drastically, but I didn't care. It was like one of those tennis matches that just *turns*— someone is losing, and then they hit a perfect shot and, wham, the game is in their pocket. I knew it was a turning point for Steven and me, and I swore to make it the best night of his life."

The Excitement/Hope/Despair Cycle

It is in this dramatic turnaround that the essence of Barbara's excitement can best be seen. In a single afternoon, her level of arousal peaked during each of three highly emotional episodes that led to an agonizing, but predictable, cycle of Excitement/Hope/Despair.

All Challengers eventually become embroiled in the Excitement/Hope/Despair cycle. It is an unavoidable consequence of creating episodic drama in the Challenger mode. Barbara's story illustrates how this cycle can begin and how we can recognize it in our own lives.

In Episode One, Barbara *excitedly* entered Elizabeth's shop, *hopeful* of this time discovering a clue to Elizabeth's lingering appeal to Steven. Her *despair* when she discovered Steven's deceit led to Episode Two, in which she was at home, crying over sad songs, gulping scotch, and wallowing in the self-generated sensation of alcohol intoxication. This tendency toward self-induced, mentally oriented stimulation—one example of the process I've termed auto-arousal —is a formidable by-product of the use of alcohol. It produces an inner drama and self-absorption that can be subjectively exciting, even when attached to events that seem objectively painful.

Barbara was unable to understand either of these scenarios or to place them in an illuminating context. She was so wrapped up in the intensity of each separate episode of drama as it occurred that she couldn't stop to ask herself the questions that were later explored in her therapy—questions about what her attachments to a man like Steven and to such a tempestuous, impossible romance revealed about her own inner needs. Because she was living episodically, Barbara was able to move smoothly from the second sensory episode into the final, climactic episode that followed Steven's phone call. Once again, *despair* was transformed into *hope,* and hope into pure *excitement.* Her luck had reversed, and the challenge was renewed.

Barbara continued on the same frantic and endless merry-go-round—Excitement/Hope, Excitement/Despair, Excitement/Hope—until it exhausted her, as it does anyone who rides it. After about a year with Steven, Barbara gave him an ultimatum: live with me, or leave me. He left, and Barbara sought therapy to help her put her life back together.

Any time we experience dizzying shifts in mood brought on by our reactions to someone else's behavior, we are in emotional trouble. In an intimate, healthfully exciting relationship, the Excitement/Hope/Despair cycle doesn't exist. But a relationship that at its core is hurtful and destructive can trigger these erratic, extreme feelings—the magnified, sensationalized (though genuinely felt) reactions that are the hallmarks of melodrama. If any of our relationships resemble Barbara's in this respect, we need to give serious thought to our deepest motives for being in them. These motives are extremely complex, and they usually have less to do with love than we may imagine.

The Signs of Challenger Drama

It might be helpful at this point to briefly review the major issues in Barbara's story, all of which are characteristic of most Challenger dramas. The following are "shorthand" versions, based on Barbara's experiences, of many of the items listed at the opening of this chapter.

- **Unrealistic Fantasies**
  Is your initial assessment of the relationship's potential based upon a fantasy? Are you ignoring obvious warning signs (such as a wedding ring) or subtle ones (such as your lover's frequent conversational references to being with other women)?

- **Competition**
  Do you have a rival for his affections or attention?

- **"Viewing" the Rival**
  Is it not enough to imagine your rival? Do you make efforts to observe her in person?

- **Provocative Questioning**
  Do you frequently urge your lover to talk about intimate details of his other relationship(s)?

- **Special Performances**
  Do you set up scenarios in which you pamper and please your lover, keeping in mind the "score" you may achieve?

- **Deterioration into Conflict**
  At some point in the relationship, do you have fights that revolve around the topic of you versus the other woman?

- **"Yes, but . . ."**
  Is this your response when friends warn you about the outcome of the relationship?

- **"I can make him . . ."**
  Is this your goal?

- **Jealousy**
  Are you jealous of the other woman's claim on your lover? Are you obsessed with thoughts of their relationship?

- **Tunnel Vision**
  Are other aspects of your life relegated to last priority or genuinely suffering as a result of your relationship?

- **Excitement/Hope/Despair Cycle**
  Do your moods shift considerably as a result of most contacts with your lover?

The Truth about Relationship Contests

Barbara was attracted to a married man, but if we substitute the words *unavailable* or *hard to get* for *married,* many women who are honest with themselves will relate to the theme that predominated in Barbara's life. Any woman can get caught up in dramatic competitions that ultimately sap her energy and sabotage her worldly successes because they demand so much intensity—which is exactly what makes them appealing.

There is always more than meets the eye to contests like Barbara's. When a woman is repeatedly entranced by the potential for conquering men who are involved with another woman or women, she hopes that in the outcome of these challenges will lie proof of her worthiness, as well as the assurance that she is very, very special. In a world where *special* for a woman usually means "in the eyes of a man" and "relative to other women," it is not surprising that many women expend their energies in trying to feel special by winning hard-to-get men. That is why their dramas continue to stem from a preoccupation with displacing the other women in the lives of the men whom they pursue precisely *because* they are not free.

In spite of the difficulties that result from the choices she makes, no Challenger really likes to lose. Yet, losing is the price many women pay for taking on love-challenges. Not only do they lose the contest, but they lose their sense of personal power as well, along with any chance for intimacy or emotional security. Whatever their other goals and aspirations, these become secondary to—and eventually obscured by—the emotionally exhausting, energy-depleting episodes of high drama.

Men are as likely as women to be initially tempted by the excitement of love-challenges, whether they are the pursuers or the pursued. However, they rarely allow the drama to become as all-consuming as women tend to do. The difference is that men are not *defined* by women or by their personal relationships. In contrast, women are even today defined first by their relationships and only second by their achievements. These definitions are imposed by social convention, manifested in the judgments of both men and women, and reinforced by women's individual self-perceptions. As a result, some women prefer to joust for the partner who is most desirable to other women—the man who for that reason alone is the most valuable and *validating* acquisition of all, whether it's for a one-night fling or a forty-year marriage. The paradox is that it is the presence of another woman that, for the Challenger, validates the man and lends him a greater aura of desirability.

Only rarely does a Challenger attain rewards that last; even if she wins her lover, they don't necessarily live happily ever after. During a courtship composed of competition, there is little chance for partners to determine whether they are potentially compatible, whether they have the depth of love or the ability to develop the kind of intimacy that keeps a long-term relationship exciting. They only know how to subsist on dramatic episodes. Trouble often rears its head at the point where challenge ends and a real relationship is expected to rise out of the ashes of the contest. At the beginning of the endless list of problems that can crop up is a most predictable one: the question of trust.

The betrayal of the other woman that is a necessary part of many romantic challenges often continues to be a serious stumbling block after the victory. A woman may begin to wonder, "Since he cheated on his wife/girlfriend to be with me, how do I know he won't do the same to me? Am I really *that* special?" Suddenly, when he says he's working late at the office, she begins to question his whereabouts. The illicit quality that made the affair exciting in the first place now boomerangs. The woman knows the deception of which her lover is capable, and she wonders if some other determined woman isn't out there right now, trying to snare him.

Also, some women forget their own center-stage role in having created the original challenge-drama and explode with repressed anger over what "he put me through," either during the initial stages of the relationship or during the breakup of his other relationship. In the midst of all this unhappiness, it is easy to find glaring flaws in the same man who not long ago seemed perfect. Once the fireworks sparked by his previous unavailability have died away, the exciting man may become a less interesting—and maybe even stodgy, dull, or sexually imperfect—day-to-day partner. Some women are amazed when a prince turns into a frog shortly after the challenge has been won. Immersed in the contest, these women were likely to overlook —or remain blind to—traits and personality characteristics of their lovers that were there all along. When they finally wake up to reality, their disappointment and anger surface rapidly.

When the contest becomes an active relationship, the drama may continue through conflict. Since in the heat of challenge the couple haven't really come to *know* each other, and certainly haven't grown to trust each other, they are left with plenty to argue about. When the contest is over it is often their conflicts that keep them going. The drama in the relationship changes in format, and Challengers temporarily become Fighters. Fighting *with* him may replace fighting to get him. This way, for a while, it may seem that the passion lingers on.

Excitement in the Conquest of Impossible Men

Although it is common for challenging relationships to demand the presence of a rival, not all are structured that way. Some men are so impossible to please, so difficult to attract on their own merits, that their emotional distance *is* their appeal. The excitement, in these cases, is sparked when their sexy disinterest is mingled with the woman's thirst for attention and approval. She doesn't need the presence of another woman, for the man alone is challenge and trouble enough. When women tend to go after men who aren't especially kind or loving to them or who don't seem to want them at all, the drama and excitement are culled from the challenge of trying to reform the men.

The "conquest" of an impossible man can occur on many different fronts. The excitement and validation we seek isn't always derived from exclusively romantic or sexual liaisons. Today, the business suite can be as fraught with interpersonal challenge as the bedroom suite. Though the workplace may offer a fruitful, invigorating source of excitement, it can also be turned into a home away from home, replicating all the drama that we have been conditioned to seek in our love relationships.

Jillian: Beguiling the Boss

When Jillian began her job in the offices of the Copy Corral, it was just that—a job and a stepping-stone to bigger and better things. As the new executive assistant to the president of a chain of quick-print shops, she was finally getting paid for skills she had honed during twelve rocky years of marriage to her ex-husband Frank, for whom she had faithfully served as typist, file clerk, answering service, and accountant, in addition to her duties as wife, cook, and mother.

When the marriage ended, Jillian was crushed and came to me for therapy. Her chief concern was that no matter how hard she had tried to please her husband, she had felt she could never do enough. She blamed herself for the breakup of the marriage, but she had never been able to figure out what she should have done differently, or better.

Jillian found working long hours for a demanding new boss far easier than working round-the-clock for her ex-husband, but she also found it a lot lonelier. She had never been alone before, and though she rallied bravely, she often felt sad, empty, and without direction.

Jillian took her job seriously, as she had always taken responsibilities of any kind. But it wasn't until she had grown accustomed to her new position that she opened her eyes to the office intrigues that swirled around her.

Like her ex-husband, her boss Jerry was a taskmaster. He was impatient, autocratic, and emotional; *tact* was not in his vocabulary. On the other hand, he rewarded loyal and productive employees freely, but they had to earn his trust and pass stringent tests that they didn't even know they were taking.

In her third week on the job, Jillian witnessed Jerry angrily firing the personnel manager. She told me that afterward Jerry asked her to bring him a cup of hot coffee, and she was so rattled that she spilled half of it over the papers on his desk.

"Don't bother about that," he'd said with an uncharacteristically understanding smile, mopping up the coffee. "I didn't really want to answer those letters anyway."

For Jillian, Jerry was suddenly more than the man who signed her checks. "He's such a challenge, because he's such a *bastard,*" she said to me. "But I think he thinks *I'm* terrific, which is what counts."

Suddenly, the Copy Corral became an arena in which Jillian set out to perform for Jerry's attention and approval. The job took on dramatic proportions. The nervous anticipation with which Jillian approached "what might happen next" gave her a focus, a renewed and exciting sense of purpose. Though Jillian was not having an affair with Jerry, the intensity of her involvement and attachment was just as consuming. Each day was an exciting cliff-hanger, and at first she couldn't wait to get to work.

Every morning, Jillian dressed for Jerry. She knew his favorite colors and wore them religiously. If he complimented her on an outfit, she felt ready to burst with pleasure, and she wore it again. If he made a nasty comment about something she wore, the offending clothes were shoved to the back of her closet. It was not that Jillian was trying to appeal to Jerry sexually, but that she simply wanted to impress him with whatever assets she had. Her looks had always been one of Jillian's calling cards, and it was automatic for her to use this attribute to be noticed by a man—any man.

When she arrived at the office each day, she was careful to gauge Jerry's mood so that she could anticipate his every need. If she sensed he was upset, she immediately brewed him a pot of tea; if he was in a jolly mood, she would excitedly amuse him with a new joke. Sometimes when he was working intently and she expected that he'd be having lunch at his desk, she ordered sandwiches early in the day so that she could take them in to him at just the right moment.

"I never know what to expect from him from one hour or one minute to the next," she would say. "The only thing predictable about him is that he's utterly *un*predictable. That's what makes working for him so stimulating!"

Jillian endeavored to excel in her work, and she usually put in twelve-hour days. She had to be perfect. If Jerry noticed how well she had followed through on an assignment, her day was made. If he criticized her, it was all she could do to choke back the tears. Occasionally, Jerry was unsparing in his ridicule: "What the hell's the matter with you? How could you be so *stupid?!*" he might scream. Jillian would begin to shake, unable to speak. A few moments later he'd apologize profusely, ask her to forgive his outburst, and tell her how much he needed her, how no one else would ever put up with him, how no one could do a better job than she. Jillian, relieved and grateful, would once again turn excitedly to her work. She absolutely refused to accept that her relationship with Jerry could be part of an ongoing, damaging pattern in her life.

Once in a while, Jillian would sit in Jerry's office and chat with him amiably about a movie or television show they had both seen; on such occasions she would return to her work floating on a cloud of happiness. Sometimes she was able to draw him out, encouraging him to talk about his family, his past. Those times were almost as special and as stirring as the rare occasions when she accompanied him to lunch at the coffee shop next door. Almost as if she were a schoolgirl on a date, she applied her makeup carefully before they left so she would look especially attractive. But she tried not to show that she felt slighted because he usually took the managers to lunch at the French restaurant down the block. Well, that was something to look forward to eventually, she rationalized.

Jillian wanted to be more important to Jerry than anyone else in the office was. When she believed she was succeeding, she felt like someone on a drugged high. If it appeared for a moment that another staff member was becoming intimate in his or her exchanges with Jerry, Jillian reacted angrily and jealously, subtly snubbing the offender and plotting secret ways to keep them at arm's length from her boss.

In her own way, Jillian was swept up in the same Excitement/ Hope/Despair cycle in which Barbara had been involved. Jillian's drama may have been less observably feverish, but it was equally powerful, all-encompassing, and self-defeating, for in her relationship with Jerry she had crossed a definitive line. When she no longer viewed her job as an opportunity for professional challenge, when she went further than desiring a pleasant, comfortable relationship with her difficult boss and began to rely on him to define her feelings about herself, Jillian stepped beyond healthy interactions into emotional drama. When she lost sight of her personal career goals and began to perceive each individual scene or dramatic episode in which Jerry figured as an all-important event unto itself, she gave him tremendous power over her life. It was a power completely unwarranted by his role as an employer, and it re-created her difficult marital relationship in the workplace.

Some of Jillian's friends simply tuned out as she recounted episode after episode of her workday drama. Jillian noticed, and was deeply wounded. Her friends didn't understand the importance of Jerry's role in her life, the excitement she felt when he showed special trust in her or conveyed his appreciation, the sharpness of her pain when his cold stare was leveled in her direction. For Jillian, as for all women for whom an impossible man becomes the center of the universe, those feelings were very real.

The unfortunate aspect of this kind of dramatic involvement—like all melodrama—is that our efforts to achieve something worthwhile are usually wasted on episodes that seem exciting at the time but that leave us feeling emotionally depleted and only marginally special. In time, it was these feelings that forced Jillian to face the self-defeating pattern she had perpetuated in her work life and to begin the real process of therapeutic self-discovery.

Jillian's case was that of a competent, hardworking, responsible woman who needed "impossible" men to keep telling her she was valuable. The drama in her life was created as she tried to arrest their attention, time and time again. It was never enough to be valued by people who were consistent in their appreciation of her, who let her know regularly how important and genuinely special she was to them. She had lost sight of the potential for excitement that could be procured from tackling non–relationship-oriented competitions and challenges, as well as of the potential for happiness in personal relationships based on intimacy rather than obstacles. For Jillian, validation that she mattered had to come from a power source who was always male and—whether lover or boss—always withholding.

Women like Jillian can be found in almost every professional environment, though their preoccupation with their bosses is sometimes invisible to observers. Lori, a former trauma-center nurse, told me of the challenge she experienced while working with "Dr. F.," whom she described as an "obsessive, workaholic surgeon."

"For him I became an obsessive, workaholic surgical nurse," she said. "I was never happier than when I was working side-by-side with him, high on the excitement and drama of sharing a subdural hematoma."

When Dr. F. stopped working such long hours, Lori was shocked and felt as though she had been jilted in some way. "How dare he prefer to stay home over performing exciting, life-and-death surgery with me!"

Just as Jillian had done with Jerry, Lori had learned to anticipate Dr. F.'s every need, and her self-image had become bound to the nods of appreciation he bestowed each time she placed the proper surgical instrument in the proper position at the proper moment. Dr. F.'s demanding, obsessive nature made him an "impossible man," and Lori's ability to satisfy him made her a "special woman." When he became less demanding, she grew less special. Lori eventually experienced the letdown that results from allowing one's world and self-concept to revolve around the emotional vicissitudes of one man.

The Specialness Factor

"I would rather be dead than ordinary."

"I hate the idea of being just like everybody else."

"He said I was special, and that means everything to
    me."

"I want people to think I'm someone really special."

In my work as a therapist, I hear such statements often. Nearly everyone wants to stand apart from the crowd and be special. Few people, deep down, feel otherwise.

The question of whether or not we are special, and the proving ground we choose to resolve it, is often dealt with at an unconscious level. And, while specialness is not an issue connected exclusively with sensation-seeking, sensation-seeking almost always encompasses the concept of specialness. Within the dramas we create—or the healthy excitements we pursue—there lie priceless opportunities for establishing our specialness. And most of us take advantage of them.

The struggle to find one's special place in the world is not gender-specific, nor is the experience of excitement that stems from the challenge aspect of that struggle. For men, however, these challenges seem to be related most commonly to expressions of independence and achievement in traditionally masculine areas of performance—sexual, athletic, or financial. For many women, specialness and excitement become overly aligned with affiliation, approval-seeking, and dependency.

Jillian and Barbara chose the most taxing kinds of relationships in the attempt to satisfy their needs for excitement and specialness. An impossible man is immediately exciting to such a woman, for if she can conquer him—or even come close to doing so—she has proof that she *must* be special. Specialness is validation; it is permission to *be.*

The concept of specialness comes up again and again in therapy, particularly in women who evidence the highest level of sensation-seeking drive. It may be that such women *were* quite special as infants and young children—more active, more talkative, more exploratory. Adults respond differently to babies who have energy and personality, and though every parent is said to see something unique in each child, it is true that all babies don't pop into the world equally adorable. "Special" children always know, in a place deep within, that they are chosen. The message is communicated, in one way or another. The problems arise at the point when caretakers fail to validate a special child—an accident that is inevitable and can occur at any time.

The "fall from grace" that Barbara experienced after her mother's death would have happened sooner or later even if her mother had lived. No child can amass reinforcement, or "strokes," indefinitely. For many such children, the strokes are snatched away quickly. The child's majesty as the center of the universe becomes a short-lived dream, often only barely remembered yet subconsciously everpresent and psychologically dynamic. It is likely that these children then become torn by a lifetime challenge: to regain lost paradise by proving oneself worthy of inhabiting it again. And for women, by and large, it is through relationships (Challenger style or otherwise) that proof is established. Once again, that is *our* "special" domain.

The rewards of relationship challenges are similar to the rewards of all other styles of drama-seeking. If we come out ahead we feel especially prized—for a while. If we don't, our self-worth is diminished, and we sink into feelings of failure and misery—for a while. But either way, *we are aroused in the process.* Stimulation becomes an end in itself, and the excitement inherent in the stirring cliff-hanger—Will I make it, or won't I?—is temporarily self-sustaining. The dramatic questions we force ourselves to answer also become a luxurious source of tension in these situations. Will he call, or won't he? Will he be angry at me, or won't he? At least *one* hunger, the hunger for excitement and sensation, is being fed, and it is being fed in a decidedly "feminine" manner. It is the adventure that we come to savor, not the specific outcome. While we may need some conquests to spur us on, any conclusion—win, lose, or draw—will mark the beginning of a new competition and a new drama.

It is partly because of their need to be special that some women lose interest once they've penetrated their lovers' emotional armor—once the quarry, so to speak, has been bagged. This is a characteristic that we have been more willing to attribute to men than to ourselves. The unwelcome truth is that some women get bored once the formerly unattainable objects of their desire are within reach, or once they have discovered the flaws and weaknesses in the paragons of masculinity they thought they had conquered. These women then need someone new—someone as unattainable as *he* used to be—to fire them up, to make them feel challenged, aroused, and, most of all, *special* again.

Power and Specialness

An additional thread running through the lives of all Challengers, and linked to the specialness factor, concerns power. When a woman pursues impossible men, and appears to "get" them, she feels not only special but powerful. It seems that she's tamed a tiger, and the power of victory gives her a rush more ferocious than that of any drug. High on the conquest, she is filled with the force of her own, suddenly exaggerated ego strength. But the power derived from romantic challenge is illusory.

Consider this: if you have absorbed the belief that men are superior to women—a belief inherent in the feeling that you "need" a man or that you are "nothing" without one—and you are then able to capture and control the most unattainable man, you will feel as if you possess amazing power, power that is even greater than the power of that man to resist you.

However, just as the other side of specialness is ordinariness, the other side of power is helplessness. And just as most people run from the fear of being ordinary, they also rush to escape the helplessness they so often feel. In conquering an impossible man, a woman may achieve respite from a sense of enveloping helplessness. Capturing such a man is, in a sense, a symbolic victory over all the miseries and tragedies that are otherwise out of her control. The subtle self-deception is this: If I can achieve this kind of "impossible" goal, then perhaps I can control anything. But our triumph is usually short-lived, for in most instances our captives have more control over us than we have over them. Since we've come to need them so desperately to bring us a sense of power and specialness, we are incredibly vulnerable to the slightest change in their manner. The moment they show any sign of detachment, any small indication that we can't control their behavior toward us, we sink into feeling powerless again—and we are right back where we started, seeking a new drama.

Quick Fixes and Letdowns

Barbara and Jillian found exciting challenges and empty conquests to keep them going. Yet, except for the excitement, neither of them found what they were looking for in these relationships. The love and self-respect, the feeling of true specialness and personal power they yearned for, remained out of reach. And both of these relationships were visibly lacking in intimacy.

Exposing oneself to intimacy is rarely in the best interests of meeting a relationship challenge. Since so much of the contest involves "making" the lover do something or otherwise strategizing and manipulating his feelings, for a woman in such a relationship to permit herself to be genuine and self-revealing would be to risk an undesirable response and perhaps to reduce her odds of outperforming the competition. If the goal is to win a person, not to establish the most sincere relationship possible, the honesty and guilelessness that is so much a part of intimacy would only get in the way.

Quick-fix, episodic excitement alone could not produce intimacy, even if we wanted it to. Intimacy demands a certain level of stability and consistency; it demands trust and mutual respect; and it demands a level of friendship and interdependence that is impossible to achieve in a roller-coaster relationship. In a healthy, loving, intimate relationship, we feel truly special inside; we feel lucky, and blessed—a sensation with which the erratic highs of romantic challenge can't compete.

Excitement alone promises neither intimacy nor love, but intimacy and love do promise excitement. When we aren't sure of ourselves, intimacy is the ultimate emotional risk. To open ourselves up, to move past games and control, would be to place ourselves in mortal danger of being *known* to another. We fear that if we were then rejected or abandoned, we could never recover from the pain— because the rejection would be of *us,* not of an act or an image.

As long as we chase excitement in challenging, dramatic relationships, we will accomplish the following, thus continuing to impede our own personal growth and sabotaging the happiness we desire:

- We will satisfy, at least partially, our taste for excitement—but we will neglect healthy goals and ambitions that provide thrills without cost and that stir pride in genuine achievement.
- We will remain safely entrenched in our "appropriate" gender role—but we will never know the freedom of going beyond its limited boundaries.
- We will occupy a place in which the worst that can happen is familiar to us, probably compatible with the worst that happened during our childhoods, and therefore the most consistent element in our lives—but we will never know the excitement of independence from, or resolution of, the past.
- We will continue to see other women as adversaries rather than as friends united by similar struggles and joys—but we will deny our responsibility for perpetuating a drama that forces other women into the role of antagonist.
- We will repeatedly test our specialness against the same narrow criteria—but we will never give ourselves a grade high enough to justify an end to the testing.
- We will avoid facing the fears or risking the pressures, responsibilities, and confusions of intimacy—but we will never know its joys or rewards, and we will continue to wonder why we aren't fulfilled in our relationships or in our lives.

Having explored the patterns manifest in the lives of Challengers, we now turn to the Rebel. In the next chapter we will examine one of the Rebel's primary ways of culling sensation from personal drama, the especially risky and defiant style of sexual thrill-seeking.

6 &

The Rebel, Part I:
Sex and the Sensation-Seeker

Terry is a single, independent woman who works as an associate producer on a local television talk show. In the course of her work she meets many attractive men, and she has slept with a great number of them. She tells her friends that the *most* exciting part of her job is "turning on all those gorgeous men."

Karla has been married for nine years and has two sons. Her husband thinks that every Wednesday night she plays tennis and has a late dinner with female friends. Actually, she joins her single friends at a disco and often picks up men, with whom she has quick sexual flings. When she arrives home at two or three in the morning, her husband chalks it up to the fact that "women are like that—they can talk and talk all night."

Rita arrived home from her vacation in Cancun especially exuberant because on the return trip she had become a member of the thrill-seeker's "mile-high club"—that is, she had met a man on the airplane and had had sex with him during the flight. She hadn't "bothered" to ask him to use a condom.

In this chapter we'll be talking about the kind of sexual/erotic excitement-seeking (distinct from romantic excitement-seeking) that can reasonably be considered "playing with fire." It is a pattern that reflects one aspect of the dramatic style that is fueled by risky and socially defiant behaviors, the style of drama-seeking whose adherents I call Rebels. Women who are sexual thrill-seekers find drama and excitement in being sexual renegades, in defying rules about what makes a girl "good," and in approaching situations that are both sexy *and* perilous.

This chapter is not about relationships, since the sexual adventurer's partner is, to a certain extent, her sexual "toy." The partner either hints of being, or actually *is,* a source of emotional or potential physical danger (and these days, amidst the tragedy of the AIDS epidemic, casual sex of any kind is dangerous). For some women, danger itself is a tremendous erotic stimulant.

In exploring the world of the sexual Rebel we are dealing with extremes. In my experience, only a minority of women prove to be hard-core sexual thrill-seekers; this is especially true today because of the added health risks. Yet, the emotional lessons that are magnified in the lives of sexual Rebels can hold meaning for all women, even those whose sexual style is, comparatively, far less adventuresome.

What Is Sexual Thrill-Seeking?

There are many stages of titillating sexual interplay that resemble or lead to, but are not exclusive to, sexual thrill-seeking. Consequently, it's important to delineate which behaviors are part of a thrill-seeking scenario and which are not. In commenting upon these behaviors, it is not my intent to moralize or judge but only to explore their potential for cost or reward.

Teasing

Flirtatious teasing—an exciting but seemingly harmless act—can be either an end in itself or the prelude to a sexual encounter. It may constitute a mild (non–thrill-seeking) or dangerous (thrill-seeking) form of playing with fire, depending upon who is teasing whom, in what context, with what intent, and with what frequency.

The flirtatious repartee between single people interested in exploring a one-to-one relationship is not playing with fire at all; rather, it is usually just one of the first steps in a typical dating waltz. On the other hand, teasing between strangers *can* be playing with fire, either mildly or seriously, depending on the context and degree.

Take the example of two strangers, a man and a woman, seated next to each other on an airplane and engaging in conversation that has light sexual overtones. When such repartee is meant to be a meaningless pastime on a long, boring flight, there is only a small fire—that is, a small risk—between them, one that is naturally extinguished when the plane lands. If the man were to take the flirtation seriously and forcefully press the woman for more than talk, the fire would suddenly be fueled—though usually controllably. For the woman the situation might prove uncomfortable, exciting, or both. But her experience, although it would entail an element of playing with fire, would not *by itself* constitute rebellious thrill-seeking.

In the above scenario, it is possible that the come-on contained in the teasing is sincere on the part of both people. They might genuinely like and be attracted to each other and wish to carry their dialogue further. If they are single, that might not present a problem. But if the woman is married and the teasing holds the potential for a sexual encounter, she would be playing with a raging fire. Nevertheless, the teasing itself, risky as it may be, would not *in this isolated context* denote a pattern of erotic thrill-seeking.

The kind of sexual teasing indicative of the sexual Rebel is frequent and reckless. Some women—whether married or single—*constantly* tease people indiscriminately and inappropriately (their boss, their best friend's husband, an important client, the driver of a car stopped beside them at a red light). For these women, the "teases" are often first scenes in very risky, personally compromising larger dramas that quite often *do* lead—deliberately, "unintentionally," or even forcibly—to sexual acts.

Extramarital Affairs

Among married women, having affairs *can* be an ongoing means of procuring sexual thrills. In most cases, however, affairs are sought for different reasons. The needs that propel a woman into one go far beyond thrills for their own sake. A married woman who has an affair usually seeks the combination of emotional and sexual satisfaction, attention, and companionship that is missing in her marriage.

Different dynamics are usually at work when a married woman (or a woman in a committed relationship) engages in a *series* of sexual liaisons. Married women who sleep with multiple partners often expose themselves to ongoing personal and health dangers and at the same time seriously jeopardize their primary relationships. Such women are attracted to, and generally motivated by, the heightened excitement, danger, risk, and consequent drama inherent in sexual adventures. They are sexual thrill-seekers.

Multiple Sexual Partners

Among single women, engaging in multiple or serial sexual relationships may constitute thrill-seeking, but it may also be otherwise motivated. Many single women engage in brief periods of sexual adventuring that some critics judge to be immoral, but which most therapists would agree are rarely *psychologically* harmful. These women, often upon gaining a previously withheld freedom (such as moving away from home or getting a divorce), feel the need to affirm their independence by exploring the world of sexual sensation. Unlike thrill-seekers, they are likely to be discriminating in their choice of partners, relationship-oriented in approach, and careful about birth control and safe-sex practices. Although these actions occasionally still lead to unfortunate consequences, they generally represent a stage in a process of personal growth rather than part of a drama-seeking lifestyle.

In contrast, some single women have numerous one-night stands over an ongoing period of many months or years. They sleep with men whom they don't know well or whom they may not even like or respect—partners who are wild and exciting sexually, but who often treat them without caring or consideration when they're *out* of bed. These women deny their feelings about such treatment for the sake of the intrigue and exhilaration of each interlude.

In essence, sexual thrill-seeking is distinguished from "typical" sexual exploration by its inherent risk and danger. The possible costs of sexual risk-taking may be personal, professional, and emotional, or they may be physical, even life-threatening.

If You Are a Sexual Thrill-Seeker . . .

Sexual thrill-seeking and sexual drama usually put their stamp upon the quality of our lives in a self-diminishing way. The *ongoing presence of risk and danger* in one's sexual relationships is a clear indication that they are thrill-seeking exploits. In addition, sexual thrill-seeking frequently evokes dramatic conflict in other relationships.

If you are a sexual thrill-seeker, many of the following statements will reflect thoughts, feelings, and actions that are familiar to you:

- When you are feeling especially bored, frustrated, or lonely, you often go someplace where there is a good possibility of meeting someone with whom you can be sexual or at least engage in an arousing and suggestive flirtation.
- Much of the excitement in your sexual adventures is in the buildup, in the suspenseful or titillating interplay that occurs long before you ever get to bed. The tension of wondering whether it will happen and, if so, how it will feel is often more thrilling than the sexual event itself.
- You often tease people with whom you have no wish to have sex. Teasing makes you feel so powerful that you often do it with people who take you seriously, even when you yourself are not serious. You've experienced, or barely skirted, being physically threatened or hurt as a result of this.
- Many of your adventures involve lovers who would probably be unacceptable to you as long-term partners. You may consider them too young, too old, too tough, too crude, or too weird—but their very inappropriateness is part of their appeal.
- You often feel emotionally unfulfilled and empty during or after a sexual encounter. What felt exciting initially suddenly seems meaningless.
- You try to live out most of your sexual fantasies, even if doing so is frightening and means trusting people who are strangers. You are sometimes aware that the danger and risk are your most potent turn-ons.
- You are often anxious to "get rid of" your lover after sex; you usually don't like to spend a whole night with anyone.
- Part of the drama in your adventures stems from "playing for an audience"—that is, when a friend asks you what's new, you entertain her with the whos, wheres, and how goods of your last sexual encounters. Sometimes you make them sound a lot better than they were.

- It is not unusual for you to sleep with someone only once or twice.
- Your sexual adventuring has caused trouble in at least one personal or professional relationship that was important to you.
- Sometimes after a sexual encounter you feel guilty and tarnished.
- Your adventures are episodic; you get involved when the mood strikes you, sometimes without respect to conflicting plans already on the night's—or the next morning's—agenda.
- You rarely take the potential consequences of your adventures seriously. Saying "I won't get caught" or "Nothing bad will happen to me" is your way of dealing with the question of possible pitfalls.

In every act of sexual rebellion, the costs and payoffs of personal melodrama are potentially present. While sexual thrill-seeking can evoke the sense of heightened aliveness, the suspense, the feeling of specialness, and the command of center stage that make drama appealing, it can also produce deep pain, reinforce a sense of low self-esteem, limit personal power, and help submerge important feelings. An act of sexual adventuring is a full-scale, archetypal melodrama. The more dangerous or risky it is, the more representative of drama it becomes.

Sexual Rebellion versus Sexual Addiction

Having distinguished between the Rebel's erotic thrill-seeking and the sexual exploration typical of many contemporary women, it's important to discuss briefly the difference between sexual thrill-seeking and sexual addiction. These two patterns are separated only by a fine line and can be easily confused.

The most critical difference between the sexual addict and the sexual adventurer is that the addict is at the mercy of her compulsiveness, while the sexual thrill-seeker is not. In some cases this is the only distinction between them, but it is a major one. To understand this difference fully it is necessary to look at the sexual-addiction cycle.

According to Patrick Carnes, Ph.D., author of *Out of the Shadows: Understanding Sexual Addiction,* sexual addiction involves a four-step cycle that intensifies with each repetition. In the first step, *preoccupation,* the addict becomes obsessed with the search for sexual stimulation. The source of stimulation may include masturbation, strip shows, porno shops, telephone sex, prostitutes, heterosexual or homosexual relationships, exhibitionism, voyeurism, molestation, and even rape.

In the second step, *ritualization,* the addict engages in his or her own special routines that intensify the preoccupation and add arousal and excitement. The addict rarely deviates from these rituals, because they contain sensory cues that automatically trigger sexual arousal.

In the third step, *compulsive sexual behavior,* the addict completes the sexual act. *Addicts are unable to stop or control this behavior.*

The fourth step is *despair,* which is described by Carnes as the feeling of "utter hopelessness addicts have about their behavior and their powerlessness."

The element that distinguishes the sexual addict from the sexual thrill-seeker is compulsivity. As Carnes states, "Sexual addicts are hostages of their own *preoccupation.* Every passerby, every relationship, and every introduction to someone passes through the sexually obsessive filter. More than merely noticing sexually attractive people, there is a quality of desperation which interferes with work, relaxation, and even sleep."

In the grip of compulsivity, the sexual addict leads a secret life. Even her closest friends may never suspect her preoccupation. Her addiction forces her to remain isolated and removed from intimate associations, lest others discover the truth. She is aware of the unmanageability of her habit, and, like addicts of any kind, she lives in an agony of self-hatred and self-pity.

Sexual thrill-seekers, on the other hand, usually share tales of their exploits with close friends. In the absence of rigid rituals and compulsivity, their adventures seem to them like "fun and games," at least for a time. While excitement and suspense are present in, and crucial to, the experiences of both the addict and the thrill-seeker, the thrill-seeker is able to stop her behavior when the potential consequences become serious. The sexual addict continues her rituals in spite of penalties as severe as arrest and public humiliation.

Sexual addicts generally come from severely dysfunctional families. Their backgrounds commonly include family alcoholism, physical abuse, emotional abuse, and sexual abuse. The child who is sexually abused receives the message that in order to have a relationship, she must be sexual. Consequently, *all* relationships are sexualized.

The sexual thrill-seeker does not necessarily come from such a background. More likely, her family was either emotionally abusive or nonabusive but highly traditional and restrictive, with male and female roles clearly delineated. For such a woman, sexual thrill-seeking might have become a means of coping with the internal conflict between her natural yearnings for freedom and the exhortations of her traditional upbringing.

We shall now look more closely at the sexual Rebel's various methods of playing with fire, and at the unique appeal and costs of each—from teasing and seduction to daredevil sexual exploits.

The Thrill of Seduction

Sexual flirtation, teasing, and seduction are related means of playing with fire. Teasing holds power. For women dominated by men, teasing is a means of momentarily gaining control of a relationship. Having the ability to arouse a man, to manipulate him, is to command dominance. In a system that still diminishes women in relation to men, the sexual manipulation of men is for some women a primary, and sometimes the only, means of asserting power. For these women, sexual teasing that culminates in seduction is an intense, thrilling, sensation-rich means of affirming their power over a man's legendary—and often very real—"weakness."

Seduction also produces tremendous risk and suspense. "What will happen next?" and "Where will this lead?" are questions that, by themselves, allude to both exciting and frightening possibilities. Consequently, the act of seduction carries with it degrees of psychological and physical arousal unmatched in ordinary interaction. And the seduction ritual offers subtleties of sensation that are not inherent in more straightforward exchanges. To capture the essence of the experience, stop for a moment and play with the following fantasies:

> You are dining with a man to whom you are highly attracted. You desire him. You want to seduce him. You want him to want you.
>
> Imagine you are carefully, deliberately teasing him with your words, with your eyes, with the suggestively lingering strokes of your fingertips over the back of his hand. Enjoy his response; see the arousal mirrored in his gaze. Notice that you, too, are becoming more sexually aroused, more emotionally excited, even more anxious, as his temperature rises.

Now, imagine deliberately withdrawing, calming yourself and changing the topic, appearing to disregard the previous mood. You pull back just enough to unsettle him. Observe his discomfort, his confusion, perhaps his annoyance, and know you are controlling and manipulating his emotions. Know you can tease him again in a moment, and force another change in his feelings. Experience the power of playing with him in this way; feel your heart beat faster and your breath come shorter as your own excitement, fueled by that thrilling rush of power, suddenly swells.

Now, imagine the same seductive ritual directed toward someone to whom you are not especially attracted but who is in a position of authority over you. Immerse yourself in the emotions evoked by the sudden rebalancing of power when he is no longer in control—and you are.

The above fantasies encompass just the first five or ten minutes of a seduction. But if such intense excitement, such heady affirmation of power can be experienced in such a brief time, it is no wonder that a long, protracted seduction dance can be so compelling.

Many sexual thrill-seekers do not limit their seductions to men with whom they hope to have an ongoing relationship. They tease, seduce, and attempt to mesmerize nearly everyone. The sexual thrill-seeker may pursue the combined sensations of excitement and power so indiscriminately that she finds herself swept away by the velocity of the teasing, which is often carried out of control into full-fledged sexual interludes that she never intended. And it is in these situations that she can get hurt—emotionally and physically.

When power and validation are derived from the thrill of seduction, the emotional costs are often far greater than the benefits. No one can be totally successful in all her seductions. When a woman's sense of self-worth rests upon this kind of validation, a rejection may trigger depression, plummeting self-esteem, and feelings of helplessness.

Even in a successful seduction, if we were to view the elements related to power as a predictable formula we would see a sequence that looks something like this:

Powerlessness → teasing → arousal (his) → arousal (yours) → validation → feeling powerful → sex acts (or end of seduction) → powerlessness → teasing the next man → arousal (his), and so on.

For many women, the stimulation generated by the seduction ritual is continued in a sexual encounter. In some cases a woman may be more psychologically turned on by the power she feels than sexually aroused by the man she is teasing. In either case, however, the sexual act can leave her feeling more emotionally vacant, lonely, and helpless than before. Try as we might, most women have great difficulty separating sex from emotion once the excitement wanes. After the sexual interlude, many women feel as though "something" is missing—usually, this something is caring, love, a relationship—and it is an unpleasant recognition. Unfortunately, it is one that is often forgotten during the next seduction, in the heat of renewed passion and power.

In instances when teasing does not lead to sex, once the teasing has ceased and the effects of the "power fix" have dwindled away the woman must face herself. The feelings of inferiority and helplessness that are part of the woman's self-perception resurface. In most cases, the cycle revolves 360 degrees: powerlessness is reexperienced, and another teasing, seductive ritual is begun.

One of the betrayals in teasing for power is that real power is never affirmed. The woman who feels so powerless that she must play on what she considers the weaknesses of others to feel worthwhile cannot find genuine personal power in sexual exploits. A sense of personal power emanates from within. It includes the recognition that you are in charge of your own life and responsible for yourself and your actions. It includes having confidence in your ability to set goals and achieve them. It constitutes the belief that you are a worthwhile and important individual, just the way you are. A sense of personal power comes from valuing yourself. Sexual thrill-seeking never confers real power, no matter how many people a woman seduces. These adventures, while risky, energizing, and stimulating, neither demand nor instill the genuine courage, integrity, and self-worth that are the basis of a sense of personal power.

Married Thrill-Seekers

Married women comprise the smallest percentage of sexual Rebels. For them, the perils in sexual thrill-seeking are compounded. Should their adventures be discovered, they risk losing the security that their family lives provide—yet this is precisely the risk upon which their excitement often turns.

Chris's story illustrates how and, most importantly, *why* such women pursue dangerous sexual adventures, and it also reveals the pain and confusion their exploits so often bring them.

Chris's Story

During her first therapy session, Chris sat curled in a chair opposite me. She was a gray specter: her sweater was gray, her jeans were faded gray, and her skin was like gray marble. She stared into her lap, then at the walls. She never looked at me.

Chris had come to see me because her sexual adventures were threatening to destroy her marriage. And her husband didn't even know of them.

"Sometimes I think I'm going to explode," Chris said. "I think I'm going crazy." Her eyes met mine for the first time.

"I have it all, you know. A husband who loves me, the best twelve-year-old daughter, a lovely house . . . a perfect little world."

She shook her head. "I know I should be happy. I have so much more than most people. So why did I do this? Why did I put myself and my family in jeopardy?"

Chris had begun to have short, unemotional, purely sexual affairs with young men she picked up in bars, restaurants, even at work. She came to see me following her eighth episode in only four months. She realized that the man involved in her latest episode was "really quite crazy"—a quality she had initially found intriguing but now realized she had underestimated. At the end of their only evening together, he had forcefully insisted upon seeing her again. She had refused, but had considered his aggressiveness sexy. However, she became frightened when he followed her home and, in the street adjacent to her house, loudly threatened to reveal her indiscretion to her husband if she didn't agree to meet him the following week.

> It was the strangest moment. Part of me found it thrilling. Here was a man who wanted me *so* much he would do anything to see me again. I was tingling inside, my heart was pounding, my mouth was so dry I could hardly speak. I was physically, sexually, totally turned on. But there was another part of me saying wait a minute, this guy's a nut and could ruin my life!

Chris agreed to see him again, in part because she wanted to play out the scenario to its conclusion, and in part because she was terrified of what would happen if she didn't agree. Two days before they were to meet she called him and said she was afraid she'd contracted a venereal disease. As she expected, he backed off—but she was shaken badly, suddenly aware of the real jeopardy in which she had placed herself.

> I feel like I'm pulled in two different directions, and it's killing me. I appreciate and love my family, but I still think about that moment on the street with that crazy man. I don't know what's wrong with me . . . Sex has always been good with my husband, but the excitement of someone new, someone different, is just incredible.

As Chris told me more about herself I began to see that for most of her life she had behaved in ways most people consider to be appropriately "female." Although she had been "a little bit wild" in college, when she met her husband, Ron, in her senior year she found him to be the picture of kindness and stability, a man with whom she felt she could happily "settle down."

Chris and Ron had a daughter after three years of marriage. A few years later, Chris began working in real estate part-time, and she eventually built a full-time career. Like the majority of women who married in the early seventies, she also took on complete responsibility for running the home. With three full-time jobs to juggle—homemaker, mother, and professional—she grew secretly angry and resentful. She began to view her home life as mundane, exhausting, and tedious. She even began to dislike her job—another arena in which "someone was always demanding, demanding, demanding!"—but she was just as afraid of reevaluating her career as she was of suggesting to her husband and daughter that they take on more responsibility for the home and for themselves.

"I felt I should have been able to do it all, but I was stressed out. There was no excitement, and not even much satisfaction, in getting up every day."

Chris's first sexual adventure occurred when her frustrations reached the boiling point.

> I had come home from work, and it seemed like everyone was placing more demands on me. "Help me with my homework, Mommy." "What's for dinner, hon?" I said I had to go show some houses and that they'd have to fend for themselves. That alone surprised them—I'd always made sure they were fed before I met with a client at night.

I remember getting in the car and just *going.* I drove up the coast and was hours away from home when I stopped at a roadside restaurant for a Coke. I don't know what made me start to do it, but I began flirting with this man at the bar. He couldn't have been more than twenty-five, good-looking in a sort of punk way. He responded as though I were someone really special. I hadn't felt so alive, so turned on in months. I spent the next four hours in a motel with him, then I got up and went home. I felt . . . powerful. I thought, ha ha, everybody thinks I'm just a middle-aged *hausfrau*—well, have I got news for them! I was thinking at the time of Ron, of everyone who knew me as "Mrs." or "Mom."

For Chris, rebellion through erotic thrill-seeking had become a reaction to the constraints of her traditional life and a way of imposing a sexual identity upon her otherwise asexual self-perception, momentarily turning "Mrs. Mom" into a suburban siren. In each sexual episode she could briefly escape her daily world and experience all the tantalizing sensations that were otherwise muted by its stresses. Above all, she could revel in the feelings associated with risk, danger, and power—three strong stimulants that were absent from her "real" life.

Sheltered Risks

What makes sexual rebellion so alluring to some women, at least at some point in their lives? The answer is complex and is only partly related to sexuality.

Some women become sexual Rebels in part because it seems to be a way of reconciling the emotional conflicts imposed by their upbringing and background—a highly individual matter. They also turn to sexual rebellion partially because there is immense potential for excitement, sensation, and drama in sexual interplay. In addition, this style of drama-making is a way of spurning the rules about what it means to be "good." Many women perceive sexual rebellion as a symbol of freedom.

Rebellion implies defying rules of conduct that are accepted and adhered to by the general population or by the groups with which we are affiliated. Those rules may range from "You do not wear clothes without a designer label" to "You must not sleep with your neighbor's spouse."

There are special rules that dictate the behavior of males and females. These include such rules as "Girls should not be aggressive" and "Boys should not cry," as well as "Husbands should make more money than their wives" and "Wives should do the laundry." They also include such subtle rules as "Women should listen raptly when men speak" and "Men can interrupt women at any time during conversations."

There are two categories of rules that women, specifically, might seek to break or try to change. The first encompasses rules that have to do with being "a girl." To break such rules means to defy convention in an obvious way—such as being aggressive—and to risk being called "unfeminine," having women judge you and men reject you. In lieu of that, women who wish to rebel can break rules that concern being a *good* girl. In rebelling against good-girl rules we can be bad, and do "bad-girl" things, without risking the censure of acting inappropriately for our sex role. For example, since good girls are permitted to cry, bad girls not only cry but also have tantrums and throw plates.

For many women, "being bad" means just being a bad girl. And to many men, bad girls are quite appealing. Driving too fast, associating with dangerous men, taking drugs, shoplifting, and sleeping around are among the means of twisting the rules of what makes a girl good without defying the "girl" rules about what is appropriately female.

Playing with the rules that define our female role would mean defying, or working to change, the social, economic, political, and power structures (including the power structures within our intimate relationships) that demand different behaviors of, and provide unequal opportunities for, women and men. Charging an employer with sexual harassment means breaking the girl rules. So does insisting that your husband share the household chores fifty-fifty, or putting your career plans ahead of your fiancé's pressure to get married. So does starting your own business and fighting for the "equal opportunity" loan that you qualified for but were denied. Famous breakers of the girl rules include Gloria Steinem, Amelia Earhart, Gertrude Stein, Lily Tomlin, Bella Abzug, and Gloria Allred.

It is often much more frightening to risk breaking the girl rules than to risk rebelling against the good-girl rules. In being a bad girl, women are still attached to and protected by men, but in defying the girl rules they are, in a sense, cast adrift to fend for themselves.

For many women the lure of defiance against the girl rules repeatedly clashes with the desire for security. The imagined adventures of freedom and independence conflict with the longing for stability, approval, love, and protection that seem only to accompany dependency. As Colette Dowling wrote in *The Cinderella Complex*, ". . . in early childhood, *girls become convinced that they must have protection if they are going to survive.*" She suggests that as a result, when most women have a chance to become more independent, they retreat "[because] women are not used to confronting fear and going beyond it. We've been encouraged to avoid anything that scares us, taught from the time we were very young to do only those things which allow us to feel comfortable and secure. *In fact, we were not trained for freedom at all, but for its categorical opposite—dependency.*"

I believe it is our deep-seated fear of independence, coupled with the fantasies of power and its pleasure that might lie beyond the fear, that taunt us, excite us—and lead us into moments of reckless abandon. In this respect, fear can be both a barrier and a lure. Rather than entirely avoiding *anything* that scares us, I find that we are often selective in confronting our fears. We often test ourselves by gingerly approaching the source of our fears in the same way a child might slowly move toward a dog she wants to pet but is afraid will bite her—neither backing away entirely nor reaching out to touch. Like the child, we struggle painfully between our own opposing, but often equally strong, desires.

We want excitement, but we want security. We don't want to be constrained, but we don't want to be abandoned. We want the fun of being bad girls, but we want to be protected like good girls.

Some women cope with these contradictions by finding ways of rebelling, playing with fire, teasing themselves with fear, amassing sensation, and feeding their hunger for excitement by taking *sheltered* risks. In essence, they take only the risks associated with breaking the good-girl rules. I call these risks "sheltered" because no matter how much danger is involved, they permit a woman refuge in her acceptable, essentially traditional feminine role.

Sheltered risks allow us to flirt with fear and defiance, to brave certain dangers and their consequences. But they don't require us to rebel directly against "the system," the social structures or relationships that place demands upon us to fulfill our prescribed roles. In addition to sexual adventuring, there are many other paths to sheltered risk for women, such as shoplifting, compulsive behavior, and drug use. Such issues will be dealt with later on.

Chris's sexual adventures might have incurred far more serious consequences than they did. Her acts were risky, but her risks were sheltered. Her life began to change when she stopped rebelling by being a bad girl and began to break the girl rules. When she felt free to say, "This way of living isn't working for me, so I'm going to make some changes" and became respectful enough of her own feelings to take a strong personal stand, sexual risks lost their exaggerated appeal.

Between Actions and Consequences, Fear and Pleasure

The excitement Chris found in each episode of sexual adventure was not related just to the eroticism of the sexual act nor simply to being a bad girl. Her arousal—both sexual and psychological—also emanated from the knowledge that for the sake of the sex and the rebellion it implied, she was facing danger and gambling on avoiding the consequences. Like all women who seek sensation through rebellion, Chris found excitement in those special moments when fear and pleasure mingle.

Playing with fire *always* opens us up to the possibility of getting burned. One of the most thrilling aspects of being bad is that it allows us to ride an exhilarating wave of fear between the commission of an act and the moment when we either come face-to-face with its consequences or realize that we've escaped them. Whatever danger we dabble in, from the moment we first contemplate the act the burning question is this: Will we get away with it—or won't we?

Many women not only enjoy riding a wave of fear, but also strive to force it to a crest again just as it's about to ebb. Sexual thrill-seeking offers many opportunities for increasing the risk factors exponentially in order to maintain the exquisite, excruciating tension some women crave. The more partners one has, the more uncontrollable they are, the more there is to lose, the more "kinky" the sexual behavior, then the more risk, the more fear, the more lingering tension there can be.

In order to really enjoy functioning at such a dangerous level and to derive pleasure from her fear, a woman must minimize the genuine likelihood, that she will come to harm. She must hold two oppositional thoughts in her mind at the same time: "I *could* get hurt" and "*I* won't get hurt." Knowing that she could get into trouble generates the fear, which creates the excitement; trusting that she won't makes her feel confident, special, and justified in her behavior.

The relationship between fear/danger and excitement/pleasure is not nearly as bizarre or abnormal as it may sound. The fact is, at a biological level fear and excitement are linked sensations.

Any dangerous situation produces the human stress-response described in earlier chapters. The physiologically induced by-products of fear-invoking situations can include increases in feelings of personal competence and strong sensations of pleasure. Any risk that provokes fear can be subjectively experienced as pleasurable, especially to the high-sensation seeker, whose system is built to thrive on increased levels of arousal.

Once we recognize that fear and excitement are intertwined, we can understand why fear and sexual excitement are partners in intense sensation. Risk can be an aphrodisiac, because the thrills of fear and sexuality are generated by the same internal mechanism.

The sexiness of fear and risk is well known as it relates to men in battle, who often become sexually aroused during or after an especially dangerous mission. Both female and male athletes have reported becoming sexually aroused by engaging in daredevil sports. Even our language patterns allude to this fundamental connection between fear and sexual excitement. Skiers, for example, often describe perilous jumps as "orgasmic" experiences. And the term *risk* is actually rooted in the French word *"risque."*

Risky sex among committed partners has been frequently documented as a favorite means of spicing up a tired sex life. Secret sex in public places or under circumstances that could prove embarrassing are common exploits, even among otherwise sedate people.

The sexiness of fear also partially explains the appeal that the "bad guy" holds for so many women, whether in real life or in fantasy.

Just as sexual thrill-seeking is related to the experience of fear, it also encompasses the stimulation of being in an agitated state of suspense. As in all our dramas, in sexual drama the question of what will happen next is a running theme. When there are no debilitating aftermaths, the sexual thrill-seeker feels special for having survived unscathed. If her experience was also sexually satisfying, her orgasm becomes a powerful reinforcer that draws her toward the next sexual adventure.

The feeling of specialness that comes from having escaped the consequences of sexual thrill-seeking is exciting in itself. For many women, the surge of confidence and self-esteem is particularly stirring because it is novel. In the midst of sexual drama, the feeling of confidence combines with the intense sensations of erotic arousal to bring about a level of excitement that can be literally breathtaking.

If we find sexual thrill-seeking appealing because it blends the sensations associated with risk and fear, suspense, sexual arousal, and specialness, it becomes even more inviting when certain aspects of an adventure—such as teasing and seduction—evoke a feeling of power. For women who have felt trapped in traditional female roles, the mixture of power and thrill in sexual adventure may be without parallel in their experience.

Sexual Adventuring with Desirable "Undesirables"

The sexual thrill-seeker is often unconscious of the sheltered quality of the risks she takes, but she is always wildly aware of trespassing upon forbidden ground. After all, she remembers the rule: Good girls *don't.*

Some women enhance the excitement of being bad girls by choosing lovers who are truly bad themselves. Such partners seem sexier because they are socially less acceptable, and perhaps even quite dangerous. In addition, for women who deep down fear the insurgent, defiant aspect of themselves, coupling with men who symbolize this aspect is as close to genuine rebellion as they may be willing to get.

Poet Rosemary Daniell once fit the above profile. "I enjoyed the notoriety of the naughty-girl image," she admits. She even wrote a book, *Sleeping with Soldiers: In Search of the Macho Man,* chronicling her adventures seeking the "ultimate excitment." Rosemary was intrigued by the frankly macho men who live dangerously, drink too much, live too fast, and often exhibit a violent form of male chauvinism. She set out on a sexual odyssey to understand their appeal, a journey that embodied both the pleasures and dangers of seeking high sensation through sexuality. I have worked with many women whose sexual thrill-seeking exploits were quite similar to Rosemary's in both expression and intent. Her insights in our personal communications and in her book speak not only for her but for those women as well.

Rosemary was both the embodiment of pristine, cloistered Southern womanhood and the raunchy renegade who strained to escape the "prison of the bourgeois" in which she was raised. In her forties, following three marriages and motherhood, Rosemary turned to sex as adventure, as a means of finding sensation and exploring the world. To her this meant sex with "macho," adventuresome men—soldiers of fortune, oil riggers, paratroopers, contemporary cowboys—whose maleness was exaggerated almost to the point of caricature.

Although Rosemary recognized the appeal of these men, she couldn't face her identification with the qualities that made them attractive, for she considered her own highly adventurous impulses "an aberration." Though she believed that "masculine" risks were out of her league, she settled for getting close enough to them in the grip of lovers who acted out her "secret wildness" and "hidden desires for anarchy." Through them she could reconcile her drive for danger and excitement with her need to remain appropriately female. As she put it, "The more macho the man, the more traditionally feminine—passive and virtuous—I felt. . . . I never experienced anxiety about sex roles with the macho man. With a man who was a Real Man, I was certain of his masculinity and, thus, my femininity."

Rosemary's adventures, like those associated with any kind of drama, had their costs. She told me of a number of incidents in which the men she picked up became threatening. She believes that she survived without getting hurt by handling the men nonconfrontationally, relying on her abundant Southern charm. For example:

> I was spending some time up in the Georgia mountains. I picked up a very good-looking, husky guy, about 250 pounds, and took him back to the cabin—there was nothing around for miles. He was high on Valium, so he had trouble performing sexually and we just went to sleep. The next morning, the snow was falling outside, and we just lay in bed watching it when he turned to me and said, "You know those women in the next county that were raped and murdered? Well, I'm the one who did it."
>
> I laughed, and pretended he was just kidding. I tried to act real cool, real casual, but I was scared. When I got up to get dressed I remember standing with my back to him, putting my sweater over my head—and he suddenly came up behind me and put his big forearm around my neck. I quickly leaned into him, all lovey-dovey, as if he was just being affectionate, and I told him I had to hurry and get dressed because someone was going to be here any second to take me to breakfast. A little while later, thank goodness, a Jeep did pull up . . ."

Rosemary writes in her book of the time one of her lovers, a black-market millionaire dubbed "the Pirate," jerked her diaphragm right out and flung it across the room because he didn't want there to be *anything* between them—"the most macho thing a man had ever done to me." It was the same man of whom she wrote:

I knew in my heart of hearts that my relationship with the
Pirate was sick. But as long as I was uncommitted, I felt I could
afford it. . . . Besides, it was fun to play out in caricature the
roles I had been brought up as a Southern woman to fulfill.
It felt *right* for me to sit beside the bathtub, scrubbing his back
as he talked. *Right*—despite his lack of interest in my life,
career, problems—for me to listen as he obsessed about his
smuggling, business deals, even his wife. *Right*—though he
rarely reciprocated—for me to massage the tension from his
calves, spasming from too many deep sea dives. *Right*—for
him to come to my apartment, fling my towels around, drink
my booze, fuck me, and then leave.

Eventually, sexual adventure grew empty for Rosemary, and she
found herself "encapsulated in perfect loneliness," a prisoner of her
own freedom. However, her experiences had helped her to realize
how much she really needed to *be* the men she sought, how strong
her own yearnings for excitement were, how trapped in convention
she had been in many ways. As she writes, "I could no longer delude
myself that being feminine automatically meant being passive. . . .
The dictionary definition of *'camofleur'* is *'one who conceals military objects
by camouflage,'* and I had long concealed my more masculine impulses behind
my feminine facade"* (my emphasis.)

Today, she is in touch with her own potential for aggression and
adventure. "Instead of making any man a metaphor for the risk-
loving part of myself," she told me, "I have begun doing some of the
things that male adventure-seekers thrive on, and nurturing the adventurous, assertive spirit within myself. Now I take more creative
risks—I use my abilities more adventurously."

At fifty-two, Rosemary is married again ("faithfully"), to a man she
has known for six years. While it was hard for her to take the plunge—
"I am committment-phobic; I fear feeling claustrophobic or lacking
options"—she did it because she regards this man as "the most
prized possession" in her life.

Looking back on her adventures, Rosemary regards them as having
been broadening:

Breaking class barriers, stepping out of my usual milieu at
times, have been highly educational experiences for me.
. . . I don't regret a bit of it. It's been other factors—my early
life and marriages, obligatory or destructive one-on-one relationships, conformity, and boredom—that have been harder
by far for me to deal with in my life.

Many women who have had similar experiences would concur that, in spite of the risks and potential dangers, their sexual adventures were part of a growth process, a learning experience. Other women, especially those who were hurt by their exploits, would vehemently refute the idea that there are overriding benefits to sexual thrill-seeking. While one's position on the subject is certainly an extension of one's unique, personal experiences, I believe that Rosemary illuminated one aspect of the question that holds validity for all women: the issue of being a *"camofleur."*

We cannot live satisfying lives as *"camofleurs."* We cannot deny our drives and our impulses (including our more "masculine" ones), misuse them or, attempt to vicariously feed them without in some way suffering for it. By relating to men as *symbols* rather than individuals, by allowing them to represent an aspect of ourselves that we fear expressing directly, we limit our full development and lose out on the potential for the intimacy we crave as much as we crave adventure. It is difficult for intimacy to grow out of a rebellious sexual encounter, because our hidden motives restrict our ability to relate with trust and emotional integrity. And it is impossible for true adventure to coexist with sheltered risks, for the limitations imposed by such risks are the antithesis of what it means to explore the world freely.

As long as we seek excitement in sexual thrill-seeking, we will accomplish the following and will thus continue to suppress our personal power and growth:

- We will escape the tedious, the obligatory, and the boring—but we will fail to enrich our lives with excitement that offers lasting rewards.
- We will find brief pleasure in our sexuality—but we will remain caught in a web of conventional expectations and inner desires that conflict desperately with one another.
- We will caress danger, safe in the *illusion* of protected femininity—but we will overlook our own inner strengths and fail to develop genuine confidence or find emotional security.
- We will have thrilling adventures that take us beyond the limitations of *proper* feminine behavior—but we will remain bound by the social structures and inequities that diminish us.
- We will come close to venting our aggressive, insurgent impulses by consorting with men who are

"wrong" or "bad"—but we will remain *camofleurs,* stifling very real aspects of our personalities.

- We will wield momentary power over men who want us—but we will grow more out of touch with the genuine power lying dormant inside us.
- We will occasionally feel desirable and special—but only rarely will we feel respected, cared for, or loved.

If sexual adventures provide intense means of seeking drama and sensation in the dangerous or forbidden, they are clearly not the only types of adventure that do so. In the next chapter we'll complete our understanding of the Rebel and explore a diversity of possibilities for sheltered risk-taking.

7 ❧

The Rebel, Part II: Crimes, Compulsions, and Addictions

Paulette: "I'll walk into a store and buy a lovely evening gown I'll never wear. I don't live a fancy lifestyle, but while I'm shopping I pretend I do. I love shopping, but I hate how I feel afterward when I can't pay the bills, and the dunning notices come in or the bill collectors call. Now when the phone rings I get this sick feeling, and I'm afraid to answer it."

Jean: "I've had a love/hate relationship with food almost all my life. It's my friend when I need something to soothe me or make me forget about my problems. When I'm eating, food is all there is, and the rest of life disappears. Afterward, I hate myself for pigging out again. Lately, I've been telling myself over and over that tomorrow I'll go on a diet—but I don't. I've been bingeing almost every day for a month, and I've gained twelve pounds. Nothing fits. I feel disgusted with myself, but I can't stop . . . or maybe I really don't want to."

Randy: "When I was a teenager my parents used to say I was too boisterous, too excitable. They thought I was hyperactive and took me to a psychiatrist, who gave me pills to calm me down. I've been on drugs of one kind or another for almost ten years now. I used to do Valium and Percodan . . . I stole prescription pads from my doctor and wrote my own ticket. Now I'm into mushrooms, MDA, Ecstacy—trippier drugs. I like traveling far, far away, sort of on my own planet . . ."

Paulette, Jean, and Randy are Rebels, and their drama-seeking styles thus always involve a form of playing with fire, of risk-taking and exposure to either emotional or physical danger. Like the sexual thrill-seeker, their risks are "sheltered"—that is, they defy society's expectations of *good-*girl behavior without breaking the rules about what is appropriately female. Women who take sheltered risks become "bad girls," deliberately or unconsciously acting out against social, parental, or spousal injunctions in ways that are far more self-defeating than individualistic or self-actualizing.

Much of the excitement derived from taking sheltered risks is the result of the auto-arousal that inspires, or is provoked by, those risks. As noted earlier, auto-arousal is the process of self-inducing or self-generating stimulation and sensation, of creating drama out of our inner experience. This is not the same as making a big production out of a small event or overreacting to a minor crisis. While in those situations we may transform an externally existing set of circumstances into a drama, to induce auto-arousal we must create the circumstances that trigger a brand-new inner drama—one not initiated by other people or occurrences.

The patterns of auto-arousal toward which the Rebel is drawn are generally negative, obtained through such activities as lawbreaking, overeating, compulsive shopping and gambling, or excessive drinking and drug-taking. Just as the sexual thrill-seeker's exploits involve partners but really have nothing to do with relationships, in these other types of endeavors a woman's primary relationship is not with a lover nor with the substances or behaviors she abuses. The relationship that really matters is the narcissistic, sensory one she has with herself.

While auto-arousal is the *primary* drama-making mechanism for the Rebel alone, it can also appear in the dramas of Fighters and Challengers. The woman who creates conflict and crisis in the lives of others by making trouble enjoys the self-induced stimulation of fantasizing about the agony she causes her victims. The relationship-Challenger's obsessive jealousy of her rival is a form of auto-arousal, as is her preoccupation with every nuance of her troubled love relationship.

It's important to realize that auto-arousal *can* be a positive experience. Daydreaming, fantasy, self-hypnosis, and meditation can all produce safe, constructive, pleasurable experiences of auto-arousal. The creative process is one of auto-arousal, as is the experience of savoring fine food and wine. All of these avenues can be enjoyed without risk or damage to ourselves and the relationships we hold dear.

Auto-arousal loses its constructive nature when it is used in the service of drama-making. Yet, even drama-based auto-arousal can yield certain emotional "benefits"—especially in the way in which it is used by the Rebel. By self-generating specific, preferred sensations, the Rebel effectively blocks her ability to experience other, less desirable feelings. In that sense, auto-arousal serves as a kind of internal buffer, distracting her from, or substituting heightened arousal for, unpleasant emotions.

While auto-arousal offers a perfect blending of stimulation and escape from the painful facets of one's inner life, it offers little else. When old hurts are systematically numbed by drugs or camouflaged by self-induced excitement, there can be no insight, resolution, or freedom from the past. And no matter how hard one tries to keep excitement alive, most highs are followed by plummeting lows, during which the very pains one intended to drown rise to the surface, intensified.

There is great similarity among the Rebel's use of auto-arousal, the Challenger's use of contests, and the Fighter's use of conflict and crisis. In each case, drama substitutes for inner truth and genuine excitement. And, in each case, the drama-seeker is at best only dimly aware that there is a chink in her "reality." The Fighter allows conflict and emotionality to substitute for intimacy; the Challenger allows contest and competition to replace sincere love; and the Rebel permits self-induced sensation to supplant self-awareness and self-expression. Each is actually trapped in a unique "*un*reality," a warped mirror-image of the life she seeks.

In the stories in this chapter, many of the dramatic elements we've seen before—specialness, episodic living, playing for an audience, magnification, and so on—will be evident. Rather than focusing again on these features, we'll center our attention on the unique pleasures and pains experienced by women who find drama in playing with many different types of fire, and we'll discover the complex motives and truths behind their activities.

Getting Started: Adolescent Rebellion

A few years ago at a professional luncheon, the subject of adolescent pilfering came up. Out of eight upright ladies seated around my table, six had found shoplifting a reliable, rebellious thrill. In fact, one of the women at the luncheon admitted that even today she is tempted once in a while to slip "just a little something" into her purse while out shopping to see if she still has "the touch," though she doesn't act on her impulses.

The teenage "selves" within most adults are still very much alive, ready and willing to come out, given the chance. There are times when allowing them to do so is to our advantage—for example, taking one's husband to a drive-in and "necking" in the front seat of the car. But when our *rebellious* teenage selves strive to act out in the same way they did when we were fifteen or sixteen, the results can be disastrous.

Janet used to go to "off-limits" parties during high school. "I'd tell my folks I was going to the movies, and I'd slip into the CYO [Catholic Youth Organization] dances, where all the hoods hung out. You had to say part of the Our Father to get in, so I had to learn it, too. My parents would have been furious—a 'nice Jewish girl' memorizing a Catholic prayer and dancing with 'greasers'!" Today, Janet is still sneaking—but now she does so behind her husband's back, to go barhopping with her single friends. "I don't *do* anything—I just flirt a little and have some laughs. But I know he'd be angry if he knew," she tells me. It seems that once sneaking around had become a part of her life, it remained as a necessary, exciting activity.

As a teen my friend Donna used to cut school, smoke cigarettes in the hallways, and eat lunch off-campus just to see how many rules she could break before being sent to detention. Today she is an avid "ticket collector."

I remember one incident that occurred when I went to see a movie with Donna. She drove, and as we pulled up around the corner from the theater she stopped in a red "No Parking" zone.

"You're in the red," I alerted her, figuring that she hadn't noticed.

"Oh, I know," she replied matter-of-factly. "I'll be fine here—don't worry."

I thought: It's her car, her ticket, her money. Obviously, the twenty-eight dollars couldn't mean as much to her as parking close by. So we saw the film . . . and when we came out we found a parking ticket slapped on the windshield. Donna spent the next five minutes cursing parking enforcers and their silly quotas, the skinflint city government, and the entire system that dared to impede her right to leave her car where she pleased.

"I don't know why you're getting so upset," I said. "You knew you were parking where you could be ticketed."

In response she opened her glove compartment to reveal a stash of tickets an inch thick. She shoved the new ticket on top of the rest.

"Sure," she replied. "But I didn't expect to *get* one!"

As Janet's and Donna's stories exemplify, it is common for behaviors that offered great sensation-seeking value at one stage of life to become habitual later on, leading to a variety of dramatic interludes. For example, in Donna's mini–cliff-hanger, if she wins by not getting ticketed, and thus proves her power over the odds, she experiences great *internal* excitement. If she loses, she has the chance to create another, different kind of internal drama by refusing to pay the ticket. She can also generate an *interpersonal* drama by fighting the ticket in court.

The little buzz of self-generated excitement Donna gets from shrugging off parking restrictions, becoming incensed when she's penalized, and taking dramatic follow-up action is unlikely to bring harm to her or anyone else. However, Anna's exploits are not nearly so benign.

Anna went much further in her teenage rebellion than either Janet or Donna. She hooked up with the leader of a neighborhood gang, tatooed his name on her forearm with a razor and black ink, and hid property stolen by the gang members under her pink canopy bed. More recently, she was charged with possession of five ounces of cocaine, which she insists she was merely "holding for a friend." If so, she apparently still finds it dangerously exciting to keep guilty associations.

Many women endanger themselves (and others) through adult versions of adolescent acts that represent *sheltered* risks. Anna's "adventures" in cocaine possession, for instance, are sheltered because they do not involve statement-making or self-actualizing risks; rather, they are self-defeating.

The Bad Girls of Crime

Like the sexual thrill-seeker, the Rebel who takes illegal risks achieves her excitement in the realm between actions and consequences. Part of her internal drama, her auto-arousal, is generated in that in-between state where the line between fear and exhilaration is blurred.

Crime can hold great allure for any high-sensation seeker, but it often holds a special attraction for middle-class women who don't turn to crime out of economic hardship or peer pressure. By toying with the forbidden and dangerous they can both defy society's rules and, in many cases, create enough strong (and self-selected) sensation to snuff out their inner pain.

Many women who feel personally powerless and insecure and who are concealing a deep, denied reservoir of past anger or hurt thrive on the risk and excitement of breaking laws. These women are the bad girls of crime. Helene's story is in many ways typical of what drives such Rebels to seek excitement through criminal behavior.

Helene: The High Priestess of Mail Fraud

Helene was the youngest of four children. When she was ten, her impoverished parents shipped her off to live with a prosperous aunt and uncle and their two daughters. To this day she angrily wonders, *Of all the children, why me?*

Helene always felt like an outsider in her relatives' home. Even worse, on brief visits to see her parents she felt unwelcome and unloved. But she managed to make herself into a celebrity at school, where, from junior high on, she got noticed by taking chances. Shoplifting, driving without a license, drinking, and going "too far" on dates all gave her an identity and a position of respect among the wilder crowd at school. She was nobody when she was good, but she was special and life was exciting when she was bad.

Helene discovered a comparable thrill only in being onstage. When a teacher urged her to audition for the school play, she proved to be outstanding, and a new world opened up to her. Onstage, she didn't have to be Helene; she could be *anyone.*

Whether stealing or acting, she was able to rise above the others, to rise beyond the everyday. Accustomed to being painfully separate at home, Helene found it thrilling to be *above* instead of merely apart.

As an adult, Helene failed in her attempt to become a success in the theater. Though she landed some good small parts, it was not enough for her to be simply an actress—she wanted to be a *star.* When she left the stage she married a diplomat, a man who was high-powered enough to help her hold on to the illusion of being on top. She soon found that life a bore compared to her theatrical past. Her boredom, mingled with her buried anger at her early rejections, brought her back to that surefire high: crime.

Helene set up elaborate mail-order scams. When I first met her, she told me all about the con game she played. Talking about it clearly excited her tremendously. It was apparent that she not only loved the riskiness of it but also thrived on the excitement of waiting to find out whether she'd be caught. There was an incongruity about watching Helene, the picture of chic, speak in a polished voice about having committed a felony. To understand what motivated her, it is necessary to see that Helene's con was not primarily a game geared toward making money. It was a source of intense auto-arousal, a drama of another, very personal kind, which began and ended within Helene.

"I am the one, true high priestess of the world's most elite coven of witches," she giggled. "I place ads in occult magazines, inviting people who feel they might qualify to apply for membership. I demand a lengthy application and a hefty membership fee. Lots of people are crazy enough to pay it. When enough applications are returned and the checks are cashed, I close my P.O. box and bank account and disappear."

"Do you ever worry about being caught?" I asked.

Again she giggled, a childlike bubble of laughter that didn't quite match her sophisticated veneer. "Of course I think about it! Sometimes when the doorbell rings I get terribly frightened, and I begin to picture myself locked up behind bars. I even start to think about ways to escape and run away. But afterward, when I find it's just the mailman or a solicitor, I get this rush, this feeling of, 'Ha! I've pulled it off again.' When I go to the P.O. box or to the bank to cash the checks, I'm shaking inside. But there's a part of me that's sailing through on a high, and I expect I'm going to get away with it this time, too."

Helene had been pulling this scam for years. She said that her husband knew about it but couldn't stop her. Helene felt special each time she got away with ripping off the naive would-be witches who answered her ads, and special each time she foiled her husband's stern injunctions to quit the game—knowing that because he wouldn't leave her, in his position he could only rage but do nothing. However, deep down Helene felt as invisible, powerless, unwanted, and unexceptional as she had twenty-five years earlier when her parents had sent her away.

Helene might be considered a "successful" con artist, if success is measured by one's ability to keep from getting caught. She might also be considered successful if success is measured by the level of excitement achieved through one's exploits. But Helene feels that these are her only "successes"—and they are not enough to make her happy.

Rebels like Helene satisfy their hunger for excitement through the intensity of the self-induced drama that surrounds their risky acts—the plotting, the anticipating, the suspense, the fear, the relief. Multiple physical, mental, and emotional sensations associated with each of these experiences often rush at them in waves—fear crashing down upon suspense, relief engulfing fear, anticipation inundating relief. As long as they can maintain the flood of sensations, as long as they can continue generating the auto-arousal, these women feel good. But when for any reason the pace of their drama slows, they often experience severe depression.

Depression is in many ways a *non*feeling state. Though it is accompanied by recognizable sensations—for example, lethargy, apathy, and numbness—it is not a state of clear, distinct emotion. Because it is nonfeeling, depression protects us from feeling. We might say it fills the same function as auto-arousal, but in reverse. Auto-arousal conceals undesirable feelings beneath selected, intense sensation. Depression conceals them in a state that is distinguished by the absence of feeling. We might envision depression as a dark cloud that envelops and shrouds all strong, deep feelings that are unacknowledged or unexpressed—a cloud that descends each time a lapse in one's excitement and internal drama occurs, giving it space to gather. While depression can also be the biochemical downside, or "crash," that follows the high of self-induced excitement, for women like Helene it is also evidence that they have not yet plumbed the depths of their feelings. Even when these women are successful in their cons or crimes, they never succeed in soothing their inner pains.

The bad girls of crime are not alone in their tendency to take rebellious, self-defeating, sheltered risks. Some Rebels gravitate toward other activities—especially those that can become addictive or compulsive—that offer risks, rewards, and results quite similar to those found in lawbreaking, and which sometimes actually cross over the line into crime.

Patterns of Abuse

Multiple manifestations of the same essential internal drama, the same kind of auto-arousal, can be played out by driving a stolen car, racking up impossible-to-pay bills at Bloomingdale's, gambling another paycheck in Las Vegas, eating oneself sick at a fast-food restaurant, or smoking crack at a "rock" house. Surrounding all of these situations are similar dramatic rituals, patterns, and elements.

All of these setups for drama involve abuses that frequently lead to addiction or compulsive repetition. There exists today a vast array of literature on the subjects of addiction and compulsion. There is also some debate about the definitions and disease nature of these problems, the point at which an abuse becomes a compulsion or addiction, and the genetic or historical causes of these problems. While these issues are significant, the overall dynamics of addiction are not our focus here. Our concern is with the Rebel's abuse of substances or activities and the means it offers her for defiance, excitement-seeking, and drama-making. While a woman who abuses any drug or activity does so for a multiplicity of reasons, understanding these sensation-seeking components is critical to her understanding and learning to change her behavior.

For our purposes, limited, working definitions of abuse, compulsion, and addiction are in order. We can consider an *abuse* to be any utilization of a normal activity or common substance for other than the legitimate purpose for which it is intended. Eating, for example, is intended to provide nourishment and enjoyment. When we eat in order to cope or until we get sick, we abuse both food and the activity of eating. Certain drugs, such as alcohol and Valium, are intended to be used occasionally, either for purposes of socialization and pleasurable relaxation or as legitimate medication. When they are ingested to excess and used for coping, they are abused.

We can consider a *compulsion* to be a pattern of ritualized abuse, repeated despite obvious consequences. And we can view an *addiction* as a physiological dependency stemming from abuse of a mood-altering substance.

Whether the Rebel's typical drama-making scenarios involve compulsion or addiction, the following four elements are always present:

1. *Auto-arousal.*

2. *Sheltered risk.* Sheltered risk-taking may lead to auto-arousal, or it may follow it.

3. *The potential for interpersonal drama that augments auto-arousal.* This is the secondary level of drama provoked by the Rebel as a result of sheltered risk-taking; it usually takes the form of conflict or crisis with family and friends.

4. *The danger/fear/excitement connection.* This refers to the experience of excitement stemming from the fear-invoking, potentially dangerous quality of an act—that is, the feelings produced in the realm between action and consequence.

A variety of behavior patterns are illustrated in the stories that follow. In each story we can see how the four common elements above are manifested somewhat differently. If you recognize yourself in any of these stories, reading them might be painful or might even make you angry. I urge you to bear with them, however. In the next chapter we'll see that some of the same elements present in these self-defeating scenarios—elements you might be inclined to view as weaknesses—are potential strengths that can become valuable assets in your life.

"When the Going Gets Tough, the Tough Go Shopping"

I recently saw a woman in a shopping mall wearing a T-shirt with the above phrase printed on it. It's one of those "cute" lines that sounds amusing—until we stop to think about what it really means. When the going gets tough, shopping is the *last* place we should go. For many women, however, buying often provides a high that gets out of control.

Marcia, a former member of an organization for compulsive shoppers, was a firstborn child, as are many self-described "shopaholics." Women who shop and spend compulsively frequently come from rigid family environments where there was great pressure to both achieve and conform. That pressure is often greatest for the firstborn.

While Marcia's family had high expectations for her, her needs for affection and self-determination were ignored—first by her parents, and eventually by Marcia herself. As a teenager she shoplifted occasionally. No one ever found out, but she stopped because stealing was just too dangerous for a girl still wed to the approval and security offered by home. As an adult Marcia took to overspending. She was $32,000 in credit-card debt before she stopped. "When I walked into a store, it was just like being drunk," she told me. "I felt euphoric, invulnerable. The sensation was the closest thing to flying I've ever experienced."

Marcia rarely left the house for the express purpose of going shopping, but somehow she always "wound up in a store."

> There were even times when I felt like someone who'd been knocked unconscious—only *I* was revived in the middle of

Saks. I guess I just blocked out my intention and put myself in a sort of mental trance. I could hardly remember *getting* to the store, but there I'd be. Then I'd walk around, not buying yet but just touching and smelling everything—the leather goods with their sweet, heavy scent; the lingerie department, so fragrantly perfumed. Sometimes I'd buy things by smell or touch—a sweater that was especially soft, for instance. Everything took on greater color and texture—I suppose the feeling could be compared to being high on grass.

After an intense, sensory episode in the store—a vivid illustration of the auto-arousal process—Marcia usually tumbled from the heights, wracked by anxiety, guilt, and remorse. This sudden plunge was often translated into further internal drama. Marcia found another, shaky kind of auto-arousal in dramatic self-recriminations, in the constant juggling of bills, and in making herself sick with guilt over her constant financial crunch.

At times, her fears about the potential consequences of her activities (fantasies of bankruptcy and personal humiliation) were mingled with memories of the excitement of shopping. In this way the danger/fear/excitement connection was made within the realm of fantasy. Unlike sexual thrill-seekers and lawbreakers, for compulsive spenders the experience of excitement is unrelated to concrete danger. Yet, their mental images of danger and their fears of embarrassment, of having credit cards rescinded and cars repossessed, or of being unable to continue their shopping sprees are equally stimulating and even more consuming. As Marcia said:

> I used to quake, waiting for the bills to come in, hoping each month that the computers would err and the charges would miraculously disappear. Then I'd put them aside, as afraid to open them as if they were letter bombs. I would scream at myself "How *could* you? Never ever again!"—then I'd go to my wallet to cut up my credit cards, but I'd be unable to go through with it.
>
> I'd think about what would happen if I kept this up, of what people who knew me would say if they found out what I did. Then I'd focus on what it felt like to shop, and I'd start to get excited about it again. "Well, maybe I can just go look around—I won't buy anything expensive," I'd tell myself. But I always did. So, after all that self-torture, I'd go out and spend all over again.

As a compulsive shopper, Marcia took financial and emotional risks nearly every day. But they were sheltered risks, for no matter how in debt she was, in appearance she was just doing what all women supposedly love to do: shop.

Women brought up to be unselfish, to exhibit self-restraint, to be "perfect" and "good" often rebel against the controlled life and all the expectations attached to it by shopping and spending excessively. By abusing an otherwise appropriate activity, they create internal excitement, play with fire, and manage to "flip off" the rest of the world. The primary problem with this bad-girl method of rebelling is that the discontent isn't translated into positive action that changes, or truly reconciles, the very confinements these women oppose. Thus, women like Marcia never feel a sense of real accomplishment or earned confidence.

> Looking back on that period, I see how dissatisfied I was with my life as a whole. I had reached a dead end in my job, but I was afraid to compete for a promotion. I didn't want to fail. I was single and confused about it. I was brought up to believe that I should be married, but part of me was glad not to be. I avoided dealing with any of my feelings. And I did nothing but shop. My closet was jammed with beautiful, expensive clothes and shoes that I never wore because I rarely *went* anywhere. My life was empty, but my wardrobe was full.

Marcia's shopping habit became the central drama, the primary source of stimulation, in her life. She didn't have to risk stretching out toward the world or facing her underlying fears and insecurities. Dramatic episodes were momentarily satiating and completely sheltering. And the ultimate cliff-hanger—waiting to see how far she could go before it all caught up with her—infused her with the final tremor of suspense.

In the act of compulsive shopping, a woman's excitement is self-induced and self-contained. For many women, overspending can also lead to dramatic encounters with creditors, fights with husbands and family members over money, and angry expressions about the unfairness of it all to understanding friends. It is at this point that rebellious risk-taking gives way to Fighter-style conflict and crisis-making. As interpersonal drama briefly replaces internal drama, some women—especially the high-sensation seekers—adeptly cross drama-seeking boundaries to "have it all."

Gambling Against Ourselves

Gambling is exciting. It's a challenge, a thrill, for those of us who do it occasionally—at the racetrack, in the lottery, or during a weekend in Las Vegas or Atlantic City. But for people who abuse this pleasure—people who gamble with money they would otherwise use to pay monthly bills, fund a child's college education, buy a new car, or start a business—an otherwise entertaining diversion becomes a serious affair.

Gambling with chips rather than taking meaningful, real-life risks can generate drama without providing satisfaction or resolution. Like all styles of personal melodrama, this one is episodic and always suspenseful, and it always places us in the spotlight. Much like Challengers, who may "win" a man but can't stop looking for a romantic contest, Rebel-gamblers may win a roll, but they can't stop the game.

Joan makes a decent living as a hairdresser, but she drops so much of it at the racetrack that money is always tight. Her friend Tina occasionally accompanies her to the track, though she is much more apt to jump into "Pyramid" games whenever they pop up in her area. Both women manufacture great internal drama and create powerful inner dialogues around the tension, fear, excitement, and hope they experience during the time span between making a bet (the action) and learning whether a horse or a Pyramid cycle will make them a winner or loser (the consequence). When either of them loses, she makes great drama of her losses, her deprivation, and the optimistic possibility of recouping "next time."

Although Tina and Joan gamble excessively and experience financial discomfort as a result of their losses, they are not compulsive. For women who are *compulsive* gamblers, the stakes are much higher, involving their businesses, their relationships, even their lives. The example of Charlene shows us the pattern of drama-making that such a dependency can create.

Charlene was an Atlantic City homemaker who was, from all appearances, a *Better Homes and Gardens* variety wife and mother who was content with her life, her husband, and her three children. "But inside, I was restless," she told me.

> I had dreams of opening a boutique, but either my husband's dental practice was down, or his office needed new equipment, or his folks needed his support. I don't think he

ever took my idea seriously, and I was angry that he always
found a use for the money that didn't include my dream.

When Atlantic City became a gaming town, Charlene began to
fantasize that maybe *she* could be the superspecial, lucky lady who
achieves the impossible—beating the odds, BIG.

I imagined I could make enough money to get the shop
started on my own. The first time I played blackjack I won
$382, and I thought I could keep winning. Of course, I
didn't—no one does. I kept going back to try my luck again,
and suddenly I was hooked. The boutique idea seemed like
nothing compared to the excitement of gambling.

From then on, while the kids were at school and her husband was
at work, Charlene was at the table, betting her life on 21.

After a while, whenever I walked into the casino my insides
fluttered and my skin tingled as if someone was running a
feather down my body. It was absolutely sexual. My heart beat
faster, my breathing changed, and my focus became laser-
sharp. Sitting at the blackjack table, I saw and heard nothing
else. I can't tell you what kind of power I felt. I loved winning—it was better than sex. There was an excitement in
beating the dealer and the house that I hadn't found in anything before.

Charlene tried to hide her gambling from her family:

When I was on a losing streak, I lied so easily I barely recognized myself. I began to feel very brave—I opened a secret
bank account, I siphoned off household funds, I even ran-
sacked the petty-cash box at my husband's office. There was
always a tinge of excitement about doing it. I knew that if
anyone saw me it would be terribly embarrassing and that if
my husband found out about the bank account he'd be furious, but that was part of what made it worth doing.

At the tables, when I was winning I was on such a high it
couldn't be concealed. When I was losing, depression drained
every ounce of energy I had. One of the casinos extended me
credit, and when I kept losing there I got really scared. I
imagined horrible things—someone going to my husband to

demand the money I owed, his finding out about my habit and divorcing me, some thug beating me up for the debt. I saw myself in a B-movie, or in newspaper headlines: "Suburban Housewife Slain over Gambling Debt." . . . It was all I thought about.

Charlene was creating internal drama, auto-arousal, by carrying on an "affair" with the gaming tables. Although winning and losing yielded different sensations—winning produced pleasure and a sense of specialness, while losing created the danger/fear/excitement connection—all of those sensations were intensely stimulating.

Charlene's exciting double life was revealed the night she and her husband were scheduled to entertain six couples at their home. The guests appeared, but neither Charlene nor the dinner did. While everyone was frantically calling hospitals, Charlene was cemented to the blackjack table, having lost $2,300 and incapable of leaving until she recouped her losses. When she was down $4,000, Charlene gave up and went home. Having forgotten entirely about the dinner party, she was completely unprepared for her family's barrage of anger.

It was just too much—all that money and then their hysteria. I broke down, sobbing out the whole story. They were stunned. I had played my role so well that no one had ever suspected.

Charlene's dramatic confession shocked her husband, who was appalled by the degree to which gambling had taken over her life. The confession also sparked a new interpersonal drama between Charlene and her husband. They fought over the fact that she had not only lied and stolen to get money but had seemed to enjoy it. They argued over the hidden bank account—he wanted her to close it, and she refused. They battled over *why* she gambled (she blamed him, and he blamed her), the kind of treatment she needed, where she could get it, and which friends and family members to tell. There were endless possibilities for interpersonal drama in the situation, and Charlene and her husband took advantage of many of them.

Only later, in therapy, did Charlene come to understand that gambling had been her way of defying the very important, but unspoken, edict that ruled her household: *a good wife should make sacrifices to satisfy the needs of her family.* For many years she *had* sacrificed, with her husband's, in-laws', and children's financial needs all taking priority. But by gambling—taking a sheltered risk—she secretly rebelled against that rule and thus became a "bad" wife, while at home still appearing to follow the "good wife" rule.

In therapy, Charlene realized that she had acted out of deep anger and hurt over her husband's lack of emotional or financial support of her boutique venture. Not only would his support have meant a great deal to her, but she also believed that she was helpless to amass the needed capital on her own. In gravitating to the thrill of gambling, she temporarily acquired a feeling of power, an experience of passion, and a starring role in her own secret drama.

Consumed by Drama

The cycle of bingeing and dieting—the agony of overeating—makes up perhaps the most common substance-abuse experience known to American women. If drama is a means of sensation-seeking, then bingeing—whatever else it may be—is drama.

The reasons women eat compulsively or become fat are complex and manifold. The initiation of these patterns often reflects the same type of social entrapment, media messages (especially about beauty and thinness), and family dysfunction that leads women to create various types of interpersonal drama. But whatever the underlying causes of a particular woman's problematic relationship to food, this relationship is one that sets the stage for a fevered, rebellious *internal* drama.

Women who maintain a pattern of overeating to the point of discomfort and who then embark upon a stringent diet may not perceive themselves as Rebels, or even as drama-seekers. Yet there is defiance in their pattern, a message to anyone or any social system seeking to control them that they cannot be completely dominated. "I will eat as much as I want to eat, I will diet when I want to diet, and *you* can't stop me. It is *my* body, and *I* have the power," they say through their actions.

In this act of defiance there are both physical risks (for the binge/diet cycle is damaging to the body) and social risks (if they become fat, these women may risk society's censure, the disapproval of men, and criticism from their loved ones). As serious as these penalties may be, the risks binge/dieters take are sheltered; no matter how extreme her behavior, it is not radical enough to efface her appropriately female persona.

Two other eating disorders are worthy of mention: bulimia (bingeing and purging through vomiting and laxative-induced elimination), and anorexia (a terror of gaining weight that results in self-induced starvation). These disorders are devastating to the body, sometimes leading to death through starvation or physical trauma. Because the underlying disturbances here are far more elusive, complex, and severe than are those of most rituals based on sensation-seeking, I have not included these disorders in my exploration of Rebel behavior.

Food as Drama

It's common for people to occasionally "abuse" food by eating to the point of uncomfortable fullness while devouring fattening or "bad" foods that they don't typically consume. However, these binges rarely last more than a day or two. For the average person, this type of binge may be a pleasurable indulgence or a temporary way of coping with sudden anxiety. In either case, if an individual does not agonize over the behavior and it is not part of a repetitive, debilitating pattern, it is unlikely to represent either rebellion or a source of drama.

In contrast, millions of women binge for periods of weeks, and even months, at a time. They may be of average or large size, but they abuse food and the act of eating repetitively, with a ferocity that either borders on being a compulsion or is one. They are obsessed with food and with their own behavior, and they tend to agonize over everything they eat. At some point even the most compulsive binger stops overeating, if only briefly, to go on a rigid diet in an attempt to make up for the damage done.

Bingers tend to use the act of eating as a way of creating both stimulation and sedation. Like all forms of auto-arousal, bingeing can be a way of stirring up desired or familiar sensations while simultaneously numbing unwanted feelings or obliterating pain. For the binger, the activities of thinking about food, finding food, devouring food, avoiding food, saying "no" to food, and recovering from food are at the heart of an endless, exciting internal drama in which she is both director and star.

The Binge as Drama

A binge is not about tasting and savoring but about swallowing and filling—in an attempt to fill emotional needs. "At the core of the binge is deprivation, scarcity, a feeling that you can never get enough," says Geneen Roth in her book *Feeding the Hungry Heart,* a stirring chronicle of the experience of compulsive eating. The woman who binges needs nourishment, nurturing, and stimulation—but of the emotional, not the edible, kind.

The drama begins when a woman does things during a binge that at other times she would find horrible, shameful, or disgusting. For example:

- Throwing food away so as not to eat it, but two hours later sifting through the garbage to find it and eat it.
- Stuffing down heaping mouthfuls of ice cream from the carton, and then, hearing her husband's key turn in the lock, quickly shoving the dripping carton back into the refrigerator.
- Eating carrots and celery for dinner, then waking up ravenous at two in the morning, spooning dry cake mix down her throat and polishing off all the peanut butter left in the jar.
- Ordering enough pizza for ten people when only she is there to eat it.
- Driving for hours from one fast-food joint to another, ordering meals for two at each and eating it all in the car.

These acts initiate the process of auto-arousal. They trigger strong physical and oral sensations, as well as intense emotions that are revealed in the binger's constant, droning internal dialogue about food, fat, self-hate, remorse, guilt, and punishment:

"Stop this, don't eat anymore—enough is enough, you disgusting pig!"

"This is the *last* time—I'll *never* do this again. Tomorrow I'll start a strict diet."

"I'll have to wear something loose tomorrow so no one sees my stomach protrude. Oh God, my caftan's in the cleaners—maybe a big T-shirt . . ."

"This is sick. Why am I doing this?? It doesn't even *taste* good! I just hate myself. Look at those fat cheeks—*ugh!*"

"Just one more order of french fries, and that's *it!*"

"Tony will be home in thirty minutes—I can't forget to dump the garbage. He'll kill me if he finds out I did this again."

"This binge probably put four pounds on me—but some of it is water, so maybe if I'm good all week I can drop the rest by Friday."

"My stomach is killing me—I have to take off my jeans or I'll split them open, even with the zipper down. I can hardly breathe. I feel so bloated and heavy—like a dead body."

Sometimes the binger tastes her food, and sometimes she is aware only of the experience of chewing and swallowing and of the pressure of too much food in her belly. Everything she consumes precipitates new, engrossing dimensions of sensory and emotional experience. By stuffing herself in the privacy of her own self-contained world, the binger is being as bad as she knows how to be.

"The inside of a binge is deep and dark," writes Geneen Roth. "[It] is a descent into a world in which every restriction you have placed on yourself is cut loose. . . . The forbidden is obtainable."

For many women, being bad by bingeing—and perhaps by getting fat—is the only way they feel they can say no to the demands of society, spouses, parents, lovers, friends, and their own internal voices that they act like the good girls they were brought up to be. To such women Roth says, "[This may be] your way of telling [them] that you don't have to be the way they want you to be." Binges are acts of rebellion, she affirms, just as being fat is an act of defiance.

The Diet as Drama

The counterpart to The Binge is The Diet, and the coconspirator in The Diet is The Scale.

The diet is fashioned to cut the costs incurred by binges—costs related only to weight and size. Rarely, *rarely* do diets succeed for bingers, because where each diet ends a brand-new binge begins. As Roth puts it, "For every diet there is an equal and opposite binge."

The diet offers as much potential for auto-arousal and drama as bingeing. During the diet, the binger still thinks about food constantly: what she can or can't eat, how often and how much she can eat, and how much she can lose. She diets as compulsively and dramatically as she eats.

While there is melodrama in bingeing only for a woman who does it repeatedly, there can be drama in dieting for almost any woman. Let's look at how a diet drama might be played out by two different women—Mary, a normal eater who has put on five pounds over the holidays, and Janice, a binger who has been on a six-week binge.

Though Mary and Janice often behave in *outwardly* similar ways while on a diet, their overall drama-seeking styles are quite different. Janice, the binger, would qualify as a Rebel. Mary, who is not a compulsive binger, tends to create diet drama in a Fighter mode. She likes to turn being on a diet into a crisis, magnifying and exaggerating both the importance and the pain of it and using it to make herself the center of attention. For example, if at a party Mary were to gaze longingly at a piece of cake and announce loudly, "Oh, I couldn't possibly eat *that,*" she would essentially be playing for an audience, making a production out of her self-denial. Theoretically, her announcement could generate some desirable responses—for example, "You look great to me! I don't see why you have to lose weight."

If Janice were to make a similar statement, playing for an audience would be only a secondary element in her drama. The *real* action would be taking place internally. While for Mary the diet would simply be a new means of creating drama in her primary style, for Janice, auto-arousal would remain the primary constituent of the diet drama.

The following scene illustrates a common internal drama played out by bingers when they are dieting:

> While watching television, Janice begins to think about food. She gets up and cautiously approaches the refrigerator door. "NO!" she berates herself. "I can't do that." She turns away from the gleaming white monster, then comes back. All right, she'll just *look* at it. She opens the freezer door, and there sits a pint of double chocolate-chip ice cream. She immediately slams the door.
>
> Janice quickly moves into the living room and resumes watching TV. A commercial comes on—for Burger King. Oh, no. "Don't even move," she commands herself. "Just sit still," she says, already rising from the couch. She goes back to the freezer, opens the door, takes out the carton of ice cream, and grabs a spoon. "Just *one* spoonful, just *one* . . . well, okay, two. Let's see, that's about fifty calories. Not bad." She returns the container to the freezer and leaves the kitchen, her mind still on the dessert.

This little drama is not over. It will go on all night, and whether or not she eats all the ice cream, the obsession, the preoccupation, the agony will be the same.

The next morning, it's time for Janice to check the scale. "Oh, no! Up three-fourths of a pound." She drinks a cup of coffee, estimating the amount and weight of the liquid as she sips. Then she visits the bathroom, mentally noting the approximate weight of her deposits. She subtracts the amount consumed from the amount eliminated. There is, she figures, about a six-ounce difference. She is back on the scale. Aha— she has *really* gained only a third of a pound! Janice is momentarily relieved and begins to plan the day's menu, promising herself she'll be good.

Janice, like most bingers, has been on almost every diet known to humankind, and she knows the *Brand Name Calorie Counter* backward and forward. The binge/diet cycle is the primary drama in her life.

One week, the binger may bring her own food to a dinner party or refuse to eat at all (creating interpersonal drama by making everyone else uncomfortable and forcing herself into the spotlight), and the following week she may dine with the same people and eat enough for three large construction workers. The binger talks incessantly about her diet but celebrates each loss of a pound with an edible reward. She has clothes in her closet that span at least three sizes. She may be thin, fat, or in-between. While the problem is more visible for the obese woman, it is no more subjectively agonizing, dramatic, or rebellious than it is for the small woman. A binger is a binger.

So much ado about eating may seem silly to people who have never lived in the black hole of bingeing and dieting. However, the binge/ diet cycle is a wretched, painful way of life. No matter how abundant the food consumed or how temporarily successful a diet, the pain of emotional deprivation that underlies the binger's drama is never eased.

Bingers seek varied sensation as well as emotional comfort in the internal drama of food abuse. In that sense they are similar to drug abusers, who also look for highs as they systematically—usually addictively—seek to blot out their lows.

Turning On and Getting High

Alcohol and drugs induce a state of consciousness that is provocative because along with new and heightened sensations, a significant change from the status quo is produced. Many people who have used marijuana and psychedelic drugs to alter their consciousness say that they do so because they love the feeling. This type of experience is classic sensation-seeking, pure evidence of a drive to seek novel stimulation, and the willingness to take risks in the service of that drive.

The use of any drug produces auto-arousal. Some drugs result in increased appreciation of many sensory experiences, such as eating, listening to music, being sexual, watching a movie, or giving a massage. Other drugs generate levels of perception, psychic phenomenon, and emotionalism unavailable to many people in a sober state. Even the paranoia experienced by some drug users while they are high on hallucinogens or marijuana can be a subjectively intriguing source of internal drama.

"I love the feeling of being just on the verge of being crazy," one such user told me. This woman, normally a controlled, rational thinker, loves to experience the metamorphosis induced by certain drugs and is even excited by the possibility that she might lose control and drift psychically away from herself, never to be the same.

In each of this woman's experiences with drugs, all the components of Rebel drama-seeking are present: the auto-arousal, the danger/fear/excitement connection ("I might go crazy"), the sheltered nature of the risk, and the potential for interpersonal drama ("I have said things to people while I was high, and they weren't, that haunted me later and created some serious problems"). Despite these drawbacks, the drastic alterations in mood, inner vision, and self-concept effected by drugs are what make them so attractive to her.

It is the consciousness-altering attributes of drug use, the potential for a highly personal, self-induced journey from one state of mind to another, that may explain why studies show that high-sensation seekers are more likely to be recreational drug and alcohol users than people with smaller appetites for sensation. Recreational drug use, however, can quickly lead to drug abuse, which can culminate in addiction. When addictive processes take on a life of their own, the arousing sensations that were initially appealing to the drug user become muted or lost, while the addiction remains. In such cases the drama of the drug experience itself gives way to the drama of addiction.

The Drama of Drug Addiction

> We had been cutting lines for about an hour. We wanted to snort more, but there was nothing around. My friend Maureen said she'd go out with her boyfriend and make a buy. I

was so high, and the coke had made me so fidgety, that I didn't want to just sit around and wait. I told her to take me with them. She said it wasn't safe, especially because I was dressed so expensively. I said, "Who cares?"

We drove down to this seedy part of town and entered a dark, dingy apartment that smelled very strange. Walking in, I couldn't see much except for a few men on the floor smoking something. I assumed they were free-basing, but I'd never been around it before. One of them looked at me and said, "Baby, you the feds?" and laughed. He grabbed my leg and started to stroke it. I was scared to death, but then Maureen's dealer came over to us and he let up.

I kept wondering if the place was going to be busted any second—I was thinking to myself, *What* are you doing here?— but I was fascinated with the whole scene. I still couldn't wait to get out of there, but when we hit the fresh air I thought, how exciting!

Seated in my office, Jennifer was describing this scene from her recent past. She had come to see me shortly after leaving the hospital where she had been treated for cocaine addiction. She hadn't touched drugs for three months, and she was finally beginning to feel "human" again. Her experience illustrates the drama inherent in the progressive use of any mood-altering substance. Whether the tragedy occurs in a bar, a "shooting gallery," a "rock house," or one's own living room, for the Rebel the same dramatic elements are always present.

"I'm still amazed that it got so out of hand," Jennifer said softly, shaking her head.

I initially tried coke because I was curious about how it would feel, and I thought it might give me a boost at work when I was tired. I never thought of myself as an addictive type, but somehow the drug—and all the rituals that surrounded it—became the center of my life. Before that I had been such a high achiever . . . I didn't drink too much, or party too much, or even date that much. The only thing I suppose I was extreme about was working. Maybe I was setting myself up for a fall.

Cocaine had destroyed everything that Jennifer had spent eight years working for. An executive recruiter, she had gone from being top producer at a large agency to successful owner of her own small firm. But as her habit grew, her business deteriorated, and she was finally forced to close her doors. It was then that she checked herself into a hospital.

Jennifer's devotion to her business had left her little time for fun, or for being in touch with the range of her emotional needs. The child of two highly successful parents whose relationship she described as "lukewarm," Jennifer grew up believing that all of life's rewards could be found in hard work and material success. "I didn't love my work," she admitted. "I did it because I knew I could make a lot of money, and I'd always felt that's what I was expected to do."

Jennifer had complied with those expectations for years, but had then rebelled against the structure of her life by becoming a very "bad" girl. As Jennifer continued to describe her experiences as an addict, I began to see that they contained a compelling drama, an adventure story, that had been very appealing to her. In light of her background, it was no wonder that after her first trip to the dealer Jennifer had become almost as hooked on the excitement, danger, and counterculture of the drug world as she had on the drug itself.

After a few visits to Maureen's dealers, I decided to make my own connection. I didn't want to be dependent on Maureen or her boyfriend and I wanted to take the risk, taste the danger, on my own. I wasn't getting high every day at that point; I binged mostly on weekends. So one Thursday night, straight, I dressed in old jeans and a T-shirt and made the drive myself.

I tried to tell myself I wasn't scared, but every imaginable fantasy flew into my mind—I'd be stopped by the cops for some small infraction on the way home and be busted with all that coke, or I'd be robbed, raped, and murdered . . . I was carrying a lot of cash.

I was nauseous and sweating, and my jaw was clenched so hard it hurt. I almost turned back twice, but when I got there everything went pretty smoothly, and I left all excited and proud of myself for being so brave. When I got home I saw a cut on my lower lip. I realized I'd been so scared that I'd bitten it but hadn't felt a thing! Two days later I heard that the place had been raided—everybody there had gone to jail.

As Jennifer's habit increased, she made new drug contacts, and in so doing she developed new opportunities to indulge her penchant for the mingled sensation of danger, fear, and excitement. Her auto-arousal was produced in equal measure by her reactions to the drug and by her sheltered risk-taking: seeking drugs, buying drugs, and eventually (in a failed attempt to save her company) even doing a bit of drug dealing.

At the same time, each workday presented Jennifer with its own drama, as she tried to fend off the impending bankruptcy of her business. Her business relationships were also deteriorating. Like most addicts, Jennifer developed mood and personality changes. She was alternately hostile, agitated, morose, elated, or depressed as a result of the neurochemical changes that were the by-products of her drug abuse. Jennifer's secretary, unaware that her boss was using cocaine, knew only that she had developed a hair-trigger temper and a foul, insulting tongue. The secretary quit.

Jennifer's clients began to realize that her judgment had become clouded, her conversations unprofessional, and her attitude snippy—and they began withdrawing their accounts. One moment Jennifer would plunge her energies into trying to salvage these relationships, and the next she would turn stubborn, telling her drug buddies—the only friends she still saw—that her clients could "all go to hell."

Jennifer suspected that she was addicted to the drug, but she didn't want it to be true.

> I knew I wasn't really getting high anymore. Toward the end I was depressed no matter how much coke I did—but I kept hoping for one more rush, just to get through the day. You know, that's part of the mystique of cocaine. No matter how many times you feel bad, you remember what it was like to feel good, and you chase the excitement and look for the high even when it's no longer there.

That, of course, is the betrayal that exists in all addictions, in every false promise of stimulation and sensation to be found in substances.

Whether a woman turns to alcohol, cocaine, marijuana, psychedelics, or pill abuse, there is equal potential for drama. Similar self-directed questions can provoke similar suspense, fear, and excitement in anyone, no matter what they ingest:

> How much can I get away with taking before I get sick, pass out, or OD?
>
> Will I get stopped while driving drunk or loaded?

Will I get caught in possession of drugs, or in the car
with an open bottle?

Can I keep it a secret from my husband, parents,
friends, and employers?

Will I get ripped off by a dealer?

What if someone slips me contaminated street drugs?

Because there is no limit to the questions or to the possible dangers and consequences, there is no limit to the potentials for drama in drug abuse.

Multiple Abuses

Women attracted to one form of abuse often engage in others as well. For example, cocaine addicts frequently also abuse alcohol. Gamblers may abuse food or drugs. Alcoholics may also abuse food or sex. Excessive shoppers may alternately diet and stuff themselves, their weight bouncing up and down, thereby generating even greater drama and interjecting a rationale for their binge shopping. The same women may even abuse the feeling of being "in love," because their systems crave the sensations that they have learned to acquire through intense, self-induced, chaos-producing auto-arousal. In the name of sensation, and out of their inner pain, Rebels jeopardize their physical, emotional, and economic well-being.

The betrayal of addiction, summed up so well by Jennifer, is to some extent the betrayal of any abuse. The initial satisfaction promised by these activities first becomes elusive, then illusory. The activities no longer deliver what they promised—but the danger remains.

It is difficult to stop a pattern of abuse once it has begun. Yet, if health is to be regained, the importance of coping with all components of abuse—including rebellion, auto-arousal, sheltered risk-taking, excitement-seeking, and drama-making—cannot be underestimated. Our tendencies toward compulsive behaviors evince far more than a "disease" process, which is the restricted angle from which even the most dedicated self-help organizations often approach the problem. Attraction to these experiences is always, in some part, the expression of a *healthy*—if seriously misdirected—desire for stimulation and excitement. It is also a manifestation of an equally healthy need for freedom from the attitudes, social structures, personal relationships, or painful pasts that bind us. But when this need goes unacknowledged and our drive for sensation becomes trapped or is simply unsupported, it is inevitable that the healthy pathways through which we fulfill ourselves will become constricted. We turn, instead, down the only roads we sense are open to us.

Whether we are Rebels, Challengers, or Fighters, to change our lives for the better we must do more than merely stop our self-defeating behaviors. Because all of us are inclined to seek sensation in some way, we must also examine our overall lifestyles and explore exciting possibilities for achievement and growth. By reconciling the painful dramas of our past, learning to take risks that are meaningful, and concurrently replacing our means of negative excitement with *equally* arousing positive means, we offer ourselves the well-deserved chance to lead lives filled with passion, confidence, and self-love.

The process by which we can attain these goals is the subject of chapters 8 and 9.

Part Two
The
EXCITEMENT

Before We Begin...

The preceding chapters have been about a many-faceted problem with diverse origins and manifestations. Nowhere have I referred to this problem—the tendency toward making melodrama—as a sickness or a disease, because I do not believe that it is one.

Since I do not believe that you have been ill, the material that follows cannot be about "recovery." It is, instead, about rediscovering and regaining ownership of the love, strength, creative force, excitement drive, and natural wisdom that you have indentured, all or in part, to various traditions—the often tragic emotional traditions of your childhood, and the demanding traditions of our culture.

Those of you who are grounded in the tradition of the "Anonymous," Twelve-Step programs, which embrace the disease model of dependency, may find this departure from the illness orientation difficult to accept and perhaps even contradictory to your deeply held beliefs. I realize that many people have received help within this tradition, and many skilled therapists espouse it. I do not discount the success of such programs. I can only point out the path that I believe in, the one that the women I've worked with have grown to trust.

8 ❧

Toward an End to the Agony: Preparation for Change-Making

*T*ransforming melodrama into healthy excitement is akin to an act of magic. Like all magical acts, it appears as a mystery to the uninitiated and as a triumph of mind and spirit to the trained. This chapter and the one that follows will offer you an initiation, an unraveling of the mysteries, and a way of bringing the magic of personal power to bear upon your life.

Thus far you have been reading of the misuse, and perhaps the waste, of your potential. You've learned of the methods by which you may have turned attributes of personality into deficits, undermined your deepest self, and exhausted your greatest source of personal power. Now you'll learn how to reclaim all the vitality and spirit that have been dissipated in dramatic but unsatisfying episodes, and you'll learn that you can experience passion without suffering for it. Yet this cannot occur unless you have the willingness to be truthful with yourself—and the courage to risk changing.

The idea of change carries frightening implications for all of us. We fear that change may mean the loss of something dear to us—a relationship, a way of life, even our very identity. Not until we have crossed beyond the borders of our fear can we see that what lies on the other side is greater and dearer than anything we may have left behind.

As you step out of the drama and bring true excitement into your life, you will recoup many of the costs of your drama. The energy you

189

sapped will be restored and expanded; the self-esteem you depleted will be renewed and increased; the personal power you denounced will be recovered and strengthened; the feelings you numbed will be touched and enriched; the intimacy you lost will be brought within reach; and the self-love you denied will be acknowledged and deepened.

Further, all the *rewards* of drama are yours to keep, and in healthy excitement they will be multiplied. You will feel exuberantly alive. You will know in your heart that you are special; no further proof will be required. You will be able to command center stage with pride, dignity, and genuine authority. And you will create as much thrilling suspense as you choose to enjoy.

For all this, however, there will be agonies—different from the ones you will be leaving behind, but agonies nonetheless. You will discover all the agonies of living, all the *true,* inevitable dramas of existence. You will discover real feelings, and some of them may hurt. You will begin new ventures, and some may fail. You will reevaluate old relationships, and some may end. But your agonies will be authentic. Both the pleasure and pain of being genuinely who you are, at this time in your personal history, will be real. Your life will be real.

Stepping out of your melodrama does not mean forfeiting the unique qualities of personality and temperament that, until now, have been given into the service of drama. The very style of drama-making you have chosen is an extension of the unique constellation of traits, abilities, and experiences that distinguish you from anyone else in the world—and it is essential that this uniqueness, this genuine specialness, be preserved. Your primary style of dramatic sensation-seeking can become your foundation for achieving all the true excitement you desire.

Similar preparations are required for letting go of any self-defeating pattern of living. Whether we make drama in the style of the Fighter, the Challenger, or the Rebel or in a blend of all three styles, we must all face the same demands in readying ourselves for change-making. This chapter illuminates those demands, in the form of eleven essential challenges. It is up to you to decide whether to move forward or to remain where you are. Some of you will be eager to make changes; some of you will not be. Whenever you are ready to begin, these pages will be here to guide the way.

In facing the challenges presented in this chapter you will be preparing—emotionally, mentally, and spiritually—to take the specific, action-oriented, change-making steps that will be detailed in chapter 9. Just as the cost of one solitary drama is minimal compared to the damaging, cumulative effect of all the dramas in your life, each single change-making step you take has only minimal power—but all the steps together, faithfully taken one after another, can produce the magic of your own transformation.

Challenge #1: Become Dedicated to Change and Self-Renewal

Nothing I will be asking you to do is easy. The patterns of drama-making that shape your life were not ingrained in a day, and they cannot be changed in a day. In order to achieve anything worthwhile, in order to step beyond the drama and bring real excitement into your life, you must be nothing short of dedicated. Rediscovering and renewing yourself must be the most important thing in the world to you.

In my clients, I have often seen dedication to change emerge as a natural extension of their willingness to embrace their own basic inner wisdom—the sometimes forgotten side of personality that intuitively "knows" what is right, meaningful, and good for an individual. Their dedication to change springs from this "higher" self's absolute certainty that making changes is a necessary, essential part of the growth process.

The *higher self,* as I am using the term here, is not meant to be a religious or spiritual concept, although it can certainly incorporate what we often call our "soul" or "essence." Your higher self is simply the purest, most natural side of yourself, uncorrupted by even your most painful past experiences or most repressive social conditioning.

If this concept seems alien to you, it may help you to recall those times when you "knew" something that you had no concrete reason to know, or knew exactly what someone else felt or thought, or even when you knew who was calling when the telephone rang. There are moments of such incomprehensible, intuitive "knowing" in all of our lives, but we often discount them, shrugging them off as coincidence or luck. In actuality, these experiences are sometimes the only evidence we have of our pure inner wisdom, the highest selves within us.

There are many ways to tap directly into your higher self. Meditation is one. Another is visualization, a technique we'll be exploring a bit later. Sometimes, you only need to sit quietly for a moment, listen for the sound of your own inner voice, and be willing to trust it.

Being in touch with this deeper, wiser aspect of yourself is akin to calling upon a reserve of strength. Just as a tired marathon runner calls upon her physical reserves for a last push to the finish line, in tackling the mental/emotional marathon of change-making you can get a "second wind" by drawing encouragement from the wisest, strongest part of yourself. No matter how dedicated you are, at times you may become frightened or frustrated with the self-renewal process, and you may even consider giving up. That's when you might want to look to your higher self to remind yourself that YOU CAN DO IT, and to give yourself a sudden shot of energy to help you renew your dedication to change.

In practical terms, dedication to change is an enormous commitment. It is not something to take lightly. It is not something you can do partially—you can no more be a little bit dedicated than you can be a little bit pregnant. Dedication stems from a deeply felt, genuine *want,* a brimming desire to be the best that you can be, and from a determination to grow. You must be willing to say, "My life is not the way I want it to be—but the world is not going to change for me, and the people I know are not going to change for me. If I want to see a difference in my life, that difference has to come from *me!"*

Dedication to change requires that you do more than simply say, "Okay, I'm dedicated." It demands that when you wake up each morning you say, "Today I will not create drama or behave as I have in the past." And it demands that when you go to bed each night you say truthfully, "Today I avoided doing at least one thing that was self-defeating in the past" or "Today I took one specific step toward being a better me." Dedication demands that you do more than just read through the challenges in this chapter and the steps in chapter 9. It demands that you embrace them and follow them faithfully.

Through dedication, you naturally abdicate your episodic style of living. *Dedication to changing yourself becomes the thread of meaning that can connect all the events in your life.* When you are dedicated to creating change, each event takes on significance beyond the moment. Suddenly, you see important questions where once there were only episodes of empty sensation: Why am I treating everyone like an adversary? Where is sexual adventure really taking me? What is this impossible relationship telling me about myself?

When you allow the events in your life to be more than random occurrences or compulsive acts, you will begin to see them as concrete evidence of your feelings, thoughts, and attitudes. When you are dedicated to change, you will be able to learn from your actions.

I have seen over and over in my clients the transformation that dedication to change brings. If you, too, are willing to dedicate yourself to preparing for and making changes, all of your actions will become aligned toward those goals. Drama-making will never be the same, because even when you engage in a drama you will be *incapable* of doing so without acknowledging it and striving to understand it, and you will be *unable* to set up a scene without learning from it. Thus, you will cease to live only for the episode and will begin to live contextually, with a purpose.

Challenge #2: Take Responsibility for Your Life

"Taking responsibility" is not merely a catchphrase of the human-potential movement of the sixties and seventies; it is a cornerstone of modern psychotherapy. Taking responsibility for your life does not mean blaming yourself for everything that goes wrong. To do so would only be to make yourself a victim of your own behavior. Taking responsibility is the antithesis of victimization. It is an act of power.

Taking responsibility means, simply, acknowledging that in every moment you have the opportunity to make choices. You choose whether to wake up early or late, and whether or not to go to work. You choose your friends, and you choose your lovers. You choose whether to yell, speak softly, or walk away when you're angry. You choose whether to drink alcohol or use drugs, whether to spend more money than you make, or whether to have sex with any man who wants you. Always, at a conscious or unconscious level, *you* choose.

I recall a session with a client who insisted she didn't make choices:

Client: I didn't *choose* not to go back to school—I *can't* go, I have to work because we have two kids and I'm pregnant, and we need the money! I'd *love* to go back to school—I don't *choose* not to!

Therapist: Well, I understand that the idea of going back to school is appealing, and I also understand that you aren't in school. You say it's because you have to work to support your children. They are *your* children?

Client: Of *course* they're mine!

Therapist: How did you happen to have them?

Client: What do you mean . . . ?! We *wanted* them—we planned them. I love children.

Therapist: So, you did choose to have them?

Client: Well . . . sure. But wait a minute—it's still not my fault I can't go back to school!

Therapist: Of course it's not your fault. But it is your decision, based upon what you see as the present needs of your family. You've made a choice that their needs come first right now, haven't you?

Client: Yes, I suppose I have.

Therapist: And you've made a choice not to go back to school because you fear that your family would suffer if you did, haven't you?

Client: Yes . . .

Therapist: You know, we can't really talk about how you feel about that choice if you keep denying that you've made one. And you can't make new choices, should you want to, if you continue to deny the power with which you made your initial choice.

Client: So, you mean that even if the pressures of the situation made me feel like I had no choice, I really did? I suppose I did make a choice to give in to the pressure . . .

Like this client, we all make choices constantly, whether we acknowledge them or not. No matter how difficult your personal circumstances, you make choices about how to *respond* to them; no matter how troubled your personal relationships, every interaction with intimates is grounded in choice. The choices may be small, such as what to do when your lover accuses you of leaving the cap off the toothpaste or of never being on time, or they may be large, such as what to do when he comes home drunk again—or whether to stay with him at all.

When we make drama in our lives, we make a multitude of daily choices about how our dramas are to be staged, about our dialogue, props, and climactic scenes. Drama is not "forced" upon us. We create it. And that creation is an act for which each of us is personally responsible.

It is true that much of our drama-seeking is motivated by beliefs, attitudes, and childhood decisions buried in our unconscious minds. That is why we do not always understand *why* we choose to behave as we do, or recognize that even "automatic" acts stem from choices that are sometimes made more quickly than the conscious mind can grasp. Yet, the unconscious energy that drives us to choose destructive methods of meeting our basic needs is not an external power. It is as much an aspect of who we are as is our behavior. And because it is *of* us, we can choose whether to allow it to dictate our actions or whether to harness its power. In order to take the change-making steps in chapter 9, you will need to begin taking responsibility for your choices right now.

All the episodes from childhood and adulthood that have left scars upon our emotions are lived over and over again in the unconscious, and often in the conscious mind as well. But there comes a time in life when we must choose whether to be at the mercy of the past or whether to exorcise our memories and create our own present and future.

No matter what hand you have been dealt in life, you choose how to play it. We witness every day the life-enhancing choices made by people who could easily have said, "I have no choice": handicapped individuals who triumph over their disabilities, and educationally or socially deprived people who build fulfilling lives. They have chosen, and so can you.

You can argue this point and prove to yourself over and over that you are a victim and, therefore, not significantly responsible for the quality of your life—and your life will remain the same. Or, you can accept the premise that you are always making active choices and that it is in your power to begin making different ones.

If you are dedicated to self-renewal and willing to take responsibility for your life, you are prepared to meet the next challenges. Many of them will help to give you an awareness of the unconscious processes that contaminate your ability to make wise, constructive choices toward a truly exciting way of life.

Challenge #3: Embrace Your Pain as You Grow

This challenge is not a glorification of masochism. However, I don't know of any instances where real growth occurs without some pain, some loss. If you expect pain and can respect the necessity of it in the preparation for self-renewal, you will find that it can only make you stronger.

Each forward motion leaves something behind. No matter how much good you extract from meeting each new challenge, there will be pain in letting go of what has always been.

One woman, Ellen, experienced many sensations as she let go of viewing herself as a victim and began to take responsibility for her life. She felt excitement, relief, anticipation, and satisfaction—but, to her surprise, above all she felt grief. Before Ellen could welcome the recognition of her own strengths, she had to pass through a period of mourning for the loss of her perceived weakness. She had to cry for the days when she had "gotten by" by acting scared, timid, and helpless, when she had been able to induce auto-arousal by wallowing in self-pity over the slightest rejection. She had to weep and mourn because this "victim" had represented her persona, part of her outer self, and her actions had been part of a meaningful phase in her personal evolution.

In acknowledging her victim-self, Ellen also had to acknowledge the squandered victim years, the time and opportunities lost while she was immersed in drama. For the first time, she took responsibility for the quality of those years—a bittersweet process of joyous awakening and somber reflection. "I feel as though a mist has been lifted," she told me. "But what I see isn't all pretty. Still, I'd rather have the vision than ever lose myself in the mist again."

Though preparing to change demands that we experience moments of pain, grief, and sadness, we acknowledge that these are our authentic pains—not exaggerated, sensationalized, or dramatized pains. In experiencing them, we grow more "visible" to ourselves, more real. And as we see ourselves better, we stop allowing ourselves to be invisible to others.

Just as there can be pain in growing, there is often pain in remembering. No transformation can be complete until we have released the remnants of the past that intrude on our ability to function purely in the present. The relinquishing of the past is begun with a challenge all its own. Rising to it is one of the most affirming, life-enhancing choices you will ever make.

Challenge #4: Place Your Past in Perspective

As important as this challenge is, many women find it the most difficult of all. Certainly, it is one that often demands the most committed, concentrated work. Placing your past in perspective is an ongoing process that may take many months—or even years—to complete. While I can offer you a foundation for beginning this important task, for further help I suggest that you seek out other books devoted primarily to this topic. A list of those I recommend most highly appears in the Appendix.

The overriding challenge now before you encompasses a number of more limited challenges, expressed below as a series of questions about your past. It is by no means necessary for you to answer each of these questions completely before you can consider yourself ready to move on. What is important is that you remain dedicated to the process of discovery and that you encourage the flow of feelings and memories buried in your unconscious. Releasing these feelings will remove the need to engage in acts and dramas that are designed to restrain or numb them. Once you have faced these feelings, you will no longer need to protect yourself from your own past—nor will you allow yourself to be its victim.

I suggest that you go back to chapter 3 ("The Family Melodrama") and glance through it again, perhaps rereading the parts that you identified with most closely. Using the issues raised in chapter 3 as a guide, it is important for you to begin exploring the following questions:

What was the nature of your family drama?

How did you adapt to it?

In what ways do your adult relationships and dramatic scenarios reflect the ways you adapted to your family drama?

What lessons about life and relationships did you learn from your family drama?

What lessons did you learn about yourself?

What feelings were evoked by your family drama? Which were the most pleasant and the most unpleasant? How, when, and by whom were those feelings evoked?

When you experience these feelings today, what do you do to increase or decrease your perception of them? How do these actions add to or detract from your fulfillment and happiness today?

The above questions are always explored in effective psychotherapy. While entering therapy is an option you may wish to consider (a guide to choosing a therapist can be found in the Appendix), many women prefer to work on themselves in other ways. In either case, if you are willing to search within yourself for answers, chances are that you will find them.

Since the challenge before you involves both delving into your conscious memories and releasing those stored in your unconscious, I offer you a technique known as "visualization" for opening up your mind to find the knowledge you seek. I suggest that you read through these instructions two or three times before following them.

Visualization.   Find a quiet spot where you can be alone and where you will not be interrupted. Be ready to explore *one* of the questions listed above, and decide in advance which it will be. Settle into a comfortable chair so that you can relax your body completely. Close your eyes.

Begin to concentrate on your breathing, inhaling and exhaling deeply, slowly, and rhythmically. Focus only on your breathing, and begin to count the seconds between inhaling and exhaling. I like to keep to a rhythm of 2-2-5—that is, first inhale and hold your breath for a count of 2, then exhale; again inhale and hold your breath for a count of 2, then exhale; finally, inhale and hold for a count of 5, then exhale . . . and repeat. Some women find that it helps to think of the word *relax* instead of the numbers—inhale and "relax, relax," then exhale; inhale and "relax, relax," then exhale; and so on.

Continue focusing on your breathing as you consciously relax all of the muscles in your body. You may want to imagine that you are floating on a cloud, or lying on a raft as it is taken slowly down a flowing river. When you feel calm and your body is relaxed, turn your attention to the blackness in front of your closed eyelids. You are about to seek the "wise person" within you—the energy of your highest self and guardian of your deepest truths. You are about to enter into communion with the reaches of your unconscious mind.

Ask yourself how the energies of your higher self would be perceived if they were to be manifested visually as a wise person, a guide. Instruct yourself to place on the "screen" in front of your closed eyes an image of this guide—what she, he, or "it" would look like in a visible form. Do not bind yourself by what you think the guide *should* look like. Some people find that their guide takes the shape of an animal or of an inanimate form, such as an ocean or mountain. Whatever comes to you is fine.

When your guide appears, ask it what name, if any, you should use in referring to it. Then ask the question you have prepared. Ask that it show you the way to the answer.

In response, you may receive a deluge of visual images or rambling thoughts, a one-to-one conversation with your guide, a physical sensation, or any combination of these. If the message is not clear, ask your guide specific questions, such as "What does this feeling mean?" or "Can you show me more?"

Remember, you are not speaking with some estranged entity. You are merely beginning to experience direct communication with your innermost, highest self, in a manner that may seem uncomfortable at first but will become increasingly familiar over time.

When you have as much information as you want or can receive at this time, thank your guide and bid it good-bye. When you are calm and have cleared your "screen," open your eyes.

Many of my clients have had highly emotional, intense experiences using the visualization technique, and some have had informative but unremarkable experiences. Others have experienced little more than slight relaxation. Still others have fallen asleep. Even if your initial results are minimal (or laughable), if you are willing to persevere I believe that you will be rewarded.

The purpose of conducting such a deep excavation of your past is to determine which feelings and attitudes you currently experience are throwbacks to past situations. Let's look at how gaining perspective on the past affected one woman's dramas.

As a child, Teresa was excluded from her older siblings' inner circle. In spite of the sadness and anger she felt, she pretended her exclusion didn't matter. However, as an adult she created crisis-drama whenever her own children appeared to keep secrets from her. She yelled, screamed, and demanded that they tell her what they were "up to." She felt threatened by their attempts to achieve privacy, just as she had when she was shut out of her siblings' private world. As Teresa delved into her past, she recognized that her buried feelings about her siblings were being inappropriately directed at her children. In recalling her own childhood pain, Theresa was able to separate the emotions linked to the past from those relating to the present. Suddenly, she could see her children's secrecy as a normal part of their growing up and developing their own identities.

Many other gains are achieved by exploring your past:

- When you place your past in perspective, you no longer need to bury feelings; thus, you can diminish self-destructive behaviors that keep emotions underground.
- When you place your past in perspective, you can realistically assess the beliefs about yourself that were created out of your acceptance of adult author-

ity when you were a child. Now *you* can decide if they
are true for you, and you can free yourself of those
that no longer apply.

- When you place your past in perspective, you can
  begin to understand the emotional forces that pre-
  vailed upon the adults who may have hurt you. You
  can then begin to let go of the anger toward them
  that may be shaping your present relationships.
- When you place your past in perspective, you learn
  that your past is not your potential. Your past is
  merely your past, and you can put it where it really
  belongs—behind you.

Challenge #5: Develop a Method to Aid Self-Discovery

Placing your past in perspective requires intense self-examination.
Most of the further challenges in this chapter, and all of the change-
making steps in the following chapter, demand that you thoroughly
explore aspects of your emotions and your behavior. In order to
benefit most from this process, it's important that you develop a
method for capturing and reviewing your experiences. The one that
has worked best for the majority of my clients is the journal, or diary,
method. The difference between thinking about the issues and questions raised in this book and writing about them in your journal is like
the difference between thinking about exercise and doing it.

A journal is an instrument of communication with all levels of the
self. It can be practical, serving as a place where you can respond to
the questions asked of you here, and where you can record your
dreams and memories, list your goals, and express your feelings. It
can also be more abstract, serving as a means for you to discover your
own voice, to develop your inner vision, and to create a synthesis of
spirit and deed. The journal experience is always an interesting,
exciting one; it is never precisely what you expect or plan it to be.

There are many styles of keeping a journal. Depending on which
of them you follow, you will adopt either a structured method or an
informal, fluid method. If you prefer structured experiences, I recommend the work of Ira Progoff, in which he describes his INTEN-
SIVE JOURNAL (see appendix II). Personally, I prefer a less formal
approach, but there are some elements in Progoff's book that are very
useful, even if you do not adhere strictly to his methods.

To begin, you need to buy a notebook to be used *exclusively* for the purpose of keeping your personal journal. I often recommend to my clients that they also carry a small notebook with them at all times, because big thoughts know no limitations of time and place.

In approaching your journal, remember that it is a personal, private, intimate resource. There are no restrictions on when you write, how you write, how much you write, and how you spell or punctuate. Many people are uncomfortable with the idea of keeping a journal because they believe they "can't write"—that is, they don't write as they've been taught they *should* write. There are no "shoulds" in keeping a journal. Some people write in brief phrases, some in poetry; some write full narratives, while others have dialogues with themselves; and some draw pictures and record images rather than writing in words.

Just as there are no rules about how and when to write, there are no restrictions about *what* to write. As Tristine Rainer, author of *The New Diary,* suggests to the beginner, "Write fast, write everything, include everything, write from your feelings, write from your body, accept whatever comes."

I would only add that you allow the ideas, questions, and exercises in this book to stimulate your writing. Write *anything* that comes to mind as you approach the challenges and steps in this and the next chapter. Do the exercises, but don't limit yourself to them or follow them religiously. Go with your own energies, feelings, sensations, and insights, and trust them—they will take you exactly where you need to go.

There are many books available that offer descriptions of writing techniques that can add dimension to your journal work. I highly recommend Rainer's book for its heartening and useful advice, especially about using the diary as a "time machine" to rediscover your past. I also enthusiastically recommend Joanna Field's published diary, *A Life of One's Own,* which is a beautiful, inspirational account of Field's seven-year journey toward "Self." This book is especially relevant to those of us who have been drama-seekers, for Field appears to have been a kindred spirit who determinedly charted her own path toward renewal and found a richly textured, purposeful life at the end of it.

Challenge #6: Anticipate Your Resistance to Change

At some point (or points) in therapy, *every* client experiences resistance. A client may resist delving any further into her past or reexperiencing the feelings she has denied. She may resist taking a specific action that would produce an important behavioral or emotional change. She may resist allowing the therapist the "power" to "make" her talk about events or thoughts she is reluctant to reveal.

There are myriad ways in which a client can demonstrate resistance: arriving late or canceling appointments, coming to sessions "too tired" to pay attention, lying, "forgetting" either an important insight she had during the last session or *everything* she talked about in that session, surprising the therapist by bringing a husband or lover to a session, turning the conversation to movies she's seen or friends who have problems . . . and so on. No matter which ploys a client uses, her resistance is usually manifested as a creative form of avoiding issues and feelings.

Resistance is normal. You, too, will encounter psychological resistance to making changes—even the ones you *really* want to make. And if you are not in therapy—if you are, in essence, your own therapist—you will direct your resistance toward yourself. As a result of your resistance, you may say such things to yourself as "I *knew* better than to exaggerate that incident when I told everyone about it—why did I do it anyway? or "Why did I eat two pints of ice cream? I only feel sick to my stomach now! It doesn't make sense."

But it *does* make sense. When your behavior obviously contrasts with your intentions, it is because you are experiencing resistance to change.

The positive side of resistance is that it usually occurs just before an emotional breakthrough. After all, if something significant were not about to happen, there would be nothing to resist. If you allow yourself to deal with your resistance, you will be rewarded with new insights, revelations, and freedoms. However, you must also remember that the personal-growth process is "three steps forward, one step (sometimes two steps) backward." Just when you've leaped one hurdle, a new one appears. Just when you're breathing a sigh of relief at having confronted a difficult memory or admitted an embarrassing truth, *another* issue will probably tug at you, demanding attention. Another issue, another moment of resistance. It can certainly become tiresome!

You might want to think of your periods of resistance as the times during which you stubbornly dig your heels into the earth and refuse to budge, like a pack mule who just won't carry its load another step. In a sense, you, too, are carrying great burdens that sometimes feel too heavy to carry any further. Your resistance is a message from your unconscious to your conscious mind and active self: "Enough is enough! Don't make me go any further right now." These feelings must be respected, not ignored. However, in order to appreciate the message, you must know the subtle signs through which your unconscious mind communicates.

Most of us communicate with ourselves in a kind of code. Instead of sending a message directly, our unconscious sends it in the form of a vague feeling that we usually proceed to act out, oblivious to the motives behind it.

It's important that you learn to recognize your own particular style of acting out so that you can become conscious of your resistance and begin to address the feelings underlying it. The following exercise will help you to do this.

In your journal, fill in the following blanks:

When I was a child, if I didn't want to do what my parents asked me to do, I showed my feelings by ⎯⎯⎯⎯⎯⎯⎯⎯⎯⎯⎯⎯⎯⎯.

(For example, did you pout, cry, do it but plan your revenge, do it badly, refuse to speak, hide in the closet? Be specific—Where did you go to pout? What kind of revenge did you plan?)

As an adult, when my boss or lover asks me to do something I don't want to do, I show my feelings by ⎯⎯⎯⎯⎯⎯⎯⎯⎯⎯⎯⎯.

(For example, do you snap, sulk, withdraw, do it grudgingly, do it poorly, get angry? Again, be specific.)

When I know I should do something that is good for me (such as studying for a class or going to the gym) but I find doing it unpleasant, I ⎯⎯⎯⎯⎯⎯⎯⎯⎯⎯⎯⎯⎯⎯⎯⎯.

(For example, do you find more pressing things to do, do it halfway, make up reasons why it isn't that good for you anyway, forget about it? Be specific.)

When I feel afraid of facing a problem or taking an action that is new and different, I avoid it by ⎯⎯⎯⎯⎯⎯⎯⎯⎯⎯⎯⎯⎯.

(For example, do you tell yourself it's not really a problem, get so wrapped up in your work that you forget about it, have a fight with your best friend to give you something else to think about, become wrapped up in your children's school projects, spend all your money? Be specific.)

As I set out to meet the challenges in this book, I will show my resistance by _____.

(For example, will you sit around and mope, spend all your money, get bored, pick a fight with someone, forget to buy your journal, buy your journal but lose it, get angry at yourself and overeat, avoid doing this exercise, avoid finishing this book? Be specific.)

Now list all the ways you might conceivably demonstrate or act out resistance to your own forward progress. Be very specific about the behaviors or thought processes you might use so that you can recognize them in action. List everything you can think of, no matter how farfetched or unlikely it seems. Allow your ideas to flow uncensored. Anything goes.

(*Now,* list the ones you censored anyway!)

Knowing how you might express resistance is a first step toward understanding it. Catching yourself *acting as you anticipated* is a second, crucial step. Dealing with the feelings that underlie each episode of resistance is the final step—and your next important challenge.

Challenge #7: Face Your Resistance to Change

To the extent that you can catch yourself engaging in behaviors that signify emotional resistance, you are well on your way toward change. However, recognizing resistance is not enough. You must delve beneath your resistance and discover its source. Facing resistance does not mean that you must immediately push past it. When you identify a resistance, you can merely say to yourself, "I see that I'm acting like I'm resisting something—I want to know what and why. *Then* I can decide what I want to do about it."

Resistance can sometimes be your way of reminding yourself that you can't move ahead too far, too fast. You need a moment to catch your breath and revel in how far you've already come. That is what happened to Julie, who experienced this kind of resistance after a few weeks of intense journal writing and exploration of her past.

As a physically abused child, Julie had survived in her household partially by squelching the anger she felt toward her abusive parents. Had she dared to express that anger, she would have been further abused. Instead, Julie tried to win her parents' love and approval, thinking that the abuse would stop if only she were smart enough and good enough. It was a futile challenge, but as a little girl Julie couldn't know that. Her adult dramas were understandably of the Challenger style—and were equally futile. Through her journal work, Julie began to face the repressed anger that she had been accumulating for a lifetime. It was painful for her to feel, and frightening for her to express the anguished fury of her childhood. But it was even more devastating for Julie to experience the slow death of her inner child's picture of who her parents were and of why it had seemed so important to her back then to obtain their love.

Shortly after gaining these necessary but painful insights, Julie put her journal in a drawer and avoided touching it for some time. "I'd tell myself I was too tired or too busy to write," she told me. "For a while I forgot about everything I had written in it, including all the little steps I was planning to take to stop building pointless relationships with men. Then one day I just opened the drawer and took it out. It was like greeting an old friend."

Julie had stopped using the journal when she reached an emotional plateau—a natural point of resistance. She needed some time to absorb what she had already discovered about herself. Based on her inner wisdom, her intuitive "knowing," she brought her progressive actions to a halt, then started them up again when she was ready to continue.

Julie's resistance problem solved itself because it was caused by emotional exhaustion, not fear. When resistance is grounded in fear, it doesn't always dissipate by itself. That's why it is so important that you recognize your own resistance when it occurs, and that you be willing to question whether you are having a bout with emotional fatigue or facing a deep-seated fear.

Let's look at a hypothetical situation in which resistance is based on fear. Imagine that you have been creating conflict-drama with your husband or lover and that you simply want to stop it. You know why you do it, you know what your payoffs are, you know how it's damaging your relationship, and you even know how it relates to your childhood experiences. Let's say that you also have a plan for stopping the fights—something concrete, such as going jogging whenever you have the urge to pick a fight. Now, let's imagine that you approach your husband, say the words you know will trigger an argument, and think to yourself, "I shouldn't be doing this. I should go running instead"—but there you are, continuing the fight anyway. You are only sure of this relationship as it has been played out in the past. Your resistance is based on your fear that if you really change, instead of just thinking about it or writing in your journal, the relationship will also change—or end.

No matter how dedicated to change you may be, your fears about revising the patterns that feel familiar and safe can create ambivalence and deter your best efforts. Fears can blend so well into the background of your mind that you may not even notice they're there until you begin to make a major move in your life; then they can jump out and stop you in your tracks.

The fears that keep many women from progressing are very similar. At one point or another, most of my clients have faced the following fears:

> If I change, if I don't go along with the way things have always been, I'm afraid my partner will leave me. And I'm afraid I won't make it without him.
>
> If I change, I fear that no one will pay attention to me anymore. I'll be "nobody."
>
> If I change, I'm afraid life won't be exciting anymore.
>
> If I change, I'm afraid I'll hurt too much.
>
> If I change, I'm afraid I won't like what I discover about myself.
>
> If I *try* to change, I'm afraid I'll fail.
>
> If I change, I fear I will not know who I am.
>
> If I change, I fear I'll cease to exist.

It is necessary for you to know which of your fears are likely to create resistance. To help you discover your own fears, think about the specific changes you wish to make in your life, and then make a list of all the thoughts and/or physical sensations that come to you in response to the following questions. Keep asking yourself these questions until you have multiple answers for each one. Think about your responses and what they mean in your life. Write them out in your journal, or discuss them with your inner "guide" so you can learn more and grow from your insights.

If I change, I am afraid that I _____.

If I change, I am afraid my friends will _____.

If I change, I am afraid my husband/lover will _____.

If I change, I am afraid my mother will _____.

If I change, I am afraid my father will _____.

If I change, I am afraid my children will _____.

If I change, I am afraid my employer will _____.

If I change, I am afraid my job/business will _____.

If I change, I am afraid my future will _____.

Sometimes fears have no basis in reality. The failures you anticipate never come to pass; the people you think will reject you may,
in fact, be the people who will provide you with the greatest support.
Often, the abandonment you fear is rooted in your childhood experiences. It's important that you approach your fears by asking yourself
the following questions:

> Have the things I fear ever happened to me before?
>
> If so, when? How?

You must take the time to sort out whether you are contaminating
the opportunities of the present with the painfully etched memories
of your past. Ask yourself:

> What are the connections and similarities between
> past and present circumstances?
>
> If there are many, did I somehow set them up that
> way?

And you must look into your heart to discover whether you are
willing to risk both the agonies and the rewards of departing from
your timeworn script.

It's necessary to realize that your fears may represent what you
know deep in your soul to be true, especially as they relate to present
relationships that already have shaky foundations. You may fear that
if you grow stronger, certain relationships will crumble. If those
relationships are grounded in your perceived weaknesses and exist
by grace of your drama, you may be right. If you choose not to

safeguard those relationships at the expense of your own vitality, you will eventually burst through your resistance.

By choosing to end the drama and include true excitement in your life, you have embarked on a very exciting journey. However, like much of the negative excitement you already know, this journey, too, has its dangers. And like more melodramatic risks, it evokes the heightened sensations of fear and the possibilities of pain or loss. You were probably willing to encompass those elements in your search for drama, though you betrayed yourself in the process. Now you must reach inside yourself for the courage to face fear and the prospect of loss as you seek the magic of self-renewal. In this act there is no betrayal, only veneration of your inner truths and your highest self.

Challenge #8: Reframe Your Deficits as Strengths

It is easy to stand back and watch drama-seeking women make "big productions" out of small crises, work to manipulate "impossible" men, steep themselves in the auto-arousal of obsessive love relationships, or compulsively thumb their noses at society, and to say about them, "Isn't that *sick* and disgusting?" or "Oh, that poor, insecure little thing, look what she does to herself," or "She has a disease; she can't help herself." While all of these responses are understandable in light of what dramatic behavior often looks like, none of them takes into consideration the tremendous capacity and strength that goes into perpetuating dramatic scenarios. None acknowledges the creative forces, perseverance, courage, or ambition inherent in the act of making drama. Such responses demean the powers of mind and spirit—misused and mischanneled though they may be—of these women.

One of the keys to transforming the quality of our lives is to *reframe and redefine the negatively perceived nature of our own experiences.* Words carry tremendous power in themselves. We base our self-image on the words that we believe define us, and we base our actions on that self-image. When, for example, we label our experience as "sick," we come to think of ourselves as sick, generally acknowledging our weakness and powerlessness. We either keep acting sick—thus making ourselves "sicker"—or we search for something or someone that will make us well. Often, we grow dependent upon that someone, or on a multitude of someones, because we believe that others have the answers, plans, and potions that will bring us to recovery. Even if they try to tell us we are making *ourselves* well, most often we know better, because if we deviate from *their* prescription for wellness we get "sick" again. Aha, we say to ourselves, we knew all along that they, not we, held the power!

Personal power is a very elusive and precious thing, an energy we all too easily disdain. The problem with following the "sickness" approach to problem-solving—for women, especially—is that in so doing we further disdain our personal power. We are brought up to relinquish our power, to deny it, hide it, misuse it, and even turn it against ourselves. What we are rarely informed of is that the power of the human mind, will, and spirit is *energy,* and that this energy cannot be destroyed or given away. Thus, the power that is within us remains within us from the day we are born to the day we die—and perhaps beyond. We can pretend that we have no power, we can say we are powerless, and we can believe we've surrendered our power. In reality, however, all of that is only representative of a belief about the way we've disposed of our power. In holding to those beliefs, we are *really* using our power to unwittingly sabotage and betray the best part of ourselves.

It is absolutely critical that we, as women, begin to accept and relish our innate power—and that we determine to practice using it with wisdom. All of the power you wield in the creation of drama (*creation* in the best, most natural, and formidable sense of the word) can be used to stop the drama and to re-create your life by design.

For some women, the concept of having power is frightening. These women have either been ridiculed for years every time they've attempted to exercise power, or they've been brainwashed by family and society into believing that they not only have no power but are entitled to none. I recall a therapy session with one such woman, Kathy, during which I guided her in a visualization exercise designed to help her acknowledge the power within her. I asked her to call upon her higher self to show her the source of her power, and to "see" her power in image form. Within a few moments Kathy's eyes flew open, and she sat bolt upright. She stared at me and stammered, "I saw my power—it was a shimmering globe of brilliant light energy . . . but it was so strong, so intense, so . . . *powerful,* that it frightened me! I had to open my eyes to make it disappear."

A few weeks later, I guided Kathy through a similar exercise, and this time she was able to really see the energy within her and to be warmed instead of frightened by it. "It's beautiful . . . I had no idea something like that was inside me," she marveled.

Like Kathy, you may discover that the concept of having power takes some getting used to. One way to ease into a powerful frame of mind is to redefine your own experience in words that imply power, not weakness. Just as a glass of water filled to the halfway point can be seen as half full or half empty, your actions can be viewed as arising from strength or from weakness. It is important that you immediately begin to reframe your perception of the efforts and energies with which you sought and made drama; it is essential that you transpose the negatives into positives. I promise you that by reframing and redefining your experiences, you will redefine your future.

If, as a Challenger, you manipulated or tried to control the men in your life, begin to think of your basic action in terms of a neutral, potentially positive, or positive ideal. Perhaps the word *manipulate* should be replaced by *strategize,* since you did, in fact, develop and implement a complex strategy for achieving your goal. You failed because your pursuit was unworthy of your abilities, and your powers were directed toward controlling another person—an absolutely fruitless, impossible, self-defeating task. If you also exhibited tunnel vision by focusing so intently on your romance that other priorities fell by the wayside, you can reframe that vision to reflect concentration or diligence, for these qualities certainly came into play. Although your energies were misdirected, it is important that you acknowledge your overall process and take pride in the drive with which you worked toward success. It is now a question of developing greater wisdom in choosing your objectives.

If, as a Fighter, you frequently made the mundane exciting by picking trivial fights, instead of in hindsight characterizing yourself as having been "mean" or "petty," think about the creativity that was involved. Had you turned cold leftovers into a gourmet feast, you would have been applauded for utilizing essentially the same ability. Likewise, if you frequently generated crisis out of minor incidents, chances are that in order to create and respond to those "crises" you had to be very resourceful. In a genuine life crisis such resourcefulness would be highly valued.

If, as a Rebel, you repeatedly induced auto-arousal by engaging in compulsive acts, you might be wondering what positive values could be found in such elementally self-destructive behavior. There are many, including persistence, concentration, sensuality, curiosity, defiance of social rules, and a willingness to take risks. The direction in which you channeled your energies did not became problematic because you rebelled, defied convention, or took risks, but because the risks you took were *sheltered.*

In taking sheltered risks, you may have channeled your power and energy into creating drama around an addiction or compulsion. It's important for you to remember that the power you misused toward that end is still power nonetheless. You are not now, *and never have been,* without power, choices, character, or valuable assets. For you, the greatest challenge of all may be to allow yourself to accept this.

Challenge #9: Be Willing to Forgive (and sometimes laugh at) Your "Failures"

I said earlier that the process of preparing for change (and the process of change itself) is a "three steps forward, one step (sometimes two steps) backward" procedure. Consequently, there will be many, many times when you think you have mastered a challenge, only to find that you have "forgotten" what you learned and have slipped into old patterns of thinking and acting—*again!*

It is important for you to accept that backtracking will be an ongoing part of the journey you have begun. The goal is not to avoid backtracking, but rather to *learn* from each retracing of your steps so that you won't have to go over the same ground more often than necessary. Part of the magic of change is that you may go over the same territory again and again, until you think you'll *never* march forward, and then one day you wake up to find yourself miles ahead of yesterday's position—without knowing how you got there. Leaps of progress occur frequently, and because they are often so sudden and unexpected, they feel magical. In fact, no one really knows exactly how the mind/spirit produces these results—but it does. *That* is a truly exciting mystery.

Since with all of your determination, inner wisdom, and power you will *still* often fail to be "perfect," the willingness to forgive yourself for each failure and to laugh at yourself whenever possible will become a priceless attribute.

Melanie was in the process of altering the way she created dramatic upheaval in her marriage when she found herself halfway through a raucous scene with her husband.

> I was standing in the kitchen, about to pick up a plate and throw it, when I realized what I was doing. I stared at him, and I just blurted out "Oh, NO!" and put the plate down . . . and something came over me. . . . I started to laugh and couldn't stop, because I realized how silly I looked and how unneces-

sary it was. I was crying from laughing so hard when I finally looked up at him and said, "You know, I think we should talk about this calmly." He thought I'd lost my mind, but we did talk, for hours. It was the first time.

Melanie's success in stopping the drama related directly to her lack of shame or guilt for having started it in the first place. Having accepted the tenets of Challenge 8, she was aware that positive character traits were contained within her dramatic style. She didn't feel "small" or "stupid" for having started a scene, and she wasn't embarrassed to stop smack in the middle. She didn't have to keep the drama going and then defend the necessity for it. She could face herself and her husband honestly and with a hearty dose of humor, because she was past the point of *making another drama out of having created the first one.* She could let go of it, forgive herself, and move on.

Like Melanie, all of us learn more from our so-called failures than from our successes. If we don't forgive ourselves for lapsing into drama, we can't make productive use of those lapses. Instead, we only perpetuate the drama itself.

In meeting the challenges in this chapter, you may realize that yesterday or last week you behaved in a way that signified emotional resistance. Instead of catching yourself at it you ignored the meaning of the behavior—and consequently ignored dealing with the resistance. You may observe yourself in the midst of a tirade in which, instead of taking responsibility for your choices, you blame everyone but yourself for your predicament. You may try to run from the pain of the losses that herald the beginning of real change, or you may hesitate to face the fears that keep you from taking healthy action. All of that is to be expected, understood, and forgiven. Rather than harassing yourself over what you failed to achieve, commend yourself for acknowledging your hesitancies or momentary lapses. The fact that you are capable of recognizing them is progress in itself, a sign that you are growing.

Challenge #10: Expect to Feel Discomfort as You Shed Your Old Self and Give Birth to the New

As you evolve through the process of recovering your strength, creative force, excitement drive, and natural wisdom, your "old self" will give way to a "new self." In effect, the drama-making grown-up child will be transformed into an exciting, adventuresome, vital woman. There is a kind of magic in this metamorphosis—magic of your own making, achieved through your own power. But there will also come a time when you experience great discomfort, when you have shed the skin of your old self but have not yet become one with your new self. It will be a time when you are likely to feel, "I am no longer who I was, but I'm not sure yet who I will be."

Challenge 10 can be compared to Challenge 3 ("Embrace Your Pain as You Grow"), although in some ways it is even more dramatic. While there is pain in confronting your past and facing certain truths about yourself, throughout most of that process you are still your old self and are, therefore, less likely to experience the identity confusion that is at the heart of this major transition.

It is important that you mentally prepare yourself for the eventual coming of this time. It is also important that you realize there is little you can *do* about it. You cannot avoid it or escape it; you can only expect it and accept that it will be a natural, normal part of your growing process. Of course, you will continue to grow and evolve emotionally, spiritually, psychologically, and physically throughout your lifetime. This initial transformation, however, can be the most uncomfortable. The transition period may be brief, lasting one or two months, or it may be lengthier, lasting up to a year or more—but if you desire change, this time must come.

For some of you, this period will be dramatic, exciting, suspenseful, and pleasurably frightening. It may in many respects be the quintessential "What will happen now?" experience, for a cliffhanger will exist not externally but internally, within your very being. What in life could be more thrilling?

For others, this interval between being and becoming can bring unwelcome fear—and consequent danger. Should the discomfort and unfamiliarity of your unfolding seem too great to bear, you might be tempted to seek safety in old, self-defeating patterns and relationships, because these at least provide a discomfort that is known. It is the difficulty of this period that makes critical your initial dedication to change and your ongoing willingness to accept the fact that growth can cause pain. As a dedicated, committed, faithful change-maker, you will not impulsively seek well-known ground. Instead, you will be able to experience both the sadness of loss and the joy of rediscovery.

Your journal can be a valuable companion during this transition period. As you try on new attitudes and styles of communication, experience shifts of mood and feeling, and practice unaccustomed behaviors, you will need a way of sorting out your emotions and perceptions. In your journal you will be able to capture and gain perspective on the inevitable day-to-day changes and moment-to-moment revelations.

One of the most trying aspects of this transitional stage is the tendency of intimates to attempt sabotage of your growth. Friends and family can easily pick up the scent of change on the wind—and they often unconsciously strive to repress that change. It takes great courage—and, again, dedication—to confront them and to repel their attempts to keep you as you were. It is not that they are malicious but that, just as you may have feared losing *them, they* may fear that if you change you will no longer need them or allow them to depend upon you. They may try to impede your evolution by getting angry, withdrawing, making greater demands on your time, criticizing you, telling you you're "not yourself," escalating crises of their own, or becoming testy or sarcastic.

The next challenge includes some suggestions for dealing with these unsupportive relationships. The honesty with which you do so will be a test of your dedication to yourself.

Challenge #11: Develop a Community of Loving, Supportive Intimates

Your final challenge concerns your community of intimates—the friends, family, and even coworkers who either nourish your growth or try to arrest it. It is important to nurture and ease your transition in a climate of support and encouragement. If you feel safe, you will not be drawn to the self-defeating familiarity of drama-making.

Challenge 11 could just as realistically be Challenge 1. It is last only because its critical nature might not have been clear to you before you had gained a broader understanding of the demands of preparing for change. There is much to be aware of, to learn, to overcome, to achieve, to relish—and the community of intimates you choose to include in your life will enhance or detract from the excitement and joy of the process.

As you seek self-renewal, much of your own resistance to change can hinge upon what you fear will become of the relationships on which you depend. If you are surrounded by critical, rigid, unaccepting people, you will naturally be more reined in by fears of their judgment and censure. If you are surrounded by clinging, insecure people, you will be held back by guilt about letting them down as you grow and expand. If you are surrounded by emotionally dishonest people, you will naturally restrain your urges to express yourself freely. But if you are surrounded by love and understanding—or even by simple acceptance—you will begin to flourish.

It has been my observation that the relationships we invite into our lives are perfect reflections of the way we feel about ourselves. The people you invite into your life treat you the way you believe you deserve to be treated. They discount you as you discount yourself; they restrain you as you restrain yourself. Consequently, it would be unrealistic to blame them for your difficulties in preparing for change, or in any other endeavor.

If your community of intimates is a manifestation of your own view of yourself, then even if you were to somehow make everyone disappear tomorrow your problems would remain, because your self-perception would remain the same. But if you were to actively build more supportive relationships—with the same and/or different people—the *action* of desiring, seeking, and generating those relationships would reveal a shift in your own self-perception. Your action and your belief would become one; you would receive the kind of support you sought, the kind you believed you deserved.

I suggest you make a list of the people who have the greatest impact upon your day-to-day life. Include lovers, friends, family members, and any coworkers or business associates to whom you are especially close. With respect to each of them, answer yes or no to the following questions:

I feel that he/she genuinely likes me.

I feel that what I do for him/her is appreciated.

I feel that I in some way receive back as much as I give to him/her.

I notice that he/she never snidely puts me, or women, down—even "in jest." If a criticism is offered, it is done respectfully.

I feel that he/she listens attentively when I speak.

I believe that he/she is always honest with me.

I notice that he/she doesn't discount or ridicule my feelings or beliefs, even if he/she disagrees or feels differently.

I feel that he/she is loyal and faithful to promises made to me.

I feel that he/she encourages me to reach for my
dreams and achieve my highest goals.

I find that he/she does *not* encourage me to talk about,
seek out, or act out the dramas in my life.

If you answered no to any of these questions with respect to anyone
on your list, it is important that you begin a dialogue with yourself
about the nature of your relationship with that person. Why are you
permitting yourself to be discounted? Why do you choose friends
who reinforce or encourage your dramatic behaviors? To what degree do you fail to take yourself seriously?

If right now you are saying to yourself, "I can't imagine answering
yes to all those questions regarding *everybody!* That's expecting way
too much of people," I say to you: No, you are asking far too little
for yourself. If you honestly don't believe you are entitled to truly
supportive relationships, you must begin to think about, and write in
your journal about, the possible reasons why that may be. If you *do*
believe you are entitled, you must question your motives for not
inviting more such relationships into your life—and for not eliminat-
ing relationships with people who belittle your worth.

I am not suggesting that you callously "dump" people who have
been important to you. But if your relationships are not mutually
supportive, I strongly urge you to share your concerns honestly with
the people in question. If there is love and caring at the core of a
relationship, your willingness to reach out and discuss your feelings
may mark the the beginning of a new era of open communication. If,
on the other hand, someone discounts, ridicules, or ignores your
concerns, you must then reconsider the wisdom of putting more
precious energy into that bond. As difficult and painful as it can be
to say good-bye to someone you have cared about, if that person is
lacking concern and respect for you, ending the relationship is an act
of self-love and self-respect.

If your current love relationship or marriage is among the relationships that are unsupportive, it is especially important that you begin
to talk with your partner about the personal changes that you intend
to make. Reassure him that by changing yourself you are not withdrawing from him. Perhaps you can even share parts of this book with
your partner so that he can begin to understand exactly what you
want to achieve, and why. Remember, change is about *you,* not about
your partner. If you go to him hoping that you can make him change
his behavior, you are defeating your purpose.

If you can't seem to bring yourself to communicate, or if you refuse to try, this is the first problem you must face. I know it will be difficult, and that you will be risking a lot. You partner may become angry, ridicule you, blame you, or ignore you—especially if he, too, has grown accustomed to a dramatic, self-defeating style of living. But if this is his final response to matters that mean so much to you, it is time you saw his position clearly. Even more important, it is time you looked honestly at the relationship you've chosen. I ask you: Is this all you are worthy of? If not, the only way to preserve your emotional health may be to end the relationship. While this may not be an option you are willing to entertain initially, I urge you to develop strong links to the rest of your community of intimates so that you can receive the love and support you desire.

On the brighter side, you may discover that your partner is more concerned about your happiness, more willing to explore ways of growing closer, more eager to support your search for self-renewal and true excitement than you ever dreamed. Don't presume the worst without discussion; instead, have the courage to speak what is in your heart.

As you begin the change-making process set forth in the next chapter, you may find opportunities to initiate many new relationships. As you do, nothing could be more important to your growth than your willingness to seek out those who can support your evolving vision of yourself. While it is true that your community is a mirror of how you see yourself, the face it reveals is one you have the power to endlessly refashion. If you are willing to always reach for the best that is within you, there will be no limit to the transformations you can create in your life.

9 ❧

Change-Making:
The Thrill of It All

As a therapist I have helped many women prepare for change and then slowly, methodically, and actively take steps to produce the changes they desired. I've helped them stop seeking sensation in self-diminishing ways and stop reinforcing the belief that they are unworthy of anything better. And again and again I've watched as something more than behavioral and emotional change took place, something I can only call a transformation of consciousness—a qualitative, generous shift in the way these women came to accept, respect, and empower themselves. I believe that this essential transformation is part of an alchemy of mind, deed, and spirit that occurs within all those who welcome and work toward real change.

I believe this inner magic can be achieved by any woman willing to dedicate herself to change-making. In each practical, concrete step beyond melodrama and in each instant of newfound excitement, a touch of that magic is found.

The Path to Change-Making

In the previous chapter you encountered eleven challenges that, when met, will have prepared you for change-making. In contrast to the general nature of those challenges, the change-making steps are very specific and, in most cases, quite practical and concrete. Each step offers suggestions to all women, and some also provide individual advice for Fighters, Challengers, and Rebels.

The six steps are a distillation of the change-making process much as it occurs in therapy. Just as in therapy a client experiences a forward/backward/forward progression, you will undoubtedly find yourself moving backward and forward through these steps. You may begin by working them in order and realize as you do Step Four that you haven't really completed Step Two, or you may discover that you experience some resistance as you do Step Six and must delve further into the challenge of exploring your past. All of this is a natural and expected part of change-making, the part for which no amount of instruction can truly prepare you. If you are willing to pay attention to your feelings and your bodily sensations as they arise, you will be blessed with wisdom about your own needs—wisdom of a sort that no one else could possibly provide you.

Following are the six change-making steps:

One: Self-Reassessment

Two: Choosing Healthy Excitement

Three: Anticipating Your Next Drama

Four: Replacing Old Behaviors

Five: Seeking Support

Six: Rewarding Yourself

A detailed "how-to" of each change-making step could conceivably fill its own full chapter, even its own whole book. Within this single chapter I can offer only a territorial map of the emotional and behavioral terrain you need to cover—a way of finding your starting point, your direction, and your best route, but certainly not a day-by-day guided tour. I have faith, however, that herein lies a wonderful beginning for a journey that will transform your life. While for some of you this chapter may provide all the guidance you require, I believe it will be worthwhile for you to seek a more detailed navigational guide to the emotional realms we will be exploring, especially those that are most unfamiliar to you. Until I can offer my own workbook for that purpose, I refer you to the listing in the Appendix of the excellent material written by my colleagues. Dedicated as you now are to change, searching out these books and reading and using them can only further seal your commitment to yourself.

In any case, I urge you to consistently follow the six change-making steps. These are the steps that I know can produce results. These are the steps that I know are empowering. Take them, use them, and practice them. You *can* change your life!

Change-Making Step One: Self-Reassessment

A sense of values, both spiritual and pragmatic, and an acknowledged, meaningful set of personal priorities give your life continuity and provide a context for all that you do. When your actions are consistent with your values and priorities, you experience a rich and *contextual*—as opposed to *episodic*—way of life.

When I speak of "context," I mean the awareness of how every event in your life and every day, week, and year are connected to all other events and times. I mean a sense of overarching purpose, against which everything you do can be measured. Just as words can lose their intended meaning when taken "out of context," events in our lives become mere episodes, disjointed and senseless, unless they are viewed "in context." In this step, you will begin to examine your life, your personal priorities, and your values as a means of bringing a thread of meaning to all you do.

Our personal values consist of the qualities of living that we hold in high esteem (for example, kindness, honesty, family loyalty, marital fidelity, friendship, religious commitment, or spontaneity). Our personal priorities consist of the attributes and endeavors we hold most dear (for example, expressing creativity, spending time with loved ones, making money, becoming famous or powerful, doing good work, finding love, or being a caring mother). When we know what we believe in and what matters, we have a gauge with which to check whether or not our words and deeds fit the context we've created for ourselves.

Perhaps you can imagine this concept as a piece of cloth being woven upon a loom. The warp refers to the solid threads tied to the loom, and the woof to the color and pattern brought in across the warp. The warp is like the context I am speaking of—a solid base upon which to hang all of the color, texture, and excitement of your life. The warp is stretched upon the loom so that it carries the tension of the weaving; in a similar way, the context of your life provides the strength to bear the stresses that the "woof," or activity, might bring to bear.

If we are aware of our values and priorities, we can seek sensation that is bolstered by the attributes we hold dear. If we have no consciousness of what matters, if there is no basic meaning to our lives, sensation-seeking becomes a haphazard, hit-or-miss affair with no foundation.

When threads of meaning link the days of our lives, our actions begin to reflect a certain continuity. People often misconstrue "continuity" to mean "sameness," carrying the implication that we should get up and do the same damn thing every day. *That,* for most of us, is deadly. Rather, acting with continuity means that whatever you do, no matter how much variety or excitement you factor into your life, your activities will fit into a personally moral, self-respectful, integrated, and purposeful framework—and that when they don't, you'll know it, and you'll learn from the repercussions.

Living with a sense of context and continuity does not mean that your values and priorities will, or should be, cast in stone. Our priorities change over time and our values are always evolving, in an ongoing process of attitude and belief formation. But these changes build upon themselves, one leading to the next in a natural progression as we continue having, and seriously examining, our own beads of experience.

We are not all going to embrace the same priorities, values, or spiritual ideals. But we must believe that the goals and values guiding us are relevant to us, individually. Then we can measure our decisions about the relationships we choose, the actions we take, and the excitements we pursue against this deep, personal foundation.

I hope that you will allow self-love and self-respect to become increasingly important values. In addition, you must begin to explore and acknowledge other ideals and endeavors, letting them become the warp through which the stunning new motif of your life can be woven.

Start by answering the questions below in your journal, and then spend more time writing about the feelings that come up in response to them. Go slowly, savoring each question and thinking about how it applies directly to your own behavior. It may take many nights, or a full weekend or two, for you to explore these issues; the process should be leisurely. Your discoveries will make this procedure both pleasurable and profitable. Treat it as though it were a song you have chosen to sing to yourself: the point of singing is not to get to the end of the song but to hear the notes, words, and messages along the way.

What does "God" or "Higher Power" mean to you?

Do you believe that what happens to you after you die
   is a consequence of the way you live now?

What do you value most about humanity?

What do you value about friendship?

What do you value in a love relationship?

What does it mean for someone to be "the best person he/she can be"?

If you knew you were going to die in five years, what would you do with your time? If you knew you were going to die in one year? In one month?

What is your philosophy of life?

What is your parents' philosophy? Does it differ from yours? If so, how and why?

How would you like to make your mark upon the world?

What gives your life meaning today?

What do you *want* out of life? Make a list.

What *must* you have in order to be happy? Make a list.

What would you miss most if you became deaf? If you became blind? If you were unable to speak? If you were unable to walk or move about?

What would you like to be able to say if you were writing your own epitaph? Can you say it now? If not, why not?

Consider how your reactions to these questions reveal your deep-seated sense of beliefs, values, and priorities, which are either put into practice or ignored in your daily life. Consider what it would mean to your life if for just *one week* your every word and deed were absolutely consistent with the demands of your innermost values and priorities. How would that change your love relationships, your friendships, your work, your self-image? What would you do and say differently, from moment to moment, for each of those seven days?

In helping you to discover the values and priorities that can create a context for your life, the above questions provide you with an auspicious beginning—but you must be willing to take the time necessary to explore them fully. I suggest that after you have mulled them over, answered them, and written about the feelings they evoke, you put your journal aside for two or three days, then come back and reread it. Then, quickly, without thinking it through, complete the following sentences by writing the first thing that comes to your mind.

My five most highly regarded current values are _____.

My five most important current life priorities are _____.

Now add a brief sentence to each item, defining what the terms mean *to you.*

Here are some completed sentences, borrowed from clients who have followed through on these exercises. You are by no means expected to mirror these examples; I offer them only to illustrate the diversity of results that can be achieved.

Angie: Forty years old, married; sales representative

Values

integrity—to do what I believe in, to finish what I start, to remember what I promised

intelligence—to use the wits I've been blessed with

loyalty—to my husband, to myself

compassion—to never lose sight of someone else's troubles; to always vote Democratic, even if I was promised I'd make more money in a Republican society

passion—to care enough to have emotion about things, whether a play, a book, a person, a movie, or politics; to have feelings and not be afraid to express them

Priorities

money—to make more money than I'll ever need

my marriage—to nurture the love relationship I have for the rest of my life *self-improvement*—to continue improving myself mentally and physically, and to learn more about my interests

career success—to become a sales manager

health—to maintain good health

Loretta: Twenty-eight years old, divorced mother of one son; office manager

Values

friendship—being a caring, responsive friend

beauty—surrounding myself with lovely, aesthetic environments, and having beautiful things in my home

attentiveness—paying attention to the little things that make life more enjoyable: a sunset, music, a rainstorm

forgiveness—being able to understand and forgive myself and others for some of the hurtful things we do

humor—being able to laugh a lot, even at silly things

Priorities

my son—being there for him, but trying not to be overprotective

my friends—making the effort to spend time with them, even though it sometimes seems like there is no time

exercise—being physically fit, and being outdoors as much as possible

culture—going to plays and films, or reading and learning about the arts

job excellence—doing the best job I can; not letting people down who count on me

As awareness of your personal values and priorities grows, it will become natural for you to weigh your actions against these criteria.

And because you're threading the "warp," when you begin weaving vivid new patterns through your everyday life the result will always reflect your own special design.

Change-Making Step Two: Choosing Healthy Excitement

In this step you are reminded of what healthy excitement really is. For perhaps the first time in your life you will focus on the question of what brings excitement to *you.* You will learn how to extract the vital seeds of true excitement from your current drama-seeking style, and you will begin to choose means of bringing personally meaningful expression to all of your sensation-seeking needs.

It's important to first reiterate the differences between dramatic and healthy excitement. In contrast to melodramatic highs, pure excitement is the kind of stimulation that brings renewed confidence, a feeling of glad-to-be-aliveness, and an affirmation of your greatest gifts and abilities, with no backlash of despair. Unlike drama, healthy excitement will never betray your highest self, and never demean you in your own eyes.

Healthy excitement differs from dramatic excitement in two other concrete, essential ways. First, where drama is self-defeating, healthy excitement is self-actualizing. This means that the experience maintains or strengthens self-esteem, furthers goals and ambitions, or enhances growth as an individual on the mental, emotional, spiritual, or physical plane. Second, where drama offers ephemeral emotional rewards but cannot deliver any that last, healthy excitement offers both substantial immediate pleasure *and* the potential for lasting reward.

Healthy excitement can be "agonizing" in its own way. Many of the serious endeavors that bring true excitement—especially those pertaining to professional and personal growth—can also encompass struggle, failure, anxiety, fear, embarrassment, pain, and other sensations that are occasionally similar to those evoked by drama. In such cases, distinctions between drama and true excitement are not based strictly on the emotional content of selected moments of experience, but rather on the overall effect they have upon one's sense of self. Drama betrays the beauty of your individuality; healthy excitement is faithful to it. Drama misappropriates your power; healthy excitement illuminates it.

The Seeds of True Excitement

Within every drama lie the seeds of true excitement. Each rewarding element in your personal dramas can be replicated without tragic repercussions. In that respect, you have everything to gain and nothing to lose by bringing healthy excitement into your life.

Writer Alice Walker has said that "to suppress any part of the personality is to maim the soul." This is especially true in terms of sensation-seeking. The road to true excitement will *not* be found by ignoring the dramatic orientation to which you've become most attached. Instead, you'll find your direction by respecting the elements of drama that are already "thrill sources" for you and seeking their replicas in more productive endeavors that are consistent with your values and priorities.

In the previous chapter, you encountered Challenge 8, "Reframe your deficits as strengths." I asked you to consider the faculties you have used to create your favorite dramas, and to view these faculties in terms of innate strength rather than weakness. In this second change-making step, you will continue the same reframing process—only now, instead of merely redefining the abilities and powers you used to create drama, you will begin to select alternate activities. These activities will be those that incorporate both your strengths *and* the particular elements of drama that have characteristically produced the most excitement for you.

Remember that the process of responding to the suggestions offered here cannot be completed in a few hours, or even days. You will need to spend time considering these suggestions, talking about them with friends, writing about them in your journal, and dreaming about them. You may want to seek additional sources of inspiration, ideas, and questions. But I promise that this step, if undertaken seriously and with dedication, will produce almost immediate changes in your life.

Choosing True Excitement: An Overview

The first thing I want you to do is turn to a fresh page in your journal. At the top of it, preferably in a color different from the one you normally use (for quick reference later), write down your essential values and highest priorities. In moving on to consider new sources of excitement, remember to *always* measure them against this essential, personally meaningful foundation. For example, if you should become suddenly thrilled by the idea of learning to race automobiles, and one of your priorities is "providing security for my children," it would be obvious that you need to think long and hard about whether racing would productively fit within the context of your life.

Before we tackle the specifics of extracting true excitement from your own drama-seeking style, I will set the stage by clarifying the beliefs with which I approach this step.

There are many venues in which healthy excitement can be found: work, recreation, volunteer efforts, creative outlets, personal growth, romantic relationships, and parenting, to name the broadest categories (many of which also overlap). In the process of change-making, I believe that it is important for you to focus on involvements outside the romantic province, and that you limit those specifically involving parenting. Of course you want healthy family relationships and romance in your life. However, this step is not about that kind of excitement. As we've seen throughout this book, you can't successfully confine your sensation-seeking to intimate relationships without becoming mired in drama.

While this step may not be about romance, it *is* about passion, about dreams, and about making those dreams real. We often live our lives according to someone else's plan, failing to experience, or go after, our hearts' desires. We negate their importance or deny our ability to achieve them, relying instead on the drama in our lives to make us feel alive. This step is about acknowledging those yearnings, both little and grand—buying that puppy you've always wanted or that property you're dying to renovate; scaling that mountain you've been longing to climb, or starting that business you've often envisioned—and about bringing them to life.

This step is also about discovering the dreams you never knew you had, and about finding the excitement you never knew you were looking for. If this is the first time you have given thought to identifying and demanding satisfaction of your excitement-seeking needs, you will have to do a great deal of exploration in order to uncover your dreams and desires before you can begin to actualize them.

Since so many women today are able to engage in work they love if they take the time to consider their options and pursue them, I believe in—and will be emphasizing—the excitement to be found in a *career* that is consistent with your values and favored sensation-seeking style. I will also emphasize it because I believe that both economic independence and a sense of achievement are critical to self-esteem.

But what about those of you who may simply not be interested in having a career? Perhaps you are a homemaker who is financially comfortable and not inclined to work, and who disagrees with my viewpoint about its importance. And what about those of you who must take jobs that are difficult and unexciting just to survive? Perhaps you are a single mother with a job you don't like, but that you feel you must do because your children have to eat. Finding a thrilling career may not be an option many of you can—or wish—to pursue, but adding healthy stimulation to your life certainly is. I ask you to consider the pastimes, creative projects, community affairs, and political issues that bear directly upon your economic or social situation. I urge you to think about the sports, the pleasure in nature, the self-improvement and educational opportunities that might strike a chord within you. There are myriad activities to choose from, many of which require little or no financial outlay.

I believe that healthy excitement will mean something different for everyone. Just as we all have personal preferences in clothing, food, entertainment, and companionship, we all perceive various circumstances to be less or more exciting—and, as we now know, we all have different levels of demand and tolerance for arousing, high-intensity experiences. In seeking to bring true excitement to your life, it is crucial that you allow no one's ideals, perceptions, demands, values, or priorities *but your own* to determine your choices. ("No one" includes me—I will be offering some hard advice, but it is *you* who must determine whether it fits.)

The following sections provide specific suggestions for Fighters, Challengers, and Rebels. If you've found that your own drama-seeking style is a hybrid of two or more primary styles, then each of the pertinent sections will be helpful to you. It is important that you pay close attention to which suggestions seem to "jump off the page," as though they were speaking directly to you. Chances are that these will contain germs of ideas that can be successfully translated into your life. You have many useful skills to channel into true excitement-seeking. You may want to find a way of applying all of them, or you may realize that only a few are meaningful to you. You have a buffet before you—and *anything* is possible.

True Excitement, Fighter Style

If your excitement has been found in Fighter-style drama, it will be important for you to consider new adventures that utilize the skills and replicate the thrills and rewards you have achieved. If you have frequently fought with lovers and family, if chaos has swirled around you for many years, you are not likely to find large doses of peace and quiet tempting. Instead, you are accustomed to acting out, to making big productions of relatively small events and minor problems. You've learned to extract some pleasure from conflict and crisis, and it would be a shame not to take advantage of what you already know. Instead of seeking true excitement by further acting out, you must look for new stimulation and satisfaction in a similar, but more productive endeavor: taking ACTION!

To begin, think about the reframing and redefining of deficits to which you were introduced in the previous chapter (Challenge 8). Make a list of the action-oriented skills and attributes with which you approached creating your Fighter-style dramas, and add to them. Have you included the following?

- willingness to take a position
- willingness to stand by your position
- ability to function under high levels of stress
- ability to engage other people's immediate attention

Now consider the elements of drama that most of your scenarios included:

- exaggeration and magnification
- playing for an audience
- seeing others as adversaries
- making the mundane exciting
- intense, unresolved episodes

It seems to me that "intense, unresolved episodes" are at odds with the very purpose of taking action, which is to generate resolution to problems. And I cannot see how continuing to engage in "exaggeration and magnification" or to view "others as adversaries" will add quality to your life. However, both "making the mundane exciting" and "playing for an audience" can be highly enjoyable aspects of many healthy Fighter-style adventures.

For example, Anne began a career in catering because it is a crisis-oriented business where even mundane kitchen chores such as chopping vegetables can become urgently exciting. Invariably, a client will demand something at the last minute—maybe three huge baskets of sculpturally arranged crudités to be added to the order (on the same afternoon that the catering truck blows a tire or a key employee calls in sick). Anne enjoys taking *action* in the midst of this type of crisis, solving all the problems, and keeping the client happy.

Ginny was a client of mine who viewed herself as someone to whom bad things happened, and she loved to share "poor me" stories with her friends. In one month alone, she rear-ended a car at a stoplight, her cat ran away, and she was audited by the IRS. Shortly thereafter, a thief broke into her new condo and stole her stereo and jewelry. But this time, instead of wallowing in her victimization, she got mad—and took *action*.

"I thought, *enough!* I'm going to do something about this," Ginny told me.

> I formed a security committee of homeowners. We called meetings, invited the police department to speak to us about safety measures, and advised homeowners on what they could do to protect their property—the whole bit. I felt, for the first time, that what I did during and after the crisis was worthwhile. People came up to me and thanked me for the organizing and the planning I had done, and I felt great.

As a result of her involvement with the homeowners' association (as well as her determination to feature healthy excitement in her life), Ginny proceeded to learn everything she could about home security. Today, she is an expert in the field of residential security and has built a successful business as a consultant to homeowner associations and residential developers. Most often she is called in to revamp existing systems after there has been a series of robberies or vandalisms. It is this intervention at a time of crisis within the community that Ginny most loves.

Now is the time for you to find new "action adventures" to satisfy your own sensation-hunger. Following are specific suggestions based upon what I've found to be successful outlets for other Fighters. Later on I will suggest techniques for ferreting out creative possibilities that are applicable to all types of drama-seekers.

There are innumerable outlets for women who find excitement in conflict and crisis. There are causes to be served, people and issues that need representation, and emergencies that require attention. Many women with this orientation have found success in emergency-care services as firefighters, paramedics, trauma surgeons or physicians, police officers, and 911 operators. Others have lent themselves to "good" fights as attorneys, paralegals, legal secretaries, union representatives, mental-health advocates, lobbyists, and political activists. Some have found other fast-paced, crisis-ridden occupations: news reporter, travel-tour director, construction supervisor, restaurant manager, chef, stockbroker. The possibilities are limited only by your willingness to imagine or seek them.

In order to introduce excitement to your work you may need to change careers or return to school—exciting endeavors in themselves. But if neither of these is a realistic or desirable option, there are many alternate efforts you can make. For example, if you are a secretary working in an insurance office and are bored with forms and numbers, you could consider a lateral move, perhaps into a different, more heated environment—such as a criminal-law office—where you can be part of a team that is involved with real drama. If you are in sales, and the product or marketing strategies of your company do nothing to excite you, you might think about moving into an industry that "grabs" you.

It is also possible, no matter what your job, to make it more exciting by becoming dedicated to excellence. In Charles Cameron and Suzanne Elusorr's book *T.G.I.M.* ("Thank God It's Monday"), advice for "zenning it" or developing an "undercover" job is offered to help people derive a sense of adventure from even the most tedious position. The book also offers excellent techniques for discovering the work you were "born to do," or in which you can make the most satisfying contribution. I heartily recommend it for all types of drama-seekers.

All of the attributes of stimulating work-for-pay can also be found in volunteerism and commitment to such causes as the nuclear freeze, environmental conservation, help for rape or child-abuse victims, funding for AIDS research, human-rights advocacy, women's issues, and so on. Perhaps you have been the genuine victim of injustice or crime. If so, you will have strong feelings about issues related to your own experience. Instead of allowing yourself to deny your feelings, ignore them, or make greater drama of them, you can take action. By doing so you will find both excitement and resolution to the sense of helplessness and powerlessness that tragic events often impose. These are arenas in which your penchant for "fighting with or fighting for" can make an important—perhaps even life-and-death—difference to humanity.

Athletics and team sports also offer outlets for healthy, exciting conflict and crisis. On playing fields we can fight to the finish, with a vengeance, and keep our personal lives intact!

As a Fighter you have *so many* admirable abilities. Use them purposefully, have fun with them, and become excited about them. They are worth far more than you may have known.

True Excitement, Challenger Style

If most of your dramas have centered around romantic competition, your task will be to channel the very same skills that served your dramas into challenges worthy of these skills, challenges that reflect your values and personal priorities.

Like the Fighter, you will need to further the reframing and redefining of deficits that you began with Challenge 8. Make a list of the skills and attributes with which you approached the creation of your Challenger-style dramas. Have you included the following?

- being a "go-getter"
- drive and endurance
- willingness to set goals and tenaciously pursue them
- ability to strategize
- willingness to compete

Now, keeping your special skills in mind, let's look at the major elements of Challenger drama:

- orientation toward striving
- excitement in the realm between desire and attainment
- an "I can" attitude
- search for specialness and validation

Each of the above elements has a counterpart in healthy excitement. Every challenge, no matter how worthy or destructive, is an act of striving. That is the very nature of challenge. The excitement, or high, of healthy challenge arises from the fever of desiring something, of having a *want,* turning that want into a goal, and striving to achieve it. Of course, the excitement of striving is always fraught with its own emotional push/pull and its own "agonies," but it is thrilling, nonetheless.

Taking on any worthy challenge demands that you have faith, confidence, and the belief in your ability to meet it. In dramatic challenge, this "I can" attitude is directed toward a person. In healthy, exciting challenge, it is directed toward a genuine accomplishment.

Involvement in a purposeful challenge (whether or not you ultimately succeed in meeting it) is a powerful validation of your abilities, drive, and determination. And, should you meet your challenge, there is no question that accomplishment produces well-deserved feelings of specialness. As a Challenger you probably need to learn how to enjoy *having* as much as striving. By beginning to tackle worthy, realistic challenges, you will begin discovering the joys of attainment.

Joan is a Challenger who finds excitement in the challenge of learning and becoming an expert. She has become adept at such varied activities as gardening, computer programming, knitting, and tarot-card reading.

> I decide that I'm going to learn about something new—not just dabble, but learn it well. Learning is very exciting and challenging to me. I love to take classes, but I'll also go to the library or the bookstore and get ten, twelve books on a subject. There was a time when I knew nothing about gardening and could barely keep a plant alive, but I learned about it. Now I have a backyard full of exotic blooms that I've grown from cuttings. I also learned to read tarot from books—I remember when there were cards and charts and diagrams spread all over my kitchen table for at least six months.

Stephanie seeks challenges of a very different kind—she is a professional stuntwoman. She challenges herself both mentally and physically on a daily basis as she sets up and implements the feats that make most of us gasp and cringe in the darkness of a movie theater.

Amy runs a day-care center. She loves children, and she thrives on the challenge of striving for excellence in her profession. She started her business in the backyard of her home, and she now has a six-room center in its own building.

In order to help you focus on the kinds of exciting, purposeful challenges that might provide outlets for your drives and your talents, refer to the techniques described later in this section. Remember, there are as many potential challenges available as there are personal interests, talents, and passions. Anything you care deeply about can be converted into a challenge, whether the contest is with others or with yourself. That is why it is difficult for me to provide specific suggestions for Challengers, but easy for Challengers to generate their own. Anything goes.

If you have a creative bent, set yourself a creative challenge. If you have technical or mathematical abilities, set yourself a challenge of that sort. If you are athletic, an avid cook, have a sales personality, or are able to build things with your hands, select challenges that match your attributes. Remember, this step is about seeking your dreams and living your passions. Don't settle for a challenge to which you cannot honestly dedicate yourself, for you will find excitement only in striving toward what you genuinely, deeply, intensely *want*. Nothing else will do.

One of the most exciting elements of challenge is the suspense it generates. Since your excitement in the past stemmed from romantic cliff-hanger scenarios that became more thrilling as the outcome became more uncertain, you may already be hooked on suspense. By involving yourself in challenges worthy of your highest level of accomplishment, you will find all the suspense you can handle. If you should choose the challenge of actualizing your dreams in the form of a new business, you will be overwhelmed with suspense! I am a great proponent of women becoming business owners and entrepreneurs, and I can think of few endeavors that produce more genuine drama than starting up a business. All the rewards of melodrama are there: suspense (Will there be customers? Will the suppliers ship the goods on time?), command of center stage (you *are* the boss!), a sense of aliveness (wanting and striving certainly makes you feel alive), and a sense of specialness (imagine if your business *really* takes off!). Think of it—all the benefits and thrills of drama, and none of the costs. *That* can be your future.

True Excitement, Rebel Style

If you have found excitement in sheltered risks, you will discover greater satisfaction and self-respect the moment you begin taking more meaningful, expressive, *un*sheltered risks. You will need to call upon all your courage and all the strengths of character you have recently defined, because the task will demand much of you.

Looking back at the attributes you began to list when you faced Challenge 8 in the previous chapter, see if you can supply any additions. Have you included these?

- generally hearty appetite for sensation
- willingness to risk failure or danger
- inability to accept at face value many of conventional society's limitations
- natural curiosity

As you consider the strengths in your dramatic behavior, it is also important that you begin to recognize the "education" with which your drama-making provided you. What do you now know about life that you might not otherwise have discovered? About yourself? About the psychology of being human? It would be worthwhile for you to spend some time writing in your journal or talking into a tape recorder about the kinds of "lessons" your history provided. Whether your experiences were objectively good or bad, they are worth something because they are yours, and also because they contain messages that might be beneficial to others.

It is critically important that you now ask yourself the following questions:

Am I willing to engage in activities that are neither "bad girl" nor "good girl," and that may even defy the "girl" rules altogether?

Am I willing to risk being judged or rejected by people who don't agree with me or who don't care to understand what is meaningful to me?

If your answer to either of these questions is no, you are in effect saying that you are not willing to expand your excitement-seeking repertoire by taking risks that are not sheltered. If that is the case, I urge you to seek therapy, because you are probably not ready to make further moves on your own.

If you answered yes to both questions, you are in for a wonderful experience. Using your power and skills to find exciting ways of expressing yourself will shake the foundation of your existence and dramatically change your life.

To begin, let's look at the two major elements of Rebel-style drama that can also be found in true excitement: auto-arousal, and the danger/fear/excitement connection.

First, auto-arousal: there are positive as well as negative means of creating auto-arousal. Examples of auto-arousal experiences through which you can find true excitement include creativity; safely altering your consciousness through visualization, self-hypnosis, meditation, or fantasy; and exploration of your sensuality through taking pleasure in giving and receiving massages, enjoying food and wine as a source of varied, delicate sensation (as opposed to filling up and getting drunk), and developing greater appreciation of nature and art.

Next is the danger/fear/excitement connection. All of the sensations associated with this trinity can be found in healthy excitement. There is nothing intrinsically wrong with desiring these feelings. If your dramas produced them, your new activities can do so as well, particularly when they involve meaningful, cause-related rebellion or authentic creative expression.

It has been my consistent experience that women whose sensation-seeking is heavily weighted in the Rebel category have a particularly strong need to express themselves through creative means. The creative process is one of distinct auto-arousal and is, therefore, highly compatible with sensation-seeking tendencies. The act of exposing one's "guts" through creativity is one of tremendous personal risk. It is dangerous, exciting, frightening, suspenseful, and invigorating. In creation, you experience an inexhaustible range of intense sensations.

Over and over again I have seen Rebels who tended toward criminal or compulsive behavior find self-renewal, regain their power, and become aligned with their highest selves through the act of creation. And in their own rediscovery, I have seen them lose the drive for activities or drugs that once filled the void where emotion and inner truth now come to reside. However, with this change-making step I am not yet asking you to give up the drama of sexual adventure, drugs, or compulsive behaviors. I am only asking that you begin *now* to bring creative, exciting activities into your life. Use the techniques of journal dialogue, visualization, sentence completion, and clustering described in the section that follows, and let these techniques inspire you.

Often, our greatest inspirations are other women who have themselves achieved the seemingly impossible. Erica, for example, is a former sexual adventuress and occasional shoplifter who now works as a production assistant for a company that produces investigative documentaries. "I used to have an incredible drive for danger," she admits. "Many of my affairs were with mobster types. There's plenty of danger in my work, too, in checking out subjects like industrial espionage. But it's also very satisfying. I feel as though I'm doing a service as well as living a thrilling life."

Tracy is a former alcohol abuser and the mother of four children. She doesn't work at a full-time outside job, but she has become an expert in still photography and recently sold one of her photographs to a national magazine. Linda, a former compulsive spender, has found fulfillment and exciting action as an art director for an advertising agency. Pam, an ex–cocaine abuser, loves her work as a special-effects makeup artist. Sandi, who once called herself a "self-stimulation junkie" because she engaged in almost every auto-arousal mechanism possible, has just completed a novel based on her life story. She hasn't sold it yet, but for her, waiting to see what will happen produces almost as much excitement and suspense as the process of writing.

Some Rebels, such as Sandi and Tracy, prefer avenues of creative expression that involve working alone. Others, such as Erica and Linda, prefer to work with other people. All of these women have in one way or another found means of courageously and expressively seeking artistic adventures of the heart and the spirit. Whatever their creative product, it is a reflection of who they are and what they believe in.

Some Rebels pursue a different kind of creativity. They create change—in society, politics, the workplace, their relationships. These women may or may not take "artistic" risks, but they apply their personal stamp—their beliefs, values, and priorities—to everything they do. If social or political rebellion is fomenting within you, express yourself through action. Like the Fighter, it will be important for you to promote the changes you value and to become involved in causes or issues you believe in. Obviously, doing so can entail risk and danger—but certainly not of the sheltered variety. Such activities are forms of rebelling purposefully and with integrity.

Sometimes it isn't necessary to take a major stand or to pursue an exhaustive creative dream. It may be that, for you, true rebellion will mean expressing your real feelings to people who try to put you in a mold that no longer fits. It may be that risking a confrontation with your boss at work or demanding rightful compensation for work performed will constitute the only "revolt" necessary. And it may be that if you begin to live your life creatively—whether that means taking the time to put a fresh rose on the table at breakfast or going to a punk-rock concert for the first time—you will be expressing the sentiments and taking the stands that are important to *you*. In action you will finally find the genuine, meaningful excitement you've been missing.

Techniques for Choosing True Excitement

Journal Dialogue.   You can release creative ideas by writing a dialogue with a relevant aspect of yourself—in this case, your drama-maker side—focusing on the subject you wish to explore (for instance, positive excitement). For example:

Karen: Okay, what do you think we could do that's exciting and good for us?

Drama-maker: Well, it had better be *very exciting,* because you know how nasty I can get when I'm bored.

Karen: Okay, okay—but give me an idea. What do you really love to do?

Drama-maker: I love to be *right,* I love to right wrongs, to fight for us, to "kick ass"—*you* know!

Karen: Yes, and you're good at it, too. But now why don't you think about the kinds of fights that really matter—not the little petty arguments you always get into.

Drama-maker: Well, I was thinking lately . . . no, you'll think this is dumb . . .

Karen: No, I promise I won't. Tell me.

Drama-maker: I was thinking that I'm not very happy with the way the union is handling the personnel problems we've been having at work—*someone* ought to intervene, get more involved with the union, and fight for some changes.

Karen: Someone like you?

Drama-maker: Someone like *us.*

Visualization.   The kind of visualization we did in the previous chapter (in search of the "wise person" or "guide") can be effectively used to help you focus on new avenues of excitement-seeking.

Just as you did in the earlier exercise, find a quiet place to be alone, close your eyes, and focus on your breathing until you have achieved a state of calm relaxation. Then, do one of the following:

- Focus on each of the values from the list you made earlier, and allow your mind to drift in search of images that show you taking actions that reflect those values.
- Picture a scene in which you have previously acted out a drama. Now, one by one, exchange the place, the faces, and the dialogue for those that reflect service to a worthy cause, one that is meaningful to you. Allow the level of intensity or urgency to remain consistent with the level in your drama. Focus on the details: What are you involved with, what is your role, and what are you achieving?
- Picture yourself playing, doing things you've never before attempted. For example, imagine yourself

scuba diving, hang gliding, belly dancing, surfing, playing basketball, skiing, driving a racing car, running a marathon, or flying an airplane. Try on as many activities as you can think of, and notice which ones generate the greatest sense of aliveness and exhilaration.

- Picture yourself creatively occupied. Imagine yourself writing a song, a poem, a novel; creating a work of visual art, taking photographs, designing clothing, soldering jewelry; landscaping; acting in a play; or making a video—again, try on as many activities as you can, and notice which ones produce the most pleasurable feelings.

Sentence Completion. Take the time to write in your journal, speak into a tape recorder, or discuss with friends your feelings about your responses to the following questions. Allow yourself to answer each question over and over until you can think of nothing else to add, and listen at a deep level to your answers. In what direction are they pointing you? How can you go about achieving those goals?

All my life I've wished I could do_____.

Nothing excites me more than_____.

I'm utterly fascinated by_____.

I'd love to learn to_____.

If I could start all over again, I'd_____.

I'm happiest when I_____.

I lose track of time when I'm_____.

Above all, I want_____.

Clustering. In her book *Writing the Natural Way,* Gabrielle Rico describes a powerful technique that can be used for getting in touch with many kinds of ideas and feelings. This technique is called "clustering." For our purposes, all you need to do to cluster is place the word *excitement* (or *thrill,* or *adventure*) in the middle of a blank sheet of paper, and around the word begin to jot down all the other words that enter your mind in association with it. Then, clustered close to those *new* words, write down all the additional words that enter your mind in association with each one, until your stream of associations is exhausted. It's a good idea to circle each word and connect it with a straight line to the "root" word with which it is associated. Now take a good look at the clusters you've come up with. What kind of message is hidden amidst all those associations? What unusual avenues for creating excitement have come to mind? How do you feel about each of them—and when can you start implementing them?

Monitoring Your Thoughts and Feelings

Change-making requires not only that you engage in new behaviors but also that you become aware of the feelings that arise as you do so. For example, it will do you no good to take up a new sport if you then lie to yourself about whether you enjoy it, fear it, or feel inept at it. Now is the time to focus on the important, deep feelings— including fear, resistance, self-criticism, and disbelief—that arise as you begin new adventures. This is also the time to try something else, something different, if one experiment fails. If the change-making process is to work, you must regard it as a process made up of trial and error, not of perfection.

It is important to recognize obstacles to your ability to enjoy new endeavors, and to move beyond those obstacles by telling the truth about your feelings. The more truth you see, the more thrilling your adventures will become.

Let's imagine that you've always dreamed of acting in community theater (one place where drama pays off), but you have been reluctant to risk being rejected or to face being bad at playing a part. Let's also imagine that you decide to take the plunge, so you excitedly set off for an audition. You're all charged up, you give a terrific reading, and you get a role—that's good. But you don't get the size role you wanted—that's not so good. Suddenly, instead of being excited, you're disappointed. You wonder why you ever bothered to audition in the first place, and you begin to doubt whether acting will bring you the excitement you expected. Now what do you do?

I said earlier that true excitement contains agonies of its own. In a sense, you've just experienced one of them. You set your sights on a goal, and you only partially achieved it. Of course you're let down— but now is the time to explore *all* your feelings about the activity and to use your journal for reflecting upon them. Imagine that you were in the situation just described. What would your answers likely be to the following questions?

> What mixture of sensations and emotions did you experience when you decided to audition? When you first entered the theater? When you stood up to read for the part?
>
> What fantasies did you bring to the situation? How did the reality measure up?
>
> Was your overall experience positive or unpleasant? Was your involvement thrilling or disappointing?
>
> What differences were there between your feelings about the involvement and about the outcome?
>
> What fears or resistance toward changing old patterns do you still carry with you? How are they getting in the way of your *honest* assessment of your experience?
>
> Have you given the new venture a real chance—attended rehearsals, experienced the thrill and/or fright of performance—or are you making snap decisions because the outcome didn't immediately match your fantasy?
>
> Do you really want to be involved in the new activity, or are you doing what people have told you "you ought to do"?
>
> Can you get past the fact that the initial result of your efforts was imperfect in order to enjoy the sensations evoked by the activity itself?

All of these questions can be translated into terms relative to any endeavor. When you begin a new, exciting activity—whether you have mixed feelings about it or feel totally enthusiastic—use the questions above as guidelines for looking beneath the strongest, most obvious emotions to explore *everything* you might feel.

Now, let's look at another, similar scenario. You've auditioned for the play and won a small role, but instead of being disappointed, you're thrilled with the fact that you received anything at all. You fantasize about the fun of rehearsals and about inviting your friends and family to see you perform . . . but when you arrive home still high from your achievement and share the good news with your husband, he just glowers at you. "What am *I* supposed to do while you're at rehearsals every night? And who do you think you are—Meryl Streep?!"

Here, it is essential that you focus on the feelings evoked by your husband's ridicule of your activity. Rather than responding directly or allowing yourself to be provoked into a dramatic conflict, you must take the time to sort out what *you* feel and what *you* want to do. If you are tempted to give in to his bullying, you need to explore why, and in what ways, you might be willing to succumb to the pressure. You must consider all of your feelings before you discuss them with him. Above all, you must ask yourself how much you are willing to love and respect your own needs.

Sometimes the pressures you feel will be far more subtle: children worrying about dinner or getting help with their homework, a spouse who sincerely misses having you at home. You may be legitimately torn between their needs and yours, and you may be hesitant to actualize your new priorities because you are afraid of hurting the very people you love and depend upon, and who depend upon you. There is no easy solution to this dilemma, but I believe that if you faithfully monitor your feelings and trust in your inner wisdom, the best answer will become clear.

No matter what your individual circumstances, if you take the time to assess your feelings as you embark upon new, exciting adventures, you can't really go astray. And when it comes to deciding how (or whether) to confront people you love, the decisions will be consistent with your inner truths.

There are many books on decision making and communication that can help you cope with the interpersonal dilemmas that may crop up as you seek self-renewal. You may initially have to deal with guilt about attending to personal needs, and you will need to learn new ways of clearly, assertively stating your needs and expressing your feelings. The Appendix includes resources that address these issues.

Change-Making Step Three: Anticipating Your Next Drama

In this step you will begin to concentrate on the dramas you make. You will begin to seriously observe yourself as you create or enter into a drama, and to note the inner feelings and sets of circumstances that precipitated it. Once you have learned the cues that trigger a drama, you will be ready for the process of learning to take evasive action (the focus of Change-Making Step Four). I've waited until now to suggest that you begin this process, because it would have been unfair to ask you to give up drama's rewards before you had found invigorating, energizing ways to achieve similar sensations.

Imagine yourself pulling a switch to stop the drama in your life—it's a lovely fantasy. In reality, when you've been making drama for a long time, you operate mostly on "automatic." No matter how dedicated you are to change, you'll often find yourself well into an episode before you realize that you've just created another scene. Don't let that discourage you. Giving up drama need not be done cold turkey. In fact, this step is not about giving it up, but rather about taking the time to learn the cues that repeatedly trigger your dramas so that you'll be able to catch yourself readying for an episode.

I've found that most drama-seeking women have the ability to sense a dramatic episode coming on (rather like a cold!). There are certain emotional and physical precursors—"symptoms," if you will. Some women describe feeling "antsy" or "itchy." Some become tense and their muscles tighten, as though they were preparing for a confrontation. Others feel vaguely bored, discontented, or neglected. It's important to pay very close attention to the feelings you experience shortly before you find yourself in the thick of an episode or a scene. One way to recognize them is to wait for your next dramatic moment (there *definitely* will be one), and afterward sit down quietly with your journal and rerun in your mind the minutes, hours, and days that preceded the scene. Ask yourself the following questions: What bodily sensations did you experience within the five minutes preceding the episode? The hour? The day? What emotions? What were you thinking about? Who was with you who might have had an emotional influence upon you?

Try to be very specific in tracking your circumstances—for example, "I was sitting alone on the couch, worrying because John was late getting home. My stomach was churning, and I was biting my nails," or "I couldn't find a comfortable position, my body ached all over for no reason I could pinpoint, and I kept pacing back and forth across the room."

Now see if you can recall other dramatic moments from the past, and look for similar preconditions. You may discover that there are four or five circumstances or general bodily sensations that inevitably precede a dramatic episode. These are your *cues.* Make note of them in your journal, and begin to watch for them in your life. *Anticipate* that when you experience these feelings, *unless you do something deliberately to avert creating a drama*—as you will learn to do in the next step—you will most likely become embroiled in an episode. Recognize that you have choices about what kind of action to take, and that it is up to you to make the most productive choices of which you are capable. This doesn't mean, of course, that you will never create a drama again. But when you do, you'll be able to understand and learn from it.

As you begin to work on this and the next step, you may at times deliberately and consciously choose to create a drama despite the fact that you could take action to avoid it. This happens to most of us once in a while, and it is to be expected. It doesn't do any good to harass yourself over it. Instead, explore it. What emotions were rumbling around inside of you at the time? What was your need? Why did you choose that way to fulfill it? What were the consequences, if any? What did you gain or lose as a result of the experience? Who else was affected? Would you do it again? If so, why? If not, why not?

When you take responsibility for generating drama, you can take equal responsibility for cleaning up any messes you make along the way. If other people are harmed in the process, that is not fair or right, and you must be willing to acknowledge the extent to which you may have hurt them. Even here, guilt is no salvation. Remorse only creates more drama and makes you and your feelings the central issue. If you have had negative impact on another person because of your decision to engage in drama, that person's feelings now need to be considered first. Action is far more meaningful than remorse. Perhaps some reparations are in order, or some in-depth communication and explanation of your behavior. Perhaps you have learned from the experience and can put that knowledge to use for the future. In either case, you gain nothing by sinking into embarrassment over your behavior. You need to accept it, take responsibility for it, take the appropriate next step, and continue forward.

Change-Making Step Four: Replacing Old Behaviors

This step is concerned with specific, concrete behavioral change. Here, you will learn to take action to avert creating drama by replacing dramatic behaviors with simple, growth-oriented acts. The acts are not necessarily "exciting" in the sense in which we have been using the term, but they will produce interesting emotional—and sometimes physical—sensations to replace those you are accustomed to experiencing during dramatic episodes. In this step you will be given detailed suggestions for *doing something different* when faced with the very set of circumstances or feelings that previously led to predictable drama. This is a key step—but it is not to be tackled until you have spent time on Change-Making Steps One through Three.

I have divided this step into sections for Fighters, Challengers, and Rebels. However, it is important for two reasons that you read all the sections thoroughly. First, even if you are primarily one style of drama-seeker, you may from time to time engage in scenes more representative of a different style. Second, you may discover that a particular method for changing a noncustomary behavior appeals to you, and you may want to "customize" it for use with behaviors from a different drama-seeking category altogether. I hope you'll take advantage of whatever you suspect might be helpful.

Before I move on to suggest individualized behavioral changes, I want to share two techniques that work well to halt the drama, no matter what your dramatic style.

One of the best ways to release the energy behind the drama is to acknowledge that you are *feeling* like being dramatic, like acting out. Announce it to those around you, and let them support you in your effort to understand, instead of burst out with, dramatic action. Saying it aloud often relieves the pressure—you've said it, so now you don't really have to *do* it. In fact, you may wind up laughing at yourself, with more humor than you thought you had in you. Talking about what you'd *like* to do, even taking it to silly extremes, is a great way of letting off steam without incurring the damage that would usually accompany the actual deed.

Another way of getting a drama out of your system is to put it on paper or speak it into a tape recorder. There are no holds barred—really get into it! Go further than you might have if you had acted it out. Become a scriptwriter, and give yourself some truly outrageous dialogue just for the thrill of it. Since no one, including yourself, will be hurt by anything you say or do on paper or tape, you can go to extremes—just as you probably always longed to do in reality. This is your chance to really flush out the agony of it all!

You might also play back old tapes of similar outbursts. These might be enlightening or funny, but they will always be useful in helping you to siphon off the urge to create another drama.

Behavioral Changes for Fighters

In Change-Making Step Three, you learned to anticipate your drama. Now you will see how the behaviors characteristic of your drama can be turned around or changed. When the patterns of behavior that make up your drama no longer exist, the drama no longer exists.

From Exaggerating to Underplaying.   When you are tempted to exaggerate a situation, underplay the problem instead. If the dog makes a mess on the carpet and you're tempted to carry on about how the carpet is RUINED, don't. Say nothing. Clean up the mess. Ignore the spot.

If the freeway is backed up and you are tempted to begin tearing your hair out—and, on arrival at your destination, to rave about how you were STRANDED FOR DAYS—don't. In the car, sit back in your seat, turn on the radio, take some deep breaths, and relax. When you get to your destination, apologize briefly if you are late. Otherwise, say nothing.

It will be difficult to say nothing in situations such as these, but it is essential. Literally bite your tongue if you have to, or place your hand firmly over your mouth as a reminder. One client of mine put a small teddy bear wearing a handkerchief gag in her desk drawer at work. Whenever she was tempted to magnify or overplay, she opened the drawer and looked at the bear. It always made her laugh, and its very presence helped her to let go of the drama.

From Complaints to Action.   When you are inclined to make a big production out of complaining, take action on your problems instead. If the car dealer still ignores you after you've been in the showroom for ten minutes, don't go marching up to blast him for his behavior. Simply ask for assistance, and if you don't receive it, take your business elsewhere.

If your back hurts, instead of moaning and groaning each time you move so that everyone around you notices your discomfort, see a doctor. If you don't like your job, instead of complaining about it, start looking for a new one. When a complaint begins to form on your lips, ask yourself if you've taken firm action to change the situation. If not, say nothing until you do. Don't make a drama out of your problem; create a dramatic solution instead.

From Center Stage to Centered.   When you are tempted to display your sore spots to an audience of intimates, hold back. Look into your soul and write in your journal about what you feel. Rather than parading your problems, begin to solve them.

When you are inclined to spend all night on the phone relating details of your troubles to three or four friends, don't. Choose one person whose advice you respect and whose solution to your problem *you will seriously consider,* and call that person. If there is no one who can offer help you will appreciate, speak with no one. Spend your time focused upon the action *you* can take to resolve the troublesome issues.

From Passive Language to Responsible Language.   If you tend to use "victim" phrases, such as "He made me feel like . . ." or "It's her fault that . . . ," STOP. Take responsibility for your feelings and for your life by using active language, such as "I feel . . . ," "It happened because *I* . . . ," and "I need . . ." Instead of saying, "He made me say those awful things," say, "I felt hurt and put down by the things he said, so I chose to say things I knew would hurt him back."

Also, if you hear yourself saying such things as "You never . . ." or "You always . . . ," STOP. "Never" and "always" are generally exaggerations, and they rarely lead to nondramatic resolutions. If you are tempted to say, "You never say you love me," say instead: "It makes me feel wonderful when you tell me you love me. I need to hear you say it more often."

From Antagonism to Understanding.   If you are tempted to be accusatory and to regard others as natural enemies, *act as if* you are more understanding, accepting, and forgiving. As your behavior changes, you'll find that your feelings will change, too. You will *become* more understanding, more open. If you don't go into every situation as though you were under attack, chances are that you won't be.

If a coworker seems to snub you, assume that she's had a bad day and offer to bring her a cup of coffee or tea. When you are tempted to phone a lawyer, first ask yourself if you have tried to resolve the situation in more humane ways.

If you are tempted to bad-mouth or create trouble for another person, just DON'T DO IT. Instead, do something nice for someone you love. Or do something nice for you—take a bubble bath, read a good book, or go to the beach. When you consistently treat yourself with kindness, your self-esteem will grow. And as your self-esteem grows, so will your compassion for others.

From Criticism to Connection.   Each time you feel that you are about to jump down someone's throat over an irritating habit, try instead to find a positive way of *connecting* with that person. You can connect in many ways, but the simplest is to verbally acknowledge the highest level at which you can identify the relationship. Say "I love you" or "Just think how many *years* we've been friends!" or "You're very special to me."

You may believe that it's easier to think about these feelings than to verbalize them—and you're probably right. That's why it's so necessary that you actually say them. *That* is change; that is growth. And when you speak your positive thoughts aloud, your irritation all but disappears. It is, at worst, reduced to discussable—but not dramatizable—size.

From Ultimatums to Time-Outs. In a dramatic, conflict-ridden relationship, when you are tempted to hurl ultimatums, take time out from contact with your partner. Leave the room, leave the house, leave the car . . . but leave. Have a fail-safe plan, and always do the same thing: go jogging, visit a friend, go to your office, go to the supermarket, or go to a movie. Let your plan become a predictable action. Don't return until you know you can do so without drama.

When you are tempted to tell your partner "where to get off," say nothing. Do not respond to provocation. Leave, and activate your fail-safe plan.

If you have an essentially communicative but occasionally conflictual relationship, and a quarrel begins to escalate in a way that *cues* drama, say to your partner: "If we continue this talk now it will turn into drama. I don't want that. I'm stopping now. We'll talk again later." Then, leave the room. Think through what is happening. Explore your feelings. Express them in your journal.

From Point of No Return to Successful Turnaround. When a conflict gets out of control and an emotional point of no return is reached, change history. Turn it around. Be willing to stop in mid-sentence and say, "I'm sorry if I hurt you. Let's stop before more damage is done." When you hear your partner say, "You're right" or "I'm sorry," STOP. Do not escalate the situation further by continuing to make your point or press your "rightness," and do not challenge. Say "I appreciate your saying that. Let's stop fighting now. We can talk tomorrow about how to keep this from going so far next time." End of episode. And end of drama.

Behavioral Changes for Challengers

Behavioral changes for women who are attracted to relationship challenges encompass two stages in the drama: acting on one's attraction to unavailable men, and engaging in the competition once the relationship has begun. The first three behavioral changes apply if you are *not* currently involved in a challenging relationship but are still susceptible to one; the others apply if you are now in a challenging relationship.

From Signs of Passion to Warning Signs. Instead of throwing yourself into a challenge drama, look for warning signs that tell you THIS PERSON IS ATTACHED. Is he wearing a ring? Does he live with someone? *Ask* him! Does he talk about other women?

If he is attached, when you begin to fantasize about being with him, STOP. Remember the pain a past relationship challenge brought you. Really argue with yourself if you start to believe that this one will be different. Argue in your journal in the form of a dialogue with yourself. Or distract yourself by focusing on a worthy, active challenge—your work or a sport, for example.

You can stop yourself from fantasizing about or focusing on your attraction by saying STOP! or NO! to yourself—again and again, if necessary—as your fantasies arise. Or you can put a rubber band around your wrist and snap it HARD when you begin to fantasize.

From Desperation to Self-Respect. If you find yourself intrigued by someone who is dispassionate, distant, or difficult to please, and you are tempted to begin "doing somersaults" to get his attention, STOP. *Immediately* remove yourself from his presence. Say to yourself: I deserve better than this. I will conserve my energy for someone who likes me, some someone who respects me, someone who is worthy of me. Take some deep breaths. Remember who *you* are! Do the same thing *every single time* you catch yourself trying too hard to please.

From Rivalry to Empathy. When you are tempted to regard another woman as a rival for your lover's affections, STOP. Imagine yourself in her shoes. Think about what she might be feeling. Do not allow yourself to label her as the enemy or as a competitor. Think of her as a friend. When you use her name, mentally precede it with "my friend." How would you feel about *you* if you were really her friend? Remember, she is a woman, just like you; looking for love, just like you; and possibly misguided about how to find it—just like you.

You might also think about an actual friend of yours who has been betrayed. Remember her pain? Do you want to cause that kind of pain?

From Other-Focused to Self-Focused.   If you are already involved in a love triangle, substitute probing questions to your lover about his other relationship with questions to yourself about the degree to which your own needs are being met. Instead of asking him, "Does your wife understand you as well as I do?" say *nothing*—but ask yourself, "Am I receiving the attention and understanding that I give?" Instead of asking, "Why did you say 'Me, too' when you hung up the phone? I know she said 'I love you'!" say *nothing*, but ask yourself, "Why am I willing to be an accessory to someone's life?"

From Fantasy to Reality Checks.   If you catch yourself saying things to friends like "It will all work out in the end" or "I know we're *meant* to be together," STOP—in mid-sentence, if necessary. When you are tempted to use these phrases, ask yourself: "Why are people saying things to me that trigger defensive responses? What are *they* seeing in me that I am not acknowledging?" Really pay attention to what people who care about you have to say. They can be quite objective about how your relationship is *observably* affecting you.

From "I Can Make Him" to "I Can . . . for Me."   If you are in a challenging relationship, you may be activating an essentially unconscious set of "I can make him's." Sit down and write up your "I can make him" list. Now there can be no more subtle manipulations that you can tell yourself were done for him. If you're going to be crafty, at least be honest about it, and make that list. What do you want your lover to do? What are your goals, from start to finish? When you have finished the list, you will be able to see what an overwhelming and unrealistic task you've set for yourself.

Each time you catch yourself figuring out a way to make your lover do something on your list, STOP. Let it go. Let him do whatever he does, let him be whoever he is. Take all the energy invested in that manipulation and turn it toward *you.* Do something kind, something efficient, something meaningful for yourself. Make dinner for a friend, go to a movie, go to the gym, or direct yourself toward the new, healthy challenges you've already begun.

Behavioral Changes for Rebels

These behavioral changes can be applied to any form of Rebel drama. However, if you are physiologically addicted to drugs or alcohol, additional measures may be needed. The steps here can reduce the *drama* surrounding your addiction and can provide alternatives to using, but they cannot entirely address your dependency at the biological level. If you are addicted, I strongly urge you to find a qualified therapist or to involve yourself in a substance-abuse program.

The following set of behavioral changes is geared toward helping you refrain from setting out to engage in the self-defeating, auto-arousal–producing acts that form the crux of your drama. Whether your dramas involve sexual thrill-seeking, bingeing, gambling, law-breaking, using drugs, or shopping, I use the term *cruising* to describe the act of setting out to acquire the substance or to do the activity that is destructive for you. You can "cruise" a bar, a refrigerator, or a shopping mall. You can cruise anything or anybody; you can cruise anywhere.

From Cruising to Conscious Choice. If you are tempted to go cruising, *DO NOT*. Instead, *do something different.* Try one or a combination of the following new behaviors:

- If you are having an especially difficult time resisting the urge to cruise, it may help to begin a written dialogue between your "wise person" or "guide" and your compulsive or drama-making self.

Take a moment to close your eyes, breathe deeply, and reach for your inner wisdom. It is there; never doubt that. I suggest that you draw upon the image of your guide to help you begin.

It can also be meaningful to call upon an image of your compulsive self. What does she look like? Is she an adult or a child? Does she have a name that is different from the one you use every day? Are you more comfortable referring to her as your CS (compulsive self)?

Now begin a written dialogue between your guide and your CS. Surely, they have much to say to each other. Step back from controlling the process and simply allow the words to flow. Don't censor anything, no matter how ridiculous or frightening the dialogue may seem. It is just another way of getting at your inner truths.

In my experience, it is very rare for a client to create this dialogue and then go cruising. It is a highly effective tool. I urge you to use it.

- Turn on the radio. Find a station playing the kind of music you don't usually listen to. Really listen. Get into the melodies, the lyrics, the emotion behind the music. Or, play your favorite music and dance alone until the urge to go cruising passes.

- Turn to a creative project begun with Change-Making Step Two. This is the time to find refuge, excitement, and self-renewal in work that reflects your essence. If you should feel blocked, try a creative exercise using a totally foreign medium. If you normally paint, turn your images into words, and write them. If you usually write, try turning your thoughts into abstract images, and draw them.

- Pick up your journal and express your immediate feelings. What is going on mentally and physically? Who or what are you angry at? What do you feel needy for?

Take action on your feelings. If you are lonely, call a friend; if you are involved in a substance-abuse program, phone a member of the program. Say, "I'm lonely. I'd like your company." If you are angry, face your anger; talk to the person you are angry with and express your feelings. Say, "I am feeling angry with you, and I want to talk about it so we can sort it out." Or, write a long letter (which you don't have to mail) or speak into a tape recorder, telling this person everything you are angry about.

If you feel helpless, get in touch with your power. Take concrete, constructive action of *any* kind to remind yourself that you *can* make choices, that you *are not,* in fact, helpless. And if you are bored, find a novel means of occupying yourself. Go to the theater on the spur of the moment. Take a moonlit walk on the beach. Read an action/adventure novel. Call everyone you know and pull together a bowling party. Above all, let yourself have FUN!

The following behavior changes are geared toward reducing the drama surrounding the act and outcomes of cruising, should you choose to go. Make no mistake—going cruising is, indeed, a choice.

From Denial to Deliberateness.   When you set out to play with fire and you begin to say to yourself, "I won't get caught; nothing bad will happen to me. I can do it just this once and get away with it," STOP. Catch yourself in the midst of these thoughts. DON'T DENY THE DANGER. Instead, say, "I know that what I'm doing is dangerous. I know the consequences. If I must pay them, it is my responsibility. I have made a choice." Be deliberate about your acts. Be responsible. There is little drama in taking responsibility.

From Self-Recrimination to Responsibility. After an episode of drama—after drinking too much, spending too much, gambling too much—when the thrills are gone and you begin to hate yourself, when you are tempted to induce further auto-arousal through exaggerated remorse and self-recrimination, STOP! Say to yourself instead, "I made a choice. This is the aftermath of it. If I don't like these feelings and consequences, then I need to remind myself of that next time, *before* I go cruising." Let your feelings go. Turn to a healthy activity and get on with your life.

Finding Calm

Whether you are a Fighter, a Challenger, or a Rebel, making the foregoing changes involves many new actions, new feelings, and new ways of thinking and perceiving. But if I were to strip these possibilities down to one essential element, it would be *choice.* Time and again you will be facing a moment of choice—a choice to acknowledge the way you make drama, and a choice to act on or ignore that recognition; a choice to set up a drama, or a choice to utilize your knowledge and wisdom to end one.

At each moment of choice it is important that you STOP, perhaps only for an instant, and calm yourself. Take a deep breath, and *consciously* consider your situation. Recognize that you are about to take *action* in some way. In order to enter into the drama you will have to take familiar action; in order to evade the drama you will have to take new and different action. Be willing to *love* yourself for creating this instant of calm, for giving yourself the chance to consider taking the new action that will bring true emotional rewards. Then, *move on* to take that action, to institute a new behavior, a new sensation, a new way of living.

Consciousness

Action

Love

Move on

Together, the above words form the acronym C.A.L.M. Remember this acronym when you are uncertain or frightened. Remember what it means. Take a deep breath, and rely on your natural ability to find the place within yourself that is always open, loving, and calm.

Monitoring Your Thoughts and Feelings

As you begin to make behavioral changes, you'll notice that many, many feelings start to rumble around inside of you. For example, if you stop exaggerating and magnifying, you may actually experience the sense of invisibility that you've been hiding in drama, since you are no longer using this tactic to make yourself feel visible or special. But you may also discover that as you experiment with new ways of creating healthy excitement, you start to feel visible and special in a genuine, meaningful way.

This is the time to examine all the feelings that dramatic episodes often cover up. You will have ample opportunity, because each behavioral component of drama serves to diminish some portion of your authentic feeling-life. As you take action to eliminate those behaviors, the corresponding buried feelings will surface. As you did in Change-Making Step Two, you will focus on your inner perceptions as you transform self-defeating acts into self-actualizing experiences. Again, you will face some discomfort, fear, and self-criticism— and even a burning desire to resist any further change. It is important that you recognize and deal with these feelings. If you bury them again, you will probably revert to old, dramatic patterns of shoveling them underground.

The true-to-self drama that lies beneath the exaggerated episode— the real, very healthy drama of exploring and experiencing your own deeply etched feelings—is worthy of your attention. It is ironic that we often steep ourselves in the sensationalism of melodrama when the truth of our own feelings and experiences is often drama enough. Leaving the stage, refusing to play out the episode, and filling the vacancy that remains by reaching inside to experience these valuable feelings are skills you can cultivate.

The feelings that arise as you let go of your dramas will undoubtedly trigger associations from the past. This is an excellent time to concentrate further on placing your past in perspective. In fact, this change-making step can be very exciting—you may feel like a detective who suddenly stumbles on fresh clues to the mystery of "Why am I who I am?"

On the other hand, you may experience some resistance to focusing on your feelings or to putting the previous step (replacing old behaviors) into continued practice. Be aware of your resistance, and be willing to slowly—and with love—face and break down those walls.

Your new behaviors are bound to have especially profound effects on the nature of your intimate relationships. In the past, when the drama in your life was centered around a certain relationship, it may have been particularly tempting to convince yourself that the turmoil was all your partner's fault. "If only" might have been a more steadfast companion than your lover: if only he would change, if only he would treat you better, *then* you wouldn't get so upset.

As you can now see, this is a typical cop-out. When you refuse to take responsibility for the chaos in your life, it never ends. Expecting a conflict-ridden, unsatisfying liaison to metamorphose into blissful passion "if only . . ." is an act of woeful self-delusion.

One way to gauge the future potential of a floundering relationship is to resolutely stop your participation in the drama. If you have already begun to do this, you will need to explore your feelings about the current state of the relationship. What do you and your partner share? How does your partner respond to the changes in you? How do you feel about that response? Each behavioral change you make will be a test of the strength of your bond and of your own ability to relate at a level of intimacy and integrity. You may uncover a true partnership beneath the previous chaos, or you may realize that you are wrong for each other. Either way, you will face many uncomfortable or frightening moments. Only by being honest with yourself about your feelings can you make sound decisions about where to go from here.

Once more I urge you to utilize your journal as a means of recording your new feelings, reflecting upon them, and noting the memories or associations they release. You'll find excellent exercises for doing this in Tristine Rainer's *The New Diary,* and a fine example of one woman's process in Joanna Field's *A Life Of One's Own.*

Dealing with your newfound feelings is a big step. Entire books have been written on the "how to," and I hope you will take advantage of some of them. For detail and incisiveness I especially recommend *Living beyond Fear,* by Jeanne Segal, Ph.D.

Change-Making Step Five: Seeking Support

Change-making is a thrilling but taxing business. As I described at length in the previous chapter, having a warm, accepting support system to anchor you during this time will make the experience far more pleasurable. In addition to friends, family, or a therapist, consider forming a peer group of women who come together weekly to help one another change outworn, debilitating, drama-making patterns. This group can be as much a tool for self-renewal as your journal. When other, fellow seekers share both the travails and delights of change, somehow the difficulties seem lessened and the joys greater.

If you are familiar with the consciousness-raising groups of the 1970s, you are already familiar with a prototype for this kind of support group. Actually, "consciousness raising" is a term that can be used to describe this type of group, too, for the group members are doing nothing if not raising, or expanding, their consciousness about their needs and feelings, their options as women, and the roles of negative drama and healthy excitement in their lives.

You might start such a group by placing an ad in a local paper, or by talking with friends and letting word of mouth bring at least five of you together. In a group such as this, it is advisable to rotate turns leading the meeting—bringing up specific topics for examination and providing any additional reading material (for example, newspaper or magazine articles, book excerpts, and journal entries) to share and discuss. You can use the organization of this book as a guide, and the challenges and change-making steps in chapters 8 and 9 as a format. Just dealing with the issues that arise as you tackle these challenges and steps will keep you very, very busy.

A consciousness-raising group is not about giving advice and telling other people how they ought to lead their lives—although that can be tempting. It is not about recounting your dramas or complaining. It is about expressing your feelings and offering one another support, because you are there for the same purpose. The focus should always be on what you are *doing* to understand and change self-defeating patterns of drama-making, and on how you are *feeling* about the changes you continue to make.

It is always hard, initially, to keep a group together. Facing and sharing feelings can be more uncomfortable than pleasing at first. Group members may have a tendency to avoid their feelings by doing the obvious—avoiding the group. During this early stage in the group's life, "hairdresser appointments" and "heavy dates" sometimes become common among members. I suggest that during the first meeting you discuss the topic of commitment and brainstorm direct ways of dealing with resistance to the group process.

If forming your own support group is out of the question, chances are that groups offering opportunities for similar growth have already formed in your community—therapy groups, women's support groups, groups for incest survivors, for divorcées, for new mothers. You may find the richness of already existing possibilities exciting, and one of these groups may suit your personal needs. You can find information about them by looking in the "women's" section of your daily paper or in the classified or community-notices section of "alternative" newspapers. You can also call your community-crisis or rape hotline, or check the bulletins at your public library.

If you are, or would like to be, involved in one of the Twelve-Step programs, such a program may prove helpful, especially if you are an abuser of drugs or alcohol. It has been my experience, however, that these groups rarely contribute to one's understanding of the importance of the drama/sensation-seeking/auto-arousal aspects of substance abuse. I have also found that groups such as Alcoholics Anonymous, Overeaters Anonymous, and Debtors Anonymous, and so on, can have detrimental influences on some women for whom denial of personal power is itself a serious issue. The essential "sickness" orientation of the Anonymous programs demands that a woman "surrender" what power she is aware of having; this can have far-reaching psychological repercussions beyond the issue of compulsion or addiction itself. Consequently, I suggest Twelve-Step programs with serious reservations.

I am, of course, fully aware that many people find these programs meaningful, and that they have provided help to millions. On the positive side, such groups offer the comfort of letting you know that you are not alone in your pain. As Jody Hayes, author of *Smart Love*, commented with reference to the Al-Anon groups:

> In the course of a week, someone will find a job, someone will lose a job, someone will be evicted from his apartment, someone's parent will be dying, someone will reconcile with a parent, someone will find a lover, someone will part from his or her spouse. We end up seeing our lives in a new perspective, and we learn, firsthand, how others manage drama in their lives.

If you do choose to become involved in a Twelve-Step program, I urge you to seek concurrent individual counseling. I find that people gain the most from these groups when they regard them as one of many resources.

Change-Making Step Six: Rewarding Yourself

This step is about pleasure and self-reward. Here, you will begin to turn previous patterns of verbal self-punishment into new habits of self-reward. Ironically, for a majority of women this is the most difficult step to accomplish. Many of us are accustomed to pleasing and complimenting others, but only to criticizing ourselves.

Each time you do something positive and healthfully exciting for yourself, each time you refrain from involving yourself in a situation that could be damaging or self-defeating, you need to commend yourself, thank yourself, love yourself. Nobody else can do this better than you. Part of changing damaging patterns entails developing a relationship with yourself that is more loving, more nurturing, and more forgiving.

In our fantasies, most of us have considered the image of an ideal parent. Few of us, if any, actually had such a parent. But we know exactly what such a parent would be like. We know how she (or he) would speak to us, encourage us, comfort us, correct us, and tenderly care for us. Our ideal parent lives within us, and it is through this parent that we can learn to nurture ourselves.

Make a list of the things that your ideal parent would do for you. This might include both emotional and practical deeds. Maybe she (or he) would comfort you when you were sad. If so, what would she say? Maybe she would soothe you when you were sick. What would she do? Maybe she would reward you when you did something that made her especially proud. Would she tell you how proud she is, tell you how much she loves you, tell you how special you are, tell you how smart or brave you are? How would she reward you when you did something for her that she especially appreciated? Would she reward you verbally, or would she do something especially nice for you in return?

You can treat yourself with the tenderness and appreciation that you imagine the ideal parent would. You *are* your ideal parent, for you know better than anyone else exactly what you need at all times.

You are probably accustomed to hearing your inner voice, your self-talk, blast you with criticism. Nothing is right, nothing is good enough. Nothing you do is fast enough or complete enough. This voice is not your friend—it is your task mistress, your ultimate critic, and sometimes your cohort in drama. Your ideal inner parent, on the other hand, knows how to correct your mistakes and guide you toward improvement in a gentle, kindly manner. She knows how to focus on the positives and on what you've achieved, not on what you've neglected. Each time you take one tiny step toward self-discovery and productive change, you need to call upon that loving, inner voice. Let her warm you with affection and consideration. *Listen* to her. Let her suggest an appropriate reward, a form of healthy pleasure to which you can surrender.

The respect you give to yourself, first, is the respect that you will earn from others later. In every way, it is all up to you.

We have come as far along the path of self-renewal as we can go together. This is where I must leave you to find your own way, to create your own magic.

No two people will make precisely the same kind of magic, and that is why the process of change—no matter how much we know or can anticipate—is still a mysterious, surprising, suspenseful, and truly exciting one. Yet, for every woman who searches her heart for truth and takes full responsibility for her choices, the magic she performs will be the precise magic she has been waiting for.

The six change-making steps and the challenges that preceded them require nothing short of dedication to a new way of living. Yet, as involved as each step can be, the whole of the change-making process distilled down to its purest elements makes only these demands:

- That you become aware of the dramatic behaviors that sap your power, energy, and spirit, and become committed to stepping off the stage and into your own life.
- That you take action to replace drama with acts of self-actualization and renewal.
- That you be willing to respect yourself for the courage to take new action, for the feelings your action evokes, for the power that is undying within you, and for the spirit with which you grow.
- That you move onward with each new experience, each moment of awareness, and each instant of aliveness devoted to renewing belief in yourself.

I trust this road to transformation, and I have every faith that on this path you will find the miracle nesting within you. I wish you love and everlasting courage throughout your remarkable journey.

Appendix I: Therapy, Therapists, and Young Sensation-Seekers

In the course of my work, I meet and lecture to many women across the country who are as committed to changing self-defeating patterns of living as my own clients are. These women frequently ask me questions about the change-making process that are not germane to the fundamental content of this book yet are important and universal enough to pay attention to. I have included material relating to two such areas of questioning in this Appendix: How do I know if I need therapy, and how do I select a therapist? And how can I bring up my daughters to keep them from making the same mistakes I made?

What You Need to Know About Therapy

For many women, the right kind of therapy can be an important, even necessary, adjunct to the scary, exhilarating, confusing process of change and growth. Therapy is, in effect, a stage upon which you can safely share your dreams, fears, and pleasures. It is a commitment to yourself. Therapy provides a place where you can cautiously take yourself apart to see what you're made of, and then slowly, lovingly, and creatively put yourself back together again.

For women, it offers a special appeal. I think that Katha Pollitt, writing in the *New York Times* "Hers" column, touched on the heart of the matter:

We live in a society that drums into women's heads from the minute they're born that they are here on earth to play supporting roles in essentially male dramas . . . [But, in therapy] a woman gets to talk about herself, in terms of issues *she* raises, in great detail and at the most intimate level. Here, for a change, the drama is *her* life, and she is the star.

That sense of being at the center of her life, rather than at the periphery of the lives of others, is what therapy offers women. It's quite an intoxicating feeling, and quite a feminist one too.

Seeking help can be a matter of choice or a matter of survival. I will give you some basic guidelines, but in general, I suggest that you ask people you know and trust for recommendations if you *suspect* that therapy could help. Then, make an initial appointment with a therapist to investigate your feelings and needs further.

If you are involved with drugs or alcohol, or have any other addictive or compulsive behavior, you should seek help. A substance-abuse program may become important to you, but my experience has been that one-on-one therapy is also necessary if you are serious about confronting your addiction within the framework of your life as a whole.

If you are depressed, if your relationships are failing, if you are involved intimately with an addict, or if you often feel frightened, anxious, guilty, or angry, you will also benefit from therapy.

If, as a child, you were sexually or physically abused, you undoubtedly bear the emotional scars, and your present problems may be a warped reflection of your early pain. You need a safe place to confront, and resolve, the past. Therapy can provide that safety.

If the changes in you provoke problems in your primary relationship and you and your partner have difficulty solving them alone, a therapist who works with couples should be sought.

If you faithfully take the steps for change outlined in chapter 9 but reach an impasse, you might want the help of a professional. She (or he) will help you to explore your present as it has been influenced by your past, work with you as you develop healthier patterns of sensation-seeking, and guide you toward building more intimate relationships. The therapist's objective questioning can help you to gain a sense of context and perspective. As you do, the disjointed pieces of your life will begin to take on significance as part of an expanding whole.

Therapy need not be long-term—in some cases, it is limited to just four or five sessions. Choosing to enter therapy does not mean that you're deranged or sick; it means that you have the wisdom to take advantage of a professional's knowledge and experience in order to benefit yourself.

Choosing the "Right" Therapist

Good therapy helps women transform drama into healthy excitement, in part because good therapy *is* healthy excitement. It is productive challenge and positive risk-taking directed toward oneself. Good therapy *is* intimacy. Therapy is not merely a setting in which client and therapist talk about such concepts as closeness and healthy sensation. The right kind of therapy *is* the concept, come to life. It is representative of what self-affirming excitement and intensity are all about.

The *right* therapist for dealing with the kinds of issues presented in this book is the following:

● One who understands that sensation-seeking is a natural, normal trait in both men and women, and who recognizes the value of healthy excitement-seeking.

● One who recognizes the special problems of women, both historically and currently, in their search for excitement.

● One who is *not* a strict Freudian psychoanalyst, because the foundation of Freudian analysis is sexist and antifemale. (This is not, however, generally the case with Jungian analysis, which seeks to healthfully balance the male and female aspects within each person.)

● One who willingly and clearly answers all of your questions about the process of therapy and about her or his professional background, experience, and personal biases. The therapist must be someone who is sincerely interested in knowing what *you* wish to accomplish in therapy, and who treats you like an intelligent, capable human being.

● Probably a woman, but not necessarily. I believe that a woman is generally better off with a female therapist because such a therapist would understand the problems and conflicts attached to being female in our culture. However, I know a few truly wonderful male therapists who are sincere in their feminism, sensitive, warm, and highly skilled. Consider personal recommendations, but don't hesitate in the first session to ask pointed questions about the therapist's attitudes toward, and style of working with, women.

• One who has had training and experience treating addictions, if you are an addict. Someone who has had extensive experience working with survivors of sexual abuse, if you have been abused. The most well-meaning professional can do more harm than good if not properly trained in these areas.

• Someone you instinctively like and feel comfortable with. You may not like or feel comfortable with the fact that the therapist asks you to look at yourself from some potentially unflattering angles, and you will probably feel awkward when you begin to reveal embarrassing or unpleasant details about yourself—but that's natural. It's important that you like the therapist herself in spite of these feelings.

If you feel put off by, or extremely uneasy with, this person—to whom you will be opening your heart—don't make a second appointment. You *must* trust your instincts here. Remember that you are paying a professional to help you gain strength in an area in which you feel unsure. Therapists, in that respect, should be treated like any other providers of services, such as accountants and lawyers. In fact, the stakes are higher. I can't stress this enough. Many people—and women especially, because we've been taught to be submissive—are cowed by medical and mental-health professionals. Don't let this happen to you. If the "match" doesn't feel right, go elsewhere.

For Parents: Bringing Up Healthy Sensation-Seekers

I was tempted to subtitle this section "Raising Daughters to be Healthy Sensation-Seekers"—but the fact is, in order to raise both daughters *and* sons to be healthy individuals, we need to raise them in basically the same way.

Sexism is not merely a political issue; it is a mental-health issue as well. I strongly believe that sexism—even the subtle sexism that exists among otherwise enlightened people—is patently unhealthy. It is just as unhealthy for boys to be raised to be "dominant," but detached from their nurturing qualities and feelings, as it is for women to be raised to be "nurturant," but submissive and detached from their power. Either state is one of emotional and spiritual imbalance. The more severe the degree of imbalance, the more extreme the resulting emotional distresses.

If you are, or intend to be, a parent, here are some basic guidelines for helping your child to channel her or his needs for excitement in healthy, productive ways. These guidelines are not surefire guarantees; no one I've ever encountered can offer those. But they *will* increase your odds of success.

• Remember that the old adage "Do as I say, not as I do" is a prescription for disaster with children. Children learn as much, if not more, from your behavior toward them, toward others, and toward yourself as they do from anything you tell them. If you exhibit positive patterns of sensation-seeking and make a point of sharing your own excitement and enthusiasm with your children, you will teach them more than any set of instructions can. If you model healthy risk-taking, they will learn not to be afraid to take meaningful chances.

• If you are willing to encourage both daughters and sons to explore the *same* (reasonably nonendangering) forms of positive stimulation—whether that means playing football or writing poetry—your children of either sex will grow up believing that their worldly options are limited only by desire and aptitude. Girls won't have to turn to self-defeating styles of personal drama later on, just for the sake of excitement. Boys won't grow up to be afraid to show their sensitive, "softer" sides, and they won't have to forfeit the personal rewards that sharing this facet of themselves can bring.

On the other hand, if you imply by word or deed that "some things are okay for boys, but not for girls" and vice versa, you not only create unnecessary handicaps for your children to contend with, but you also provide them with a set of rules against which to rebel, often self-destructively.

• It is important to recognize that your children may be constitutionally higher- or lower-level sensation-seekers than you. Be tolerant of their individual temperaments.

Instead of attempting to constrain high-energy children, work toward helping them find a variety of outlets for their cravings for stimulation. Remember that children who are high-sensation seekers have a greater need for novelty and may have shorter attention spans than other children. Cooperate with nature by being enthusiastic about what your child is capable of achieving in a short time. The more you try to tie children down or force their focus, the more resistance you will encounter, and the less will be accomplished.

• Allow your children to take the lead in determining the activities and involvements that excite them. Certainly, you'll want to make suggestions and introduce them to pastimes that you find especially engaging, but pay attention to the cues that tell you what *their* special interests are. Above all, DON'T make fun of or criticize their choices, no matter how outrageous they seem to you. If you feel that something is unsafe or objectionable on moral grounds, stay calm and discuss your feelings clearly without belittling the child or disparaging her or his ideas. Remember that the more distressed you appear, the more appealing the original idea will be to most children—especially teenagers.

These five points are just a beginning, but they are a solid one. As most parents know, there is no simple formula to being a "good" mother or father or to raising a child. Many factors—genetics and social influences, for example—are for the most part out of your control. But I find that the most energized, excited, and secure children have the most self-actualized, emotionally well-nourished parents. It all comes down to the fact that you can't give what you don't possess. If you have rewarding excitement in your own life, if you have love for yourself, and if you have respect for relationships that enrich the quality of your life, then you have rare and precious gifts to share not only with your children and husband but also with the world.

Appendix II:
Recommended Reading List

The following resources are organized according to the chapter of this book in which they were originally mentioned or to which they most directly relate. While they occasionally reflect philosophies or positions that conflict with my own (and with one another's), I believe you will find each book valuable and thought-provoking in its own way.

An asterisk (*) beside the title indicates that it is, in my personal opinion, particularly outstanding.

Chapter 2

Phyllis Chesler, *Women and Madness* (New York: Doubleday, 1972).

*Riane Eisler, *The Chalice and the Blade* (San Francisco: Harper and Row, 1987).

*Judith Hooper and Dick Teresi, *The 3-Pound Universe: Revolutionary Discoveries about the Brain, from the Chemistry of the Mind to the New Frontiers of the Soul* (New York: Macmillan, 1986).

Harvey Milkman and Stanley Sunderwirth, *Craving for Ecstasy: The Consciousness and Chemistry of Escape* (Lexington, Mass.: Lexington Books, 1987).

Jean Baker Miller, *Toward a New Psychology of Women* (Boston: Beacon Press, 1976).

*Merlin Stone, *When God Was a Woman* (New York: Harcourt, Brace, Jovanovich, 1976).

267

Marvin Zuckerman, *Sensation Seeking: Beyond the Optimal Level of Arousal* (Hillsdale, N.J.: Lawrence Erlbaum Associates, 1979). (Note: This book predates Zuckerman's CSA theory.)

Chapter 3

Ien Ang, *Watching Dallas: Soap Opera and the Melodramatic Imagination* (London: Methuen, 1982).

Ellen Bass and Louise Thornton, *I Never Told Anyone: Writing by Women Survivors of Child Sexual Abuse* (New York: Harper and Row, 1983).

Susan Forward and Craig Buck, *Betrayal of Innocence: Incest and Its Devastation* (Los Angeles: Jeremy P. Tarcher, Inc., 1978).

*Eliana Gil, Ph.D., *Outgrowing the Pain: A Book for and about Adults Abused as Children* (Walnut Creek, Calif.: Launch Press, 1983).

Alice Miller, *The Drama of the Gifted Child* (New York: Basic Books, 1981).

Robin Norwood, *Women Who Love Too Much: When You Keep Wishing and Hoping He'll Change* (Los Angeles: Jeremy P. Tarcher, Inc., 1985).

Chapters 4 and 5

*Tara Roth Madden, *Women vs. Women: The Uncivil Business War* (New York: Amacom, 1987).

Lillian B. Rubin, *Just Friends: The Role of Friendship in Our Lives* (New York: Harper and Row, 1985).

Hans Selye, *The Stress of Life* (New York: McGraw-Hill, rev. 1976).

Chapters 6 and 7

Patrick Carnes, Ph.D., *Out of the Shadows: Understanding Sexual Addiction* (Minneapolis, Minn.: CompCare Publications, 1983).

David Dalton, *Piece of My Heart: The Life, Times and Legend of Janis Joplin* (New York: St. Martin's Press, rev. 1985).

Rosemary Daniell, *Sleeping with Soldiers: In Search of the Macho Man* (New York: Holt, Rinehart, Winston, 1984).

*Colette Dowling, *The Cinderella Complex: Women's Hidden Fear of Independence* (New York: Pocket Books, 1981).

Ralph Keyes, *Chancing It: Why We Take Risks* (Boston: Little, Brown, 1985).

Susan Nadler, *Good Girls Gone Bad: American Women in Crime* (New York: Freundlich Books, 1987).

Susie Orbach, *Fat Is a Feminist Issue* (London: Paddington Press, 1978).

Geneen Roth, *Feeding the Hungry Heart* (New York: Bobbs-Merrill Co., 1982).

Claude Steiner, *Games Alcoholics Play* (New York: Ballantine Books, 1971).

Chapters 8 and 9

Jean Shinoda Bolen, M.D., *Goddesses in Everywoman* (New York: Harper Colophon Books, 1984).

Charles Cameron and Suzanne Elusorr, *T.G.I.M.: Making Your Work Fulfilling and Finding Fulfilling Work* (Los Angeles: Jeremy P. Tarcher, Inc., 1986).

Jean Houston, *The Possible Human* (Los Angeles: Jeremy P. Tarcher, Inc., 1982).

*Joanna Field, *A Life of One's Own* (Los Angeles: Jeremy P. Tarcher, Inc., 1981).

Harold Kushner, *When All You've Ever Wanted Isn't Enough: The Search for a Life That Matters* (New York: Pocket Books, 1986).

Diane Mariechild, *Mother Wit: A Feminist Guide to Psychic Development* (Trumansburg, N.Y.: The Crossing Press, 1981).

Ira Progoff, *At a Journal Workshop* (New York: Dialogue House Library, 1975).

Tristine Rainer, *The New Diary: How to Use a Journal for Self-Guidance and Expanded Creativity* (Los Angeles: Jeremy P. Tarcher, Inc., 1978).

Gabrielle Lusser Rico, *Writing the Natural Way* (Los Angeles: Jeremy P. Tarcher, Inc., 1983).

Adele Scheele, *Skills for Success* (New York: Ballantine Books, 1981).

On Exploring Feelings

Claudia Black, *Repeat after Me* (Denver: M.A.C. Printing, 1985).

Eugene Gendlin, *Focusing* (New York: Bantam Books, 1981).

Harriet Goldhor Lerner, Ph.D., *The Dance of Anger: A Woman's Guide to Changing the Patterns of Intimate Relationships* (New York: Harper and Row, 1985).

Jeanne Segal, Ph.D., *Living beyond Fear: A Tool for Transformation* (North Hollywood, Calif.: Newcastle, 1984).